The Haunted

THE HAUNTED

A Social History of Ghosts

Owen Davies

First published 2007 by
PALGRAVE MACMILLAN
Houndmills, Basingstoke, Hampshire RG21 6XS and
175 Fifth Avenue, New York, N.Y. 10010
Companies and representatives throughout the world

PALGRAVE MACMILLAN is the global academic imprint of the Palgrave
Macmillan division of St. Martin's Press, LLC and of Palgrave Macmillan Ltd.
Macmillan® is a registered trademark in the United States, United Kingdom
and other countries. Palgrave is a registered trademark in the European
Union and other countries.

ISBN-13: 978–1–4039–3924–1   hardback
ISBN-10: 1–4039–3924–1   hardback

This book is printed on paper suitable for recycling and made from fully managed
and sustained forest sources. Logging, pulping and manufacturing processes are
expected to conform to the environmental regulations of the country of origin.

A catalogue record for this book is available from the British Library.

Library of Congress Cataloging-in-Publication Data
Davies, Owen, 1969–
   The haunted : a social history of ghosts / Owen Davies.
      p. cm.
   Includes index.
   ISBN 1–4039–3924–1 (alk. paper)
   1. Ghosts—England—History. I. Title.
   BF1472.G7D38 2007
   133.10941—dc22

                                        2007025497

10   9   8   7   6   5   4   3   2   1
16 15 14 13 12 11 10 09 08 07

Printed and bound in Great Britain by
Antony Rowe Ltd, Chippenham and Eastbourne

Contents

List of Plates

Between pages 240 and 241

Plate 1

Here is *A True and Perfect Relation from the Faulcon at the Banke-side; of the strange and wonderful aperition of one Mr. Powel, a baker lately deceased*. By permission of the Bodleian Library, University of Oxford. Shelfmark: Wood 401 (183).

Plate 2

Laying a Ghost! Richard Newton after George Montard Woodward (1792). By permission of the Trustees of the British Museum.

Plate 3

The Ghosts; Or Mrs. Duffy and Mrs. Cruckshanks. Written by T. Dibidin, Esq. (1805). The image mocks the St James's Park ghost sensation of the previous year (see Chapter 7). By permission of the Bodleian Library, University of Oxford. Shelfmark: Harding B 10 (37).

Plate 4

Edward Kelley raising a ghost. From [Robert Cross Smith], *The Astrologer of the Nineteenth Century* (London, 1825). Author's collection.

Plate 5

The Hammersmith Ghost. Engraving 1804. By permission of the Wellcome Library, London.

Plate 6

John Maddison Morton's farce, *My Husband's Ghost! A Comic Interlude* (c. 1829). Author's collection.

Plate 7

David Garrick as Hamlet, adopting his trademark pose at seeing the ghost. Author's collection.

Plates 8a and 8b

Ghost-making machines. An example of a magic lantern (top) and the phantasmagoria (bottom), as represented in David Brewster's *Letters on Natural Magic* (first published 1832). Author's collection.

Plate 9
Pepper's Ghost Illusion. From Jean Eugène Robert-Houdin, *The Secrets of Stage Conjuring* (London, 1881). By permission of the British Library.

Plate 10
The Haunted Lane. A double exposure stereoscope ghost card (1889). Courtesy of the Library of Congress, Prints & Photographs Division, LC-USZ62-49314.

Plate 11
The Widow's Mite. A double exposure stereoscope ghost card (c. 1876). Courtesy of the Library of Congress, Prints & Photographs Division, LC-USZ62-68335.

Plate 12
A poster advertising William Wallser's well-known Ghost Show (c. 1874). Evanion Collection, Evan 2778. By permission of the British Library.

Acknowledgements

Once again I would like to thank my family and Céline Chantier for their constant support. Richard Crangle, Michael Hunter, Tim Hitchcock, Matthew Cragoe, Jason Semmens, Graham Holderness, Richard Wiseman and Mark Fox all kindly provided information or responded to questions. The publisher's anonymous reader provided useful comments, corrections and suggestions. I would also like to thank the staff of the Norfolk Record Office, West Yorkshire Archive Service, Essex Record Office, Cambridge University Library Manuscript Department, and also the Magic Lantern Society.

Introduction

England has long had a reputation for being haunted. In 1712 the literary critic Joseph Addison, in an essay on the popularity of ghosts and spirits, wondered why 'we abound with more Stories of this Nature'.[1] A few years later, Anthony Hilliar, adopting the guise of an Arab visitor to this country, portrayed the people as exceedingly credulous with regard to ghosts. 'If you tell them that a Spirit carry'd away the side of a House, or play'd Foot-ball with half a dozen Chairs, and as many Pewter Dishes,' he observed, 'you win their Hearts and Assent.' 'Whole Towns and Villages', he continued, 'have e'er now been depopulated, upon a white Horse being seen within half a Mile of them, and near a Church Yard in the night time.'[2] Moving forward a couple of centuries, the Swiss psychiatrist Carl Jung, perhaps influenced as much by the more recent history of English spiritualism as older perceptions, expressed his surprise at finding that the belief in ghosts was just as widespread in his own country as 'among the English'.[3] To try and give a quantative sense of how haunted the country was in the past, in the 1940s a Warwickshire folklorist calculated that there was one ghost to the square mile in his district.[4] Taking this as a representative figure, it can be extrapolated that in war-time England, when according to opinion polls ghost-seeing was at a low ebb, more than 50,000 ghosts haunted the country.

Such calculations are just a bit of fun of course, and it is impossible to prove that England was more haunted than anywhere else. What can be studied, though, is the question why, over the last few centuries, it should be thought that we were such a ghost-ridden nation. For Addison the reason was that 'the English are naturally fanciful, and very often disposed by that Gloominess and Melancholy of Temper, which is so frequent in our Nation, to many wild Notions and Visions, to which others are not so liable'. The twentieth-century ghost hunter Peter Underwood suggested that it was due to 'a unique ancestry with Mediterranean, Scandinavian, Celtic and other strains, an intrinsic island detachment, an enquiring nature, and perhaps our readiness to accept a supernormal explanation'.[5] As I hope to show though, the English love affair with ghosts has little to do with a shared national temperament or the country's ancient ethnic amalgamation. It is primarily a consequence of our religious, social and cultural development over the last 500 years.

1

The continuance of English ghost-belief is a truly remarkable story considering that, as a Protestant country, the population should have rejected ghosts centuries ago along with Catholicism. During the Reformation, Protestant theologians denounced the idea of ghosts as the 'superstitious' product of the medieval Catholic concept of purgatory – the intermediate state in which the souls of the dead suffered for their sins before being allowed into heaven. That ghosts remained a vibrant aspect of popular belief does not necessarily indicate, however, the continuance of an explicitly Catholic eschatology (the theology of death and the afterlife). It tells us more about the tradition, culture and psychology of the English people than it does about their religious persuasion.

But what is a ghost? Throughout this book the term will generally be used to describe the manifestation of the souls of the dead before the living. Souls were often also described as 'spirits', though both historically, and in my usage, 'spirits' also included other entities such as fairies, devils and angels. The term 'apparition' also lacked a precise definition, denoting the visual appearance of a 'ghost-like' presence. So a ghost sensed visually was an apparition, but an apparition was not necessarily a ghost; it could be another form of spirit, a saint or a devil perhaps, or an image of the deceased created by natural forces. 'Phantom' and 'phantasm' have a long history of usage in English sources, though they were rarely used in popular literature until the influence of magic lantern shows from the late eighteenth century onwards. Although occasionally used in the sense of 'ghost', they were generally employed to denote visions or hallucinations of the dead rather than the appearance of their souls. The term 'wraith' has sometimes also been used interchangeably with 'ghost', but it represents a distinct tradition. King James I, in his treatise on the satanic threat, *Dæmonologie* (1597), clarified that 'wraithes' were those spirits that 'appear in the shadow of a person newly dead, or to die, to his friendes'.[6] So a wraith can be defined as the appearance of the human spirit at the moment of or shortly before death, and therefore prior to its ascent to heaven or its stint in purgatory. The relevance of the distinction will become particularly evident when considering Victorian investigations into the existence of ghosts.

The above terms are still widely used today, but other words employed in the past to describe ghosts will no longer be familiar to most readers.[7] King James I used the terms *lemures, umbrae mortuorum*, and *spectra* to describe the spirits of the dead. He was undoubtedly influenced by the first chapter of Ludwig Lavater's *Of Ghostes and Spirites* (1572), which was devoted to the terminology pertaining to the spirit world. James defined *lemures* and *spectra* as those spirits 'that haunted some houses, by appearing in divers and horrible formes, and making great dinne'. Lavater, citing classical sources, provided some less precise definitions, observing that 'some men call the ghosts of all dead things by the name of Lemures', while a *spectrum* was 'a substance without a body, which being hearde or seene, maketh men afrayde'.[8] In this sense it equated with 'apparition'. Before the mid-nineteenth century *spectrum* was rarely used in its modern sense to describe the colours of light.[9] 'Spectre', which appeared in several early modern texts, only entered general language during the early nineteenth century when it was employed in several popular plays. *Umbrae mortuorum* were the 'shadows of the dead'. Words equating with 'shadow' were used throughout Europe to describe both the appearance of the souls of the deceased and the souls of the living, such as witches, that travelled away from the body.[10] Finally, one other Latin word for 'ghost' that also cropped up occasionally in sixteenth- and seventeenth-century sources was *larva* (*larvae*), which referred to the 'mask' or 'guise' of spirits appearing in the form of the dead.

With such a variety of terms being employed over the centuries it is important to be sensitive to the religious and cultural context in which they were used, and how and by whom they were being expressed. I have already highlighted some broad historical and social patterns of usage, but as a modern study of the supernatural beliefs held by a group of Manchester women reveals, even in contemporary society people's use of terminology concerning ghosts is remarkably slippery. There was reluctance amongst the women to use value-laden terms. 'Apparition' and 'spirit' were rarely mentioned during interviews, while 'ghost' was used to describe malign presences rather than to express explicitly a belief in the return of the souls of the dead.[11] Historical sources seldom reveal such subtleties of personal expression regarding ghosts, but we must be conscious of their existence and meaning in the past.

Today a 'haunting' is generally associated with the repeated appearance of a ghost before someone or in a certain location.[12] Yet in the past fairies were also said to haunt places. This is indicative of a broader shared existence. Writing in the late seventeenth century, the Scottish antiquarian Robert Kirk noted how in popular belief fairies were considered by some to be departed souls that lingered on earth. The link is certainly apparent in several Scottish witchcraft trials, in which cunning-folk or healers claimed to have had relations with the spirits of the dead, who either dwelt with the fairies or were fairies – the distinction is not always clear.[13] Nineteenth-century folklorists also identified several parallels between the two entities, noting, for instance, how both often dressed in old-fashioned garb, and liked to linger around ancient burial mounds.[14] One of the foremost experts on fairies, Katharine Briggs, summarising a large collection of relevant fairy beliefs from Scotland, Wales and Cornwall, concluded that fairies were sometimes 'vaguely called "spirits", with a kind of implied suggestion that they were the spirits of the dead. Sometimes they were described without qualification as the dead, or said to have the dead among them. More often they are qualified as a special kind of dead.'[15] This explicit association between ghosts and fairies is, however, little evident in English sources other than those relating to Cornwall. Whether this is because the 'fairy as ghost' tradition is an aspect of an ancient Celtic tradition is another matter. The concept of fairies as intercessionary beings was in significant decline from the seventeenth century in most areas of England other than Cornwall, and so a similar tradition would be less detectable in the sources. As we shall see in the first chapter, though, in English folklore there are indications of a 'ghost as fairy' tradition as distinct from a 'fairy as ghost' tradition. The ambiguous identity of their nature in certain types of haunting is most evident with regard to the boggard of northern England. This was a frightful spirit that haunted places where people had died violently. In this sense it acted like a ghost, but in its manifestation it was usually more akin to a monstrous fairy.

Why would the spirits of the dead want to haunt the world of the living? There was always a reason – or to be more precise people always found a reason. Some were thought to appear to memorialise the tragic end to human lives, such as those of suicides, while other souls were so attached to their earthly routine that they returned out of habit to repeat their daily actions over and over again. Some ghosts were restless due to an unsatisfactory burial. The Yorkshire clergyman, the Rev. J.C. Atkinson (1814–1900), heard that ghosts returned if the corpse was not carried up the customary 'church road' to the burial ground. Any deviation from what was considered a sacred route would result in the dead person 'coming again'.[16] Other spirits returned briefly to show their disapprobation if their earthly remains or the sanctity of the dead were disturbed.

The ghosts that most typified medieval and early modern hauntings, though, were those that actively intervened in the affairs of the living rather than merely appearing before them. Their righteousness enhanced by their heavenly residence, ghosts sometimes returned to haunt the sinful and plague the consciences of moral transgressors. In 1650 an Essex alehouse servant named Susan Lay deposed to a magistrate that she was haunted everywhere she went by the ghost of her mistress Priscilla Beauty. Lay had given birth to illegitimate children by Beauty's husband and her son William. Both children were put out to wet nurses and died. A few days after Priscilla's death in 1650, Lay, now living in the Beautys' barn, began to be haunted by her ghost 'all in white', which called to her 'Sue, Sue, Sue'. Susan interpreted this as a vengeful act. 'Oh this woman will be the destruction of me' she told a companion. William reinforced this view with evident relish. When Susan threatened to commit suicide, he said: 'this is a just judgement of God upon you for if she walks, she walks to you and nobody else'.[17]

Pre-modern ghosts also liked to correct legal injustices. When the second wife of Sir Walter Long (c. 1591–1672) tried to have her stepson disinherited, the legal process was impeded by the ghostly intervention of the first wife, whose disembodied 'fine White-hand' appeared between the parchment and the candle as the clerk sat up one night trying to draw up the legal documentation. He threw down his pen and refused to do it. In another instance the ghost of a woman whose legal settlement for her children had not been carried out after her death appeared to the sister of Doctor Turbervile of Salisbury. The ghost pointed to where the settlement had been hidden behind a wainscot, and informed the woman that she had 'wandred in the Air' but now, finally, she could go to God.[18] Similarly the philosopher and theologian Henry More (1614–1687) received an account of how the ghost of a Mrs Bretton, wife of a Rector of Ludgate, had appeared to her maid to ensure that some land she had bequeathed to the poor was returned after it had been wrongfully denied them after her death.[19]

The most sensational purposeful ghosts were those of the murdered who returned to wreak revenge on their killers. This was an ancient literary role played out time and time again on the stage, yet such was the social and intellectual currency of the notion that, up until the early eighteenth century, it was taken seriously by at least some of the magistracy. In 1660 a Westmorland justice of the peace launched a murder investigation after he was informed by one Robert Hope of Appleby that the ghost of Robert Parkin had appeared to him in the parish church crying, 'I am murdered I am murdered I am murdered.' A few years later, in 1668, a justice of the peace in the West Riding of Yorkshire ordered that people be summoned to give evidence against William Stones of Heeley, Sheffield, regarding the suspicious death of Stephen Starling 'and the apparition of his spirit before him'. As late as 1728 the body of a boy of Beauminster, Dorset, was exhumed on the orders of the coroner after several witnesses said they had seen his ghost. There had been no inquest on the boy's body, but if his spirit had returned then it indicated foul play. The coroner's investigation concluded that the boy had, indeed, been murdered.[20] The moral purpose of ghosts in detecting murderers was also related in numerous instances of providential interventions reported in popular literature through until the late eighteenth century. Chapbooks with titles such as *A Dreadful Warning to all Wicked Persons* reinforced the message: murderers beware; the ghosts are out to get you!

Occasionally the spirits of murderers rather than their victims appeared, yearning to assuage their torment by revealing their crimes. A pamphlet and ballad printed in 1679/80 told how in Middle Row, Holborn, the ghost of a midwife appeared half a year after her death to urge a servant maid to take up two tiles in the hearth of her former house and to bury what they found beneath. Following the ghost's instructions the bones of two children were discovered. They were the remains of illegitimate children that the midwife had murdered 15 years before.[21]

The concept of the vengeful ghost was so engrained in popular belief that it was thought that the living could determine to haunt someone after death as an act of malice and retribution. Such ghosts were, in effect, a curse. In April 1609, for example, a poor woman named Frances Barker was brought before an Essex magistrate regarding an illegitimate child she had with a tailor named John Banson. Banson much abused the woman, moving her between different towns to avoid her pregnancy being detected. One of the threats he made against her was that if she did not follow his orders 'he would kill himself, and that when he was dead his ghost should tear her in pieces'.[22] Similar alarming pronouncements were still being made over two centuries later. In 1858 magistrates who reopened an investigation into the unsolved murder of a Dagenham police constable twelve years before, heard from the wife of one of the suspects, William Page, who had died two years after the foul deed had been committed. She recalled how, as he lay ill, he told her that 'if I said anything he would rise from the grave and crush me'. After he died she said, 'my husband's ghost followed me about. I saw him in three different cottages, and my eyes were wide open. I could seem him as plain as noon day.' The jury at another murder trial a few years later also heard how a man swore that, 'If he died he would torment the prisoner with his ghost for the wrong he had done him.'[23]

The opposite of the ghost curse was the notion that the living could make pacts that the first to die would return at the other's time of need to forewarn of imminent danger. An oft-repeated story concerns the Royalist Major-General John Middleton's escape from the Tower of London in 1652, dressed in his wife's clothes. Middleton and his great friend Laird Bocconi had made a pact along the lines just mentioned. As Middleton languished in his cell the apparition of Bocconi appeared to him to say that he had died and that he was now a ghost, 'and told him, that within Three Days he should escape'.[24] Ghosts' premonitory gifts also led them occasionally to inform the living of their imminent departure from earth. In December 1706 Robert Withers, the vicar of Gately, Norfolk, inserted in the parish register of Brisley the following account of a ghost seen a few months before by a Mr Shaw, a fellow of St John's

College, Oxford.[25] Withers obviously thought the parish register an appropriate place to record what he considered was an example of 'the moral certainty of the truth' regarding the afterlife. A later entry underneath, in what looks like a nineteenth-century hand, gives a rather different interpretation: 'I am sorry to see this story inserted here, which appears to me to have been no more than a dream.' Anyway, as Withers recounted, Shaw was smoking a pipe in his study late one evening when there appeared the ghost of a Mr Naylor, another fellow of the college, who had died four years previously. Naylor's ghost sat down and they conversed for about two hours. Shaw 'askt him how it far'd with him. Very well says he. Were any old acquaintances with him? No! (at which I was much concern'd) but Mr. Orchard will be with me shortly & your self not long after.' As Naylor was about to depart Shaw asked 'if he would call again. No. He had but three days leave of absence & he had other business.' Withers noted that Mr Orchard died soon after and Shaw a couple of months later.

Although from a theological point of view ghosts could not appear on earth without God's permission, the notion that he used them as messengers had always been problematic. Why use a ghost when the angels usually fulfilled that function? The interpretive dilemmas raised by the issue will be discussed in detail in Chapter 4, but a case heard by the Leicester magistrates' bench in July 1829, in which a Mrs Bridgart charged her servant girl with imposing upon her, provides a useful, initial example. Around ten o'clock one night the Bridgart family were in their yard when they heard the servant girl screaming loudly. On opening her bedroom door they found her lying on the floor apparently unconscious. When she recovered consciousness she said 'she saw something white, in the shape of a woman'. Someone sat up with the girl for the rest of the night but no further disturbances occurred. The next night the girl fainted again. Bridgart thought she might be suffering from a guilty conscience and told the girl, 'If thy heart condemns thee, speak the truth, for God knoweth all things.' The girl said nothing incriminating in response and so Bridgart concluded that the apparition was 'probably a supernatural call for one of them; but said they were not to be frightened to death if it was so'. Under further questioning the girl implied that the ghost had been sent by God as a warning to the 'wicked' boys in the household, whom she claimed were 'all liars – you don't know how they all swear and tell lies'. Still, God had told her that they would not be disturbed again by the ghost. Bridgart subsequently suspected the girl was nothing but a troublemaker. Questioned as to her Revelation by the Leicester magistrates, the girl replied, 'I did not say that the Lord had told me so; but that it might be the Lord's will to send it (meaning the ghost), as the boys were in the habit of swearing.' The magistrates could find no grounds for prosecution and so let her off with an admonishment.[26]

Writing in the late nineteenth century, the perceptive historian of ghosts and self-styled 'psycho-folklorist' Andrew Lang concluded that the age of the purposeful ghost was over. The modern ghost was a 'purposeless creature' who 'appears nobody knows why; he has no message to deliver, no secret crime to reveal, no appointment to keep, no treasure to disclose, no commissions to be executed, and, as an almost invariable rule, he does not speak, even if you speak to him.'[27] The basis for his assertion, which has been repeated by other commentators since, derives from the contrast between the evidence provided by the various collections of spirit manifestations published during the late seventeenth century, and the huge archive of contemporary cases accumulated by the Society for Psychical Research (SPR) two centuries later.

Most studies of ghosts from the eighteenth century onwards, including this one, have relied considerably on the numerous cases of haunting collected by the clergyman and philosopher Joseph Glanvill (1636–1680), the philosophy professor George Sinclair, the minister Richard Baxter (1615–1691) and the Somerset gentleman Richard Bovet.[28] All four men had a purpose for recording accounts of purposeful ghosts and turbulent spirits. They were trying to uphold a crumbling system of religious philosophy based on the Neoplatonic conception of a world that was infused with and functioned through the interconnection of a myriad of spirits. Ghosts and angels served to demonstrate the working of providence, in other words the direct divine guidance of human affairs, while witches and evil spirits provided confirmation of the Devil's constant attempts to undermine the Christian faith. So they would undoubtedly have had little interest in ghosts that made no attempt to contact or disturb the living, and simply acted as silent, self-absorbed memorials of the fate and activities of the former living. Many examples of such ghosts can be found in the folklore collections of the nineteenth century, and it is very likely that they were as ubiquitous in early modern popular culture. What I am suggesting, therefore, is that it should not be assumed that the purposeful ghost is representative of the experience of haunting in the period.

Founded in 1882, the Society for Psychical Research gathered a huge body of material on apparitions during its first 20 years, including many accounts of ghosts. Cases were reported and discussed in its *Journal* and *Proceedings*, including a report on the huge Census of Hallucinations, conducted between 1889 and 1894, which elicited some 17,000 responses after requests for personal experiences were advertised in the press. This came after another major and more influential survey conducted by two key members of the society, Edmund Gurney and Frank Podmore, which was published as *Phantasms of the Living* in 1886 and contained just over 700 cases of apparitions. The information accumulated by members of the Society for Psychical Research represents an important resource for studying the recent history of ghosts, but I have limited my use of the material for two reasons. First, a lot of the cases have been extensively analysed and reprinted in numerous books over the last century. Second, and more significantly, relying too heavily on the SPR sources can distort our understanding of the nature of ghosts at the time. Those who provided the SPR with information were predominantly from the middle and upper classes. Their social, educational and religious experiences undoubtedly shaped their views on the nature of ghosts, and consequently how and why they were thought to manifest themselves. The SPR sources tell us little about the experiences, beliefs and legends of the rural and urban working classes, in other words the majority of the population. It is certainly evident that the ghosts reported by the Victorian middle classes were largely purposeless, but an examination of other sources, particularly newspapers and folklore, confirms the continued significance of purposeful ghosts in popular culture. As we shall see, ghosts continued to wreak revenge on murderers, returned to warn people of imminent danger, and retained the habit of locating hidden treasures.

This is not the first book to provide a general history of English hauntings,[29] and it benefits considerably from recent work on the meaning of ghosts in the medieval and early modern periods.[30] When it comes to the modern era, however, historians lose interest in traditional ghosts as their attention switches to the rise of spiritualism during the mid nineteenth century. This is understandable considering the cultural influence of the spiritualist movement, but it has led to the neglect of the equally significant ongoing history of popular hauntings. As to the general structure of this book, previous histories have adopted a chronological approach, tracing the changes in ghost belief from antiquity through to the present. This works well enough, but I thought a thematic approach would better demonstrate how pervasive and enduring the significance of ghosts has been in English social history over the last 500 years or so. As a work of social history this book is not concerned with proving or disproving the reality of ghosts. It is up to the reader to draw what conclusions they want from the centuries of evidence and debates presented here. I have, however, refrained from constantly using the adjective 'supposed' when mentioning ghosts. When examining people's belief in and experience of ghosts, I discuss them as if they were realities to express better how they were understood in the past. Whether you believe in ghosts or not, there is no doubt they make ideal guides for exploring the thoughts and emotions of our ancestors.

Part One

Experience

ONE

Manifestation

How did people know they had seen a ghost? What distinguished the spirits of the dead from their former earthly selves? When someone known to have died appeared to the living then it was an obvious deduction that the vision was a ghost, but in numerous cases ghost and percipient were not known to each other. There had to be other diagnostic characteristics. The reality of existence itself would have been thrown into doubt if the living could not be distinguished from the dead. Translucence and pale opacity were obvious determinants but by no means all ghosts exhibited these qualities. Some did not even appear in human form. As we shall see, though, there was usually a tell-tale sign that one was in the presence of a spirit, even if its exact nature was not always clear. Ghosts shared certain characteristics with fairies, angels and devils, and the tricky task of distinguishing between them often depended on the context in which they appeared; and this in turn changed over the centuries according to religious, philosophical and scientific developments.

PERSONAL CHARACTERISTICS

Ghosts usually preferred a solitary sojourn on earth. Apart from battlefield hauntings and the occasional funeral procession they hardly ever made collective appearances. Seeing ghosts was likewise usually a solitary experience. Rarely has more than one person seen a ghost at the same time, though they often appeared to different people at different times. This has always been one of the key arguments against their reality. According to folk tradition, though, some people were unable to see ghosts due to their date of birth. Some said that first-born sons could not see ghosts, and in the opinion of others neither could those born on Christmas Eve.[1] Perhaps this was a better birthright than being particularly sensitive to the appearance of spirits, which in Somerset was a gift bestowed on those born between midnight and dawn on a Friday.[2]

13

Regarding the gender of ghosts, it is true that in the medieval English and continental sources most were male, as were most percipients.[3] It has to be taken into account, of course, that the authors were usually members of the clergy living in exclusively or predominantly male social circles. The gender imbalance is less obvious in post-Reformation English sources. Although authors and publishers were still predominantly male, in the age of print there was a significant female readership, which may have affected the way in which ghosts were presented. Women were also actively involved in the reporting of ghostly experiences to the likes of Glanvill and Baxter. During the nineteenth and twentieth centuries, women, as spiritualist mediums, folklorists and members of the SPR, were at the forefront of experiencing and investigating encounters with the spirits of the dead. This increasing public female involvement generated a more even proportion of female and male ghost sightings.

It is an intriguing fact that from the medieval period to the present the ghosts of children have rarely been seen in England. The ghost of a murdered child that haunted the countryside near Graythwaite, Cumbria, in the nineteenth century is an unusual example.[4] Infant and childhood mortality was shockingly high for most of the period covered by this study, yet the tragedy of infant death did not seem to translate into a tradition of spiritual manifestation. The deep cultural as well as religious significance of this paucity is suggested by a comparison with the strength of the child ghost tradition in Scandinavian and Baltic folk belief. A survey of nineteenth-century Polish ghost-lore found that 11 per cent of hauntings concerned the spirits of aborted children. In Finland the nightmare experience was sometimes blamed on the ghosts of dead babies, and a diverse array of traditions have been recorded in Sweden and Norway concerning the ghosts of children who were murdered, abandoned, stillborn or who died before baptism or name-giving.[5] As a study of this tradition observed, the position of such infants was 'problematic in that they have never really belonged to the living social group'.[6]

The significance of child-ghosts in Poland is understandable, as are the numerous Irish and French legends of the spirits of unbaptised children appearing as lights or birds.[7] In Catholic countries the medieval concept of limbus puerorum, the intermediate state between heaven and earth where the souls of unbaptised children resided for eternity, remained a strong theme in popular belief right through to the present day. While the similar prominence of child ghosts in nineteenth- and twentieth-century Lutheran Scandinavia may also reflect the continuance of old Catholic traditions in post-Reformation folklore, the lack of a similar tradition in England suggests that the absence or presence of child-ghost legends reflects pre-medieval patterns of belief rather than the success of English Protestant reformers.

There are, however, a few intriguing references in seventeenth-century depositions to the ghosts of adults appearing in the shape of children. In Somerset, during the 1630s, the ghost of one Mother Leakey was seen by a woman 'in the shape of a little child shining very bright and glorious'.[8] A woman who claimed to have seen Priscilla Beauty's ghost in 1650 stated she saw it 'in the shape of a girl about a dozen years old walking up and down the yard'. In 1662, Isabel Binnington of Hull said that the ghost of Robert Eliot, murdered 14 years before, appeared to her 'resembling a boy about twelve years old', as well as in adult form with 'long flaxen hair in green cloaths, and bare-footed', and also 'in white, like a winding sheet'.[9] These seventeenth-century examples presumably reflect the long tradition of Christian pictorial representation of souls ascending to heaven in the forms of naked children. They, along with doves, symbolised the innocence and purity of the soul once freed from the polluted body.

HAUNTING TIMES

Hallowtide, which consists of the Catholic feasts of All Saints' Day (1 November) and All Souls' Day (2 November), is particularly linked with the appearance of ghosts, a brief period when the boundary between the living and the dead was more permeable than at any other time in the Christian calendar. However, the association is, perhaps, not as venerable a tradition as might be thought. In medieval Europe neither day served, as Jean-Claude Schmitt put it, 'as privileged anchoring points for apparitions of the dead'.[10] As far as one can tell from medieval accounts of apparitions, ghosts were more associated with the period from Christmas to the Epiphany. Even then the Christian significance seems less important than the environmental factor of midwinter darkness. Moving eastwards to the Orthodox churches of Europe, Easter and Pentecost were most associated with the communion of the living and the dead, while in Estonian tradition ghosts were thought to prefer appearing in the autumn, or more specifically in the period between Michaelmas (29 September) and Christmas.[11] In fact it could be argued that All Saints' Day was the least likely time to see a ghost as communities made a concerted effort to keep them at bay. The religious observance most associated with the day in pre-Reformation England was the ringing of the church bells. As Ronald Hutton has shown, it proved one of the most stubborn of Catholic practices, with the Elizabethan church authorities pursuing numerous prosecutions up and down the country. Other commemorative customs, which were not reliant on the church, continued clandestinely amongst Catholics and by Protestant communities down the centuries.[12] There is some debate amongst historians as to whether the practice of bell ringing on All Saints' Day was popularly perceived as intercessionary, comforting and thereby propitiating the souls of the dead, or was a more aggressive act of protection intended to ward them off.[13] Either way, it was not a good day to see ghosts, and, anyway, in post-Reformation England there is little evidence that, despite the suppression of bell ringing, ghosts were popularly thought to have recolonised the country at Hallowtide.

Today Halloween is, of course, most associated with the imitation of ghosts and noisy spirits rather than concerns over their actual appearance. As we shall see later in this book, people have been donning white sheets and roaming the streets for centuries, and the practice was particularly common in nineteenth-century towns and cities. But analysing all the numerous court cases that arose from such pranks there is no sense that this was a Halloween tradition. In fact, ghost imitators were just as likely to jump out on people or flit across fields on warm summer evenings as long winter nights. This comes as no real surprise, as Halloween as we know and observe it today is largely a twentieth-century phenomenon derived from America, which developed out of a strong Irish tradition of making mischief and mimicking malicious spirits on All Hallows' Eve.[14]

The time of day rather than the time of year is a more significant issue in the study of hauntings. While ghosts have certainly been seen in daylight, over the last thousand years the vast majority paid nocturnal visits. There was no obvious explanation why this should be, and it was evidently an issue that puzzled many over the centuries. The night was popularly thought to be the most conducive time for devils, fairies and evil spirits to emerge from the depths of hell or the bowels of the earth. From a religious perspective of inversion, if God, the angels and the saints were radiant, casting light wherever Christianity was practised (as iconography depicted them), then it stood to reason that darkness, by contrast, was the natural home of the ungodly and the damned. Neither was purgatory illumined by God's effulgence, and so in the medieval period the spirits of the dead visiting from purgatory would not be allowed to appreciate the divine light of earthly day. When one medieval ghost was asked, 'Why do you appear to me at night rather than during the day?', it replied, 'As long as I cannot go to God, I remain in the night.'[15] But most ghosts were not considered evil, the Devil's minions, or the eternally damned, and furthermore, after the Reformation they were not bound by purgatorial punishment. They often helped the living, returning to right wrongs and reveal injustice. As one eighteenth-century sceptic observed, 'in common reason, spirits have no more to do with night, than day-light; and if any information was really providentially intended by them; day-light, and publick places of resort, would be the properest for their apparition'.[16]

In post-Reformation England, then, other explanations were required, and those proffered were couched in either demonic, scientific or psychological terms. The explanation put forward by the Elizabethan writer Thomas Nashe was simple. He believed apparitions were nothing more than devilish delusions, and, since God had allocated the night as the Devil's kingdom, it stood to reason that he would cast his apparitions in the dark. 'There is no thief that is half so hardy in the day as in the night; no more is the devil.'[17] Nashe's explanation was only satisfactory if one rejected the possibility that the spirits of the dead returned, but many educated people did not. Perhaps science could justify this faith. The philosopher Henry More believed he knew the answer as to why 'Apparitions haply appear oftner in the Night than in the Day'. It was, he suggested, to do with the quality of night-time air and the ability of spirits to spin a physical form for themselves out of aerial matter. He thought that the damp, clammy air of the night was 'more easily reduced to visible consistency' by the 'imagination' of spirits. He was adamant, though, that human imagination could not generate such physical materialisations.[18] The anonymous author of Aristotle's New Book of Problems, which was printed several times for a general reading public during the early eighteenth century, further added that, because ghosts were formed from air, the heat of the sun would dissolve their vaporous mantle.[19] By the early eighteenth century, however, the Neoplatonic conceptions that inspired More's theory had been largely discarded in intellectual circles. Ghosts were not realities but figments of the imagination. When the Rev. Henry Bourne puzzled over the matter in the early eighteenth century he focused on the introspection that the night encouraged. Darkness brought on intimations of the Day of Judgement and so 'inclines us to grave and serious Thoughts, raises in us Horrour and Dismay, and makes us afraid'.[20]

MATERIALISATION

An acquaintance of the Victorian Cornish antiquarian Joseph Hammond once described how the ghost of a miner he knew appeared first as a puff of smoke. It 'circled round and round and then gathered itself into a sort of tiny cloud, which hung suspended a few feet above the ground. Surprise gave place to terror, as the smoke gradually assumed the form of his dead comrade.'[21] In

1790 it was reported that the deceased wife of a London bookseller appeared to a friend of her husband 'entirely encircled in a thick blue vapour, and which, upon her disappearing, always left a very strong scent'.[22] Most accounts of ghosts, however, say little about the manner in which they appeared. People rarely had time to sit and stare at ghosts for hours on end. Unless they had some terrible burden to get off their ethereal chests or a task to complete (behaviour most common in the early modern period), ghosts usually only appeared for seconds or minutes before disappearing. On first seeing a ghost, then, the attention was fixed immediately on its appearance and the senses were stunned by the initial shock.

A little more detail is forthcoming about how ghosts disappeared. This was the culmination of the experience, the senses had adjusted and concentration was intense. In 1662 a ghost was described as vanishing by 'glideing away without any motion of steps'.[23] An old labourer of Satterthwaite, Cumbria, recalled how, around 1825, as he rode in a cart one day, he saw the ghost of a woman, 'dressed well but old-fashionedly, suddenly leave the highway and rapidly ascend into the air, finally disappearing from sight'.[24] Ghosts hardly ever exited by sinking into the ground, as they traditionally did on the stage, and rarely did they disappear by walking through walls or other solid objects, as in films. Despite the cultural influence of modern media, even in twentieth-century reports the latter behaviour is relatively uncommon.[25] Ghosts evidently respected physical entrances such as doors and passageways.

Over the centuries ghosts have often been reported to have a luminescent quality, and sometimes, particularly outdoors, manifested themselves as lights, often of a bluish hue. A man of St Austell told Joseph Hammond how he was going home one summer evening when he saw a pale, bluish light. In typical pixy-led fashion, he lost his way, and, as he began to feel exhausted, the light went out and in its place he saw a man wheeling a barrow. He cried out as it approached and the ghost stopped and melted away. Some locals subsequently told him that a few years before a miner pushing a barrow had fallen into a disused mineshaft near the spot.[26] The appearance of the soul as an indistinct luminescence is found in the tradition of death lights or corpse candles. They were described as blue lights about three feet high, which left the house just before or at the moment of death and followed the path that the funeral procession would take. They would then enter the church and rest at the spot where the coffin would be placed, lighting up the whole church before moving to the grave plot and disappearing. The appearance of a death light was considered a good a sign for it foretold the soul was at peace. A detailed seventeenth-century account of similar mysterious lights in Wales described how, 'If it be a little Candle, pale or blewish, then follows the Corps either of an Abortive, or some Infant, if a big one, then the Corps of some one come to Age, if there be seen two or three, or more, some big, some small together, then so many, and such Corpses together.'[27] In the early twentieth century it was observed that although the belief in corpse candles was once widespread, it was by then held by only a few old people.[28]

These dead lights have long been equated with the strange gaseous lights emanating from damp and boggy places, known variously as will-o'-the-wisps, Jack o' Lanterns or ignis fatui. The phenomenon was widely interpreted in popular cultures across Europe and beyond as the manifestation of either the spirits of the dead or fairies, and England was no exception.[29] In Somerset, for example, spunkies, as they were also known, were thought to be the souls of unbaptised children.[30] It was the apparent deliberateness of their movement and predilection for following people that gave them a supernatural quality. It would be wrong to assume, however, that people thought every blue light they saw on a dark night was a ghost. There was popular awareness that some ignis fatui had natural causes. It was the context in which they appeared and their behaviour that shaped the interpretation of their existence. This is apparent from the Rev. Sabine Baring-Gould's interview with William Henry Shopland, of Broadwoodwidger. One evening at harvest time around 1860, Shopland and several others saw a strange light dancing about in the spot where, not long before, two girls had been gleaning. The girls were the daughters of a neighbour, William Hicks, whose son had recently died. According to Shopland, the light 'ran from place to place as though tracking their footsteps ... we saw it perfectly, as a blue candle flame. It moved up and down and finally settled on a mow.' Shopland and others saw the light in the same field for three or four months. Because it was dry ground he did not think it was a Jack o' Lantern. 'We thought that young Hicks who had died was troubled in his mind about something, and that this was his spirit.'[31] The Northamptonshire poet John Clare (1793–1864) had also seen many will-o'-the-wisps and considered them nothing more than bog vapours, until one night he and a companion were entranced at seeing two seemingly playing with each other. It 'robd me of the little philosophic reason[in]g which I had', he confessed; 'about them I now believe them spirits'.[32]

DRESS

In his survey of popular beliefs the eighteenth-century antiquarian Francis Grose remarked that 'Ghosts commonly appear in the same dress they usually wore whilst living; though they are sometimes cloathed all in white; but that is chiefly the churchyard ghosts.'[33] This is an accurate observation apart from the last statement. White-sheeted or shrouded ghost were also sometimes seen in homes and on the streets. John Clare wrote how there had recently been 'a great upstir in town about the appearance of the ghost of an old woman who had been recently drownd in a well – it was said to appear at the bottom of neighbour Billings close in a large white winding sheet dress'. He and a neighbour spent several nights waiting for it to appear, but saw nothing.[34] Up until the nineteenth century it was common for the poor to bury their dead in such winding sheets or shrouds. Only the wealthy could afford a wooden coffin. After the corpse had been washed and laid out, a white sheet, sometimes the bedsheet on which the person died, was wrapped around the body allowing only the face to be seen, with the cloth fastened at the head and feet to ensure the corpse did not slip out when being placed in the grave. The sheet had traditionally been made of linen, like Jesus' shroud, but a law of 1666 ordered that they be made of wool to help boost the textile industry. Towards the end of the seventeenth century the wealthy elite increasingly discarded the traditional winding sheet, clothing corpses in tailor-made funerary outfits consisting of a white shirt or smock and a cap.[35] John Aubrey recounted that the Oxford philologist Henry Jacob, who died on 5 November 1652, appeared a week later to his cousin, the doctor William Jacob, 'standing by his Bed, in his Shirt, with a white Cap on his Head', which was presumably how he was dressed in his coffin.[36] However, only a minority of ghosts were seen in their winding sheet or shroud, and the image was more of a stereotype, exploited by hoaxers and used in literary and pictorial representations over the centuries. Medieval illuminated manuscripts sometimes depicted the apparition of the prophet Samuel in a shroud.[37] During the seventeenth century one woodcut of a ghost in a winding sheet tied up at the top of the head but loose at the bottom, and with taper in hand, was used over and over again to illustrate ballads and pamphlets concerning ghosts.[38]

Because of the stereotypical image of ghosts swathed in white fabric, the wearing of pale clothes, such as workers' smocks, could be risky on dark nights. In December 1851 it was reported how a couple living in Alum Street, Great Ancoats, Manchester, were returning home from the market when the wife looked down a dark alleyway near their home and saw 'something very white', which frightened her. She clung to her husband and exclaimed, 'Oh dear me, there's a ghost!' The intrepid husband pursued the white figure and managed to catch it. It turned out to be a young thief named James Devine who had just robbed Taylor's Mill in Alum Street and was making off with a swathe of white calico cloth, which he had draped around himself. He was subsequently prosecuted.[39] A less satisfactory intervention by the police followed the sighting of a spooky white figure that kept appearing by a lane in Hollybush Hill, Hampstead, in November 1836. Several people had been terrified to suddenly see a white apparition flitting to and from behind a wall, and one night a young woman named Williams was so alarmed by 'the ghost' that she ran shrieking to PC Simmons, who happened to be patrolling in the area. Similar incidents had been previously reported and so that night, around ten o'clock, Inspector Aggs and two constables determined to confront the apparition. While searching the bushes around the premises where the ghost had been sighted, they were attacked by a pale figure. It turned out to be a solicitor named E.P. Sutton, who evidently had a penchant for white apparel. Sutton was knocked down by the constables, dragged to the police station and charged with assault. The magistrate at Marylebone police court subsequently dismissed the case due to conflicting evidence.[40]

Tragedy ensued in Hammersmith on 3 January 1804 when a bricklayer named Thomas Milward was shot dead around ten o'clock at night by an Excise Officer named Francis Smith who mistook him for a ghost.[41] For over a month an apparition, usually garbed in a white sheet though sometimes wearing an animal skin, had plagued the neighbourhood. It was rumoured that the wife of a locksmith had died of fright and two others were dangerously ill from the shock of being confronted by the ghostly figure. William Girdler, a local watchman, testified that the alarm caused by the ghost was 'very great', 'many people were very much frightened'. It was rumoured to be the spirit of a local man who had cut his throat a year or so before.[42] Every evening a group of young men patrolled the area looking for it. It was certainly unwise to be out at night in white clothing – as was a bricklayer named Thomas Milward on the night in question. His working apparel consisted of white linen trousers, a white flannel waistcoat and a white apron. Only a few nights before, as he made his way home from work, he had frightened a gentleman and two ladies in a carriage. The gentleman had called out 'there goes the ghost', to which Milward replied that he was no such thing, swore at him, and threatened to punch him in the head. After this incident Milward's mother-in-law begged him to change clothes: '"Thomas," says I, "as there is a piece of work about the ghost, and your clothes look white, pray do put on your great coat, that you many not run any danger."' He evidently refused.

On the night of the third, Francis Smith was in the White Hart pub when the conversation turned to the ghost. Fuelled by drink, Smith decided to put an end to the haunting and was joined in his quest by Girdler. They agreed to take separate paths in order to cover more ground, and they were conscious enough to arrange a watchword to ensure they did not shoot each other. Espying a white figure between the hedges of Black Lion Lane, Smith twice asked it to identify itself. Receiving no reply and seeing it continue to advance he shot it with his fowling gun. As soon as Smith realised he had killed a man he gave himself up to the local magistrate. He was subsequently found guilty at the Old Bailey of murdering Milward and was sentenced to death, but was swiftly reprieved and had his sentence reduced to one year's imprisonment. In July he received a free pardon from the king.

By no means all ghosts were pale visions. In the various collections of ghost sightings published during the second half of the seventeenth century, there are several ghosts that percipients swore looked just as they had dressed in life. The ghost of a gentleman of Marlborough named Edward Aven appeared to several people in 1674 'in the same Cloathes, which he wore in his life time; as a long White-Crown'd hatt, Blew Cloaths, and White Stockings'. Likewise the ghost of Mistress Bretton, wife of Dr Bretton of Ludgate, Deptford, appeared to her servant maid 'in a morning Gown, the same in appearance with that she had often seen her Mistris wore'. In such cases there was nothing visually to distinguish the dead from the living. Indeed Bretton's maid exclaimed, 'were not my Mistris dead, I should not question but you are she'.[43]

Francis Grose observed that English ghosts hardly ever wore black.[44] This was true for his time, but not for the entire period covered by this book. In medieval Western Europe the colour of ghosts' clothing was represented as changing from black to white as they progressed through purgatory.[45] In post-Reformation England this symbolism was obviously rendered redundant and black ghosts became a rarity. During the second half of the nineteenth century, however, sightings of black-clad apparitions became quite numerous again, as is evident from reports sent to the SPR.[46] This reflected, perhaps, the spread of formalised black mourning attire in Victorian England, the price of silk crepe having reduced massively over the previous 100 years.[47] For reasons to be discussed later, there was also a significant increase in the number of apparitions of nuns sighted during the late nineteenth and twentieth centuries. To give just one instance that combines both observations, a female ghost clad in a black silk gown, which haunted a farm on the Isle of Axholme, Lincolnshire, was thought to be associated with a religious house that once stood on the spot.[48]

There is a distinct tradition of the ghostly White Lady. The folklore sources are full of examples. There was the woman in white that frequented a lakeside spot near Hawkshead, and one with buckled shoes that haunted a pond at Llwynberried.[49] The Shropshire folklorist L.H. Hayward, writing in the 1930s, knew of several White Ladies in the county. One at Longnor lived in a pool and would come out and dance on the green at night.[50] Another emerged from a 'bottomless' pool near Morton, Lincolnshire and proceeded to glide over the surrounding area.[51] With their liking for deep pools and other watery places, and in some cases a lack of historical association or back-story, many of the White Ladies seem more fairy-like than ghosts. One folklorist has suggested White Lady figures in early literature had no ghostly characteristics at all, and that it seemed they had 'been degraded from a form of mother goddess to a kind of fairy and finally to a ghost'.[52] While the link to female divinity worship is stretching the evidence too far, the suggestion that the White Lady is a fairy archetype is pertinent. Across much of England, Cornwall being a singular exception, fairy belief was in serious decline by the eighteenth century. Examples of people professing to see fairies are few and far between in the folklore sources compared to ghost sightings. It is quite likely that long-held traditions regarding the appearance of ethereal fairy women, even queens, would be reinterpreted in terms of more 'realistic' female ghosts.

The conundrum of why ghosts wear clothing will be discussed later, but suffice it to say that sightings of naked ghosts were exceedingly rare throughout the period concerned.[53] There are a few medieval examples, such as the Rochester priest whose shivering, naked appearance was symbolic of the way in which his estate had been denuded by his executors.[54] One of the very few reports of a ghost in the altogether concerned a shepherd named Charles Taylor, whose experience can be dated to the early nineteenth century. Returning home one evening from folding his sheep near Bampton, Oxfordshire, he was much frightened to see briefly the apparition of a naked man beside him on the road.[55] The shepherd may not have been hallucinating. In another instance a nude ghost proved to be flesh and blood. In January 1834, George Barlow, a flashing Primitive Methodist of Winsford, was sentenced to three months' hard labour. For three years an apparition or 'boggart' in the guise of a naked man appeared every few months at night on the roads around the village, causing much consternation to the local population. The *Macclesfield Courier* reported that women 'dared not venture out of doors after dusk' for fear of the obscene spirit. The boggart was eventually laid after appearing at the window of a pub between eleven and twelve o'clock at night on 4 January, scaring a female servant who was scrubbing the floor. Her screams brought her master to the scene. He managed to overpower the naked Barlow and hand him over to the local constable.[56]

HEADLESS

The headless or acephalous ghost is one of the classic ghost stereotypes, present in folk tradition across Europe. It is also the rarest of firsthand ghost sightings, based more on legend than experience. In England we find a little evidence for headless ghosts in the medieval period. According to the fifteenth-century chronicler John Warkworth, amongst the numerous ominous tokens seen in 1473, people between Leicester and Banbury and elsewhere 'herde a long tyme cryinge, "Bowes! Bowes!" whiche was herde of xl. menne; and some menne saw that he that cryed soo was a hedles manne'.[57] Examples are more forthcoming from the seventeenth century onwards. Richard Baxter related several cases. An acquaintance of his, Colonel John Bridges, saw 'something like a headless Man' as he peered out of a window one night at Edson Hall, near Alcester. Then there was the servant who had murdered his master and fled to Ireland, and was haunted by the apparition of a headless man whenever he lay alone in bed. Despite lacking a head, the ghost would say to him 'Wilt thou yet confess?' Its repeated visits eventually drove him to give himself up.[58] A broadside reported in 1722 that the apparition of a funeral procession conducted by headless men had been seen marching towards the residence of the late Duke of Buckingham.[59] A hundred years later the Rev. J.C. Atkinson (1814–1900) recalled how in his Essex childhood he knew of the ghost of a headless lady in a blood-stained nightdress that appeared during certain phases of the moon.[60] Early the following century, a man was sometimes seen on the road near Peter's Pool, Hay-on-Wye, carrying his head in his hands.[61] Many more examples could be given from the late nineteenth and twentieth centuries.

The obvious explanation for headless ghosts is that they represent those who had their heads chopped off. It has been suggested that the absence of acephalous ghosts in Ancient Greek and Roman sources was because beheading was a rare form of punishment or modus operandi of murderers.[62] In England it was not particularly common either. From the Anglo-Saxon period hanging was the main form of execution. Still, there are examples of beheadings from Anglo-Saxon cemeteries, and in some cases the method was evidently used as a ritual act to prevent the victims' corpses from rising from the grave.[63] Beheading was rarely employed in early modern England, and the few occasions when it was meted out concerned treasonous members of the aristocracy held in the Tower of London. The most famous victim was, of course, Anne Boleyn, whose headless ghost is rumoured to still haunt the vicinity of the Tower. There are hardly any instances of people seeing headless Anglo-Saxon ghosts, however, and most acephalous ghosts did not hang around the Tower of London, nor did they have any association with treasonous activities. So there is little direct link between beheading and headless spirits.

People in the past also pondered why some of the non-aristocratic ghosts haunting their neighbourhoods had no head, and a general association was made with head and neck injuries. The headless horseman who, every New

Year's Eve, haunted a track between Penselwood and Stourton, in Wiltshire, was thought to be the ghost of a man who made a wager at Wincanton market to ride his horse to his home in Stourton in seven minutes. He cut across country and broke his neck going down the track. The headlessness of the ghost of a smuggler near Crowborough, Sussex, was attributed to the fact that he was shot in the head by a gamekeeper.[64] But rationalising headless ghosts takes us only so far in understanding them. What of the many headless animal ghosts, such as the bear-like apparition seen by a Royalist soldier named Simon Jones during the Civil War, or the headless horse and pig that appeared occasionally in the parish of Tillington, Sussex, during the mid nineteenth century?[65] There is clearly a deeper meaning.

The conundrum of headless ghosts can be situated in terms of Christian ideas about the fate of mutilated bodies at the Day of Judgement.[66] In the early modern period there were lengthy debates about what happened to those who had been eaten by cannibals or devoured by beasts and fishes. They were a more rarefied version of the classic old-style pub debate about whether a man with one leg would have the other one restored in the afterlife. The comforting orthodox theological view was that God would reunite every particle of each body with its soul, and therefore the resurrected body would be identical to the complete body of the deceased. Some argued further that the resurrected would be free from all imperfections. Either way, from this theological perspective there would be no headless men and women at the Day of Judgement. Still, these musings do not take us much further. We should focus not on the ghostly body, perhaps, but on what the missing head symbolised. One Jungian psychologist, basing her analysis on Swiss ghost-sightings in the 1950s, suggested that headless ghosts were the unconscious ideation of the moral penalty meted out to those who had committed a terrible crime while alive – the loss of personality, the 'highest value attainable in life'.[67] But this explanation does not apply to most of the English headless ghost sightings and legends, which do not concern murderers or other heinous criminals. Working on a similar level of abstraction the folklorist Theo Brown suggested the headless ghost implied 'the shadow of that earthbound side of humanity left stranded without its informing spiritual centre'.[68] A more explicit construction of the same idea would be that the headless ghost was a cultural echo of the pre-Christian pagan belief that the soul was located in the head, and that at death the head was symbolically separated as the soul departs. Only the ghostly body returned as a spiritual memory. Such speculations, while fascinating, still tell us little about the meaning of the headless ghost in the early modern and modern periods. It remains an enigmatic recurring motif.

INVISIBLE GHOSTS

Many reported ghosts over the centuries were not visible; their presence and sometimes their identity were revealed through the stimulation of senses other than sight. In late nineteenth and twentieth century studies there are numerous accounts of people feeling an indefinable sensation of a presence, which is sometimes connected with a perceived drop in temperature.[69] Sometimes this feeling heralds an apparition and other times it constitutes the entire haunting episode. The experience does not necessarily cause unease. In those cases where it is connected with the bereavement process it can evidently be a comforting feeling.[70] Considering the psychological and environmental basis for the sensation, it is likely that it is neither culturally nor historically exclusive.

Sometimes the presence of a ghost was beyond the detection of human senses. It was a long-held belief that flames turned blue when spirits were around. There is a reference to the notion in *Richard III*, when the king observes, 'The lights burn blue', heralding the appearance of a succession of ghosts. A pamphlet of 1673 recounting the recent appearance of a female ghost at a house in Deptford noted that its presence 'caused the Lights of two Candles that were burning, to be almost extinguished, and burn blue'.[71] Daniel Defoe gave some consideration to the reality of the matter, including a long account of how a London dinner party was thrown into pandemonium when the candles burned blue. A servant seeing this ominous sign fearfully exclaimed, 'I think the Devil is in the Candles to Night', thereby frightening the wits out of the ladies present.[72] The idea that animals have a greater sensitivity to spirits than humans is also venerable and widespread.[73] There are numerous examples in the English records. Baxter recounted the case of a mastiff that awakened a household with its howling having sensed a ghost outside. Francis Grose noted that dogs had a greater faculty for seeing ghosts, showing 'signs of terror, by whining and creeping'. In the nineteenth century an 'eminently unsuperstitious' farmer told Henry Cowper that his cattle and horses became remarkably frightened when they passed near a haunted spot at Hawkshead poor house.[74]

Returning to less refined human senses, people occasionally claimed to have smelt the spirits of the dead. Early modern pamphlets sometimes reported that troublesome ghosts left behind the sulphurous smell of brimstone. A seventeenth-century gentlewoman whose bedroom was haunted smelt an even fouler odour. The ghost or spirit left an 'impression on the Bed, as if some Body had been lying there, and opening the Bed, she smelt the smell of a Carcase some-while dead'.[75] However, such stenches suggested the whiff of the demonic rather than the dearly departed, indicating that they either emanated from the spirits of the dead who had journeyed from purgatory or hell, or were evil spirits masquerading as ghosts. Less obnoxious but unidentifiable spirit odours were even more of a puzzle. John Aubrey recorded an apparition seen not far from Cirencester in 1670, which, when being asked whether it was a good or bad spirit, 'returned no answer, but disappeared with a curious Perfume and a most melodious Twang'. Whether it was a ghost was debatable, and Aubrey noted that the astrologer William Lilly decided it was a fairy.[76] While evil smells clung to evil spirits, so in Christian hagiography angels and saints exuded sweet fragrances.[77] One might expect to find that a little of this perfume rubbed off on ghosts from heaven, but descriptions of ghost odour are rare until the evidential material produced by spiritualism. The latter development may explain the popularity of noxious and perfumed ghosts in Victorian and Edwardian ghost literature. In Wilkie Collins's short novel The Haunted Hotel (1878) a playwright who is planning to write a ghost drama remarks to himself, 'a terrible smell from an invisible ghost is a perfectly new idea. But it has one drawback. If I realise it on stage, I shall drive the audience out of the theatre.'[78] In the twentieth century there is more reported evidence of ghosts revealing their presence by smell, but still only in a small minority of cases. Green and McCreery found that 8 per cent of their respondents reported odours associated with apparitions.[79] As recent interviews with the bereaved indicate, ghosts were more likely to exude mundane scents which people intimately associated with their loved ones. One woman said she could feel her deceased husband's presence and smell the cigarettes he used to smoke. Another woman once felt her husband's presence by the manifestation of the odour of the muscle rub he used regularly.[80]

Invisible ghosts were more frequently heard than smelt. Noises resulting from violent or aggressive actions, such as slamming doors, or knocking on walls, were usually associated with poltergeists, and will be discussed later in this chapter. In the past, passive auditory ghosts were generally identifiable by the repetitive actions that the living were associated with in life. Most common was the sound of footsteps but others were manifested by occupational sounds. A man of Longtown, Herefordshire, reported how he heard the ghost of a hurdle-maker: 'you could hear him tap, tap, tap, choppin' wood for his hurdles all about the place where he was used to work'.[81] Similarly, in the 1930s in the village of Berwick St James, Wiltshire, the former site of a carpenter's workshop was haunted by the tapping noise of the carpenter's hammer.[82] In November 1847, work on the Lancashire, Cheshire and Birkenhead Railway was halted after a man was crushed by a tunnel collapse near Stockham. When workers resumed work, for several days they heard the sound of a pickaxe emanating from the spot where the worker had been killed. It was concluded that it must be the ghost of the man, a belief that was confirmed when one of the navvies was lowered into the tunnel and emerged swearing that he had seen the white figure of the dead man working away. Subsequent investigation revealed the ghost was merely a tin powder can being blown against rocks by high winds.[83]

The rustle of silk was a more frequently reported auditory sign of a ghostly presence, usually defining both the gender and social status of the ghost. Silk was not a fabric worn by the poor. During the haunting of Mr Mompesson's house in Tedworth, Wiltshire, in 1662–63, a member of the household 'heard a rusling noise in his Chamber, and something came to his Bedside, as if it had been one in silk', while another heard an invisible entity enter room that 'rusled as if it had been in silk'.[84] An elderly Oxford man recalled of his encounter with a ghost in 1894: 'the ghost was that of a tall woman dressed in silk', for he 'heard the rustling of the dress'. Quite a few such cases were also reported to the SPR.[85] Even when the rustling accompanied visual apparitions one gets the impression that it was sometimes the sound that enabled the percipient to characterise the apparel and identity of the ghost. Consider, for example, the experience of a Wiltshire man who told a folklorist in 1894 that he was walking along on the local turnpike road – in reality a highly unusual place to encounter a well-to-do woman walking in silk – when a tall lady dressed in silk 'rustled past'.[86]

SPEECH

Francis Grose noted the tradition that 'a ghost has not the power to speak till it has been first spoken to'. This had to be done in a prescribed way, 'commanding it, in the name of the Three Persons of the Trinity, to tell you who it is, and what is its business'. Once it began to speak it was dangerous to interrupt or ask questions.[87] But, in general, ghosts were reluctant speakers and, as we shall see in a later chapter, the representation of the dumb ghost pointing at some malefactor or guilty person became a stereotypical representation on the stage. In the early modern period vocal ghosts were not rare, but during the nineteenth century they lost their voices to a considerable degree and by the 1970s ghosts were decidedly taciturn. Green and McCreery's survey found that only 14 per cent of all human apparitions spoke, noting that 'few speak at length, and the speaking is not always realistic'.[88] A similar comment was made back in 1681 regarding a ghost that made some physical contact, but could not speak beyond a whisper despite much earnest human beseeching:

This troublesome Spirit I suspect to have been the Ghost of some party deceased who would have uttered something, but had not the knack of speaking so articulately as to be understood. And when they can speak intelligibly, it is ordinarily in a hoarse and low Voice, as is observable in many stories.[89]

In the past, when ghosts did speak it was certainly not for idle chit-chat or to discourse at length on the nature of the afterlife. If they did more than repeat one's name three times and groan, it was because they had urgent news or instruction to impart, which could not be divulged by gestures alone. The late eighteenth-century occultist Ebenezer Sibly believed that only the spirits of those who had been murdered under 'circumstances uncommonly horrid and execrable' were able to speak. This was because the horrific remembrance of the event did 'more powerfully operate upon the faculties of the apparition, as to enable it to frame the similitude of a voice, so as to discover the fact, and give some leading clue to detect and punish the wicked perpetrator'.[90] Sibly was correct in that the most talkative ghosts were usually of those who had died a terrible death, but the need to right other wrongs, such as inheritance disputes or hidden goods also sometimes required a conversation.

The question of how exactly ghosts spoke without having physical organs has long been considered. There are several medieval accounts of ghosts deigning to explain to the living the nature of their vocal capacities. The response of two of them that they spoke from their guts and not their mouths hardly solved the matter, though it helped explain how headless ghosts sometimes talked. Another replied more convincingly that the power of speech lay in the soul and not the tongue.[91] In the early eighteenth century *Aristotle's New Book of Problems* plumped for a Neoplatonic scientific solution. As aerial beings, ghosts had command of the movement of air, and since sound was transmitted by percussion, 'they assume a Voice by beating on the Air, and so frame Sounds, as to be understood of us in any Language they shall please'.[92] The following century, the author Catherine Crowe, borrowing from contemporary theories of mesmerism and clairvoyance, argued that, 'in cases where speech appears to be used by a spirit, it is frequently not audible speech, but only this transference of thought, which appears to be speech from the manner in which the thought is borne in and enters the mind of the receiver; but it is not through his ears'.[93]

TOUCHING ENCOUNTERS

It has already been observed that ghosts commonly respected physical objects rather than walk through them, but that is not to say that they could not. It was their ethereal lightness that enabled them to travel through the air. Glanvill provided an account of a female ghost in which a man stated that 'If a Tree stood in her walk, he observed her always to go through it.' On one occasion the ghost requested that the man lift her up, and he reported that 'She felt just like a bag of Feathers in his arms.'[94] This was fascinating detail for Glanvill because he was engaged in a more general debate with contemporaries about the nature of heavenly substance. Over the centuries the touch of ghosts has usually been described as cold. A seventeenth-century pamphlet told how a female ghost placed a finger that 'seemed to be very cold' on a lodger in a Deptford inn. In the same period a gentlewoman visited repeatedly by a ghost described how she felt it 'cold and very smooth', and another woman who was touched by her deceased mistress affirmed her hand 'was as cold as a Clod'.[95] This was presumably explained away as representing the temperature of corpses, but it is worth noting that the touch of the Devil was also said to be icy.

Ghosts rarely applied much pressure to the flesh of the living, usually merely brushing past or giving a gentle prod or embrace. The gentlewoman mentioned above described it as like 'a cold blast or puff of Wind'. Occasionally, though, they liked to throw what weight they had around. Samuel Wesley, father of John Wesley, described how during the haunting of the family home at Epworth in 1716–17, he had 'been thrice pushed by an invisible power, once against the corner of my desk in the study, a second time against the door of the matter chamber, a third time against the right side of the frame of my study door, as I was going in'.[96] In 1802 a spirit haunting a house near Cambridge took a particular dislike to people's clothing. The case was recorded in a letter from Benjamin Smith, then a student, to his father the Nonconformist and politician William Smith (1756–1835). For two weeks past, wrote Smith, a 'ghost' had plagued the house of a tanner, ripping to shreds the clothes of its inhabitants: '18 or 20 of the neighbours, who went in to examine, were served by the spirit just the same way. – multitudes of people soon flocked from all quarters to have their clothes spoilt, and all went away satisfied and in rags'. A local doctor launched an investigation but no evidence of fraud was found. Smith was satisfied that the reality of the spirit manifestation was 'beyond the possibility of doubt.'[97] In recent decades some people have claimed to be sexually assaulted by ghosts, but such instances are rare in the historical record.[98] The sensation of nocturnal molestation was usually attributed to the Devil or witches, and some cases were certainly the result of a condition known as sleep paralysis, which will be discussed in a later chapter.

The actions of aggressive invisible forces take us into the realm of the obstreperous poltergeist, where the boundaries between the activities of devils, witches and ghosts become blurred.[99] The term 'poltergeist', meaning 'noisy ghost', was first used in print by Martin Luther (1483–1546), but it only entered English vocabulary during the nineteenth century when Catherine Crowe referred to the poltergeists of the Germans in her compendium of ghost stories *The Night-Side of Nature* (1848).[100] It was the psychic investigator Harry Price (1881–1948) who then popularised the term and the phenomena in the twentieth century through his public investigations and publications. Poltergeist activity, which was nearly always associated with the haunting of buildings, typically consisted of the throwing or moving of objects, the slamming of doors, the rattling of windows, and the rapping on walls and furniture. Occasionally spirits would communicate through such knocking. Sometimes they pushed, pinched and bruised people. As one nineteenth-century study of ghosts astutely observed, 'a ghost's power of making a noise, and exerting what seems to be great physical energy, is often in inverse ratio to his power of making himself generally visible, or, at all events, to his inclination so to do'.[101]

Stone-throwing or lithobolia, as such spirit activity was called by one seventeenth-century pamphleteer,[102] was a particularly common feature of historic poltergeist activity. Richard Baxter reported the case of a house in Lutterworth plagued by stones for several weeks in February 1646. Large crowds gathered to see the mystery but 'no search could discover any fraud'.[103] John Beaumont, writing in 1705, recounted a similar instance that had occurred recently at the house of a Mr Pope of Butley, in Somerset. Pope's adolescent son suffered from recurring fits during which he said he saw spirits that threatened to burn the house down. For days stones were thrown through windows, 'no Man perceiving from what Hand they came', until the day when the house and oxen stall were set on fire.[104] Through rumour and gossip, the act of stone-throwing, if continued for long enough without detection, could accrue supernatural associations that were not present in the first place. In the Lutterworth case mentioned above, Baxter reported that the stone-thrower also targeted the crowds that gathered but, strange to say, the stones 'hit them, but hurt them not'. The *West Briton* newspaper, reporting on a stone-thrower who targeted a military depot in Truro in April 1821, patronisingly observed that 'The lower classes, who have always a taste for the marvellous, are fully persuaded that this is a supernatural visitation by some troubled spirit, and numberless tales of the most extravagant nature have been circulated.' These included assertions by some that the stones smelt of brimstone and that they continued to rain down in rooms even though the windows and doors were shut.[105]

The haunting of the Wesley's home, which is now usually referred to as the 'Epworth Poltergeist', demonstrates well the fact that up until the nineteenth century in urban areas, and the twentieth century nationally, such noisy manifestations were not commonly blamed on ghosts. Emily Wesley believed the spirit, which they called 'Old Jeffrey', was the work of witches or an act of magical spite by local cunning-folk. Her father Samuel called it a 'deaf and dumb devil'. No one mentioned spirits of the dead. In other poltergeist cases the usual popular cultural explanation was witchcraft, while the puritanical and evangelical were quick to blame aggressive hauntings on obsession, in other words the external molestation of a person or persons by the Devil. The decision-making of the Independent minister Vavasor Powell (1617–1670) is a good case in point. He recalled being at prayer one night in his chamber when

> suddain I heard one walk about me, trampling upon the Chamber floor, as if it had been some heavie big man, upon which I grew so fearful, and unbelieving, that I ran down shutting, and hasping the door after me, and called up some of the family, telling them there was a thief in the room, but it proved in the end, to be no other than that spiritual thief, and murderer Satan.[106]

GHOSTS WITH NO SOUL?

In some hauntings ghosts appeared in inextricable association with equally apparitional inanimate objects, such as phantom coaches, ships and more recently cars. But if ghosts were the spirits of the dead how could such inanimate objects also be spirits? For some this was a pointless, ridiculous question that demonstrated the absurdity of the belief in ghosts. But one man, at least, attempted to construct a spiritual rationale for their existence. In his *Spirit World: Its Inhabitants, Nature and Philosophy*, published in 1879, the American spiritualist Eugene Crowell argued that phantom ships and spectral railway trains were not myths. They were the earthly creations of the ghosts of mariners and railwaymen, constructed from spiritual substances gathered from the heavens. He hastened to point out that permission to carry out such spiritual manufacturing was only granted 'to such spirits as have reformed, or have not led abandoned lives'. By building their own ships the ghosts of mariners who yearned for the sea were able to voyage the oceans once again and visit ports just as they had done in life. The ships 'glide over the waves without sinking into them', Crowell explained, 'and earthly winds propel them at rates of speed which our ships cannot attain'.[107]

What serious debate there was on the issue of ghostly inanimate objects focused primarily on the matter of clothing. That ghosts appeared in dress, armour or in winding sheets was one of the favourite rationalist arguments *against* their existence over the centuries. The philosopher Thomas Hobbes raised the point in 1651 when he queried how 'Ghosts of men (and I may adde of their clothes which they appear in) can walk by night in Churches, Church-yards, and other places of Sepulture.'[108] In 1762, the author of *Anti-Canidia*, a rationalist attack on supernatural belief, pondered, 'how is a spirit, in itself immaterial and invisible, to become the object of human sight? How is it to acquire the appearance of *dress*?'[109] A century later another critic mocked, 'how do you account for the ghosts' clothes – are they ghosts, too?' 'What an idea, indeed!' He exclaimed.

> All the socks that never came home from the wash, all the boots and shoes which we left behind us worn out at watering-places, all the old hats which we gave to crossing-sweepers … What a notion of heaven – an illimitable old clothes-shop, peopled by bores, and not a little infested with knaves![110]

That the issue was also debated widely outside the literary sphere is indicated by the editor of the *Occult Review*. In 1906 he wearily commented, 'I am not unfamiliar with the criticism. Indeed, it comes to me reminiscent of early school days and of debates on the subject in school debating societies.'[111]

In the early modern period answers to the clothing conundrum were not forthcoming from the ghost believers. Maybe it was felt there was no need. God worked in mysterious ways. The theories of mesmerism, hypnotism and clairvoyance that circulated in late-eighteenth- and early-nineteenth-century England provided pseudo-scientific theories to bolster the faith position. If the living had telepathic powers perhaps the sentient souls of the dead could also transmit thoughts and images into the minds of the earthbound. The spirits did not necessarily physically appear but they could impress their physical identity upon the minds of the living, and therefore the imagination of the clairvoyant. Catherine Crowe, whose book of hauntings and apparitions went through numerous editions following its initial publication in 1848, applied this theory to the ghost clothes issue. If a spirit could 'conceive of its former body it can equally conceive of its former habiliments, and so represent them, by the power of will to the eye, or present them to the constructive imagination of the seer'. As to their reason for choosing to appear clothed, they were naturally the same as for wearing clothes in life. To appear naked, 'to say the least of it, would be much more frightful and shocking'.[112] As others argued, ghosts obviously did not need clothing to keep them warm or attract the opposite sex. Clothes were also about personal and social identity. In 1851 Alfred Roffe observed that those who held up clothes as proof against ghosts 'never seem to consider, that even in the Natural World, Men do not use Clothing merely for Decency and Defence … Clothing is used also for its beauty, and above all, for its great significancy.'[113] The same point was reinforced in a debate on the subject in the pages of the *Occult Review*. A ghost, wrote one correspondent, wore clothes 'to identify himself with the position and period of his earthly life'.[114] The argument had a sound internal logic. How could one make sense, otherwise, of a naked headless ghost? A disturbing thought both in the past and present.

ANIMALS

Only a very small proportion of the apparitions reported to the SPR and Green and McCreery were of animals. Most reports concerned cats and dogs, which is not surprising considering they are the animals most associated with human companionship.[115] The surveys also confirm what is apparent from the historical sources, that only a very small number of apparitions were those of identifiable pets. Likewise there are few examples of animal ghosts verifiable by known deaths, such as that of a dog seen on Bengeo Common in Hertfordshire in March 1877. As a local newspaper reported, it was thought to be the ghost of a dog that had been killed three weeks before. It was reddish in colour – 'so far as can be seen at night, for it has not been seen in the day time'.[116] Unlike cat and dog apparitions, those of horses, which were common enough, usually appeared in association with human ghosts, pulling phantom carriages or carrying headless horsemen. Otherwise there have been reports of diverse other animals over the centuries including bears, calves, deer and rabbits.[117]

We have to be careful with terminology here, because it is unclear from modern and historic sources as to what extent people believed that the spirit animals they saw *were* ghosts – in other words the souls of the deceased. The issue of whether animals have souls, and, if they do, what type of soul, has long been and continues to be a matter of Christian debate in both Catholic and Protestant churches. An English survey conducted in the 1990s revealed that 77 per cent of people thought that animals had souls, with 56 per cent believing they had an afterlife.[118] From a theological point of view, of course, the reality of animal ghosts could be interpreted as confirmation that the souls of animals are immortal, but this was hardly an orthodox position in medieval and early modern England. It was widely accepted that animals possessed spiritual souls; some suggested immortal ones, but few, other than political radicals during the Civil War and some evangelicals, argued that they had rational souls or shared an afterlife with humankind.[119] In the seventeenth century the French philosopher Descartes, who rejected entirely the idea that animals had a spiritual soul, though he conceded it might be corporeal, reinvigorated the debate. However, his idea that animals were merely machines was not widely adopted in England. Following the publication of a popular edition of Descartes's work in 1694, the issue was at least widely debated in the press, with contributions from the main essayists of the day such as Defoe, Pope, Addison and Swift. Even in this Enlightenment discourse, there was no consensus on the issue. Some continued to assert that animals had immaterial and immortal souls, while the odd voice even suggested that animals joined humans at the Day of Judgement.[120] It is important to stress, though, that the debate regarding animal souls was conducted separately from that of ghosts, and that there was no conflict between adhering to the concept of their immortality and rejecting the notion of the return of the spirits of the dead.

In popular culture right through until the twentieth century there were several alternative explanations for such sightings. Witches, fairies, angels and devils were all believed to transform themselves into animals, and witches were also thought to have animal familiars. Up until the late nineteenth century most animal apparitions seem to have been interpreted in these contexts, and could be distinguished by their unnatural features, which were more demonic than ghostly. They were sometimes said to be bigger than normal animals, while others were indefinable animal forms. Some were headless. Many possessed abnormally large fiery eyes, often described as being as 'big as saucers'. A good example of this type of spirit beast was that seen in January 1878 by the inhabitants of Baldock, Hertfordshire. Large numbers gathered nightly to witness the haunting of a house at the top of the high street, causing Police Constable William Tripp some trouble in keeping the road open to traffic. Windows and doors banged open and beds were lifted up. This disruptive ghost was described as a 'small white animal, with eyes as large as saucers' and was seen by both day and night.[121] Many of the local legends of black dogs that have been recorded over the centuries fit this mould of spirit being.[122]

In early modern accounts, black dog spirits were usually overtly diabolic. Pamphlets told of a sulphurous-smelling, headless black bear that manhandled a Somerset woman in 1584, and a large, coal-coloured dog that haunted and disrupted the house of an Oxfordshire gentleman in 1591–92. Proof that such incidents were played out in the popular mind of the period, and not just on the printed page, is apparent from the casebooks of Elizabethan and Jacobean astrologers and physicians. One man who consulted Richard Napier described how the Devil appeared to him in the form of a black dog and a bear.[123] Richard Boulton, who, in the early eighteenth century, wrote one of the last intellectual defences of the belief in witchcraft, asserted that the

Devil appeared 'in divers Shapes, not only of those who are alive, but also of dead Men, or in the form of Beasts and Birds, he sometimes appearing in the Likeness of a black Dog'. His assertion was based primarily on the evidence of the witch trials of the previous century. In 1664, for instance, Elizabeth Styles confessed to a Somerset magistrate that around ten years before, the Devil had appeared to her in the form of a handsome man and a black dog.[124] But as a recent overview of the black dog tradition confirms, by the late nineteenth and early twentieth centuries the demonic traits of such animal apparitions had dwindled, just as encounters with the physical Devil dropped out of popular legends and memorates. Dog apparitions were no longer figures of fear and dread but rather subjects of curiosity and wonder. They began to take on more of the characteristics of human ghosts.[125] This is exemplified by the generation of stories of ghostly dogs haunting the spots where their deceased masters or mistresses had last been seen or murdered. The dog ghost on Bengeo Common was, perhaps, a product of its time.

As the discussion above suggests, there is little evidence for people believing in animal ghosts prior to the late nineteenth century. However there is another intriguing, and long-held popular tradition that human ghosts, as well as devils, fairies and witches could shape-shift and appear in animal form. Eighteenth-century rationalists singled out the belief for particular mockery. Writing in 1720, the satirical, anti-clerical writer Thomas Gordon divided ghosts into two kinds. One was the 'ghost of dignity', which represented 'in every respect' the same person as he or she was in life, and inhabited their own house or rattled around in their coach and six. The 'plebeian ghost', on the other hand, rarely appeared in its 'bodily likeness'. It 'humbly contents itself with the Body of a white Horse, that gallops over the Meadows without Legs, and grazes in them without a head. On other Occasions it wears the Carcass of a great black Dog, that glares full in your Face.'[126] Several decades later the author of *Anti-Canidia* wondered with considerable disdain how the 'vulgar' could imagine that ghosts appeared 'in variety of shapes; – like a dog, with saucer eyes, for instance, as well as like a human person?'[127]

While such shape-shifting human ghosts appear across the range of relevant sources – trial records, pamphlets and folklore – there is a difference in the way they were represented over time. In seventeenth-century literature they had overtly demonic characteristics. An apparition that plagued the parishioners of Spraiton, Devon, in the early 1680s, appeared sometimes in the form of the deceased wife of a local gentleman and 'now and then, like a monstrous Dog, belching out fire'. Its appearance and behaviour had Richard Bovet calling it both a ghost and a 'She-Dæmon'. An account of a haunting conducted by the ghost of a baker in 1661 described how he appeared in the likeness of a black cat and a goat as well as in his human form, and also left behind the smell of brimstone. In another pamphlet published in 1679 the appearance of the ghost of a young man of Stamford, who was murdered on the orders of his brother, was said to have 'changed itself into more fearful formes, as a Bear, a Lion, and the like with Gastly countenance, and horrid Eyes, oft sparkling fire'.[128]

Turning to nineteenth-century folkloric sources, however, we find few diabolic connotations. Apparitions of animals, usually of a more gentle persuasion, and with few if any abnormalities, were thought to haunt the spots where people died in terrible circumstances. At Wheal Vor Mine, Cornwall, the place where several miners were blown to pieces by an explosion was afterwards said to be haunted by a troop of little black dogs. The ghosts of those murdered in and around Corby were sometimes seen crossing Highstane Common, Bewcastle, in various forms including a drove of black cattle or a herd of wild horses. In early nineteenth-century Oxfordshire the spirits of suicides buried at Cowleas Corner haunted the spot in animal forms such as calves and sheep.[129] The ghost of another suicide, a farmer of Weobley, Herefordshire, was also seen in the form of a calf, while the Lincolnshire diarist Henry Winn recorded in the 1840s that a place near Fulletby was haunted by the ghost of a girl in the form of a white rabbit. She had supposedly died on the spot in 1766, after falling from her horse.[130] The Radical politician Samuel Bamford (1788–1872) recalled an old house at Stanicliffe, near Middleton, where, during the Civil War period, a man was shot dead by the fearsomely tempered servant of the local important family:

> Ever after, until a comparatively recent date, the house and premises he occupied were haunted by 'fyerin' (boggarts or apparitions) which came sometimes in the form of a calf, sometimes in that of a huge black dog, and sometimes in the human form, but hideous and terrible.[131]

The Lincolnshire folklorist Mabel Peacock was unable to get a clear opinion as to whether such animal apparitions were popularly thought to be the victims in animal guise or demons who liked to frequent spots where terrible acts occurred. After 'some consideration I have come to the conclusion that they are probably the former', she wrote.[132]

It is tempting to interpret this tradition of shape-shifting ghosts as an extraordinary remnant of animistic, pagan shamanic belief, but as the medievalist Jean-Claude Schmitt has cautioned, there is also a Christian tradition of pictorially representing souls in animal form.[133] The concept is also evident in medieval ecclesiastical literature, where the souls of angels and dying saints assumed the form of a dove, while the saints in heaven sometimes came to the aid of their future peers in the form of an eagle. However, examples of the souls of lesser humans appearing in animal form are rare.[134] The cases of shape-shifting human ghosts reported by a Cistercian monk in Yorkshire, around 1400, are unusual. In one instance a dead person appeared in the form of a haystack and a horse, while another was seen in the guise of a crow, a dog and a goat. There is some evidence from the early modern period that angels were popularly thought to appear on earth on animal forms, usually as birds or bird-like forms.[135] So it is possible that the human-animal ghost derives from Christian symbolism, though the notion that it is an archaic survival of pre-Christian belief should not be discarded.

Whether the shape-shifting ghost became less demonic during the modern period is debatable. It is possible that the gentler nineteenth-century version existed in early modern folklore as well. The seventeenth-century pamphlet literature, influenced by the educated preoccupation with the Devil, may distort our understanding, presenting us with a demonic conception of ghosts that did not reflect popular beliefs. Then again, witchcraft historians, using trial records, have shown how, due to the influence of the clergy and pamphlets spreading the idea of satanic witchcraft, the witch's familiar became more overtly diabolic in popular belief during the seventeenth century. Once witchcraft was no longer an educated concern, and the common people were no longer being inculcated with the notion of the witches' pact, the demonic aspects of familiars faded. In nineteenth-century folklore they are usually represented as simple domestic creatures once again.[136] A similar process could have occurred with the shape-shifting ghost, and so Bamford's boggarts may have been a remnant of the early modern demonising of crime.

THE SHELF LIFE OF GHOSTS

How long do ghosts last? Certainly no more than 2,000 years it would seem. Until recently there were no sightings of the ghosts of prehistoric people; no Palaeolithic hunter-gatherers roaming the landscape; no Bronze Age spirits hanging about tumuli or Iron Age phantoms patrolling hill forts. Why should there be limits on the age of hauntings?

In the medieval period, as Jean-Claude Schmitt has observed, 'the time of ghosts was the time of living memory'.[137] Ghosts appeared shortly after death, and even reported to their human interlocutors how many days or months had passed since their existence. The length of time between appearances was often dependent on the length and procedure of the programmes of intercessionary prayers and masses that were employed to speed the passage of souls through purgatory. This in turn obviously depended on the wealth of the deceased and their families. The commonest request from those with a bit of money was the trental, which consisted of a set of 30 requiem masses, usually said over 30 days, though it could be compressed into a week if the family had sufficient funds to employ a marathon relay of priests. Considering how much money was involved servicing purgatorial souls, the church was understandably flexible about the nature and length of the intercessionary services they offered. In 1546, for example, One William Crofts, of Bolsover, bequeathed that 100 shillings be paid to a priest to have him sing for his soul for a year after his death.[138] Sometimes masses were spread over several years. Whatever the arrangement, it was considered reasonable that the restless spirits of the dead might return periodically to remind or encourage those praying for their souls, with an appreciative parting visit at the end to mark the completion of their time in purgatory.

In the early modern period, limits were put on the existence of ghosts depending on various scientific and metaphysical criteria that will be discussed in subsequent chapters. In the sixteenth century, for instance, it was stated that according to some necromantic magicians the spirits of the dead could only be recalled to the body within one year of death.[139] Some scientists argued that the spirits of the dead created their visual forms from the moisture of their former earthly bodies, and so they could no longer appear once the corpses they were spiritually attached to desiccated.[140] For the same reason, a similar timescale was suggested by those who argued that ghosts were merely simulacra generated from vapours arising from decomposing corpses rather than the spirits of the dead.

Purposeful ghosts continued to appear and disappear as before in post-Reformation England, and were particularly prominent in the literature of the seventeenth century. Many of the accounts in the collections of Glanvill, Baxter, Sinclair and Aubrey concern ghosts that appeared shortly after death to friends and family, while those that hung around for longer were usually waiting for someone to facilitate their mission. This did not usually take long, though there were some exceptions. A pamphlet published around 1675 reported that a ghost had recently appeared to one William Clark, a maltster living near Northampton, and stated:

I am the disturbed Spirit of a person long since Dead, I was Murthered neer this place Two hundred sixty and seven years, nine weeks, and two days ago, to this very time, and come along with me and I will shew you where it was done.[141]

The Reformation ensured that purgatorial parameters were no longer relevant, however, and maybe this slowly but surely freed the constraints on ghostly sojourns in popular tradition. The ethnographic evidence for popular beliefs from the eighteenth century onwards suggests that certain types of ghost were appearing for longer and longer periods. These were not the purposeful ghosts that interacted with humans, but the hordes of silent memorial ghosts who walked the roads, roamed the fields or lingered by pools, sometimes haunting the spot where a person committed suicide, perhaps commemorating a sad event or merely a repetitive action. The lifespan of such ghosts, for which there was no obvious allotted occupancy on earth, depended on the collective memory and the stability of the oral transmission of local histories in communities from one generation to the next.

A ghost needed to be located in time to make sense of it. This could be achieved by matching a haunting with a real event such as a murder or a suicide. This could be a recent incident fresh in the collective or individual memory, or it could be associated with a dim and distant tragic event. Legends could be appropriated to give a ghost a back-story. Sometimes the location of a haunting provided the dating evidence. A ghost in a castle could be confidently located in medieval or early modern times. The building's physical state, whether it was in ruins or not, could further narrow down the date range. Ghosts, as troubled spirits, also became explicable if they could be situated in a turbulent period of history such as the dissolution of the monasteries. Ghostly nuns and monks are common in folklore sources. To give but two examples, near Tong, Shropshire, in the 1930s, a nun haunted the former sight of a nunnery dissolved during the Reformation.[142] The ghost of an abbot haunted Buckfast Abbey, Devon, for 300 years, but was apparently assuaged in the 1920s by the building of a Catholic chapel on the site.[143] The Civil War was another tumultuous period, strong in the collective memory and popular literature, and consequently numerous historic ghosts are dated to this conflict. Samuel Bamford (1788–1872) recalled how, in his childhood, School Lane in Middleton, Lancashire, was haunted by two men, one Royalist and the other a Roundhead, who killed each other there during the Civil War.[144] A Roundhead haunted Heath House in Shropshire, while the ghost of a Dutch officer who fought in the Civil War haunted a Shrewsbury inn until the 1970s.[145] It is clothing that enables people to date the age of such ghosts. The ubiquity of ghostly nuns, monks, Roundheads and Cavaliers is due considerably to the fact that they are easily recognisable by their habits and headgear. So clothes identify the period and the period provides the reason for the haunting.

To a large extent, then, people's perception of historic ghosts depended on their sense and knowledge of history. But this is an extremely difficult thing to gauge. Prior to the advent of compulsory mass education in the second half of the nineteenth century, most people's idea of the past was built on orally transmitted traditions passed down through families and communities, and, from the seventeenth century onwards, the tales of past events found in popular literature, such as ballads, chapbooks and almanacs.[146] There was certainly little conception of prehistory as we know it today, and the various visible remains of our ancient landscape, such as Neolithic and Bronze Age ritual and burial monuments, were popularly interpreted as the work of the Devil, or of giants and fairies from an indeterminate distant past.[147] During the sixteenth and seventeenth centuries, the furthest back that most people's sense of English history extended was the Viking invasions and settlement from the ninth century. Educated and popular publications of the time generated a strong popular patriotic sense of the English resistance to the 'Danish yoke'. Numerous local legends of valiant battles against the Danes sprang up around the country, with some enduring right through into the twentieth century, perhaps given renewed life by the national celebration of King Alfred in 1901, to mark the 1,000th anniversary of his death.[148] It is quite likely, as a consequence, that tales of the ghostly appearance of Danish and English soldiers were common at the time. But significant insights into popular beliefs in ghosts only become available from the late seventeenth century, and by this time the chronological parameters of popular history had shifted to more recent events. The Civil War had become the most prominent episode in English legendary history, smothering and replacing earlier traditions of Old English battles and monumental destruction. Oliver Cromwell 'was here' became part of the topography of many communities, while confusion with Thomas Cromwell and his role in the dissolution of the monasteries helped perpetuate the earlier folk memory of the Reformation.[149]

There is also a regional angle to this history of popular historical tradition and ghosts. In the West Country, for example, the Monmouth rebellion of 1685 and the infamous Bloody Assizes held by Judge Jeffreys became a strong legendary influence. As one Victorian folklorist noted, 'Even as far west as Lydford Castle the ghost of Judge Jeffrey is said to still frighten timid children and old women.'[150] Thomas Babington Macaulay (1800–1859) wrote in his famous *History of England* that his own childhood recollections testified to the fact that in Somerset 'many tales of terror' about the events were told over Christmas fires over a century after the rebellion. 'Within the last forty years,' he said, referring to the execution of the rebels, 'peasants, in some districts well knew the accursed spots, and passed them unwillingly after sunset.'[151]

The focus on such events was further reinforced by the popular histories that formed part of the Victorian school curriculum. The Reformation was obviously held up as a key moment in English historical progress, though some pedagogic texts recognised the brutality of the Dissolution. Similarly, the Civil War and the execution of Charles I was used to defend the righteousness of monarchy and the iniquity of political rebellion.[152] Considering the emphasis on these events it is no wonder that during the early twentieth century ghosts continued to conform to the preoccupation with these periods. The influence of popular education in creating stereotypical ages of haunting is apparent from the antiquarian Henry Swainson Cowper's debunking of the Lake District legend of the 'Crier of Claife'. This ghost supposedly scared the ferrymen of the lakes around the time of the Reformation, until a monk vanquished it. Cowper pointed out the basic historical and geographical errors in the story, as told by several writers such as Harriet Martineau in her *Guide to the Lake District* (1858), and suggested that the compilers of the story 'muddled wilfully or by accident' several traditions. Writing in 1899, Cowper concluded that 'The fact that the country people now know the story, is worthless as evidence, since it has been repeated by guide book after guide book for at least thirty years.'[153]

The most recent addition to the corpus of heritage hauntings is also the most venerable of all – the roman legionnaire. A search on the internet reveals numerous sightings in diverse places such as London, Derby, the Isle of Wight, and an old Roman road near Weymouth. Some readers will be familiar with the well-known case of a troop of soldiers seen by a plumber working in a York cellar in 1953. However, such sightings are a modern phenomenon, with nearly all of them dating to the last 50 years. The earliest reports I have found concern a Roman centurion seen patrolling the Strood, Mersea Island, which was first recorded in 1904, and a ghostly Roman army that marched on certain nights along Bindon Hill, Dorset, to their camp on Ring's Hill during the 1930s.[154] Distinguishing between the ghost of a Bronze Age warrior and an Iron Age one would be a task for an archaeologist, but thanks to 'swords and sandals' film epics, and the inclusion of the Roman invasion in school curricula, the dress of the roman soldier has become as recognisable as that of a monk or a cavalier. Clothes truly maketh the ghost.

FRIGHTENED TO DEATH

For some, seeing a ghost was a matter of life and death in more than just a metaphysical sense. The Rev. E. Gillespy, a Northamptonshire clergyman, wrote in 1793 that 'Nothing can affect the human mind with greater terror, than the dread of an interview with the souls of deceased persons.'[155] It is still common speech to say to someone 'It looks as though you have seen a ghost', to describe how they appear pale, drawn and shocked. In the past the most characteristic reaction to seeing a ghost was to feel one's hair stand on end. There is a biblical precedent. In Job 4:15, Eliphaz states that when 'a spirit passed before my face; the hair of my flesh stood up'.[156] An eighteenth-century account of a haunting on board a ship bound for New York described how 'a man sprung suddenly upon the deck in his shirt, his hair erect, his eyes starting from their sockets, and uttered, he had seen a ghost'.[157] The eighteenth-century publisher James Lackington experienced another classic symptom. He recalled that on momentarily believing he had seen a ghost as a youth, 'I perceived my hair to heave my hat from my head, and my teeth to chatter in my mouth.'[158] Even more evocative was the reaction to seeing an apparition described by the Welsh Independent minister Edmund Jones (1702–1793): 'his hair moved upon his head, his heart panted and beat violently, his flesh trembled, he felt not his cloaths about him'.[159]

While such imagery provokes a smile, in a popular culture where witchcraft was thought an ever-present threat and spirits roamed the land after dark, people were literally 'frightened to death'. The Hammersmith ghost scare was said to have caused the demise of one woman, and in 1814 the newspapers reported that an aristocratic young woman had died after a convulsive fit brought on by having seen two ghosts in her bedchamber.[160] Of course, such rumours were often nothing more than that, but as inquest records prove, people really did die of fright, though from a modern perspective we would now seek to determine and emphasise the underlying medical causes. In January 1894 an inquest on the body of a 17-year-old servant named Elizabeth Bishop, at Misterton, Somerset, concluded that she had died of excessive fright or syncope. The previous month, the ship *Olive Branch* had sunk and her master's brother, who was captain, had drowned. There was obviously much distress in her master's household in Lyme Regis, and one day when left alone in the house she saw the shadow of a man on some window blinds and thought it was the ghost of the captain. This severely frightened her and in the ensuing weeks she said she had also seen the ghost of a cousin who had been dead some 20 years. In a state of considerable distress she returned home to her parents in Misterton, and shortly after she fell into a terrible fit and died.[161] In March 1841 an inquest on the body of an elderly labourer named Patrick Hayes, who lodged at the Fortune of War in Marsh Street, Bristol, heard how he died from injuries sustained after falling down stairs while under the influence. The landlady, Mary Croker, testified that she thought he might have seen a ghost that haunted the building. She told the coroner:

> It is the ghost of a lady in silk, and has been troublesome to some former lodgers. Two or three lodgers have been killed in the same house, and no doubt frightened from the same cause. I have never seen the ghost myself.

A verdict of accidental death was given.[162]

TWO

The Geography of Haunting

S ome ghosts haunted individuals while others haunted places. Wherever humans have been so ghosts have followed: from ships in the middle of the ocean to the crowded streets of London, from the dark depths of the earth to moonlit hilltops, from the humblest cottages to royal palaces. But rarely did ghosts roam or linger aimlessly; there was usually a reason as to *where* as well as *why* they appeared. The spirits of the dead most obviously returned to those places where someone had died or where corpses lay buried or hidden. But there were other locations where ghosts lingered that did not have explicit associations with death, such as bridges, roads and pools. The Rev. John Christopher Atkinson's (1814–1900) recollection of the haunted landscape of his Essex childhood evokes well the traditional range of haunted locations. Ghosts lurked in 'houses, always old and mostly old-fashioned, barns, lanes, the moated sites of old manor-houses, "four-want-ways" or the place of intersection of two cross-roads, churchyards, suicides' graves – which were spoken of, dreaded, avoided after nightfall, as being "haunted"'.[1] One way of encapsulating and trying to understand the significance of this diverse geography of hauntings is to consider them in relation to liminal spaces.

The concept of liminality, which pertains to the state of being on the border or threshold of two defined states of existence, has been most enthusiastically employed by anthropologists to describe the symbolic and physical transitional stages in which initiates find themselves when undergoing rites of passage. But the concept also serves to describe, in various historic and prehistoric contexts, the relationship between life, death, the afterlife, and natural and man-made features in the landscape.[2] Certain physical boundaries, such as Neolithic henges, that prehistoric peoples carved into the landscape can be seen to have much deeper symbolic meaning in terms of the boundaries between the living and dead or the worlds of mortals and gods. Natural features such as rivers likewise served as liminal places where the two worlds met, and where people gathered to either reinforce the separation between them or to try to permeate it briefly for religious or magical purposes. Man-made or

45

administrative boundaries constructed for pragmatic rather than religious purposes could also assume deeper liminal significance. In Scandinavia, for instance, there was a long association between the living dead and property boundaries. This was ostensibly due to a medieval law that declared that anyone caught moving the stones marking out people's properties would be considered an outlaw. Once dead the outlaw returned to haunt the spot where in life he or she had transgressed secular and religious norms, and could be encountered groaning, trying to move the stone to its rightful place, or pointing out to the living where it should lie.[3] There are some indications that English parish boundaries also functioned as liminal places. The demonic ghost that, in 1682, tormented and abused a man of Spreyton (Spraiton), Devon, only appeared to him as soon as he crossed into the parish. Richard Bovet picked up on this, suggesting, 'it looks as if these spirits were tyed to some limits, or bounds, that they cannot pass'.[4] A study of haunted English roads has also identified that a significant number lie on parish boundaries.[5] Considering that the origins of parish boundaries date to the Anglo-Saxon period, and were delineated by linking up recognisable landscape features such as tracks, burial mounds, river crossings and streams, then some hauntings may have deep symbolic roots in the past.

As well as being sensitive to the significance and meaning of liminality, we should also be aware of how changes in the environment over time influenced the landscape of haunting. One wonders, for example, how parliamentary enclosure in the late eighteenth and early nineteenth centuries affected ghost traditions in Midland communities, and likewise how drainage of wetlands influenced hauntings in Somerset and the Fens. One indication of the impact of the latter development on ghost legends is evident from a conversation between a Norfolk woman and the Rev. John Gunn, rector of Irstead, Norfolk. She told him how before the parish had been drained and enclosed in 1810 she had frequently seen a light near a spot called Heard's Holde, where legend had it a man who had committed terrible crimes had drowned. 'I have often seen it there, rising up and falling and twistering about, and then up again. It looked exactly like a candle in a lantern.'[6] How many other such ghosts were extinguished with the receding water?

INSIDE

There is no great mystery as to why buildings should have been so frequently haunted. Whether the dwellers of castles or cottages, manors or hovels, the vast majority of people died inside their homes. It was, therefore, the natural place for their ghosts to return. It was where people mourned the dead and were surrounded by memories of their presence. For sceptics the house was obviously the centre of hauntings because it was where people slept and dreamed of the dead, or where people lay drunk, drugged or hallucinating in their sickbeds. The theory of ghosts as residual electromagnetic impulses left behind by the strong emotions of the deceased, emphasises the dampness and enclosed environment of buildings required to retain this residual memory.[7] There was, then, an explanation to suit whatever stance was taken on the question of the reality of ghosts.

As we shall see later in this chapter, and in others, numerous houses over the century attracted a reputation for being haunted because they were empty or derelict. In his memoir of working-class life in Salford during the early twentieth century, Robert Roberts recalled that houses rarely 'stood vacant for longer than a fortnight before ghosts got in'.[8] Some houses were, however, abandoned because they were thought to be haunted. The former situation represents a different category of internal haunted space to the latter. The haunting was not concerned with the intimacy between the dead and the bereaved or subsequent residents inside the property, it was about what abandonment of a social space meant to the community outside. If people failed to occupy a human environment then external forces would move in; perhaps a mysterious gang of criminals, but maybe also supernatural visitants such as witches, boggarts and ghosts.[9]

Sometimes houses were said to be haunted when to be more precise it was only certain spaces within them that attracted phenomena. The ghost might be limited to the room in which a person was murdered or committed suicide. The haunting could even be restricted to a single piece of furniture, as was heard during an unusual libel case tried at the Norwich Assizes in the summer of 1866. Honour Lingley and her husband, a shepherd, rented a house at Sprowston, which was commonly known in the village as the 'Haunted Cottage'. The Lingleys apparently did not know of its reputation before renting it, and it was a neighbour who informed them that a ghost haunted the closet. After hearing this, Honour 'felt timid' whenever she went near it. One day, when the Lingley's were out, two young men from Sprowston entered the premises and fired at the haunted closet and a picture hanging in one of the rooms. The police were called to investigate the break-in and the libel resulted from a letter Honour Lingley wrote to the Norwich Argus complaining of the constables' behaviour. She claimed in the letter that they rifled through her private belongings, mocking her and insinuating she had stolen some of her linen.[10]

The bedroom was most frequently the focus of ghostly visitations, whether they were hoaxes, hallucinations or perceived realities. As well as being where people most often breathed their last, it was also the room where deep emotions were most frequently manifested. It was a place for dreaming, having sex, exchanging intimate confidences and expressing solitary anguish. Undressed in the darkness, this was where people felt most exposed psychologically. That said, bedroom hauntings were sometimes passive even comforting affairs, such as the sight of ghosts standing still at the foot of the bed, or the stroke of an invisible hand. But bedrooms were also the scenes of some of the most violent and frightening experiences. The astrologer and occultist John Heydon (1629–c.1670) recounted how one of his mother's maids was pulled out of her bed one night by the ghost of a lover named John Stringer, who had recently been murdered by a jealous admirer. Despite three doors leading to her bedroom being locked, the maid 'had the right side of her haire and headcloths clean shaved or cut away' by Stringer's ghost.[11] A gentlewoman friend of Richard Baxter was subjected to a violent spirit disturbing her bed: 'she had not time to dress her self, such Cries and other things almost amazing her, but she (hardly any of her Cloths on) with her two Maids, got upon their knees by the Bedside to seek the Lord'.[12] The ghostly grabbing of bedcovers was a particularly common and disturbing phenomenon. In 1899, for example, a Wiltshire folklorist was told by one man that his bedclothes were once pulled off by two ghostly maidens. 'I'll throw my shoe at 'ee', he threatened them.[13] One gets the strong impression that with some physical bedroom hauntings there is an undoubted sexual component, with the gender difference between haunter and haunted being more explicit than in manifestations occurring elsewhere.

According to numerous legends, those murdered inside houses sometimes left a permanent bloody reminder of their tragic end. The ghost was in effect a stain. In January 1789 Hannah Corbridge, of Laneshaw Bridge, Near Colne, Lancashire, had her throat cut by her lover Christopher Hartley, who was subsequently executed. He hid her body near Barnside Hall and when the Hall was pulled down some years later some of the sandstone was brought back to Laneshaw, where it was reported that Hannah's blood was seen oozing from them. Such a sensation caused crowds of people from around the area to flock to the site.[14] In the early nineteenth century a parlour flagstone at Green Top, Pudsey, was thought to be stained with the blood of a murder victim. Even when the flagstone was replaced the stain reappeared.[15] More recently, in the parish of Llanigon, near Hay, a story recorded in the 1920s told that a woman who had her throat cut dipped her hand in her blood and daubed it on the wall before dying. It remained an indelible stain and subsequent tenants had to place furniture in front to hide it. Around the same time, further north in Shropshire, there was a house near Wenlock Edge where another murdered woman smeared her bloody hand on a window pane and even when the glass was replaced the hand print reappeared.[16]

The gaol cell was another internal living space that most people would have loathed to call home but where many died in torment and terrible circumstances. A young pickpocket told the Victorian social investigator Henry Mayew: 'the only thing that frightens me when I'm in prison is sleeping in a cell by myself … You can't imagine how one dreams when in trouble. I've often started up in a fright from a dream. I don't know what might appear. I've heard people talk about ghosts and that.' He went on to recount how, during one such stay, the noise of water dripping into a tin excited much agitation amongst the inmates: 'all in the ward were shocking frightened; and weren't we glad when we found out what it was!'[17] The boy's fears were understandable. Murderers spent their final hours in the their cells, some no doubt wracked by guilt and haunted by the ghosts of their victims. The corpses of the executed were often buried in the precincts. No wonder, then, that when the Quaker founder George Fox was flung into Launceston Castle gaol in 1656 he soon discovered that his fellow inmates believed that ghosts haunted the condemned cell.[18] The day before his execution in 1697, the highwayman John Shorter was very disturbed at seeing the ghost of a murdered prisoner named Lorimer, which appeared as he prayed in the chapel at Newgate. Shorter knew Lorimer had recently been murdered in the prison by fellow inmates but he had not reported it. It evidently played on his mind as he spent his last hours of life.[19] Cut off from the rest of society and living a twilight life in semi-darkness, the occupants of the cells existed in a state halfway between life and death,[20] which fostered a heightened spiritual awareness, as many 'last dying confessions' relate.

LANDSCAPES OF DEATH

Ghosts are rarely reported appearing in churchyards these days. Only a small minority of people still go to church regularly and therefore rarely find themselves passing through burial grounds. In modern urban society most dead are buried in large municipal cemeteries set apart from the lives of the living or are incinerated in crematoriums. This development, which has been described as a dechristianisation of burial, was a result of increasing public health concerns about the spread of disease and noxious vapours emanating from overcrowded urban churchyards.[21] While burial grounds obviously remain places of remembrance and mourning, our relationship with them has changed profoundly. As church records from the medieval and early modern periods demonstrate, churchyards were important recreational places as well as sacred spaces, used not only for commemoration but also for playing ball games, dancing and fighting, much to the chagrin of the clergy.[22] During the day the churchyard was a space shared by the living and the dead because the latter kept their distance, but as night fell it became a liminal place as the boundary between the two worlds dissolved.

It was a common Protestant observation that in Catholic times, as the Elizabethan gentlemen Reginald Scot remarked, 'everie churchyard swarmed with soules and spirits'.[23] Yet, as Peter Marshall has recently noted, there was nothing in Catholic doctrine that required purgatorial spirits to hang around their burial place.[24] Besides, in Reformation England churchyards remained a favourite haunt for ghosts. Further explanation was required from those who dismissed them as figments of Catholic 'superstition'. One of Scot's contemporaries, the writer Thomas Nashe, who believed that ghosts were nothing more than diabolic illusions, explained that

> If any ask why he [the Devil] is more conversant and busy in churchyards and places where men are buried than in any other places, it is to make us believe that the bodies and souls of the departed rest entirely in his possession and the peculiar power of death is resigned to his disposition.[25]

Turning to popular beliefs, we saw in the previous chapter that a reason was usually found why a ghost appeared. From this perspective ghosts did not hover round graveyards just because their bodies lay there; they were on a mission or wished to express an opinion on the activities of the living. This is clear from the numerous examples of churchyard hauntings reported in the nineteenth-century press.

Ghosts were commonly thought to appear to show disapproval when their graves were somehow disturbed. In the summer of 1875, for example, Mr Penhey, the proprietor off an oil and colour shop in Kingston, Surrey, decided to extend his cellar. Unfortunately it turned out that the excavated area was formerly part of the old parish churchyard. The workmen turned up numerous skulls and bones and it was not long before strange disturbances occurred. One night, just around closing time, Mrs H.P. Turner visited Penhey's shop and while in conversation chunks of plaster began to fall from the ceiling.[26] The notion that ghosts were awoken by the disturbance of their former earthly shells is also evident in an unusual court case heard by the Lambeth Street magistrates in 1841. Around eight years before, body-snatchers had entered Slater's Chapel burial ground and stolen the corpse of the wife of a Billingsgate fishmonger named Drake. His wife had requested that a pair of black silk stockings, a lace cap and several other personal articles were placed in her coffin. The body-snatchers had left these and so Drake, with police permission, decided to remove the coffin and its sentimental contents and rebury them in his backyard at No. 7 Gower's Walk, Whitechapel. Several years later he moved several houses down, and in 1841 he asked the current occupants, a Mr Stone and his wife, if he could dig up the coffin, saying he would like to keep his wife's belongings and make a cupboard out of the coffin boards. They consented, and Drake got to work but found the wood had rotted. Since these proceedings Mrs Stone had been in a state of terror that the ghost of the dead woman would haunt the scene. Such was her dread that each night she placed all the chairs and tables against the back door of the premises.[27]

The ghosts of suicides were unlikely to appear in churchyards, as until relatively recently they were not permitted to be buried in consecrated ground. Sometimes they were thought to haunt the spots where they killed themselves. According to a letter from Nicholas Jekyll, of Castle Hedingham, to the Essex antiquarian and minister William Holman, in the spring of 1713 much excitement was caused in the village by the apparition of a man who had recently drowned himself below Jekyll's house. It was seen haunting the place, 'acting like a fellow in deep melancholy, and at last throwing himself in to water'.[28] In the early twentieth century the rectory at Boscombe was haunted by a man who hanged himself in one of the attics. Doors opened mysteriously and people felt an invisible presence.[29]

Up until the early twentieth century the ghosts of suicides were also commonly thought to haunt crossroads due to the practice of burying their bodies in the highway and driving a stake through their chests. This profane form of burial was probably quite widespread in early modern England, though evidence is scarce as there was no requirement to record burials outside the churchyard or in unconsecrated ground. However, numerous cases were reported in eighteenth-century newspapers and periodicals, suggesting the continuation of a long-standing tradition. Consider, for instance, the corpse of the murderer and self-murderer David Stirn, which was dissected in September 1760 and then buried with a wooden stake driven through it at a crossroads near Black Mary's Hole, Clerkenwell.[30] In 1851 locals believed that an old hawthorn tree at a crossroads south of Boston, Lincolnshire, had grown from one such stake hammered into the corpse of a suicide.[31] It is no surprise that ghost legends developed round these spots. The isolation of the locations, the mental torment that led people to commit self-murder and so damn their souls, and the knowledge of how their corpses were ritually desecrated, must have easily played on the imaginations of those travelling the roads at night. In Fielding's *History of Tom Jones*, first published in 1749, there is a discussion between Sophia and her maid in which the matter is discussed. When Sophia vows that she would rather plunge a dagger into her heart than have to marry a local squire, the maid cries:

> Dear Ma'am, consider – that to be denied Christian Burial, and to have your Corpse buried in the Highway, and a Stake drove through you, as Farmer Halfpenny was served at Ox-Cross, and, to be sure, his Ghost hath walked there ever since, for several People have seen him.[32]

By 1790 one author described the practice as 'local, not general' and an Act of Parliament finally prohibited it in 1823.[33] But several centuries of its practice left numerous legends of haunted crossroads around the country, which lingered on in local tradition into the twentieth century. There was the ghost of a 'bad man' seen on a white horse at Matscombe crossroads, near Beesands, Devon. Legend had it that a suicide was buried at a crossroads near Fair Ash, Somerset, and in the early twentieth century people still thought it was consequently haunted by 'zummat'.[34] Obviously only a tiny number of crossroads were used to bury suicides, and so many of the hauntings recorded in these locations, such as those involving phantom coaches, had no relation to actual people or historical events. The association of crossroads with death meant they became general focal points for ghost legends. But in some cases ghosts can be seen as virtual roadside memorials of real events that had long since disappeared from personal remembrance. In the early twentieth century, when the rise of the car led to a major upgrading of England's minor roads, skeletons were occasionally (and still are) dug up at crossroads which locals had long held to be haunted. Human remains were found during the widening of the haunted crossroads known as Lidgett's Gap, near Scawby, Lincolnshire. Likewise when, in 1908, a new signpost was being put at a junction on the Bridgwater to Stogursey high road, Somerset, the bones of a tall man were found six inches below the surface. In the local folklore a ghost of a tall old man dressed in a ragged uniform was said to roam the spot.[35] As these legends indicate, popular belief did not suggest that the staking would prevent the tormented souls of suicides from returning as ghosts, but that it would pin them to a specific location and so prevent them from wandering too far and disturbing local villagers. The crossroads acted as a further hobble, the four possible routes confusing the poor benighted souls.[36]

Murderers too were denied a proper Christian burial. As tormented spirits they were a potentially common source of haunting. Although their ghosts more often haunted people rather than places, they were seen in gaols, and particularly from the eighteenth century onwards, those that were gibbeted lingered at the scene of their final ghoulish ignominy. A phantom black dog was thought to prowl the spot near Tring where Thomas Colley was hanged in chains for his role in the death of Ruth Osborne, who drowned whilst being swum as a suspected witch in 1751. Legend also had it that the ghost of a murderer who killed a man at the crossroads between Castle Cary and Wincanton in 1790, haunted the place where he was gibbeted.[37]

As these cases indicated, there would seem to be historical parameters to such hauntings. Gibbeting had been practised in the early modern period but it was by no means a common form of capital punishment.[38] It was in response to the perceived increase in murders during the mid eighteenth century that an act of 1752 formalised and institutionalised the macabre punishments of dissection and hanging in chains to provide a graphic warning to the public. The body or just the face of the criminal was covered with pitch and suspended from the gibbet, which was usually erected either where the crime had taken place or on a prominent spot nearby. The corpse would eventually be picked and pulled to pieces by scavenging birds. Some birds took to nesting in the cavities that opened up. By the nineteenth century gibbets were a significant part of the English landscape. In the 1770s nearly 100 gibbets stood on Hounslow Heath alone. Because some gibbets and their macabre fruits were left hanging for many years, they even found themselves being recorded on maps.[39] The practice was ended in 1832, but it took a couple of decades or so for the gibbets with their rattling cages and chains to be finally removed from public display. Workmen at Jarrow probably demolished the last one in 1856.[40]

It is hardly surprising, then, that gibbet sites attracted reputations for being haunted. The corpses of the criminals, denied a Christian burial, made them prime candidates for ghosthood. This is why gibbets were often sited on parish boundaries that traversed common land in order to prevent such troubled spirits from wandering far. In *Great Expectations* Charles Dickens evoked well the sense of the supernatural that accrued such spots. When the young Pip sees Magwitch picking his way through the marshes after their first encounter, the latter is limping towards an old gibbet, its chains, which once held the body of a pirate, clanking in the wind. It was 'as if he were the pirate come to life, and come down, and going back to hook himself up again. It gave me a terrible turn when I thought so; and as I saw the cattle lifting their heads to gaze after him, I wondered whether they thought so too.'[41] The Cumbrian antiquarian Henry Swainson Cowper remarked that a former gibbet spot near Hawkshead, was dreaded even during daylight. Writing in 1899 he noted that 'probably there are now many people who are unaware that a gibbet ever stood here', but the haunting evidently remained as a memorial.[42]

The spirits of the murdered appeared more frequently than their killers. In unsolved cases, this was a matter of identifying the murderer and ensuring justice was done. Sometimes, though, the bodies of victims were not found and so did not receive a Christian burial. Rather like purgatorial delay, it was up to the ghosts of those so grievously sinned against to return and ensure that justice was done before they could rest peacefully until the Day of Judgement. It was commonly thought therefore, that ghosts hovered over the hidden bodies. Francis Grose wondered why the ghosts of those murdered did not go straight to the nearest justice of the peace, rather than hang about their burial place frightening passers-by. 'Ghosts have undoubtedly forms and customs peculiar to themselves', he concluded.[43] To give just one amongst numerous examples of this tradition, in the spring of 1806 a butcher of Stretford, near Manchester, disappeared after some bad flooding in the town. A rumour soon spread that he had been murdered, and it was reported that numerous people had seen his ghost at midnight wandering near a deep pool of water. A town meeting was convened and it was agreed that the pool be pumped dry in search of the butcher's body. It was duly discovered, although the fact that money and valuables were found on the corpse suggested his death was accidental.[44]

Battlefields were another location in the landscape where the dead lay without a proper Christian burial. Somewhat surprisingly, though, prior to the twentieth century there is not a great deal of evidence regarding the presence of ghosts at such sites. The popular literature of the seventeenth and early eighteenth centuries certainly contained frequent reports of apparitions of armies fighting in the sky both in England and abroad. However, these were usually prophetic visions disseminated for political propaganda purposes rather than representations of the apparitions of the dead involved in recent battles.[45] One of the few reported instances of ghosts haunting a battlefield occurred a month or so after the battle of Edgehill, Warwickshire, in October 1642. The villagers of nearby Kineton heard the sound of drums, trumpets, and the noise of battle. The earth groaned with 'the weight of lives whose last beds there were made to sleepe upon'. An apparition of the fighting was seen in the night sky, while on the ground three locals saw a long way in front of them on the road 'the likeness of a Troope of horses posting up to them with full speede, which caus'd the Countrymen to make a stop as fearfull of their events. But coming neer unto them they of a sudaine sunke into the earth'. So fearful were the people of Kineton that women were reported to have had miscarriages.[46] While the Monmouth rebellion raised its fair share of enduring ghost stories in the West Country, the Civil War remains the main source of first-hand, twentieth-century battlefield ghost sightings. In 1932, for instance, a commercial traveller driving across Marston Moor saw three men dressed rather like Royalist soldiers walking along the road before vanishing.[47] Away from English soil, during World War I some British soldiers reported seeing the ghosts of their dead comrades, such as the various sightings of some stretcher-bearers blown up by a shell during the battle of the Somme. One soldier swore they had carried him to safety.[48]

TREASURE SITES

Ghosts not only hovered over the burial places of the dead, they also liked to linger where valuable goods lay buried. Daniel Defoe considered this one of the most absurd but widespread popular beliefs regarding ghosts. It was 'impossible to beat it out of their Heads', he moaned, 'and if they should see any thing which they call an Apparition, they would to this Day follow it, in hope to hear it give a Stamp on the Ground, as with its Foot, and then vanish'. They would dig in the 'hopes of finding a Pot of Money hid there, or some old Urn with Ashes and Roman Medals'. If you tried to reason with them and say there was no basis for their confidence, 'they would laugh at it as the greatest Jest imaginable, and tell you there were five hundred Examples to the contrary'.[49] The tradition was still going strong nearly two centuries later, according to the Herefordshire folklorist Ella Leather. She remarked that it was a general belief that if someone hid or buried money or valuable possessions their spirit would have to haunt the spot until someone had the courage to say to it, 'In the name of God, who art thou?' She remembered hearing the wife of an old workman, who lay ill in bed, say that she had to go and search for his tools, which he had left under an archway, otherwise 'he might have to haunt the place after death'.[50]

As this story suggests, some treasures were of recent deposition, and often based around a local miser who secreted his savings somewhere in his property. In December 1867 considerable excitement was caused in the village of Hawkchurch, Somerset, by the ghostly flitting of a candle behind the windows of an abandoned cottage. An elderly pauper had owned it, and it was rumoured that he had hidden a large sum of money in the walls. After his death the cottage was searched but no treasure was found.[51] Otherwise treasures were located outdoors and usually in association with prehistoric earthworks, particularly Neolithic and Bronze Age barrows which were often thought to be gateways to the world of the fairies and their wealth. In the early twentieth century a ghost guarded gold treasure buried in a tumulus near Minchinhampton.[52] Half a century earlier, people in the area of Chanctonbury Ring, a small Iron Age hill fort in Sussex, believed that the ghost of an old man with a long white beard haunted a spot at the bottom of the hill. Legend had it that he had been seen at dusk combing the ground 'as if in search of treasure'.

This haunting was recounted in a report on the finding of an Anglo-Saxon coin hoard near the spot in 1866.[53]

Hidden treasures were as much a part of urban as of rural tradition. As we shall see in the next chapter, the seventeenth-century eccentric politician Goodwin Wharton went on numerous treasure hunts in and around the capital. The belief was encouraged by popular literature. In 1705 a pamphlet recorded the amazing discovery of a chest full of money in an old building in Rosemary Lane, London, thanks to the directions provided by a female ghost.[54] A curious pamphlet describing another treasure-seeking escapade in London was published in the early 1820s. It was purportedly written by one Patrick Reardon, a former sailor who made a small living selling coffee to labourers at the West India Docks in London. On 22 July 1820, an apparition of a woman appeared to him around midnight and told him to dig under his house. She appeared again with the same message three days later. The following day the apparition expressed its impatience, saying, with ghosts' usual fondness for triplication, 'If you do not act agreeable to my directions you WILL RUE IT! YOU WILL RUE IT! YOU WILL RUE IT all the days of your life.'[55] He experienced no further visitations from her until 20 January 1821. Reardon finally decided to act, and with the help of an acquaintance began to dig at a spot pointed out by the apparition. Their work was interrupted by the appearance of a black serpent. Despite overcoming this obstacle all they found was a pair of shoes and an old key. Further excavations were halted by the landlord of the property where they were digging, and they were arrested and incarcerated at Shadwell police station for 24 hours. Reardon's account could be dismissed as journalistic invention, exploiting the well-worn theme of 'Authentic Narratives' common in the late seventeenth and eighteenth centuries, but it does have the ring of truth about it, and a similar scenario was played out for real 50 years later. In April 1871 two young men named Richard Ball and Samuel Savage, of Globe Lane, Woolwich, were charged with illegal entry before the Greenwich magistrates. Ball and Savage were caught entering a vacant property next to the Crown and Sceptre Tavern in Greenwich. It transpired in court that Ball's father and grandfather had once occupied the house, and on his deathbed his father had told him, 'Look under the stairs, where you will find a lot of money.' In early April, Ball dreamed over several nights that an apparition appeared to him, which pointed and said three times, 'Under the stairs.' It was with the intention of following the instructions of this extraordinary messenger that he and his friend entered the vacant property. Much to his consternation the stairs had evidently been removed, and to complete a disastrous night they were arrested. On hearing this account, and proof having been supplied that Ball's family had indeed owned the property, the presiding magistrate decided to let off the two men.[56] The historical record would seem to bear out Daniel Defoe's conclusion that 'in all my Search after those things, and after evidence of Fact, I cannot arrive to one Example, where ever an Apparition directed to the finding Money hid in the Ground or Earth, or any other place'.[57]

WATER

A significant minority of ghosts were seen frequenting lakes, pools and rivers. In boggy or marshy places these were sometimes will-o'-the-wisps, around which legends accrued. Other sightings were interpreted as the spirits of those who had drowned themselves. In the 1920s a Suffolk folklorist reported that for generations it was thought that an old woman named Mother Wakely drowned herself in a local pond, and that her spirit sometimes appeared to those who passed by the spot and tried to drag them in.[58] A few cases, such as the ghost of a man fishing, could have been generated by a repetitive action associated with a known individual.[59] Another explanation for some haunted pools and lakes in out of the way places was that clergymen had laid troublesome ghosts there to prevent them from disturbing communities. With the tradition of White Ladies and their liking for pools, particularly ones described as deep, we move to an interpretation of water sources as liminal places, portals between the worlds of the living and the spirits. A similar symbolic meaning could help explain why ghosts were also sometimes found on or under bridges.

In 1668 a tailor named John Bowman, of Greenhill, deposed to a magistrate that on returning home from Sheffield market shortly before Ascension Day:

One John Brumhead overtooke him, and they past along until they came against the cutlers bridge. And when they came at the said bridge they had some discourse concerneing an apparition that had beene seene there, as it was reported, in the shape and corporall forme of a man that they called Earle George. And as they were speakeinge of itt, of a sudden there visibly appeared unto them a man lyke unto a prince, with a greene doublet and ruff ... whereupon this examinate was sorelye affrighted and fell into a swound or trannce.[60]

Samuel Bamford recalled how in his childhood in Middleton Lancashire, the locals much feared Owler Bridge and the field that led up to it, in which it was believed a murder had once been committed. It was 'thronged by spirits, whilst "fairees" were frequently seen dancing and gambolling on the bridge, and the bank of the stream on either side'. When his father, a Nonconformist weaver, had to pass over the bridge at night, he 'seldom forgot to hum a psalm or hymn tune, whilst on his way'.[61] Scholar's Bridge, between Sapcote and Stoney Stanton, Leicestershire, was likewise a focus for ghosts and strange appearances, as were two bridges near Normanby, Lincolnshire. Horses had a tell-tale objection to passing over one of them.[62]

There was a tradition that clergymen also laid ghosts under bridges. A legend from Bagbury, Shropshire, told of how the ghost of an unpleasant old man, which tormented the village in the guise of a bull, asked a parson to lay him under Bagbury Bridge, but he was cast into the Red Sea instead.[63] In such instances, and with examples such as Owler Bridge, the hauntings have a historical, albeit legendary explanation. Other bridge hauntings did not, however, and this observation, as with White Lady traditions, seems to be significant. It is possible, of course, that by the time some legends were recorded, historical explanations may have been lost from the communal memory. But as the example of Owler Bridge indicates, the bridge acted not only as a practical, physical crossing point but also as a spirit access point. Casting a ghost under a bridge either banished it to the spirit realm or trapped it between the two worlds. Regarding those ghosts with no personal history, then perhaps, as with the White Lady tradition, they have their origins in fairy hauntings rather than human events.

Occasionally ghosts travelled beyond land to haunt sailors at sea. In February 1843 word spread through Sunderland that a mariner on board the Myrtle had been visited by the ghost of his sister while out at sea. Her body lay in a Sunderland churchyard and it was reported that her ghost would visit her brother again in port at midnight a few days later. Apparently a crowd of more than 1,000 people gathered around the church in expectation of seeing the woman's spirit make its way to her brother's ship.[64] In such an enclosed, intense and dangerous physical and social environment the sighting of a ghost, and the excitement and fear it generated, could lead to tragedy. A murder on board the British vessel the Pontiac, which was taking a cargo of Guano from the port of Callao, on the 13 October 1863, was linked to the sighting of a ghost on board. A Greek sailor named Moyatos stabbed to death a fellow seaman, Robert Campbell, and gravely injured another named George Williams. Moyatos claimed that God had revealed to him that the two men had been bribed by the captain of another ship to throw him overboard. Moyatos's paranoid suspicions were confirmed in his mind by overhearing Campbell and Williams talking of stabbing and chucking someone overboard. The conversation was actually a joke between the two men about what they would do to a ghost that the steersman and a cabin boy had said they had seen two nights before. A good number of the seamen feared that the apparition had appeared as a forewarning of a disaster that would befall the ship, though others like Campbell and Williams mocked the idea. Neither had any idea, of course, that the disaster was to befall them. No doubt for some on board the murder was confirmation of the ghost's prophetic appearance. Moyatos was brought to trial in Scotland and declared insane.[65]

MINES

The intense and dangerous nature of work in the mines was rather similar to those on board ships, but as subterranean places these were also liminal spaces where fairies and spirits were frequently encountered. Referring to fairy beings known as 'knockers', a book on 'Signals from the World of Spirits', published in 1800, remarked that 'the history of mine-working is inseparable from the observation of the existence of these visible, though untangible beings'.[66] A century earlier, the Cornishman Thomas Tonkin wrote of the 'Many strange stories we have, more especially among the miners, of fairies or, as they call them, piskeys, small people, etc.; of their discovering mines to them.'[67] These 'knackers', 'nuggies' or 'knockers' were once described as small, wizened creatures, or little old men, who some thought were the spirits of the Jews who crucified Jesus.[68] Following on from the discussions on pools and bridges, it is now understandable why ghosts would be found in such subterranean company, and, the terrible loss of life in mining accidents provided plenty of material for legend formation and first-hand experiences of ghosts. But while knockers usually kept themselves to themselves as long as humans respected their presence, ghosts served to help their mining colleagues.

During the early twentieth century some Durham miners continued to believe strongly that the spirits of those killed in the mines, and also the ghosts of children, appeared to forewarn miners of an imminent collapse. The ghosts of those killed in such accidents were also thought to linger on the spot as a reminder of their fate.[69] On a personal level a man known to the Victorian Cornish antiquarian, Joseph Hammond, was warned of an imminent mine collapse by the appearance of the ghost of another miner, who had died several weeks before at the treacherous mine end being investigated by Hammond's informant. The seriousness with which mining communities interpreted such apparitions is evident from an incident at Shirland Colliery, near Alfreton, Derbyshire in October 1867. A few days after a miner was accidentally killed down the mine, a colleague working down the pit claimed he saw the ghost of the man. The news spread quickly among his fellow workers who downed tools and demanded to be taken up, evidently fearing a collapse. When they emerged at the surface they informed the next shift of the apparition, and they refused to go down. In all, 200 men and boys refused to work until the mine was considered safe.[70]

URBAN GHOSTS

In his account of the 'present state' of England, written in 1732, the historian Thomas Salmon, with typical Enlightenment ignorance, stated that 'the People of London are not so superstitious as those in the Country; we seldom hear of Apparitions, Witches, or Haunted Houses about Town'. He concluded that those Londoners who believed in such things must have 'lately come out of the Country, and have not yet overcome the Prejudices of their Education'.[71] The paucity of urban ghosts in the folklore archives of the nineteenth century would seem to support such a view. But folklorists rarely ventured into the massively expanding urban areas of industrial England, and the countryside was assumed to be the natural home for spirits. So, did ghosts wander the backstreets of slums and the dark corners of the rookeries just as they paced the isolated byways, bridges and pools of the countryside? Not quite, but nineteenth-century urban England still teemed with ghosts and turning to other sources reveals a vibrant belief in haunted houses and churchyards.

In the 1840s the perceptive critic of human credulity Charles Mackay complained that there were many houses in London blighted by a ghostly reputation. One thinks of Thomas Salmon when Mackay wrote, 'If any vain boaster of the march of intellect would but take the trouble to find them out and count them, he would be convinced that intellect must yet make some enormous strides.'[72] In 1863 the *Court Journal*, a London paper dedicated to literature, science and art, bemoaned the fact that 'the number of so-called haunted houses that are closed and have gone to decay in and about town, under this mouldering and blighting reputation is ridiculously large. We know of half a dozen such.'[73] The reader will find numerous cases to support these views throughout this book.

While haunted houses were as common in town and country, it would appear that in the nineteenth-century urban landscape, churchyards became a more frequent focus for hauntings than they were in rural areas. This is understandable considering that there were fewer liminal features in the urban environment to attract legends. Another reason was the fear raised by body-snatchers or Resurrectionists, which was at its peak in the 1830s. This created a general concern and interest in nocturnal churchyard activity and consequently a heightened awareness of potential ghosts. Grieving mothers mounted night-time vigils over their deceased children, for example, and this led to the occasional haunting scare, such as at St Giles's Church, London, in August 1834. One night, around eleven o'clock, large crowds gathered there as rumours spread of a ghost sighting. Several intrepid men climbed the railings to investigate the shadowy figure seen moving among the gravestones. Instead of a spirit they found a poor Irishwoman, named Anne Macarthy, of Buckeridge Street. Her son had been recently buried there, and having heard that 'resurrection-men' were about, decided to set guard by his grave.[74] The concern regarding body-snatchers and ghost sightings led to a rather farcical prosecution in 1851. In August rumours circulated in the vicinity of Shadwell Church, London, that a ghost was haunting the cemetery. As usual, crowds soon gathered nightly in the hope of seeing it. As Peter Mellish, the vestry clerk of the church, later explained in court, the rumours began when a poor old woman, who lived in one of the almshouses near the church, was seen passing through the churchyard late one night with a pint of beer, choosing this route to avoid going up the steep slope of Foxe's Lane to the east of the church. One man who was unaware of this, but who did not believe there was a ghost, was a local drover named Henry Loomer. His father was buried in the churchyard and, fearing that body-snatchers were about, Loomer and a fellow drover named Garret Berry climbed over the churchyard railings, the gate being locked to prevent ghost hunters, and searched around the tombs. They found two young men in hiding and a punch-up ensued until the police arrested them. The two men, John Beasley and Henry Ridley, who turned out to be tea-urn makers from St Lukes and Hoxton, were subsequently tried for being in the churchyard for an unlawful purpose. They claimed they were only there looking for the ghost and were discharged.[75]

The need in populous urban areas for dead-houses, where bodies lay before inquests, provided another source of ghosts, who were troubled by the delay in receiving a proper burial. In the late eighteenth century James Lackington reported the haunting of a London hospital. The ghost was confined to the lower part of the building where a continual tapping on the windows was heard. The nurses concluded that it was the work of the spirit of one of the dead bodies kept close by in the dead-house. So fearful were the nurses that they refused to go from ward to ward if it required entering the haunted part of the building.[76] In July 1868 an estimated 2,000 people congregated nightly around Bermondsey Church. The vicar and parish officials tried to get the crowds to disperse but were ignored. As the police arrived, James Jones, aged 19, climbed up on to the railings and shouted to the mob, 'Don't go; there it is again; there's the ghost!', leading to scuffles with the police. It later transpired in court that, a few days before, a dead body had been pulled out of the river and taken to the dead-house adjoining the church until an inquest could be arranged. Hearing of this, some boys in the neighbourhood began to spread the rumour that a ghost was haunting the churchyard, causing large numbers of people in the district to flock to the church after work in expectations of seeing it.[77] For several decades the memory of the haunting lived on in the lore of the local community, and up until 1895 it was included in the calendar of notable events published in the *Southwark Annual*.[78]

COMMERCE AND TOURIST SPOTS

To a significant extent tourism now defines where ghosts are seen. The phrase 'most haunted' has become part of the English tourist experience, with numerous pubs, villages and towns laying claim to the title. Ghost tours and walks have recently become a popular leisure activity. Visitors to Epworth, for instance, can take advantage of a ghost trek inspired by the Wesleys' experience.[79] These tours have proved particularly successful by placing heritage ghosts in a firmly urban setting, broadening tourism's more traditional association of ghosts with castles and stately homes.[80] Haunted locations were advertised as tourist attractions in Victorian travel guides, such as Harriet Martineau's *Guide to the Lake District* (1858), and in attempts to attract English middle-class visitors to Scotland by advertising places mentioned in the hugely popular Scottish novels of Walter Scott.[81] But the tourist ghost is a largely twentieth-century phenomenon. We can see an early sign of things to come from the following advertisement placed in *The Times* in September 1936:

> HAUNTED HOUSE for SALE: XVIth-century house in quiet Sussex village: ideal for GUEST HOUSE. Freehold £5,000 or offer.

A few days later, an editorial in the newspaper pondering the continued appeal of ghosts observed: 'Ghosts may come and ghosts may go; ghosts may emigrate or be let with bedrooms to tourists.'[82] A comment by the psychical investigator William Salter, writing in 1961, indicates how overseas tourism was by then already influencing the marketing of hauntings. 'I have been told', he said, ' that enterprising travel agencies in America hold out as one of the principal attractions of a visit to the United Kingdom the prospect of seeing our historic ghosts.'[83]

The history of the haunted pub provides us with both a good example of the impact of modern tourism and also the longer tradition of the commercial exploitation of ghosts. Today there is a cottage industry of publications and websites regarding haunted pubs and inns.[84] In contrast, there are relatively few instances prior to the twentieth century. Thomas Burke's classic cultural and historical survey, *The English Inn*, first published in 1930, contains numerous tales and legends of visiting monarchs, murders and highwaymen, but little about ghosts.[85]

While neither obvious liminal spaces nor desolate places, there are reasons why pubs and inns might have attracted a reputation for haunting. Although they were convivial and social institutions, in the early modern period and the eighteenth century they often had reputations for being hubs of criminal activity. Drink and violence led to murders, and then as now, people sometimes chose such a public place to commit suicide. The seventeenth-century astrologer William Lilly recalled in his autobiography how when in service, before he became an astrologer, he found on the body of his dead mistress a small scarlet bag containing several protective magical sigils. One of them had belonged to her former husband. He had once lodged at a Sussex inn, and spent the night in a chamber where only a few months before a grazier had cut his throat. For many years following this unsettling stay her husband believed he was plagued by the suicide's spirit, which continually urged him to slit his own throat. Her husband would often shout out 'I defy thee, I defy thee' and spit at the ghost. He sank into depression and evident mental illness, so to try and put an end his torment his wife went to consult Dr Simon Forman, a famed astrologer-physician of Lambeth. He provided her husband with a charm that apparently relieved him of his haunting as long as he wore it, which he did until his death.[86]

Even back in the seventeenth century, though, we find signs of how pubs and inns could exploit hauntings. The pamphlet published in 1679 recording the appearance of a ghost in Holborn that revealed where the bodies of two children lay buried, advertised that those not convinced by the account could see the children's bones on display at the local Cheshire Cheese Inn.[87] Although the famous Cock Lane ghost of 1762 did not appear in a hostelry, the writer Horace Walpole, who visited the haunted house, remarked cynically in a letter that 'provisions are sent in like forage, and all the taverns and alehouses in the neighbourhood make fortunes'.[88] A handful of haunted pubs were reported in the mid-nineteenth century and the newspapers implied that a commercial explanation lay behind the ghost sightings. Consider, for example, the haunting of the Tiger public house, Wirksworth, Derbyshire, in June 1834. One of the guest rooms at the pub run by William Lowe was disturbed by the regular violent shutting of a box and the flapping of a table-leaf between ten and eleven o'clock at night, annoying both Lowe's family and the neighbours. As the news spread, large crowds gathered, beyond the usual drinking hours, both inside and outside, to hear the haunting. As a newspaper commented, it had caused a deal 'of money to be spent, and been the means of filling Boniface's pockets, and emptying his cellar.'[89] Boniface, it should be noted, was a literary name for the jovial landlord of a country tavern.[90] A similar lucrative outcome resulted from the haunting of the Feathers Hotel, Manchester, in May and June 1869. Staff and guests were disturbed nightly by strange noises and the periodic ringing of all the bells at once. The wiring was rearranged and muffles put on the bells to try and stop the noise. This proved successful for nearly a week until they began to ring again more violently. The rumour spread around the district that a policeman and a couple of boys had seen a ghostly figure in black, and consequently hundreds gathered nightly in expectation of catching a glimpse. As the *Manchester Examiner* punned, the crowds' 'thirst of knowledge, or other desire, have been exorbitant in their demands for spirits, to the no small profit of the landlord'.[91] However, all these cases were not really about tourism – in other words, providing entertainment for holidaymakers. These hauntings were a strategy for pulling in more local punters. It was in the twentieth-century that the marketing men and women began to see the tourist potential of sleeping, eating and drinking with ghosts.

The idea of whole communities being ghost-infested is an obvious product of modern tourism. It is a reversal of the historic position where communities desired to be rid of their spirits. Villages, towns and cities now boast of the number of ghosts they have. Prestbury has been suggested as a contender for the most haunted village in the Cotswolds, if not England. Warrington has been described as 'England's Most Ghost-infested Town', and Barnet as the most haunted borough. In 2002 York was 'officially' given the title of most haunted city in Europe by the President of the Ghost Research Foundation International.[92] The most successful winner (though some locals might say loser) in this tourist competition is Pluckley in Kent. A gazetteer of ghosts, written in 1971 described it as the most haunted village in the county, but it shot to national and even international prominence when the 1998 edition of the *Guinness Book of Records* awarded it the title of most haunted village in the country.[93] It has now become a must-visit place for those fascinated by ghosts.

Ghost hunting as a collective recreational activity is nothing new. Haunted houses and churchyards attracted large crowds in the past. What the tourist industry has done is to reformulate and package the experience by creating a synergy between visitor, place and ghost. The visitor is now a customer, the place has a brand identity, and the ghost is a desirable lodger rather than an unwelcome guest. The landscape is still full of ghosts but you are better off looking for them on the tourist trail than on a trek through the countryside.

THREE

Seeking Ghosts

Nearly all the ghost sightings discussed so far were unexpected and unwanted. Graveyards and haunted spots in the countryside were to be avoided. Encounters were startling at best and fatal at worse. It can be safely said that most people had no desire to ever find themselves in the presence of a ghost. To prevent such a meeting it fell to certain members of the community to step forward and confront the spirits of the dead in order to banish them from the world of the living. Yet it is human nature to be fascinated with the macabre, the ghoulish and the supernatural – as long as the experience is vicarious and on our own terms, and so people gained a voyeuristic thrill in glimpsing or hearing the haunting of others. Some had a more positive and earnest perception of ghosts, however, and saw them as a means of accessing the secrets of nature, providing a glimpse of divine wisdom. Due to their celestial position ghosts had knowledge of the past, present and future. Their existence was defined by the past, their presence was witnessed by the living, and most wondrous of all, their experience of the afterlife gave them intimations of the future of life. No wonder, then, that there has always been a minority who have sought their company.

NECROMANCY

Ancient Greek and Roman tragedies, plays and poems furnished early modern demonologists with numerous examples of magicians and witches raising ghosts to seek their aid and to foretell the future – necromancy, in other words.[1] In Homer's *Odyssey*, Odysseus, under the instructions of the sorceress Circe, calls up the spirits of the dead with prayers and blood sacrifice. Horace gave us the brutal necromantic witches Canidia and Sagana. Several Greek papyri discovered in more recent times demonstrate that there were specific rituals for calling up the dead, yet it is noteworthy that there is little historical evidence of necromancy actually being practised in the classical period.[2] More significantly, the Bible also held out the possibility of necromancy. The account of how the woman of Endor supposedly raised the spirit of the prophet Samuel, as told in I Samuel 28, was enigmatic enough in its description to provoke endless debate – it was still the cause of tetchy argument in the mid nineteenth century, as evident from an exchange of letters in *The Times*.[3] What was so controversial about Samuel 28? To set the scene, the Philistines had gathered for war against Israel and at the sight of their vast army Saul feared the outcome of battle. He hoped that God or his prophets would send him a message, but as no such communications were forthcoming he decided to turn to the diviners he had recently banished from the land. It is worth noting that in the first complete English Bible, printed in 1535, such people were described as 'soothsayers', 'expounders of tokens' and 'witches', while in the King James Bible, first published in 1611, they are 'wizards' and possessors of 'familiar spirits'. Here is what follows when Saul consulted the woman of Endor, as recounted in the King James version:

> Then said the woman, Whom shall I bring up unto thee? And he said, Bring me up Samuel.
>
> And when the woman saw Samuel, she cried with a loud voice: and the woman spake to Saul, saying, Why hast thou deceived me? for thou art Saul.
>
> And the king said unto her, Be not afraid: for what sawest thou? And the woman said unto Saul, I saw gods ascending out of the earth. And he said unto her, What form is he of? And she said, An old man cometh up; and he is covered with a mantle. And Saul perceived that it was Samuel, and he stooped with his face to the ground, and bowed himself.
>
> And Samuel said to Saul, Why hast thou disquieted me, to bring me up?

For some theologians, from the beginning of the Christian Church through to the modern era, this passage was the ultimate proof that through divine intervention the spirits of the dead could return to communicate with the living. Yet even in the early years of the church there was no consensus about the reality of Samuel's ghost.[4] There was certainly general agreement that the woman of Endor, or 'Witch' as she commonly came to be known, did not have the power to summon the dead, but some argued that God had, for his own reasons, commanded Samuel's spirit to arise in conjunction with the woman of Endor's pretence. Others were less willing to interpret I Samuel 28 quite so literally, suggesting that either God had allowed a demon in the shape of Samuel to appear, or that a demon had deceived Saul into thinking he had received the prophecy from Samuel. As early as the mid third century

AD such scepticism was quite widespread in theological circles. We know as much from an attack on critics by one of the most influential early church fathers, Origen of Alexandria (185–254).[5] The interpretive problems caused by the passage are also evident in St Augustine's (354–430) shifting opinions on the matter.

To counter those who held literally to the wording of the passage, those who denied that Saul had been raised from the dead had to deconstruct the language of the Bible's authors. They argued that, following their usual condensed writing style, the Bible scribes felt it was unnecessary to express explicitly that 'a demon appeared in Samuel's shape' or that the woman of Endor 'saw a vision of Samuel'. They took it for granted, asserted the sceptics, that readers would know that she was a fraud. Another argument that was repeated for centuries concerned the fact that Saul heard but did no see Samuel, and therefore the woman of Endor's use of ventriloquism could easily have deceived him. By the fourteenth century the demonic impersonation of Samuel had become the orthodox theological interpretation. The preoccupation was consequently less with the figures of Saul and Samuel and increasingly with the woman of Endor as heretical necromancer, while in the iconography of the event the Devil entered the picture for the first time.[6]

During the era of the witch trials in the early modern period, those who questioned the reality of witchcraft adopted the argument that the raising of Samuel was nothing more than human deception. The Elizabethan sceptic Reginald Scot observed: 'He that weigheth well that place, and looketh into it advisedly, shall see that Samuel was not raised from the dead; but that it was an illusion or cozenage practised by the witch.'[7] The seventeenth-century physician Thomas Ady echoed Scot in dismissing the possibility of a diabolic miracle. 'That the Devil can assume and raise a dead Body, it is most absurd and blasphemous,' he asserted, 'for it was by the divine miraculous power of Christ upon the Cross, that the bodies of the dead were raised for a time, and appeared unto many.'[8] This did not, of course, preclude the possibility that the Devil deluded Saul through illusion. The more contentious issue was whether the woman of Endor was also duped or was working with the Devil. The latter interpretation was adopted by the Puritan clergy and used as a key defence for the existence of diabolic witches. The clergyman Thomas Cooper (c. 1569–1626), for instance, denounced those 'patrones of Witch-craft' who argued that Satan deceived the woman of Endor. For Cooper, 'the witch, by vertue of the covenant with Satan, raised him up; He by his power and skill counterfeited Samuel'.[9] In Puritan England, then, the definition of 'necromancer' became, as the Calvinist clergyman John Edwards (1637–1716) described, one 'who by Magick Inchantment raised the Souls of the Dead, or the Devil rather to represent Souls, and then consulted with him'.[10]

In 1604 a new Act of Parliament was passed that reflected the deep concerns of King James regarding the necromantic activities of witches and magicians. It expanded upon the Elizabethan Act against witchcraft and conjuration, including the prosecution of all those who

> consult covenant with entertaine employ feede or rewarde any evill and wicked Spirit to or for any intent or pupose; or take any dead man woman or child out of his her or theire grave or any other place where the dead body resteth, or the skin, bone or any other parte of any dead person, to be imployed or used in any manner of Witchecrafte, Sorcerie, Charme or Inchantment.

One of the main influences fuelling James's concern over necromancy was the dissemination of the *Fourth Book of Cornelius Agrippa*, which he recommended to the readers of his *Dæmonologie* as a principal source on the 'rites, & curiosities of these black arts'.[11] By the early seventeenth century the *Fourth Book* had, indeed, become an influential and widely used manual of spirit conjuration across Europe, but Agrippa certainly did not write it. Agrippa's fame and the success of his *Three Books of Occult Philosophy* made his name an attractive marketing tool. The *Fourth Book* first appeared in the mid sixteenth century, years after Agrippa's death, and although an English edition only appeared in 1655, manuscript versions and continental editions were circulating in England long before then. The *Fourth Book* was primarily concerned with the conjuration of good and evil angels, but at the end it devoted a few pages to the souls of the dead. It advised that they were 'not easily raised up, except it be the souls of them whom we know to be evil, or to have perished by a violent death, and whose bodies do want a rite and due burial'. For this reason it was usually not safe to conduct necromantic rites where the bodies of such troubled souls lay, and instead the *Fourth Book* advised the reader to take 'some principal part of the body that is relict, and therewith to make perfume in due manner, and to perform other competent rites'.[12]

Most of the discussion on the souls of the dead in the *Fourth Book*, though not the practical advice above, referred back to Agrippa's *Three Books of Occult Philosophy*. This was not a manual of practical magic but a learned disquisition on the science and religion of Neoplatonic thought. In his chapter on 'What wayes the Magicians and Necromancers do think they can call forth the souls of the dead', Agrippa started from the premise that 'souls after death do as yet love their body which they have left' and so 'yet wander about their carcasses

in a troubled and moist spirit'. Citing the writings of the ancients, such as
Homer and Lucan, he posited that it was possible for necromancers to attract
these souls back to their host bodies by enhancing the spiritual harmony that
existed between body and soul. This could be done through the utterance of
sacred invocations and the creation of alluring 'vapours, liquors and savours,
certain artificiall lights being also used, songs, sounds and such like'.[13] The only
limitation was that the spirit raising needed to take place where corpses lay,
such as burial grounds, places of execution and battlefields, for that was where
pining souls hovered. Agrippa distinguished between two types of necromancy.
There was necyomancy, which concerned the raising of the bodies of the dead,
and required sacrificial blood; and sciomancy, in which the operator desired
to call and communicate only with the spirits of the dead. He warned that
diabolic spirits were equally at home amongst the dead and were liable to
appear at the necromancer's summoning. Unlike the author of the Fourth Book,
Agrippa reinforced the point that man alone could not raise the dead through
magic, as it 'requireth all these things which belong not to men but to God
only'. However, he also posited a scientific as well as a religious rationale for
raising the dead. Sometimes, he said, the soul continued to reside in a retracted
state in the body even though the body may seem dead. Thus the 'body can be
wakened again and live; and thus many miracles appear in these; and of this
kind many have been seen amongst the Gentiles and Jewes in former ages'.[14]

By the early modern period necromancy was often used in a more general
way to describe the conjuration of any type of spirit, as well as the use of
corpses in magic rituals and charms.[15] This makes it difficult to gauge the
extent to which necromancy in the sense of raising the spirits of the dead was
actually practised in early modern England. Those conjurers tried under the
1604 Act for entertaining spirits usually swore they were communicating only
with benign spirits, fairies or angels. During her prosecution for witchcraft
and spirit conjuring in 1653, the cunning-woman Anne Bodenham asseverated
that 'these Spirits, such as she had, were good Spirits, and would do a Man
all good Offices, all the Days of his Life'.[16] Rarely were the spirits of the dead
mentioned in such trials, and we need to look elsewhere for necromancers in
the sense that Agrippa used the term.

One of the few possibly authentic cases was that of the notorious Edward
Kelley, the assistant to the famous Elizabethan occult philosopher and scientist
John Dee (1527–1609). Dee was troubled by accusations of being a conjurer
and magician in his own lifetime and accrued the reputation of a necromancer
in subsequent centuries. But Dee's occult activities were not concerned with
talking to ghosts. He sought communications only with the angels, hoping
that they would reveal the 'true wisdome' of the natural world, while Kelley

acted as his scryer or medium, through whom the angels communicated via a crystal ball.[17] Just over 30 years after Kelley's death, the poet and antiquary John Weever related an account of how Kelley and an accomplice named Paul Waring had one night engaged in infernal ceremonies in Walton-le-Dale Park, Lancashire, to ascertain the manner and time of death of a certain young gentleman. They asked one of the young gentleman's servants which was the most recent corpse buried in the local graveyard. This turned out to be a poor man interred that same day. With the help of the servant, Kelley and Waring dug up the man's corpse and 'by their incantations, they made him (or rather some evill spirit through his Organs) to speake, who delivered strange predictions concerning the said Gentleman'.[18] Weever heard an account of the events from both the gentleman, shortly before his death, and his servant who participated in the necromancy.

The politician Goodwin Wharton (1653–1704) was another larger than life necromancer, who recorded his communications in his autobiography. To be more precise, it was his partner, a cunning-woman named Mary Parish, who acted as the medium between himself and several spirits of the dead, the most helpful of which was that of George Whitmore. Mary told Wharton that she had read in her book of magic that to conjure ghosts and keep them as spirit guides it was necessary to seek the agreement of someone before they died. She sought out Whitmore, a gentleman highway robber, who obligingly agreed to the compact and his ghost duly appeared to her shortly after his execution. He helped Parish and Wharton locate hidden treasures in such diverse places in and around the capital as Highgate Woods, Stoke Newington and Tyburn Road, though they never actually managed to find them. When Wharton asked Mary if he could meet with George's ghost face-to-face, George apparently objected strongly to the idea of also being under his command. He complained that because Wharton was only around 30 years of age – much younger than Parish who was in her early fifties – he would have to hang around on earthly business for perhaps another half a century. He was not inclined to spend such a time in the world of the living, but did agree to listen to Wharton's request in person. He refused to appear before him, however, and since only Mary could actually see Wharton's ghost this led to a rather comical scene. For being assured by Mary that George was present, Wharton set forth his arguments to the empty air. He then had to leave the room while George gave his reply to Mary. Wharton was satisfied with the results. A compromise was reached, with George's ghost agreeing to submit to Wharton during Mary's lifetime.[19]

During their various quests for treasure Mary claimed to have also called up the ghost of a man named Nicholson who agreed to show them where he had hidden some money and goods on his premises. There was also Mr Abab, a great French chemist who had lived in Montpelier, and the spirit of Cardinal Thomas Wolsey. I should not forget to mention that they also sought the help of the Queen of the Fairies and various angels. It is clear from Wharton's diary that he was mentally ill, but to what extent all or some of his accounts are the imaginings of a disturbed mind is difficult to gauge.[20] It is certainly the case that he was the dupe of Mary Parish's cunning and invention. Yet it is important to point out that the descriptions and accounts she gave him of ghosts, fairies and angels were 'realistic' or feasible in the context of those who clung to the Neoplatonic conception of the spirit world during the late seventeenth century.

GHOST PREVENTION

It would seem that, until the rise of spiritualism in the nineteenth century, the main reason for wishing to encounter the dead was in order to banish them rather than to seek their spiritual guidance. But before discussing the exorcism of ghosts it is necessary to consider strategies employed to prevent ghosts from appearing in the first place. This usually involved treating the corpses of potential ghosts, such as those of suicides and murderers, in ways that physically and symbolically hindered their passage between the worlds of the living and the dead. This could be achieved by dismembering the corpse, pinning or staking it to the ground, or weighing it down under water – all practices that had been employed back in the prehistoric period and in later Pagan and Christian times. While in early modern Europe such solutions were most associated with the physical hampering of vampires and the walking dead, in other words reanimated corpses,[21] such eschatological treatments also served to prevent the return of the spirits of the dead. A range of other prophylactic rituals were also enacted on the continent. In early modern Sweden, for example, several criminal trials resulted from 'unchristian' practices to prevent hauntings. In one instance, in 1714, a widow walked in front of her husband's funeral procession with her petticoat pulled over her head and then threw it over the grave to stop her husband's ghost from returning. In another case a fire was lit on a road over which a funeral procession had passed to ward off the potential ghost. There were several suicide panics in seventeenth-century Bavaria, with corpses being dug up to deter troublesome ghosts and avoid divine wrath. In one instance a court ordered that the corpse of a female suicide, which had been buried in a pasture, be exhumed and cremated after locals complained that the milkmaids were fearful of her ghost and refused to work in the field.[22]

As will be discussed in a later chapter, the popular belief in the walking dead had disappeared in England by the Reformation, yet as we have already seen the staking down of suicides continued into the nineteenth century. The legal and religious rationale for the practice was couched purely in the secular terms of a social and moral deterrent. As John Weever explained in 1631, suicides were buried in the highway 'with a stake thrust through their bodies, to terrifie all passengers, by that so infamous and reproachfull a burial, not to make such their finall passage out of this world'. To this end the stake was sometimes left exposed on the surface as a long-term reminder.[23] But while the general populace no doubt recognised this authoritarian message, it is likely that they also conceptualised such profane burial as security against wandering spirits.

Another prophylactic burial practice found in England and elsewhere was the interment of suspect corpses face down in graves. Archaeologists have discovered numerous such prone burials dating to the Roman period. At a Cirencester cemetery, 10 per cent of the interments were of this type, and 14 such burials were excavated at a London burial ground; two of the skeletons also had large stone blocks placed on their backs. A few have been found in Anglo-Saxon cemeteries, where they also tend to be in the deepest graves, but there is little archaeological evidence that the tradition continued into the second millennium in England.[24] Yet there is some historical and ethnographic evidence that it continued as a means of ghost prevention right through to the twentieth century. The folklorist Ella Leather was informed about a man at Longtown, Herefordshire, who in justifying his belief in ghosts remarked: 'I helped myself to turn a man in his grave, up at Capel-y-fin; he come back, and we thought to stop him, but after we turned him he come back seven times worse.' The event, if true, must have taken place in the second half of the nineteenth century. Another folklorist remembered as a child listening to a group of Somerset sextons discussing their business. One of them, who was also a village carpenter and coffin-maker, said he secretly turned over the corpses of infamous locals before nailing down their coffin lids. 'This action was apparently well-approved', she noted.[25] That such remembrances of prone burial were not merely the product of hazily remembered idle talk is evident from a report on the treatment of the corpse of the brutal London murderer Nicholas Steinberg, who killed himself in September 1834. The staking of suicides having been prohibited ten years previously, it was evidently felt necessary to enact another means of preventing the man's ghost from rising. So at the Clerkenwell poor ground two men lifted Steinberg's corpse from its cheap coffin, one by the shoulders the other by the feet, and held it over the grave. They then turned the corpse over and dropped it into the grave face down. The corpse was partially covered with earth and then one of the assistants smashed the head to pieces with a large mallet. Only then was the grave filled.[26]

GHOST LAYERS

In the first place, he got together the most powerful Exorcisms that he could find; to which, he added some new ones, as by the Bowels of such a Saint, the Bones of St. Winnifrede; and after this, he makes choice of a Place in the Field, near the Thicket of Bushes, whence the Noise came. He draws ye a Circle, a very large one, with several Crosses in it, and a phantastical Variety of Characters; and all this was perform'd in a set Form of Words. He had there also, a great Vessel, full of Holy Water, and the Holy Stole (as they call it) about his Neck; upon which hung the beginning of the Gospel of St. John. He had in his Pockets, a little Piece of Wax, which the Bishop of Rome us'd to Consecrate once a Year, commonly call'd an Agnus Die. With these Arms in time past, they defended themselves against Evil Spirits.[27]

Such was the method of exorcising a ghost recounted in a seventeenth-century translation of Erasmus's humorous story concerning an English priest's encounter with a supposed ghost, written in the 1520s. Although the Dutch Catholic theologian's account was intended to be satirical, it probably accurately represented the mix of orthodox and quasi-magical ritual methods employed by some of the Catholic clergy of the time.[28] The portrayal would have struck a chord with English Puritans. Protestant reformers considered such practices as typical Catholic 'superstition', and English Canon Law forbade exorcism in 1604. Article 72 stated that no ministers were 'to attempt upon any Pretence whatsoever, either of Possession or Obsession, by Fasting and Prayer to cast out any Devil or Devils, under pain of the Imputation of Imposture or Cozenage, and Deposition from the Ministery'.[29] There was no mention of ghosts because orthodox Protestant theology taught that the spirits of the dead did not return unless God so desired it, and, if he did so, it was for a divine purpose not to be interfered with.

The Anglican clergy were therefore prevented from providing what had been an important service aiding the laity in their regular struggle against the torments of malignant spirits. Yet as part of their pastoral duties many Protestant clergymen continued to receive requests to 'lay' spirits, as exorcism was popularly known. How could they help? In his Daemonologie King James provided some authoritative guidance on cleansing haunted houses:

By two meanes may onely the remeid [remedy] of such things be procured: The one is ardent prayer to God, both of these persons that are troubled with them, and of that Church whereof they are. The other is the purging of themselves by amendment of life from such sinnes, as have procured that extraordinarie plague.[30]

There is evidence that in possession cases some of the Anglican clergy, particularly Puritan ones, did engage in fasting and ardent prayer before and after 1604, even if it transgressed the wording of Article 72.[31] Meanwhile, evangelical Nonconformist ministers, who were not bound by Canon Law, were particularly prominent in late seventeenth- and eighteenth-century instances. The Welsh Independent minister Edmund Jones related how in 1758 some clergymen from Bangor tried to deal with a house plagued by a stone-throwing spirit. Jones said:

they did their best with a good design, but they were also beaten and obliged to go away. Reading prayers was too weak a means to drive an enraged evil Spirit away. There was a necessity of some persons of a strong faith, who had the Spirit and gift of prayer in some great measure.[32]

It was not what was said but how it was said that mattered – an important distinction from Catholic exorcism.

Popular literature of the seventeenth and eighteenth centuries also reinforced the continued role of the clergy in dealing with troublesome spirits. A pamphlet of 1674 reported how a parish minister was called in to deal with a malicious spirit that ripped clothes and fabrics at the house of a gentlewoman in London Wall. This 'worthy and learned person' went to prayer in the house and then gave 'the Woman and her Sister Encouragements from Gods word to strengthen their Faith, to resist the Tempter'.[33] There is, it must be said though, frustratingly little concrete evidence of the clergy laying ghosts. Cases of clerical intervention were usually concerned with domestic poltergeist activity, which up until the nineteenth century was generally interpreted as either manifestations of witchcraft or of satanic interference rather than the spirits of the dead. Ghosts could either be avoided by staying clear of haunted locations or disappeared from their own volition once their task had been completed.

In northern England, where the Catholic faith persisted most strongly following the Reformation, the tentative efforts of the Protestant clergy in combating spirits were popularly contrasted with the efficacious exorcisms of the old Church. The Newcastle curate Henry Bourne observed in 1725 that it was 'common for the present Vulgar to say, none can lay a Spirit but a *Popish*

Priest'.[34] The Rev. John Atkinson observed that in the mid nineteenth century Anglican parsons were still called 'Church-priests' in the district of Danby, Yorkshire. He remembered one of his elderly female parishioners requesting him to deal with some spirits that tormented her house. He wrote:

> She told me what spirits they were, and in some instances whose spirits, and what their objects and efforts were. I told her at last I could not, did not profess to 'lay spirits'; and her reply was, 'Ay, but if I had sent for a priest o' t'au'd church, he was a' deean it. They wur a vast mair powerful conjurers than you Church-priests.'[35]

Folk legends rather than priestly activity were instrumental in perpetuating this perception. In 1878, for instance, it was recorded that a Roman Catholic priest had laid the ghost of Hannah Corbridge, of Laneshaw Bridge, near Colne. She was murdered in January 1789, and her spirit had roamed the area where her body was dumped. In Kirkby Lonsdale there was a legend that three Catholic priests had laid a ghost under the local Devil's Bridge.[36]

In the southern half of England there is little evidence of an enduring popular belief in the exorcising powers of Catholic priests. Instead, in contrast with the historical record, the folklore archives are full of stories about the ghost-laying activities of Protestant clergymen. If the legends are to be believed, they were ghost-busting on a regular basis. The most powerful conjuring parsons could take on a ghost single-handedly, but they often performed in groups of nine or twelve. In the mid nineteenth century the villagers of Cumnor, Oxfordshire, believed, for example, that the ghost of Lady Dudley (1532–1560), who had died in suspicious circumstances, was laid by nine Oxford parsons.[37] Sometimes ghosts were said to have been laid in a bottle or some other small container, such as a snuff box, but most ubiquitous was the notion that clergymen banished ghosts to the depths of ponds, echoing perhaps the ancient practice of burying potential restless dead under water. Numerous such local legends were recorded in Oxfordshire in the late nineteenth century. It was said, for instance, that the restless spirit of a woman who had committed suicide by drowning herself in a pond at Stanton Harcourt Manor, was finally laid to rest in the pond by some parsons who ensured that it never subsequently dried up. Around 40 years before, some clergymen apparently laid several ghosts in a well at Woodperry House.[38] Similar tales were recorded all over the country. A spirit that haunted a large barn in Walford, Berkshire, was banished to a fish pond by twelve clergymen who stood in a circle and read a psalm, and further tempted the spirit with two live cockerels, which it tore to pieces with relish. A similar legend was known in Long Crendon, Buckinghamshire, where the ghost of a woman, who vowed to torment a thief, was laid to rest by twelve clergymen who prayed backwards and proffered a dove instead of cockerels.[39] In the West Country ghosts were also banished to perform endless tasks to keep them occupied, such as the troublesome ghost of an eighteenth-century mayor of Okehampton who was laid in Cranmere Pool, Dartmoor, and ordered to bale it out with a sieve. Others were set the impossible task of spinning ropes of sand.[40]

There was an enduring tradition that the safest place to send a ghost was the Red Sea. The earliest reference I have found to it in popular tradition is in a deposition taken in 1650 from an Essex alehouse servant named Susan Lay, who complained of being haunted by the ghost of her mistress. Susan told a friend that to be rid of it she would have to 'conjure' the ghost 'into the red sea or else she would be her destruction'.[41] Joseph Addison incorporated the same notion in his humorous play on the ghost of the Tedworth Drummer, which was first performed in 1715. In one passage several of the characters discuss how a cunning-man could deal with the troublesome spirit by capturing it within a magical circle drawn on the ground. 'If the conjurer be but well paid,' says one, 'he'll take pains upon the ghost, and lay him, look ye, in the Red Sea – and then he's laid for ever.' Another replies, 'Why, John, there must be a power of spirits in that same Red Sea – I warrant ye, they are as plenty as fish.'[42] Later in the century the student of 'vulgar' beliefs Francis Grose noted humorously that in many instances ghosts had 'most earnestly besought the exorcists not to confine them in that place. It is nevertheless considered an indisputable fact, that there are an infinite number laid there.'[43] The enduring tradition of Red Sea ghost-laying is evident from several references in the folklore record of the early twentieth century. A Wiltshire folklorist, writing in 1901, recorded a local legend of how a ghost begged a parson not to lay it in the Red Sea, while in Somerset the ghost of a wicked old man of West Harptree was first laid for a period of seven years by the local vicar, but when the allotted time expired he turned up again to annoy the locals. This time the vicar cast it into the Red Sea.[44]

Such local legends often accrued around real clergymen. Some evidently attracted reputations in their own lifetimes but it is likely new legends were generated long after their deaths. In 1823 it was noted that Richard Dodge, Vicar of Talland, Cornwall, who died in 1746, 'had the reputation of being deeply skilled in the black art, and could raise ghosts, or send them into the Red Sea, at the nod of his head'. Stories of his exploits still circulated at the end of the nineteenth century.[45] Fifty years after the death of the Rev. Hudson, vicar of West Harptree, Somerset (1837–42), a legend circulated of how he laid a ghost by putting a door key in the Bible and reading the Lord's Prayer backwards.[46] Fame could be long-lived. In the late nineteenth century, tales were still being told of the ghost-laying exploits of the Rev. Thomas Flavel, vicar of Mullion, Cornwall, who died in 1682.[47] Some of the clergy no doubt encouraged their reputation for spirit laying. The Rev. Richard Polwhele, writing in 1826, said he 'could mention the names of several persons, whose influence over their flock was solely attributable to this circumstance'.[48] There is little evidence, though, that the Anglican clergy employed unorthodox or magical means, as some of the legends would have us believe. It is highly unlikely that Hudson read the Lord's Prayer backwards, or that Parson Woods of Ladock cast out ghosts and spirits with an ebony stick engraved with planetary signs and magical symbols.[49]

It has been argued persuasively that historical processes and social change are reflected in the similar ubiquity and activities of ghost-laying ministers in the narrative legends of nineteenth-century Lutheran Denmark. In particular, the failure of ministers to lay ghosts, which represents around 17 per cent of a corpus of several hundred legends, with a further 21 per cent having an ambiguous resolution, are interpreted as representing an erosion of church authority at the national and parochial level.[50] While the English corpus of legends is not so extensive, we may be able to identify some historical messages – it obviously reflects the enduring influence of the Catholic faith and the activities of its priests in the popular traditions of northern England. As in Denmark, the power and influence of the established church in England was eroding during the nineteenth century. However, one does not get a similar sense of this being reflected in the English ghost-laying legends from southern and western England. In contrast with the Danish material, the clergy are nearly always successful, though it may be significant that the effort was often portrayed as a collective clerical action. The forces of secularism and declining church attendance were a particularly urban phenomenon, and so the legends, perhaps, reflect the continued rural perception of the Anglican clergy as a protective, unifying parochial force.

In early modern and modern England there were various lay folk who also professed to have special knowledge or powers to exorcise spirits, and who, unfettered by the professional constraints of Canon Law, made use of tried and tested Catholic exorcisms and rituals. However, as with clerical exorcism, cases of cunning-folk or other individuals offering to expel the spirits of the dead, as distinct from exorcising the possessed or relieving those persecuted by witches, are rare. For the early modern period we have to turn to the unreliable source of popular literature for detailed accounts of lay ghost-laying. In a 1679 report of the ghost of a murdered young man near Stamford that tormented the household of his brother, who had organised his murder, the astrologer called in to lay the ghost is presented as unprofessionally unprepared. When the ghost, with its blood-stained clothing appeared to him, it 'so amazed the Conjurer, that not withstanding his Maganminous art, he did begin to fly the Room, when as the Spirit bid him not to fear, though it was not in his power to lay him, till his blood was by Justice answered for'.[51]

Another pamphlet concerned the ghost of a recently deceased baker named Powel who haunted his former house and garden in Southwark in 1661. He appeared in various animal guises as well as in human form, 'his Eyes half sunk in his Head, his Face extraordinary Black, and in the same Cloaths he used to wear when he was alive'. The hideous noises Powel's ghost made caused his son Thomas to abandon the house, leaving only the servant to look after it. Word of the haunting soon reached the ears of some 'conjurers'. They stayed in the house night and day, 'Using all possible means they can to lay this troubled Spirit, and are continually reading and making of Circles, burning of Wax Candles, and Juniper-wood.' Their first attempts failed, but one night,

> Having made a great Circle in the Garden, the Spirit of Master Powel appeared, to whom one of them said: 'We conjure thee to depart to thy place of Rest.' He answered, 'Wo be to those that were the cause of my coming hither.' The rest (being eight in number) kept close to their Books, and fain would have brought him into the Circle, but could not; whereupon one of them said, 'The Son of God appeared to destroy the works of the Devil': which caused him to vanish away.[52]

Powel's ghost was merely interrupted rather than vanquished and it continued to torment the household. Rumours soon spread that the ghost was guarding a hidden stash of money and Thomas began digging about the place. It took a man-to-spirit conversation with a local minister to resolve the haunting. The clergyman asked the ghost, 'In the Name of God the Father, Son, and Holy Ghost', why he had departed his heavenly slumber. Powel's spirit replied that the cause was 'about a Grand-Daughter of his, whom he desired might have satisfaction from the Dead, it having been some way unjustly dealt by before his Departure.'

A couple of decades later another pamphlet reported how 'one who pretended to be a Cunning-Man' had sought to meet the ghost of a gentleman that disturbed the occupants of his former residence in Middlesex. The occupants had employed 'Ministers and others' to lay the ghost with initial success, but several months later it returned to haunt the house. Knowledge of the haunting spread around the neighbourhood and came to the attention of the cunning-man who, accompanied by a two or three acquaintances and several bottles of wine, undertook to stay the night at the haunted house. As part of his spiritual protection he placed two crossed swords at the entrance to the room in which they kept their watch. It apparently worked, for at midnight the ghost was seen to pass by the room and look through the entrance but did not enter. Up until this point in the haunting the ghost had been harmless but the cunning-man's meddling seems to have upset it, for now it began to pull the bedding off the servants' beds and even pinched and bruised one of them. The master of the house consequently expressed his intent to invite some divines to quieten the ghost.[53]

These popular accounts of non-clerical attempts to lay ghosts served not only as scary entertainment and confirmation of the reality of ghosts, they also provided useful information on how to deal with them. As one popular pamphlet, *A Whip for the Devil*, which provided a helpful series of exorcisms, remarked, 'Paper works Miracles. The Devil dares no more come near a Stationers Heaps, or a Printers Work-house, than some men dare put their Noses into a Cheesemongers Shop.'[54] This was actually a facetious observation and the ostensible aim of *A Whip* was to denounce papist 'superstition', but the author must have known full well that his exposé of exorcism could also serve as a valuable practical manual for would-be ghostbusters. It provided detailed instructions on how to exorcise haunted houses, including the following 'Prayer to be said when you come to the place haunted':

Give ear, O Lord, to our supplications, and enlighten this house with the eyes of thy goodness, and let thy blessing descend upon the inhabitants thereof, that abiding with safety in this habitation, they may be thy habitation also.[55]

As the accounts provided above show, though, the seventeenth-century pamphlets stories portrayed cunning-folk as ineffective ghost-layers. Their magic was either insufficient or they did not have the spiritual or moral authority to command the spirits of the dead. The negative portrayal is understandable considering the authoritarian denunciations of magical practitioners at the time and the prohibition of spirit conjuration. The paucity of nineteenth-century legends regarding lay exorcists, compared with the profusion of clergymen, suggests that the weakness presented in the biased early modern literature was also engrained in oral tradition. Ghost-laying was evidently one area of supernatural interventionism where the Anglican clergy had a decided edge over cunning-folk in popular perception.

NOISY HAUNTINGS AND THE SEARCH FOR THE TRUTH

Noisy ghosts or poltergeists have always attracted the most intellectual attention. The spirits concerned responded to and interacted with the interventions of the living. Such hauntings were about public spectacle, and treated by some as dramatic entertainment. But poltergeist activity also drew those seeking answers to profound theological and philosophical questions. If the manifestations could be found to be free of trickery then it was firm proof of the reality of the spirit world. Then came the question of what types of spirit were responsible: devils, witches or ghosts? It was from the mid seventeenth century onwards, when Neoplatonism was beginning to crumble, that poltergeist activity assumed considerable importance as a battleground for competing philosophical discourses. The most influential focus of debate was the case of the Tedworth Drummer.[56]

In 1662–63 the house of a gentleman named John Mompesson, who lived at Tedworth (Tidworth), Wiltshire, was plagued by strange noises, smells and lights. Most curious of all, a drum that had been confiscated from a vagrant drummer and petty conjurer named William Dury, who had been arrested for possessing fake documentation, began to emanate beats and even banged out whole tattoos. Dury was an obvious suspect for causing the disruption, but for some of the time Dury was locked up in Gloucester gaol on an unrelated charge. It was a mystery. Could Dury have been exacting revenge by using magical powers? Was it the Devil making mischief? A neighbour told Mompesson's wife that the fairies sometimes paid visits to humans to leave money. Glanvill was told by a curious Somerset physician that 'it was nothing but a Rendezvouz of Witches, and that for an hundred pounds, he would undertake to rid the House of all disturbance'.[57]

As usual, the balladeers were quick to make capital out of the events with *A Wonder of Wonders* telling in verse the 'true relation of the strange and invisible beatings of a drum'. The case came to achieve enduring fame, however, due to an account published in Glanvill's *A Blow at Modern Sadducism* (1668), while an oft-repeated version appeared later in *Saducismus Triumphatus* (1681). But at the time, word of mouth effectively spread news of the occurrences and before long Mompesson was being inundated with visitors from the clergy, gentry and aristocracy. Anthony Ettrick, a lawyer and close friend of John Aubrey, stayed in the house one night with Sir Ralph Bankes. They did so 'out of curiosity, to be satisfied. They did hear sometimes knockings; and if they said "Devill, knock so many knocks," so many knocks would be answered.'[58] Sir Thomas Chamberlain was amongst a company of gentlemen present when the drummer complied with a request 'to give five knocks and no more that night'.[59] Two members of the royal court, the second Earl of Chesterfield and the Earl of Falmouth, were sent down to Tedworth on behalf of the king. They were both sceptical, as were other members of court such as Lord Sandwich. Such were the numbers wishing to see and hear for themselves the antics of the spirit drummer that Mompesson understandably grumbled in a letter, 'These strangers are not onely troublesome and chargeable, but hinder us from doing our duties.'[60] Well-sourced rumours spread that during a meeting with the king, Mompesson had admitted that he had discovered the haunting to be a cheat. However, the reason for him saying as much may have been more due to the inconvenience caused to him by the legions of sightseers. John Wesley's eldest brother, who was at Oxford with Mompesson's son, inquired about the events at his family home, and asked if his father had acknowledged that the whole affair had been a trick played upon them. Mompesson explained that

> The resort of gentlemen to my father's house was so great, he could not bear the expense. He therefore took no pains to confute the report that he had found out the cheat; although he, and I, and all the family, knew the account which was published to be punctually true.[61]

The case of the Tedworth Drummer is second only to the Cock Lane ghost in terms of historic notoriety. A century on from the events at Tedworth, the Cock Lane sensation demonstrates both continuity in terms of the characteristics of the manifestation and the debates that surrounded it, but it also reflected intellectual and cultural changes as well. By now witchcraft had dropped out of the educated discourse regarding such phenomena, and there is little evidence that it was considered relevant to the case by the urban artisans in the surrounding streets. Unlike the Tedworth Drummer, the Cock Lane manifestation had a clear back-story as a ghost haunting, but those seeking confirmation of the spirit world did not rule out the machinations of the Devil. The story has been much told and so there is no need to go over the details in great length.[62] In brief, in January 1762 Elizabeth Parsons, the twelve-year-old daughter of Richard Parsons, landlord of a house in Cock Lane and also parish clerk of Sepulchre's, began to be the focus of mysterious knocking and scratching noises. The first person to be called in was a local carpenter employed by Parsons to remove the wainscoting in Elizabeth's bedroom, but nothing obviously connected with the noises, such as a rat's nest, was found. Parsons next applied to John Moore, the assistant preacher at St Sepulchre's, and a Methodist sympathiser. Moore decided to make contact with what was now considered to be a spirit, and, by knocking once for 'yes' and twice for 'no' on the bedpost in Elizabeth's room, it slowly revealed its terrible story. It was the ghost of Frances Lynes, the mistress of one William Kent, the husband of her deceased sister. She and Kent had briefly lodged at Parsons' house in 1759. She died in Clerkenwell the following year of what was thought to be smallpox. She was pregnant with Kent's child at the time. Her spirit had decided to return to Parsons' house to reveal that she had, in fact, been poisoned by Kent and wished in traditional ghostly fashion to reveal the murder so that justice would be done. For the sceptical, the fact that Parsons owed Kent money and had been threatened by him with legal action may have had something do with the ghost's appearance in his house and its grave accusation. Several decades had passed since any of the magistracy would have acted on ghost evidence, but Parsons may have only wished to have Kent's reputation publicly debased.

Reports of the events in Cock Lane spread quickly both by word of mouth through the streets of London and also via the newspapers. Kent sued the editor of the *Royal Chronicle* for libel after it published 'An authentic narrative' of the haunting, which 'raised groundless Suspicions concerning the Death of the said Frances Lynes'.[63] While the locals crowded round the building day after day, a succession of the great and the good drew up in their carriages to inspect the latest supernatural wonder. One of them was Horace Walpole who turned up one morning, but left frustrated and dismissive: 'the ghost was not expected until seven, when there are only 'prentices and old women'.[64] Moore called in fellow clergymen to bolster his own conviction of the veracity of the ghost. Those with Methodist leanings were notable by their presence. One who, after attending seances with 'scratching Fanny', came to believe in the ghost was the Rev. Thomas Broughton (1712–1777), who, although estranged from Wesleyanism, was a well-known evangelical and secretary of the Society for Promoting Christian Knowledge (SPCK).[65] Another believer was the Rev. Ross who, in the presence of Lord Dartmouth and an eminent surgeon, conversed with Fanny's ghost, seeking to solve a fundamental question regarding the nature of spirit matter. 'Are you clothed in a body?' he asked. The ghost replied with one knock. 'Are you clothed in a body of flesh?' Two knocks. Now to the crucial issue. 'In a body of air?' asked Ross. Two knocks. 'In a body of light?' he enquired. One knock was heard.[66]

It was another clergyman, the Rev. Stephen Aldrich, who organised a formal investigating committee to determine the cause of the Cock Lane manifestation. It included the Rev. John Douglas, a future bishop of Salisbury. His inclusion is understandable considering that in the previous decade he had published a well-received exposé of Catholic miracle healing.[67] There was also Lord Dartmouth, the eminent physician George Macaulay, and Dr Samuel Johnson. Thus learned spiritual, medical and philosophical imperatives were combined. Johnson sent an account of their findings to the *Gentleman's Magazine*, the conclusion being that no other agency was responsible other than the clever counterfeit noise making of Elizabeth Parsons. A sceptical pamphleteer on the case urged that such impostors 'ought immediately to be pilloried' otherwise 'new Impostures will be continually starting up in other Parts of the Town and Country'.[68] Kent subsequently prosecuted the Parsons and Moore for conspiracy to take away his life by accusing him of murder. Local public opinion, however, was evidently far more ready to believe in Scratching Fanny. When Parsons appeared in the pillory three times as part of his two-year prison sentence he was not subjected to the usual abuse and refuse flung at the pilloried. On the contrary, collections were taken for his benefit.[69]

Scratching Fanny became a byword for fraud and 'Cock Lane' was the cynical cry when new knocking ghosts came to the attention of the press. Well-reported cases of supposed possession or poltergeist activity continued to attract large crowds, but senior members of the religious and medical establishment, and the intelligentsia generally, became more reluctant to investigate. Debunking became a tiresome and unnecessary exercise for sceptics, while those who liked to keep an open mind feared being mocked for having an overly fond interest in such matters. Insinuations of Methodist credulity were quick to be directed at those who visited haunted houses. In 1772 the anonymous author of a sober report on the strange noises and missiles that plagued the house of a gentlewoman named Mary Golding, of Stockwell, Surrey, recognised that, regarding the details he furnished, 'we cannot be at all surprised the public should be doubtful of the truth of them, more especially as there has been too many impositions of this sort'. The author refrained from mentioning any hint of spirit involvement, and wished only that 'this extraordinary affair may be unravelled'.[70] Such caution, even by an anonymous author, indicates how sensitive earnest inquiry regarding ghosts had become in and around the capital.

Nevertheless, notwithstanding the haunting refrain of 'remember Cock Lane', modest, local investigations continued to be launched around the country whenever an outbreak of poltergeist activity took place. With the expansion of the regional press by the end of the century, county newspapers increasingly took on the role of enlightenment crusaders, exposing ghost frauds, instructing the 'superstitious', and thereby defending the provinces from condescending metropolitan assumptions regarding rural backwardness. There is no better example of this than the Sampford Ghost sensation. In the summer of 1810 the house and general supplies shop of John Chave, in the Devon village of Sampford Peverell, near Tiverton, was the setting for an attack of poltergeist activity. There were knockings and footsteps, most of which focused, as so often, around a teenage servant girl named Sally Case. She was the focus of particularly violent attacks, having bruising invisible blows rained down upon her. On two occasions she managed briefly to catch hold of the spirit molester and described it as feeling like a dog or a rabbit. Another time she saw the white apparition of a man's arm. A servant boy was frightened one night to see a vision of an old woman. The case would have remained a low-key affair but for the intervention of the rector of Prior's Portion, Tiverton, the Rev. Charles Caleb Colton (1777–1832).

Colton was a curious and eccentric character. He had been educated at Eton and Cambridge and his father had been the canon of Salisbury. But the spiritual duties of his position were not always on his mind. He was an inveterate gambler and seemed to prefer fishing to preaching. After having spent six nights at the Chave's home, and being perplexed by the phenomena he experienced, on 18 August he gave an affidavit, signed before the Mayor of Tiverton and three local surgeons. In it he stated:

> with a mind perfectly unprejudiced, after the most minute investigation, and closest inspection of all the premises, I am utterly unable to account for any of the phenomenon I have seen and heard, and labour at this moment under no small perplexity, arising from a determination not likely to admit of supernatural interference.[71]

As in the Stockwell pamphlet there was no attempt to explain the phenomena explicitly in terms of spirits or devils, though in a letter to the *Taunton Courier* Colton observed:

> It is not the object of this letter to make converts to a belief in Ghosts; yet, were the existence of such supernatural Beings established, I am apt to suspect the effects produced by such a persuasion, (if any) would be rather favourable to virtue, than otherwise.[72]

The fact that Colton chose to produce a popular narrative of the mysterious events with the title *Sampford Ghost*, suggests that he may have had an eye on its commercial prospects.[73] In response, John Marriott, the editor of the *Taunton Courier*, the main newspaper covering Somerset and east Devon at that time, decided it was necessary to fight back on behalf of the rationalist cause, even though Colton had been careful to highlight his own sceptical inclinations. The various exchanges between the two through the newspapers and in pamphlets were also reprinted in the national press, giving the case and the locality considerable notoriety.[74]

In his *Sampford Ghost!!!*, John Marriott set out his case that the haunting was a hoax perpetrated by Chave, his brother-in-law William Tayler, Sally Case, and a local cooper named James Dodge. Most of his evidence derived from an account of the investigation by a local property owner named Talley, who caught Taylor and Dodge in very suspicious locations when the manifestations were happening, and spotted tell-tale dent marks on the ceiling below Sally's chamber as if it had been hit with a blunt instrument. It was also alleged that Tayler had received lessons on slight-of-hand tricks and illusion from the well-known stage magician Moon who toured around the region. Tayler admitted he had met Moon twice but had never received any tuition.[75] On the 27 September Chave, Tayler, Dodge and Case also signed affidavits before the mayor of Tiverton denying any knowledge of fraud and insisting on the veracity of the inexplicable manifestations. Colton responded to Marriott in another edition of the *Sampford Ghost* with the subtitle 'Stubborn facts against vague assertions', in which he accused the editor of 'gross misrepresentations'. The affair died down after a few months, though one imagines it caused considerable, long-term social disruption to the people of Sampford Peverell who found themselves having to decided whether they were pro- or anti-Chave. Colton moved away a few years later and went on to achieve some literary and gambling success during sojourns in America and France, but shot himself in 1832 rather than face a major surgical operation. The nature of his death made him a good candidate to return to the living in spirit form, though there is no record of him ever being seen.

Colton implied he believed in ghosts, but in the climate of the time refrained from explicitly defending the notion. The sensitivities of the subject were evident four years later when a neighbouring clergyman, the Rev. William Vowles, wrote a pamphlet denouncing another noisy haunting, this time in the house of a 'respectable yeoman', Mr Taylor, who lived in Tiverton parish. It was based on a sermon Vowles had given at the Steps Meeting House, an Independent chapel in Tiverton, attacking the popular belief in apparitions and supernatural voices. There was nothing equivocal in his position. For Vowles the idea of ghosts was 'not only absurd, it is pernicious and pregnant with evil ... Spectres and ghosts are some of the vile spawn of idolatry.' They were merely the result of 'visual deceptions, dreams, opium, night-mare, and the horrors of guilt'. This damning denunciation was inspired by his inquiry into the strange sounds and voices experienced in the Taylor's house following the death of Mr Taylor's daughter, Ann, who had lain in a trance for several days. A record of the pious dreams she had during this time was printed for popular consumption, and disseminated widely. Vowles dismissed it as abounding in 'excessive absurdities', but 1814 was a good time to be peddling such accounts of religious visions and the afterlife, for it was the year that the Devon prophetess and spirit-communicator Joanna Southcott amazed the country with the announcement that she was going to give birth to Shiloh, the son of God who would redeem and rule all nations. To mark the event there was a rush of chapbooks and broadsides about the prophetess and her revelations.[76] Vowles suspected the Taylor's servant girl was responsible for the phenomena that occurred after Ann's death, and following the publication of the first edition of his pamphlet he received communications from two other families that had employed the girl. During her stay their houses had also been subjected to the 'vagaries of some frantic but invisible and undiscovered agent' – 'vagaries not unlike those acted on the *darkened* theatre of Sampford of ghostly renown'. Only when she left did they stop.[77]

What staunch rationalist consensus there was by the early nineteenth century did not last long. Several decades before the advent of modern spiritualism in 1848, two developments, one scientific and the other religious, heralded a new educated engagement with the spirits of the dead. The theory of animal magnetism or mesmerism, propounded by the Viennese doctor Franz Anton Mesmer (1734–1815), had considerable influence in certain intellectual and scientific circles.[78] In essence, the theory was that the universe was infused with an invisible, fluidic substance that connected all matter. It provided what seemed like the first serious scientific explanation for the possibility of spirit communication since the Neoplatonic theories of the sixteenth and seventeenth centuries. The need to investigate supposed spirit manifestations accrued new relevance. If natural causes or fraud could not be detected, then noisy hauntings held out the prospect for serious analysis of possible mesmeric forces at work. Mesmerism's popularity required the intellectual sceptics to re-energise their interest in practical investigation rather than merely debunking from their armchairs. It is in this context, perhaps, that we can situate the reaction to a haunting in Clewer, near Windsor, in June 1841. A household was plagued by mysterious violent knockings and rappings against the door of their water closet. A policeman who had been asked to watch over the house detected no obvious explanation for the noises. The haunting caused a sensation in the area and was reported widely in the press. A 'scientific gentleman' from London, who read of the events in a national newspaper, paid three visits to try and discover a rational cause. The floorboards of the closet were removed and both the floor and the area around the closet were excavated to a depth of several feet. He then had the drain exposed and examined. The water in an adjoining ditch was even sent for analysis. Next the local gravedigger was employed to use his sounding iron to sound the ground around the closet, but nothing unusual was detected. Only when the tenants of the house moved out did the haunting cease, leading to the suspicion that it was all a trick by a member of the household.[79]

The religious environment of England was changing during the first half of the nineteenth century. Methodism, in its various manifestations, became a major religious and social force as middle- and working-class membership expanded massively. In the face of the denunciations heaped upon them for their credulity regarding the spirit world, many members subscribed to John Wesley's view that absolute proof of just one instance of spirit communication was sufficient to confirm that the age of miracles was not over. The growth in earnest spiritualist interest during the 1840s, which seems to be linked to the success of Methodism and other evangelical denominations, is evident from the publication of a series of pamphlets on different spiritual and providential phenomena. In 1846 a tract warning of backsliding amongst Wesleyans used the vehicle of Wesley's ghost appearing to admonish his followers. The cover engraving, with its image of Wesley in a white sheet appearing to a surprised follower seated by a fireside, borrowed from the imagery of two centuries of popular ghost literature.[80] A few years earlier the Wesleyan minister Robert Young published a much reprinted pamphlet recording his person testimony of the trance visions of the afterlife experienced by a Miss D., who resided in a British colony. While in her entranced state, between life and death, she was taken on a tour of heaven and hell by her guardian angel, and saw those of her acquaintance who had only just died.[81] Then there was the case of Mary Jobson. In 1839 this sickly thirteen-year-old girl was the focus for the usual knockings, footsteps, and slamming doors, but those who came to investigate were not looking for proof of the Devil, for as the manifestations developed it became clear to some of those investigating that the agents behind these were benign, heavenly denizens. Indeed the Virgin Mary spoke to her and spirit voices provided member of the household with uplifting religious messages. The apparition of a lamb appeared on one occasion, another time a man surrounded by radiance. One of those who investigated and came to the conclusion that these were truly visitants from the afterlife was the respected physician William Reid Clanny (1776–1850).[82] At the time he was senior physician at Sunderland infirmary, but earlier in life he had achieved considerable acclaim for inventing a sealed candle lamp – a forerunner of the Davy lamp – that helped minimise colliery explosions. The fact that he was prepared to publish an account of the affair and endorse the reality of the spiritual manifestations indicates that, despite the inevitable mockery to which he would be subjected in some quarters, he also felt that he had sufficient middle-class peer support as well. Indeed, he asserted that many members of the Anglican church as well as ministers of other denominations were also satisfied with the evidence.

It is against this background of spiritual investigation and revelation that we should consider the interest generated by the more traditional haunting of Willington Mill, in Willington Quay, a town situated on the Tyne. The haunting began in 1835 and continued until the owner, a Quaker named Joseph Proctor, and his family left in 1847. There were the typical footsteps, bangings, rattling of windows and moving of beds but also ghost sightings. A transparent, white female figure was seen in a window of the house on one occasion and also a luminous priest in a white surplice. Procter wrote in his diary, 'even in modern times, amidst a thousand creations of fancy, fear, fraud, or superstition, there still remain some well-attested instances in which good or evil spirits have manifested their presence by sensible tokens'.[83] Clanny, who lived some ten miles south, seems to have known of the case, but there is no record of his visiting. However, in July 1840 a medical acquaintance, Dr Edward Drury and a friend, T. Hudson, were given permission by Procter to sit up all night in the house and await any manifestations of the spirit or spirits. Just before one o'clock in the morning the household was awoken by a terrible shriek from Drury. As he later recounted in a letter, he saw 'the figure of a female attired in greyish garments, with the head inclined downwards, and one hand pressed upon the chest, as if in pain, and the other, viz., the right hand, extended towards the floor, with the finger pointing downwards'. As it stood before him in its suspiciously classic pose, Drury made a rush for it but felt nothing and collapsed in a faint.

The Willington case attracted considerable fame. In 1842 the Newcastle bookseller and publisher Moses Aaron Richardson published a supportive *Authentic Account of a Visit to the Haunted House at Willington*, and reprinted it along with the correspondence between Drury and Procter in his *Local Historian's table book: of Remarkable Occurrences* (Newcastle, 1841–46). In 1847 William Howitt, the Quaker writer and publisher, also reproduced parts of Richardson's account, along with his own description of the setting, in his short-lived periodical *Howitt's Journal*. 'We have of late years settled it as an established fact, that ghosts and haunted houses were the empty creations of ignorant times', Howitt observed. Yet the haunting of such a respectable family, in the face of 'the incredulity of the wise, the investigations of the curious', could not be easily dismissed. When Catherine Crowe reprinted an account of Howitt's and Richardson's reports in her bestselling collection of ghost stories *The Night Side of Nature*, she described it as 'one of the most remarkable cases of haunting in modern times'.[84] This glut of published accounts of spiritual visitations was too much for one anonymous author who wrote a counterblast to Clanny, Young, Richardson and the editor of the *Wesleyan Magazine*, condemning and debunking what he called a rash of modern miracles.[85]

Mesmerism and Methodism may have created a sympathetic atmosphere for spiritual inquiry but it was spiritualism that made ghost investigation a mainstream intellectual pursuit again. It allowed the Anglican clergy more freedom to pursue their interest in the subject, while a new breed of gentlemen psychical investigators joined them and the medical fraternity in investigating haunted houses. Societies sprang up to provide a sober, impartial vehicle for assessing the evidence for the return of the dead. In 1851, members of Cambridge University founded the Ghost Club. Another Ghost Club was established in 1862 by a group of respected London gentlemen, including the Rev. Llewellyn Davies, Canon of Westminster.[86] The following year it apparently advertised for access to a well-reputed haunted house that it could investigate thoroughly on its own terms.[87] As the fires of scepticism and puzzlement inspired by the first wave of spiritualist phenomena died down, both groups seem to have fizzled out. Still, in 1879 some Oxford University students formed the Oxford Phasmatological Society, which existed until 1885, and in 1882 the Ghost Club was revived, though this time the composition of its members was more obviously pro-spiritualist.[88] One of its co-founders was the well-known medium Rev. William Stainton Moses. It functioned as a monthly dining club, with each member having to provide each year one 'original Ghost Story, or some psychological experience of interest or instruction'.[89] Although the Ghost Club would go on to have a long though interrupted life, it was the Society for Psychical Research (SPR), also founded in 1882, that was to be at the forefront of rigorous investigation regarding the spirit world. One of its first major inquiries was into haunted houses, and the debate over the reality of ghosts and spiritualism dominated the pages of its *Journal* and *Proceedings* during the 1880s and 1890s.[90] The history of the SPR has been discussed in great detail elsewhere, and there is no need to repeat it here.[91] Suffice it to say for the moment that the majority of its founding members soon came to the conclusion that the spirits of the dead did not appear to the living.

The role of the press in ghost investigations also changed under the influence of spiritualism. The unanimity newspapers had shown at the beginning of the century in dismissing and debunking hauntings was broken. Some editors, most notably William Thomas Stead of the *Pall Mall Gazette*, adopted a sympathetic stance towards the spiritualist movement.[92] Similar sympathies were also expressed in the editorials of some of the regional press, such as in George Pulman's *Pulman's Weekly News*, which served parts of Somerset, Devon and Dorset. He may not have been outspoken on the issue like Stead, but he liked to keep an open and impartial mind regarding spirit phenomena. This is apparent from the reports he published on a haunting at a farmhouse in Muchelney, Somerset, in the summer of 1868. Bangs, blows, slamming doors, shaking walls and moving furniture tormented the inhabitants. One of the first reports on the case was printed in the sceptical *Somerset County Herald*, which received so many accounts of the manifestation from readers that it decided it could 'scarcely venture to publish them without making enquiries'.[93] More than a month later, after a lull, the haunting began again. In an update the *Somerset County Herald* reported that

> scores of visitors have flocked to the house, and the inmates have been dreadfully annoyed by silly questions and absurd requests ... several religious zealots have visited the house, and there is a rumour that three of the number have since been holding special meetings to exorcise the hobgoblin.[94]

At this stage Pulman sent a correspondent to investigate. Having witnessed a mahogany table being smashed by unseen forces and heard violent, inexplicable rappings, he returned convinced that something spiritual was involved. *Pulman's Weekly News* told its readers that it was 'sheer folly to pooh-pooh the affair'. It asserted that it was 'very different from the Cock Lane Ghost' and that it was 'worthy of the most serious attention of the devout and faithful investigator into the marvels and mysteries of Nature'.[95] In a swipe at its competitor and others, the editor of the *Somerset County Herald* ridiculed their interest in the affair, referring to them and others as the 'large number of GULLS far away from the sea coast of Somersetshire'.[96]

URBAN RECREATION

'Respectable' spirit investigators were happy to visit haunted farmhouses and middle-class homes, but they would not be seen dead searching for ghosts in the streets and churchyards of Victorian cities. If they had, they would have found themselves in tumultuous and boisterous company. While the pious or earnest investigator was drawn to haunted bedrooms for profound truths or lies, the urban working classes gathered on the streets for sensation and entertainment. Yet the phenomena that attracted them were often the same. When, in 1852, word spread round Hull that a noisy ghost haunted a lonely tenement in Wellington Lane, between 2,000–3,000 people gathered in the surrounding streets waiting to hear the ghostly knockings. The *Hull Packet* reported:

Yesterday night, although it was dull, drizzly, and cold, crowd upon crowd besieged the spot, standing, in spite of the cold and wet, 100 yards from the haunted house, anxiously discussing the nature and object of the ghost's visit, and patiently waiting to learn from the police, or those who were fortunate enough to get near the house, 'when it had knocked last.'[97]

What must surely be the biggest ghost hunt ever occurred in July 1874 when a rumour circulated of a sighting in the churchyard of Christ Church, Broadway, Westminster. When an effigy of a ghost, made of white paper, was pinned to a nearby tree, an estimated 5,000–6,000 people gathered nightly to gawp at it.[98]

Word of mouth obviously spread quickly in urban neighbourhoods, but the role of print also helped generate urban ghost hunts. London's daily newspapers, and the rapid spread of dailies in other big towns from the 1850s onwards, meant that a swift momentum of interest could build up regarding the appearance of a ghost, thereby helping shape public perception and involvement in hauntings. During a court case in September 1853, a policeman testified that following the publication of newspaper reports of a ghost at No. 6 Pond Place, Chelsea, the neighbourhood had been in 'a state of uproar'.[99] Even during the first half of the nineteenth century, the publishers of ballads and broadsheets were remarkably quick to convert sensational news into print for local audiences. When, in 1835, the sound of footsteps and draws being opened in an empty architect's office on the corner of Cross Street and St Ann's Street, Manchester, were reported by the landlord of the neighbouring property, the Lord Hill pub, a broadside publisher was quick to pick up on the story, elaborate on it and disseminate it. Within days a thrilling broadside account was being hawked about the streets recounting how the noises were the work of a troubled spirit emanating from the chapel burial ground nearby. It told how five brave men determined to investigate:

Presently the dreaded sound approached; it appeared to issue from the floor close to them; nothing, however, was to be seen. This was too great a trial for their courage. They simultaneously took to their heels and with all speed rushed into the street to report the awful tidings to an already terrified assemblage of persons who were collected there. Indeed, one of the men has since been heard to declare that he actually thought that his ghostship had got hold of him and was literally tearing him to pieces.

On reading this sensational news, or on it being read to them, it is no wonder large crowds soon gathered. The sober *Manchester Guardian* felt bound to clear

up the mystery by reporting how an investigation by the local superintendent of the watch and his colleagues had proved the haunting was merely an
unintentional trick of acoustics.[100]

While it would seem that the composition of such crowds consisted of
a cross section of working class and artisan society, the most significant
component and often the catalysts for ghost hunts were boys and young
men. In early October 1845, for example, the youth of Norwich were much
excited by a ghost that had been seen taking a long perambulation, which
included walking through a wall before disappearing into a tower. Large crowds
gathered in the evenings to see further appearances but were disappointed.
A search party of some 400 people was organised, including 'a whole army
of little boys, and a pretty fair sprinkling of children of larger growth', to lay
siege to the ghost-infested tower, but the spirit was not forthcoming.[101] The
prominence of young men is not surprising considering they were often the
most conspicuous presence in other boisterous urban street gatherings such
as Guy Fawkes celebrations or the institution of communal shaming rituals
against moral transgressors such as adulterers.[102] Like these other working-class
festive events, the authorities and the press saw ghost hunts as uncouth and
vulgar, a disgraceful mix of 'superstition' and a lack of civility. One Victorian
Dewsbury magistrate remarked that 'all intelligent and thinking persons' had
nothing to do with Fifth of November celebrations.[103] It goes without saying
that such 'persons' would also have had nothing to do with ghost hunts.
However, the 'problem' of popular credulity was subordinate to the issue
of law and order. The crowds were sometimes described as 'mobs' and their
behaviour denounced as 'riotous'. Reporting on the ghost seen in Shadwell
church in August 1851, the News of the World talked of the 'disorderly characters'
that assembled nightly in front of the church railings to witness the ghost, and
how the affair had 'given rise to a good deal of curiosity and much disorder and
rioting'.[104] In May 1865 The Times referred to the 'mobs' that gathered between
nine o'clock in the evening and four in the morning hoping to see a ghost at
St George's Church in Southwark. The crowds were so great that extra police
had to be drafted into the area in order to keep the traffic moving in the high
street. One man was arrested, Henry Stanley, who had rushed around the place
shouting 'Here's the ghost!'[105]

The working classes considered the streets as a valuable social space while
the authorities saw them as both conduits of commerce and havens of crime.
Conflict was bound to ensue.[106] The police were quick to appear when a
ghost sighting attracted crowds, and ghost seekers were ready to show their
unhappiness about being moved on when their quarry was potentially in sight.
During the Bermondsey ghost sensation of July 1830 some 2,000 people

gathered nightly around a haunted property in Grange Road. An entire police division had to be called in to disperse the crowds. Some strongly expressed their irritation at being moved on, complaining they had walked for miles to catch a glimpse of the ghost.[107] Many of those living in the vicinity of a street haunting understandably considered ghost-hunting crowds, like any such street gathering, an unacceptable disturbance of the peace. In September 1828 The Sun reported that, due to a ghost sighting in Percy Street, it was not possible to get from one end of the street to the other in a direct line after sunset. Such were crowds drawn to a reported ghost in Whitechapel church in October 1842, that 'it was almost impossible for a person to pass along the pavement; and it was with no little difficulty the congregation could make their way out of the church gates'.[108]

Crowds were certainly animated and there were usually a number of pot-valiant men and women manifesting their eagerness to take on the spirit world, but press talk of 'mobs' and 'riots' was often an unfair exaggeration of the crowds' behaviour. Still, frustrated ghost seekers, usually young males, sometimes decided to create their own entertainment by resorting to petty vandalism. In June 1867 nine young men were charged before the Bow Street magistrates with creating a disturbance and resisting the police in Woburn Square. For several nights large crowds had gathered after a rumour spread that a ghost was frequenting the area. Nothing spooky having been sighted, some young men started to kick at doors calling for the ghost to appear, causing much annoyance to local inhabitants. When police arrived to seal off the square a mini riot ensued.[109] In 1882, after No. 40 Halsey Street had been abandoned by its owner for several months, rumours began to circulate that it was haunted. For several weeks in September crowds gathered, calling on the ghost to appear, while local schoolchildren targeted the building, throwing stones, ringing the doorbell and throwing filth at it. A neighbour called in the police but they said they were powerless to deal with the disturbance. They eventually acted in a rather feeble manner by arresting a drunken woman amongst the crowd.[110] In July 1876 a machine ruler named Robert Withey, aged 13, was charged with throwing stones at a house that was under repair in Bermondsey, not far from the home of the notorious murderers the Mannings, who had been executed in 1849. Withey was one of a gang of boys, amongst a crowd of some 300–400, who gathered on successive evenings outside the house shouting 'There's the Ghost! There's the black Ghost! There are the Mannings!' Some threatened to tear the haunted house down. At Withey's trial a policeman testified that 'He did not see the elder persons throw stones, but they shouted out "Ghost!" and caused the boys to throw stones.'[111] This echoes an observation regarding Guy Fawkes night aggression in Victorian Oxford, where older townsfolk encouraged the young men to target undergraduates.[112] It is likely that there was a degree of class resentment in such vicarious pleasure being had from the destruction of property, particularly of the middle classes.

As the main representatives of authority in England's urban streets the police were sometimes drafted in not only to prevent the breaches of the peace that occurred during ghost hunts, but also to investigate the alleged hauntings. By allaying public fears and curiosity they could perform a dual function of debunking ghosts and preserving law and order. Their role in investigating ghosts gives new meaning to the idea of policemen as 'domestic missionaries'. Considerable police time was sometimes expended. In 1859 a policeman did duty for several days in a haunted house in Ashford Road, Maidstone, and at one point a police cordon was placed around the property to detect who was responsible.[113] The Weymouth police made a considerable effort in January 1861 to investigate the strange noises and shaking of crockery emanating from a tenement in East Street, which attracted much public attention. As a sceptical newspaper reported, the ghost could not 'be persuaded to show itself, skulking meanwhile in the wall, and wisely eschewing all intercourse with the police, who have been vainly endeavouring to apprehend the "mysterious" visitant, or at least to detect the cause of the noise'.[114] More successful was PC Thew, who was given the job of diffusing the 1874 Westminster haunting. After a week of crowds disturbing nightly both the traffic and the church congregation, Thew hid himself in the churchyard at midnight and lay in wait for the ghost. His patience was rewarded. He saw a labourer named Frederick Grimmond climb over the railings, place a white sheet over his head and run across the graveyard. Grimmond had the misfortune to stumble over a grave, however, and Thew pounced and arrested him. In court Grimmond lamely explained that he was only looking for the ghost when someone placed the sheet over his head. The magistrate expressed his astonishment that 'people should believe in such things' as ghosts, and rather leniently ordered Grimmond to enter into his own recognisance to be of good behaviour for six months.[115]

By the early decades of the twentieth century, ghost-seeing was no longer a popular urban pastime. This was due in part to the development of more sophisticated strategies for policing urban crowds, but other broader cultural influences were also responsible. Increasing working-class sensibilities regarding authoritarian perceptions of their intellectual abilities, inspired by the growth of mass education, political consciousness and unionism, engendered a self-consciousness of what was and was not respectable in terms of expressing belief in spirits. The attraction of new forms of media, such as the working-class theatre, music hall and film show, also provided novel vehicles for encountering ghosts, albeit representations rather than the real thing.

GHOST HUNTERS

The twentieth century heralded the rise of the 'ghost hunter', the media-friendly, maverick psychic investigator who came to each case with an open mind but who, like any good detective, treated every case as a mystery waiting to be solved rationally. The ghost hunter was not so much driven by the desire to prove profound truths about religion and the human condition – the motivating force for the founders of the SPR – as by the thrill of the hunt and the prospect of perhaps one day finally coming face to face with spirits. One template for the image of the modern ghost hunter was William Hope Hodgson's *Carnacki the Ghost Finder* (1913), which consisted of a series of stories about the exploits of the fictional Edwardian psychic investigator Thomas Carnacki.[116] Even before this was published, Elliott O'Donnell (1872–1965) had already begun to make a name for himself as an authority with books such as *Bona-fide Adventures with Ghosts* (1908). He went on to write more than two dozen books on the subject and was the first to style himself as a 'ghost hunter' in his *Confessions of a Ghost Hunter* published in 1928.

Another *Confessions of a Ghost-Hunter* appeared in 1936, though this time the author was Harry Price (1881–1948), a man who, unlike O'Donnell, created an enduring reputation for himself as a psychic investigator. Gordon Meyrick probably had Price in mind when he penned his 1947 novel *The Ghost Hunters*, which followed the escapades of psychic investigator Arnold Perry. Price's reputation endures partly due to his indefatigable and shrewd investigation of spiritualists, and partly due to his enthusiastic and sometimes compromising engagement with the media. In 1936, for example, he took part in the first live broadcast from a haunted house.[117] On 10 March BBC radio transmitted two programmes recording Price's investigations into a ghost at Dean Manor, Rochester. Listeners heard how a ghost hunter went about his business, sprinkling wax and powdered starch on the floor to detect footprints, wiping powdered graphite on the walls to test fingerprints, human or otherwise, and setting thermometer to detect any sudden drop in temperature that might herald the clammy coldness of a ghost.

Although ghosts did not excite Price's interest as much as the possible existence of human psychic powers (hence his work on poltergeists), his knowledge of historical hauntings, based on a valuable collection of rare tracts and books, was impressive. Today his name is most associated with his investigation of the haunting of Borley Rectory, Essex.[118] The rectory had been built in the mid nineteenth century, apparently on the site of a Benedictine abbey. Several decades later, inhabitants began to report seeing the apparition of a nun and subsequently poltergeist-type activities began, such as the ringing of bells and throwing of objects. Local legend had it – or a legend was created to explain it – that back in the thirteenth century a monk and a nun had eloped. They were caught, the monk was hanged and the nun was walled up in her convent. In 1929 the incumbent clergyman, the Rev. Guy Smith, called the Daily Mirror about the strange goings-on, and the news editor invited Harry Price to investigate accompanied by a Mirror reporter. They were treated to a good performance of smashing glass and stone throwing. The following year a new vicar, the Rev. Lionel Foyster, moved in, and if anything the manifestations became more intense and elaborate. Writing was scrawled on the walls requesting that a Mass be said. The Foysters moved out in 1935, and two years later the by now notorious rectory was rented by Price, who placed the following advertisement in The Times, which delineated the requisite characteristics of the ghost hunter:

Haunted House.– Responsible persons of leisure and intelligence, intrepid, critical, and unbiased, are invited to join rota of observers in a year's night and day investigation of alleged haunted house in Home Counties. Printed instructions supplied. Scientific training or ability to operate simple instruments an advantage. House situated in lonely hamlet, so own car is essential.[119]

One of those who got involved in the investigation was the Rev. W.J. Phythian-Adams, Canon of Carlisle, who constructed a detailed historical hypothesis for the identity of the troubled ghost. He concluded that it was a seventeenth-century French nun brought to Borley Manor by Henry Waldegrave, who later strangled her. The rectory burned down in 1939, though the site continued to be a hotspot for psychical investigators, with ghostly phenomena continuing to be observed there over the following decades. Thanks to Price it has become the best-known haunted house in the country, perhaps in the world.[120]

There were other, now largely forgotten ghost hunters who were quite well known in their day through their books and newspaper articles. One such figure was Nandor Fodor (1895–1964), a Hungarian-born journalist and psychoanalyst, who, like most investigators down the centuries, was mostly drawn to poltergeist phenomena. Unlike most others, he generally eschewed publicity. He once described Price as 'intensely selfish, jealous, and intent on his own glory at all costs'.[121] Amongst his investigations was a bell-ringing and door-opening haunting at Aldborough Manor, Yorkshire, in 1936, and in the same year the more intriguing case of a noisy haunting at Ash Manor, Sussex. In the latter, a pair of psychical investigators had previously explained to the family that the ghost of a man who committed suicide in 1819 haunted the Manor, while a well-known medium divined that it was a man who had been tortured and imprisoned nearby in the medieval period.[122] There was also the Cornish folklorist William Henry Paynter who, during the 1940s, along with Prince Birabongse Bhanubandh as his sidekick, zipped around the county in the prince's sports car investigating haunted houses and phantom sightings, giving talks on his experiences to local societies and gatherings.[123] In the 1970s and 1980s Peter Underwood laid claim to the press tag of Britain's leading 'ghost hunter', combining the flair, knowledge and entrepreneurial drive of Price with the publishing ubiquity of O'Donnell. He thankfully refrained from titling his memoirs *Confessions of …* .[124] Today there are numerous 'how-to' ghost-hunting manuals available for budding investigators, who can also benefit from having new technology like night-vision goggles and digital cameras at their disposal.[125] In England the recent success of Living TV's *Most Haunted* series, which presents sensational, telegenic live investigations, and its spin-off publications, have also no doubt boosted renewed interest in the occupation of ghost hunter. It also highlights the rise of the medium as exorcist. Rather than adjuring or praying that ghosts depart from houses, mediums act as ghost counsellors, seeking to relieve spirits of their mental burdens. Unlike the clergy, modern mediums have no need of the scriptures, only the gift of compassion and sensitivity to the needs of the spirit world.[126]

The ghost hunters, as I have defined them, were, of course, not the only active investigators during the twentieth century. The SPR and other societies, such as the Institute of Psychophysical Research, continued to act as more sober forums for investigation. In 1956, for example the SPR published a damning report on Price's involvement in the Borley Rectory haunting, suggesting that he had colluded with the creation of fraudulent phenomena.[127] In the last couple of decades, though, due to academic interest in the subject, the serious study of ghosts has moved away from the traditional techniques of site investigation and collation of witness accounts. There have been various laboratory-based attempts to recreate psychic phenomena or to monitor neuropsychological behaviour and hallucinatory experiences.[128] Psychologists have also gone back out into the field. Their aim this time is not to record or debunk ghostly manifestations though, but to monitor the response of people to reputedly haunted environments. Richard Wiseman recently led research experiments at two well-known haunted locations: Hampton Court Palace, and South Bridge Vaults in Edinburgh. The team used questionnaires to examine people's responses to visiting the haunted spots and electromagnetic equipment to measure anomalies in the magnetic fields that might affect people's sensory perception. They concluded that those in the survey who reported characteristic phenomena at both sites – sense of presence, strange odours, drops in temperature and even apparitions – may have been influenced by localised environmental stimuli such as magnetic fields and lighting levels. Another recent, similar study of a reputedly haunted bedroom at Muncaster Castle emphasised the potential importance of magnetic variations on those who see or sense ghosts.[129]

Part Two

Explanation

FOUR

Debating Ghosts

S o far ghosts have been discussed as realities, since that is how most people in the past perceived them. Throughout history, though, there has always been debate as to whether they existed. There was a general assumption for much of the period that people really did see external apparitions of humans and animals, but as to whether they were the spirits of the dead was another matter. There were other explanations, both natural and supernatural, which, for religious or scientific reasons, were more or less acceptable to different sections of society at different periods. These questions and suggestions were usually debated as an aspect of broader, fundamental arguments about the fate of the soul, post-biblical providence, the reality of witchcraft and changing philosophical conceptions of the universe. Ghosts flitted through some of the most profound developments in intellectual thought over the last 500 years, and so to discover how they were conceived in the past is to understand how society itself changed.

THE WALKING DEAD

As we have already seen, it was a widespread belief in much of pre-Christian and Christian Europe that the bodies of the dead could emerge from their graves to torment or communicate with the living.[1] It is likely that many of the decapitated, dismembered, staked or weighed down corpses that have been excavated from the prehistoric and Roman periods were treated that way to prevent them from returning to the living. Accounts of the walking dead or *revenants* appear frequently in medieval Scandinavian legends, particularly in the Icelandic sagas, where such a being was called a *draugr*. These usually emerged from their burial mounds at night or during foggy daylight to terrorise the living, though sometimes they could be accommodating. They were best despatched by cutting off their heads or burning them.[2] In southeastern and central Europe the belief in and apparent encounters with the living dead, in the form of the vampire, continued as a vibrant concern into the modern era.

Yet the concept of the walking dead had no place in Christianity. Only God could perform the miracle of resurrection, as Jesus demonstrated to the people of Bethany when he raised the body of Lazarus. The troubled spirit or soul of the dead did not have the power to raise its own body and nor did necromancers. Biblical precedent was one thing, however, and the numerous stories of the walking dead that were recorded in medieval and early modern times were another. So, if the stories were to be believed, then the explanation for so many animated corpses led to only one generally acceptable conclusion – the Devil was up to his tricks. If he could possess the living, as was widely believed and apparently proven by many instances, then there was no reason why he could not possess cadavers for his nefarious purposes. He could, after all, assume ghostly forms, shape-shift and send out his wicked spirits, so it was understandable that he would also animate corpses to strike fear into people's hearts and lure them into sinful assumptions. King James I asserted that the Devil carried bodies out of graves 'to serve his turne for a space', but assured his readers that while

the Divell may use as well the ministrie of the bodies of the faithfull in these cases, as of the un-faithfull, there is no inconvenient; for his haunting with their bodies after they are dead, can no-waies defyle them: In respect of the soules absence.[3]

These demonic, puppet cadavers were not really ghosts then, but they could fool people into believing that they really were the spirits of the dead. One French writer on the subject thought the Devil's ventriloquial skills were such that it was impossible to distinguish between a talking demon-animated corpse and a living person.[4] Of course the corpse had to be fresh to achieve such an extraordinary deception. The Jesuit François Richard discussed the issue in 1657 in a discourse aimed at confounding French 'atheists'. Richard's views on the subject were influenced by the stories he had heard on his travels in the eastern Mediterranean, and his attendance at the exhumation of a suspected walking dead or 'false revenant'.[5] There was an element of scientific as well as religious belief in his conclusion that, for a brief period after death and the departure of the soul, the corpse remained in a physical state capable of manipulation. The mystic vegetarian Thomas Tryon, writing in the 1690s, further suggested that 'there is some likeness or Relikes of the Spirit remaining in the deceased body so long as it continues moist and full of matter'.[6] As soon as the body began rapidly to putrefy and the main vehicles of the senses, the eyes and nose decayed, however, the soul, the Devil or demons could no longer influence or animate it. It had lost its human principle.

The continental debates regarding the diabolic reanimation of corpses were, however, largely ignored by English intellectuals, which is intriguing considering that the walking dead were prominent in medieval English ghost narratives. The Yorkshire canon William of Newburgh (1136–1198) recorded instances of their activities from Buckinghamshire and Yorkshire. Indeed he considered them to be a contemporary plague, writing that 'it would be extremely tedious' to record all the instances he had heard.[7] He told, for example, how in Buckinghamshire the corpse of a sinner kept returning at night to lie upon his wife in bed. The terrified women asked her family and neighbours to keep watch, which seems to have deterred the dead man. Instead he started to disturb at night the animals owned by the family – 'this was known because of the restlessness and unusual movements of the beasts'. He next began to appear during the day, though 'if it met many people at a time, it was visible to only one or two of them'. The case was reported to the Bishop of Lincoln, who was advised that the usual remedy was to open the grave and cremate the corpse. The bishop found the idea sacrilegious and instead drew up a scroll of absolution, which was placed on the corpse and then reburied. The dead man terrorised the community no more. In another instance from Yorkshire the corpse had its heart taken out, body dismembered and burned. William of Newburgh concluded from the absence of relevant cases in books from former times that the walking dead were a contemporary problem, though he did not know why that should be. William hesitantly plumped for the satanic option in explaining how corpses could walk, though at one point he says he knew 'not what spirit' possessed the bodies.[8] The apparent profusion of such cases would have led an early modern demonologist to conclude that it was a sign of the Devil's increased work in the land, but William evidently did not see the plague of living dead in such a gloomy light.

The collection of Yorkshire ghost sightings reported by a Cistercian monk of Byland Abbey around 1400 present a clearer, orthodox theology for the appearance of the walking dead than the threatening corpses recorded by William.[9] In each of the Byland stories the dead appear explicitly to expiate sins they have committed in life, such as theft or murder. They desire the living to free their souls from purgatory by paying for their sins to be absolved. One reason for this is that the concept of purgatory only really became widely established doctrine during the fourteenth century, providing an alternative to the more problematic satanic theory of reanimation. It is possible that the Byland stories also mark a shift in English popular tradition away from the living dead to the spiritual dead, a shift wrought by the popular inculcation of purgatory. Although in the Byland stories the dead are corporeal and tangible, they are nevertheless referred to by the author as 'spirits' and some of them have the power of shape-shifting into animal form. While William of Newburgh's living dead were corpses pure and simple, given mechanical motion by means of diabolic or spirit activity, the Byland bodies seem to be imbued with the souls of the dead. Two centuries after the Byland stories were written the concept of the living dead had disappeared completely from the corpus of English popular beliefs regarding the spirit world. The transition towards a more spiritual eschatology of the troubled dead instituted by purgatory was completed by the Reformation emphasis on a spiritual rather than mechanistic preparation for the afterlife.

REFORMATION

The rejection of purgatory was potentially a fatal blow to the theological and popular rationale for ghosts. Early Protestant reformers saw ghosts not only as a pernicious product of a dangerous dogma, but also as the very foundation of purgatory. Through their deceptions and illusions monks and priests had bolstered popular support for their money-making doctrine by faking apparitions.[10] Without purgatory there were no ghosts and without ghosts there was no purgatory. Ghost belief was therefore synonymous with Catholicism. Henry Caesar, vicar of Lostwithiel, Cornwall, was investigated for being a crypto-Catholic in 1584–85 because of his 'belief in spirits and apparitions'. Part of the evidence against him, which he denied, was that Sir Walter Mildmay had conjured up the spirit of Cardinal Pole, Archbishop of Canterbury, who had died in 1558.[11] However, this Reformist equation was unconvincing. After all, purgatory only became orthodox church doctrine during the late medieval period, and ecclesiasts had been questioning the reality of ghosts long before then. Nevertheless, within several decades of the Reformation confident assertions were already being expressed that the popular belief in spirits was in decline following the rejection of purgatory.[12] Archbishop Sandys, for instance, opined that 'the gospel hath chased away walking spirits'. Ghost belief was contentedly consigned to the errors of the Catholic past. Reginald Scot, betraying his usual caution, believed in reports that ghost sightings had ceased in Lutheran German states, and by the time he was writing in 1584, he was evidently confident that with 'the word of God being more free, open and knowne' fewer English people were also being fooled by illusions and false doctrine; perhaps the ghosts were all fleeing to Italy, he mocked.[13] The notion of a Catholic golden age for ghosts was only abandoned during the nineteenth century. Despite the initial confidence in some quarters, however, it was obvious by the mid seventeenth century that the cleansing properties of the Reformation had not washed away the Catholic stain on the popular consciousness that ghosts were thought to represent. As we shall see, many of the Protestant intelligentsia, as well as the populace, found it impossible to give up the notion that the spirits of the dead returned to the living.

It is rather curious, considering the concerted attack on purgatory by English Protestant reformers, that the subject of ghosts was not a more prominent matter of debate in sixteenth-century England. There was a vast literature on the state of the soul after death but comparatively little on the return of souls amongst the living.[14] The published debate was livelier on the continent, and the only English publications dedicated to the subject were two translations of influential continental treatises.[15] First to appear in 1572 was Of Ghostes and Spirites Walking by Nyght by the Swiss reformed pastor Ludwig Lavater. It had been published in Zurich in 1569 and was quickly translated into German, French, Italian and Spanish as well as English. It consisted of a huge collection of ancient, medieval and contemporary instances of ghost sightings, and became the source and template for later collections such as Thomas Bromhall's A Treatise of Specters (London, 1658). Lavater set out clearly and in depth the orthodox Protestant theology that it was impossible for the souls of either the faithful or unfaithful to return to earth until the Day of Judgement. He did, however, accept that the weight of historical evidence and learned testimony proved that visions of the dead really did appear to the living. So he set out a range of alternative explanations. Some were hoaxes, some optical illusions, but the most significant message that Lavater wanted to get across was that many supposed ghosts were angelic or, more often, demonic visitations. As one historian has pointed out, though, Lavater's treatise was not so much a doctrinal polemic as a work of pastoral instruction.[16] He recognised that it was one thing to destroy the foundations of purgatory but another task to relieve people of the fear of the spirits of the dead.

Catholic as well as Protestant theologians appreciated Lavater's work. Although they obviously did not agree with his religious principles there were two areas of common ground. First, the acceptance that some, even many hauntings were fakes, and, second, that the Devil imitated the spirits of the dead for his nefarious purposes. Both these points were evident in an influential Catholic response to Lavater's treatise by the French Capuchin Noel Taillepied. In his Psichologie ou traité de l'apparition des esprits (Paris, 1588) Taillepied argued with simple casuistry that the Devil's resort to mimicking the spirits of the dead was proof itself of the reality of ghosts. For if the spirits of the dead did not return occasionally to the living, 'evil Spirits would not adopt this ruse, since it would be idle and vain'. The Devil pretended to be a ghost, 'because he knows that ghosts actually appear to men'.[17] Taillepied's work was not translated into English at the time and seems to have made little impact. This was not necessarily because he was arguing from a Catholic perspective. English demonological writers were happy to mine Catholic continental texts if it furthered their arguments about the iniquity of witchcraft. In this context *A Treatise of Specters* by the French lawyer Pierre Le Loyer proved more influential. The Puritan divine Richard Bernard, for instance, used cases from Le Loyer's *Treatise* as evidence of the various devilish activities of witches in his influential *Guide to Grand-Jury Men* (1627).

A Treatise of Specters was, in fact, the first major Catholic counterblast against Lavater, having been published two years before Taillepied's tome, but the first part of the book only appeared in an English version in 1605. There was a pragmatic reason for the timing of its publication. Le Loyer apparently desired to stay in England and was seeking royal protection. His translator Zachary Jones therefore used the English translation to plead his cause, appealing to King James's preoccupation with the witch threat. He recommended Le Loyer as 'a stoute and most worthie Champion' in the fight against the 'diabolicall illusions of Witches, Sorcerers and Conjurers'.[18] From a commercial point of view, Le Loyer's *Treatise* also tapped into the zeitgeist of growing Puritan influence and concern over the ineffectual progress of the campaign against witchcraft. Witch trials had reached a peak in the 1580s and 1590s with nearly 300 recorded prosecutions.[19] But for Puritan theologians such as William Perkins, those tried represented only a tiny portion of the diabolic scum they believed polluted the country. The Puritan clergy also fostered a greater theological emphasis on the threat of demonic spirit influence in human affairs, which was reflected in the 1604 statute against witchcraft and conjuration. Indeed, Zachary Jones praised the King's campaign against witches – 'the generation of Vipers, and the seede of the wicked Serpent: whose head you have also bruised, both by divine lawe, and by Act of Parliament'.

It is important, of course, not to assume that the lack of English publications reflected a lack of intellectual interest. It is likely, for example, that lively public debates took place amongst university students and dons.[20] The only English treatise dedicated to ghosts, though never published, was based on a 'semi-public' lecture on the subject given by the clergyman Randall Hutchins (1567–1603) when a student in Oxford, probably in the late 1580s. He recalled a few years later that no subject 'pleased me more than that of specters'.[21] Hutchins' main authorities were the works of the ancients, but Lavater inspired his interest in the subject. He described him as a gifted man but criticised him for relying on the accumulation of examples as a form of discourse – 'a feeble kind of disputation', he said – rather than arguing from 'firm reason.'[22] Hutchins distilled the essence of Lavater's arguments, explaining the different types of spirits that could 'take on bodies easily perceptible to sight'. He concluded that 'the Devil has not only impiously fabricated that whole doctrine of the wandering ghosts of the dead, but also iniquitously augmented it'.[23]

By rejecting Catholic doctrine on the afterlife Protestant theologians sought to conceptualise alternative theories of the soul's existence. What happened to souls up until the Day of Judgement? The debates that ensued were at times as vitriolic as the Protestant denunciations of Catholic doctrine, and allowed plenty of scope for ghosts to retain theological pertinence. One of the main threats to their existence came from mortalism; in other words, the idea that the soul either slept or died until Judgement Day.[24] This obviously precluded the return of the spirits of the dead. The notion had circulated during the early centuries of Christianity, and had been condemned by the likes of Origen and Augustine, but it gained widespread support during the early decades of the Reformation. Luther was sympathetic to the idea. However, because some radical Reformers enthusiastically propounded it, it was dropped or diluted by mainstream Protestantism. The concept of ghosts or soul walkers could even be upheld as a means of highlighting the heretical error of mortalism. As we shall see, it was such tensions between different facets of Protestant theology that gave ghosts their remarkable intellectual longevity.

The weight of evidence was obviously an important defence for the existence of ghosts, but the ultimate authority on all matters spiritual was the Bible. Yet Protestant defenders of ghosts found it difficult to draw definite conclusions from its words. When the Independent minister Isaac Watts (1674–1748) sought to draw biblical support for the reality of ghosts, his efforts were remarkably tentative. 'The Scripture seems to mention such sort of Ghosts or Appearances of Souls departed', he observed. Referring to the passage in Luke Act xxiii, verse 9, where some Pharisees ask, 'What if a Spirit or an angel hath spoken to this man?', Watts concluded, 'A Spirit here is plainly distinct from an Angel, and what can it mean but an Apparition of a human Soul which has left the body?'[25] This was clutching at straws and such claims for divine backing could easily be swatted away by the sceptics. The biblical defence had to rest on the story of the raising of the prophet Samuel, which, as we have seen, had been a source of controversial debate since the founding of the Christian church. The Reformation failed to seal the matter. While the diabolic deception thesis was certainly the majority position amongst English intellectuals, some still clung to the raising of Samuel as proof that the souls of the dead could return. So eager was he to prove the existence of the spirit world that Joseph Glanvill stuck his head above the parapet on this most contentious of biblical issues and defended the literal reading of the passage. 'Now if it were the Real

Samuel,' he explained, 'as the Letter expresseth, (and the obvious sense is to be followed when there is no cogent Reason to decline it) he was not raised by the Power of the Witches Inchantments, but came on that occasion in a Divine Errand.'[26] By the 1670s this was an isolated position even among ghost defenders. It smacked of Catholicism, with one pamphlet complaining that 'the Jesuits affirme Samuels reall resuscitation, bewitching the vulgars to believe that the dead appeare out of Heaven, Hell, and Purgatory'.[27] Yet Glanvill's willingness shows how Protestantism failed to shake off what had been widely castigated as a Catholic deception. As Peter Marshall neatly puts it, the Reformation turned ghosts into 'illegal immigrants' across a supposedly impermeable boundary.[28] They should not exist, but they evidently did. They were deeply problematic but continued to serve a theological and moral purpose.

THE DEVIL?

From the Elizabethan period onwards the Catholic threat from both abroad and within remained an ever-present concern. The authorities were watchful of the activities of crypto-Catholics and Jesuits, and the clergy and the church courts struggled to root out Catholic practices employed by the laity. Still, the country was not wracked by the confessional tensions and intense propaganda battle that permeated the main confessional battlegrounds of central and northern Europe. Consequently ghosts had less of a prominent role to play in English theological polemic. Issues regarding ghosts did, however, permeate the most pressing religious concern in Elizabethan and Stuart England – witchcraft.[29] While ghosts continued to serve a didactic purpose, highlighting the deceptions of priests and monks, it was the ghost as diabolic illusion that was the main issue of debate. Ghostly apparitions were confirmation of Puritan fears. The frequency with which the Devil confronted people with apparitions of the dead was further proof, if it were needed, of the pervasive activities of his principal agents, witches and cunning-folk. Even true ghosts could be appropriated to the anti-witch cause. Those sceptics, like the Elizabethan gentleman Reginald Scot, who challenged the reality of witchcraft, did so as part of a broader rejection of spiritual intervention in human affairs. If it could be proved that ghosts existed, then it would undermine the sceptics' bases for rejecting the idea of diabolic witchcraft.

Yet those who believed both in ghosts and that the Devil masqueraded as ghosts were confronted with a serious diagnostic problem. How to tell one from the other? The awkwardness of the quandary is clear from the hotchpotch collections of supernatural 'Relations' in defence of spirits produced during the late seventeenth and eighteenth centuries. Many of the cases were stated to concern 'spirits', but what sort of spirits was often left unresolved, presumably because of the difficulty of determining whether manifestations were the work of witches, devils, fairies or ghosts. Joseph Glanvill's definition of a spirit encapsulates this lack of clarity. A spirit was, he said, an 'intelligent Creature of the invisible World', which could be either an evil angel or a devil, 'an inferior daemon, or a wicked soul departed'.[30] Now consider Richard Baxter's diagnosis of the experience of a dissolute London gentleman of his acquaintance. Upon awakening from his drunken slumbers, he would hear something knocking on his bedhead; the noise would then follow him around the house. Other members of the household also heard it. Suspecting he was playing a trick, his brother held his hands but the knocks continued. His wife, whilst watching him, saw his shoes under the bed move by an invisible hand. For Baxter the noises were clearly a providential warning to the drunkard about his sinful ways, but what spiritual messenger had God employed?

> It poseth me to think what kind of Spirit this is, that hath such a Care of this Man's Soul, (which maketh me hope he will recover.) Do good Spirits dwell so near us? Or are they sent on such Messages? Or is it his Guardian Angel? Or is it the Soul of some dead Friend, that suffereth, and yet, retaining Love to him … God yet keepeth such things from us in the dark.[31]

It would seem that amongst the educated classes, first-hand experiences were just as difficult to resolve. The astrologer and merchant Samuel Jeake (1652–1699), son of a Nonconformist preacher, wrote in his diary of his puzzlement regarding the following strange encounter. He had stayed in a room where the bedstaff kept being mysteriously moved around as he slept. Others sleeping in the same chamber had reported similar 'like trifles'. Jeake confided:

> This seemed somewhat strange; & being pretty well satisfied; that none of the family were concerned in it, I cannot yet resolve it into any other Cause, than the ridiculous & trifling actions of some of the meanest rank among the Infernal Spirits.[32]

The Oxford don Robert Burton had no doubt in 1621 that 'Divells many times appear to men, & afright them out of their wits sometimes walking at noone day, sometimes at nights, counterfeiting dead means ghosts'.[33] The Northamptonshire physician John Cotta (c. 1575–1650) saw no reason to doubt that the Devil could create such natural illusions, so that when people saw apparitions their eyes were not deceiving them. Satan's deception lay in fooling people that the apparitions really were ghosts. Cotta pointed out that mirrors could create 'outward shapes, and figures of creatures and substances', while painters could 'represent perfectly the true and lively shape of men, and other creatures, even when they are not onely absent, and removed in farre distant places, but when oft-times they have many yeares beene swallowed of the grave'.[34] If man could recreate physical representations of the dead on flat surfaces then it was quite conceivable that the Devil could use the atmosphere as his canvas. His exceeding knowledge of nature enabled him to manipulate the corruption and condensation of air. Rainbows were cited as evidence of how the atmosphere could assume form and colour. Clouds also formed recognisable shapes so why could not the Devil create physical representations – not out of thin air maybe, but certainly out of heavy air. Evil spirits were themselves invisible, but they could cloth themselves in such aerial garments and so become visible to the human eye.[35]

Yet, if apparitions of the dead were the work of the Devil, then why was it that they often appeared to the living to right wrongs and identify murderers? The Presbyterian minister John Flavell (c. 1630–1691) thought hard on this conundrum. He accepted that God may sometimes send back the souls of the dead 'to evidence against the *Atheism* of men', but in general believed that the vast majority of ghosts were evil angels. The Devil, in the guise of a ghost, engaged in good causes, he concluded, because it was 'certainly his interest to precipitate wicked men, and hasten their ruine by the hand of Justice: and he will speak the truth, and seem to own a righteous cause to bring about his great design of ruining the Souls and Bodies of men'.[36] This was unacceptable reasoning to some. While St Paul had observed in Corinthians that the Devil could disguise himself as an angel of light, if he went around the world serving justice it would be impossible to tell the providential from the diabolic. The schoolmaster and polemicist John Webster (1611–1682), best known for his scepticism regarding witchcraft and physical diabolic relations, asserted that the Devil and his evil angels were 'not Authors of any good either Corporeal or Spiritual, apparent or real'.[37] From studying several cases where he believed apparitions of the dead had truly uncovered murders and identified murderers, he concluded that there could be only two solutions. As he did not believe in ghosts, the apparitions must have been wrought either by divine power or by the 'astral spirit' of the dead.[38] The latter was the Neoplatonic concept, espoused by Paracelsus in particular, that there were three essential components of Man: the body, soul and 'a middle substance, betwixt the Soul and the Body' that hovered around the corpse. This astral spirit consisted of matter but took longer to decompose than the body. It also preserved the 'thoughts, cogitations, desires and imaginations that were impressed upon the mind at the time of death'.[39] Hence to the percipient it conveyed the horror and cause of death of the last moments of a murder victim. As someone who rejected so much of Neoplatonic thought on spirits, Webster was unconformable with astral spirits, but at the same time he could find no other 'rational' explanation for the apparitions of the murdered.

Although he accepted the possibility of divine intervention Webster rejected the idea that ghostly apparitions were good angels come to minister divine justice on God's behalf. He saw no scriptural justification for such angelic intervention and found no proof of any examples from human experience. Yet, if the Devil was to be discounted, and few did so prior to the late seventeenth century, and astral spirits remained unconvincing, then good angels provided the only theologically acceptable solution to the reality of the apparitions of the murdered. As Daniel Defoe concluded:

> What Apparitions have been, have certainly been of those blessed Angelick Spirits, who may so far have concern'd themselves in some Cases of Violence, Opression, manifest and atrocious Frauds, to alarm the Offenders, and thereby bring them to do Right.[40]

NATURAL PHILOSOPHY

From the mid seventeenth century scientists and philosophers across Europe, both Catholic and Protestant, began to challenge the existence of ghosts not only through theological reasoning, but also on the basis of new conceptions of the constituents and workings of the world. Neoplatonism, founded on the principal of spiritual governance, came under attack and new philosophical ideas threatened to blow away all the spiritual explanations for the apparitions of the dead. One of the key destabilising influences was cartesianism. The French philosopher and mathematician René Descartes (1596–1650) said little directly on the subject of ghosts, but his concept of a world consisting only of matter meant there was little room for spirits. It was the antithesis of Neoplatonism. Everything visible and invisible consisted of particles or corpuscles that acted in relationship to each other but which could not be influenced at a distance. The world and everything in it worked through a mechanical sequence of consequential material motions, hence the idea of a clockwork universe that was later developed by the likes of Isaac Newton. The mind, too, was a substance though different from corporeal matter. Soul and body were separate entities, though in humans God had allowed a special relationship between the two. Yet the soul could only express itself within a living human body. Outside of the body, to which God had ordained its existence, it could exert no influence over matter.

Cartesian thought did not take root as strongly in English intellectual circles as it did elsewhere in Western Europe. Yet his ideas certainly influenced Thomas Hobbes (1588–1679), one of the most radical and original English philosophers. He was the first to make an absolute break with the old Reformation discourse on ghosts by basing his scepticism of spirits not only on common sense and theological inconsistency, but also on ideas of natural philosophy pushed to the extreme. For him there was no uneasy balance to maintain between attacking Catholic doctrine and upholding a belief in the supernaturalism of the Bible. In his controversial book *Leviathan* (1651) he was categorical that *all* ghosts were mere fancies, deceits, the product of fearful dreams or a troubled conscience.[41] It was impossible for the soul to assume shape or motion. This was tantamount to saying that the soul did not exist, and, not surprisingly, intellectual support was not immediately forthcoming for this radical materialist stance. Hobbes was accused of being a heretic by some and an atheist by others. *Leviathan* was refused further publication. Although he was initially intellectually isolated, his views on ghosts and witches were to influence a new, more contentious debate about the extent to which materialism was compatible with Christianity. To cast doubt on the reality of the spirits of the dead was to question the reality of the soul, and consequently the very foundations of Christianity; over the next century, cries of atheism showered down on those who doubted the reality of ghosts.

Atheism, which was a term applied broadly to those who propounded a range of unorthodox views regarding established theology, had become an increasing concern during the second half of the seventeenth century.[42] Church court records show that a variety of sceptical positions were certainly held by the laity, and it was not unusual for the faith of Puritans to have been reinforced by moments of religious doubt attributed to diabolic inspiration.[43] There are, however, few recorded expressions of atheism in the modern sense of someone who rejects the existence of God. There is no doubt, though, that questioning voices were multiplying, particularly during the religious and political foment of the Civil War and Interregnum period. Richard Baxter warned, 'There are in this City of London, many Persons that profess their great unbelief, or doubt of the Life to come.'[44] Yet the fear of absolute unbelief far exceeded the reality. The concerns can be seen more as a response to the increasing influence of a rationalist approach to religion, which began to strip away the miracles, wonders and revelations of the Old and New Testaments to uncover a rational basis of Christianity. This was not a rejection of God and his works, but an attempt to found Christianity on Reason and science. For some this was the slippery slope to irreligion and those who espoused it were denounced as crypto-atheists, too afraid to utter what they really believed. As Glanvill asseverated, 'those that dare not bluntly say, *There is NO God*, content themselves (for a fair step and Introduction) to deny there are *SPIRITS, or WITCHES*'. He was relieved to say that such people were few and far between amongst the 'vulgar', but warned that they were numerous amongst the 'looser Gentry' and 'the small pretenders to *Philosophy* and *Wit*'.[45]

Scepticism regarding spirits was not only symptomatic of atheism, however, but as Thomas Bromhall warned in his *Treatise of Spectres* (1658), it also led to 'iniquity, impiety, and dissolute living'.[46] The author of the *Narrative of the Demon of Spraiton* (1683), which concerned the 'apparition or spectrum' of a dead gentleman and his wife in Devon, agreed that disbelievers 'were capable of no higher enjoyments than the sickly pleasures of a sensual Life; whilst with Torrents of Intemperate and Libidinous Debauches, they overwhelm their pampered and deluded selves'.[47] So the blasphemy of atheism undermined not only religion but also the moral values of society. Ghost-belief provided a spiritual bulwark against this incipient libertinism. 'Hear ye Sons of the Atheistical *Leviathan*, and let the Impenetrable Off-spring of Chance and Atomes, give attention!' thundered the *Narrative of the Demon of Spraiton*. 'How long shall your Impious Incredulity Brave the Power of the Almighty ... Where are your Hobbs's, your Scots, your Websters, with their Blasphemous denials of the Existence of Spirits.'[48]

Decade by decade, though, sceptics of varying degrees in relation to the founding positions of the likes of Scot, Hobbes and Descartes, began to chip away at the intellectual underpinning for the existence of ghosts and spiritual intervention more generally. But as historians of witchcraft have shown, the struggle was not a simplistic one between science and religion, between rationalism and supernaturalism.[49] Adherents to some aspects of mechanical philosophy, such as Henry More, Joseph Glanvill and Thomas Browne, continued to propound the concept of the immortal soul and that it could, with God's permission and help, influence matter and, therefore, assume substantial form. To this end the likes of Glanvill, Bromhall and Baxter sought to bolster the defence of the reality of the spirit world through the sheer weight of personal testimony gathered from respectable friends, acquaintances, and the confessions of accused witches. Glanvill averred that it gave him 'no humour nor delight in telling Stories, and do not publish these for the gratification of those that have ... I record them as *Arguments* for the confirmation of a Truth.' Those who denied the Truth – the existence of the spirit world and therefore the whole basis of providential Christianity – he denounced as 'nullibists'. These he described variously as the 'multitudes of brisk confident Men in our days', the 'Huffers and Witlings', whose rational faculties had been distorted by Cartesianism, and who 'boldly affirm that a *Spirit* is *Nullibi*, that is to say, *Nowhere*'.[50]

One of the headiest defences for the existence of ghosts was propounded by the astrologer and occultist John Heydon (1629–c.1670). Heydon's views were characteristic of what one historian has described as the 'fertile and chaotic intellectual milieu' of the times.[51] The widely-read Heydon tacitly recognised elements of corpuscular theory but diffused them within an all-embracing Neoplatonic notion of the universe. His conception of ghosts was further influenced by his own personal experiences of various denizens of the spirit world, such as the strange 'aerial men' who visited him in 1648, and intimated they could live for several hundred years. In 1656 Heydon married the widow of the renowned astrologer-physician Nicholas Culpeper (1616–1654), whose ghost had visited her, 'bidding her vindicate him, for he was abused by some *Booksellers*'.[52] Culpeper's spirit also apparently produced a document addressed to his readership for the same purpose, which was published in 1656 as Mr *Culpeper's Ghost*. The author of its preface, Peter Cole, was not sure as to how the ghost had produced the manuscript, commenting: 'whether he delivered all this in an Apparition; or whether Spirits can write, and so he wrote it to some Friend of his, that will not be known, for fear he should be counted a Conjurer, and one that had familiarity with Spirits? I will not determine.' At any rate, Heydon cited the publication as proof that 'these Apparitions are really the souls of the Deceased'.[53]

Heydon criticised those who presented ghosts or 'unbodied Souls' as largely devoid of substance, and therefore possessors of a 'dubious transparency'. He dismissed such descriptive terms as 'shades' or metaphors likening them to the reflection in a mirror. Such notions suggested that the substance of souls were lost when released from the body, as if 'nothing but a tenuous reek remains, no more in proportion to us, than what a sweating Horse leaves behinde him, when he Gallops by in a frosty morning'. Surely God had ordained a more substantial existence for the soul? They may have had an aerial existence but the air, thought Heydon, was just as thick with matter as a cup of water. Ghosts, therefore, were actually solid entities that had a sense of touch, and Heydon furthered that it was 'a very hard thing to disprove that they have not something analogicall to Smell and Taste'.[54] Knowing Heydon's occult interests, espousal of Rosicrucian mysticism, and extraordinary spiritual experiences, it would be easy to dismiss his views on ghosts as the product of an isolated, eccentric mind. True, he was for various personal and pragmatic reasons, considered as an outsider by some of his contemporary occultists. Yet this staunch monarchist was no radical sectarian, and his conception of the spirit world should be seen not only as a product of the occult experimentation of the period but as part of the defence of providential religion espoused by more orthodox figures like Glanvill.

Even for those who rejected Neoplatonism and worked within an explicitly Cartesian intellectual framework, it was possible to construct arguments confirming the existence of a spirit world. This is just what several Dutch clergymen attempted to do during the late seventeenth century, though they were primarily interested in bolstering the principle of angelic intervention rather than the more problematic belief in ghosts.[55] Those who held the torch for theological Cartesianism, such as the Dutch pastor Balthasar Bekker were ultimately unable to go as far as Hobbes and reject entirely the reality of the spirit world.[56] Bekker endorsed Descartes's separation of spirit and matter, and therefore could find no rational explanation for how the souls of the dead could appear in a corpuscular world. Even if it were possible, they certainly could not have any influence in earthly affairs. Popular sightings of ghosts could be put down to natural causes such as dreams, frauds, over-vivid imaginations and melancholy. However, his acceptance of the reality of angels, based on biblical precedent, allowed that what people thought were the spirits of the dead may possibly, occasionally, have been angelic visions – though he did not actually say as much.

Bekker's work provoked considerable controversy, primarily in the Netherlands but also amongst French and German theologians.[57] Its reception in England was fairly muted though. An abridged English edition of Bekker's volumes on the subject, The World Bewitch'd, was published in 1695, but the only significant response to it was from John Beaumont (c. 1640–1731), a Somerset gentlemen and member of the Royal Society. On reading the complete French edition of Bekker's work, Beaumont had been provoked into contacting acquaintances in the Netherlands asking 'for all that was Writ against him, and any Reply's he had made'.[58] He was disappointed by the poor response he received, but it seems to have spurred him to provide his own detailed rebuttal of Bekker's views in his Historical, Physiological and Theological Treatise of Spirits, Apparitions, Witchcrafts, published in 1705. A cursory reading of Beaumont's defence of the spirit world suggests it was written in the same vein as the ghost-believing natural philosophers of the previous generation, like Glanvill. However, it differed in two significant ways. First, Beaumont's views, like John Heydon's, were influenced by the profound personal experience he had of spirit communications. While Glanvill, Baxter and the like may have claimed to witness spirit manifestations, they were rarely singled out for personal attention. In a second publication nearly 20 years later, Beaumont remarked:

I know many Persons laugh at all Apparitions; and it's not for those I record these things, but for those to whom such *Genii* may appear; who, as they will be much surprised at the first Sight of them, I know will be glad to find that others have had the like Experiences.[59]

A second point of difference is that Beaumont's defence of the spirit world was not intended to bolster the witch trials, which had practically ceased by the time. He certainly cited numerous accounts of spirit activity and familiars from the seventeenth-century trials in England and New England in support of his arguments, but he also showed a healthy scepticism. He posited that those who *confessed* to witchcraft were likely to have imagined their diabolic exploits during 'extatick Dreams', but 'for want of Judges knowing in this mysterious State of Mind', such people had 'been barbarously prosecuted and murthered, even to the Ridicule of Mankind'.[60] In this sense Beaumont's work marked a significant shift in the English ghost debate by uncoupling it from the discourse on witchcraft. The reality of ghosts became a separate theological issue positioned more comfortably within the debate over providence, thereby extending the intellectual shelf-life of ghosts. It was this separation from the witchcraft controversy that helped give Beaumont's *Treatise* a welcome reception on the continent. It was published in German in 1721 with a supportive preface by Christian Thomasius, a leading Protestant jurist whose work attacking the use of torture and the flimsy evidential basis of many witchcraft prosecutions helped to undermine the witch trials. Although Thomasius and Bekker are often cited together in this respect, the former was no Cartesian. Like Beaumont, he accepted that the Devil could exert a spiritual influence over people, and that magicians could manipulate occult forces to do harm, but rejected the possibility of a physical Devil. What they shared was the principle of the absolute state of God's control over the world, which the concept of diabolic witchcraft – disseminated, they said, by the papacy – seemed to threaten.[61]

THE 'VEGETABLE PHŒNIX'

The complexities of the seventeenth-century debates on spirits, and the ambiguities of some of the scientific endeavours to explain ghosts, are well illustrated by a curious and rather neglected episode in the history of science. Some scientists hoped that uncovering the mysteries of the natural world through experimentation could lead to the revelation of the greatest miracle of them all – the resurrection of the dead. But taking the Devil and his tricks out of the equation and trying to provide a natural explanation smacked dangerously of heresy. The seekers after the secret were careful to argue that they were attempting to reveal how God's divine intervention could be effected by natural processes. They were in no way trying to undermine the fundamental basis of Christian spirituality by suggesting that mankind could emulate God's miracles.

In a talk to the Society for Promoting Philosophical Knowledge by Experiments in 1660, the occult scientist Sir Kenelm Digby (1603–1665), told his audience:

> if I prove that there is no repugnance against the feasibility of it, I am confident I shall not misse of hearty thanks from those sincere believers who have nothing to shake the firmnesse of their Faith, but the suspected impossibility of the Mystery.[62]

Digby's proof concerned a series of experiments in which he believed he had succeeded in regenerating new crayfish from the ashes of deceased ones. He washed some crayfish, boiled them for at least two hours, and then made a distillation of the resulting liquor. The bodies of the crayfish were next reduced to ashes in an oven and the 'salts' extracted. The salty residue was then mixed with the liquor and left 'to putrifie' in a moist place. Within a few days tiny little animals appeared out of the mix, which he fed on ox blood until they had grown to the size of a button. Over the next few weeks he grew them on to full-sized crayfish by rearing them in a bucket of river water and ox blood, which he changed every third day.[63] We may now laugh at Digby's deluded scientific revelation, but it was based on his knowledge of decades of previous experimentation by continental scientists.[64] Rumour had it that years earlier a French chemist named de Claves had regenerated the form of a sparrow by burning its ashes in a flask.[65] However, most experiments, at least those that were claimed to be successful, were conducted on the ashes of plants. Digby had consulted an international network of scientific showmen on the matter, such as the famed Jesuit Athanasius Kircher in Rome and the Scottish chemist Dr William Davisson (c. 1593–1669), who was based in Paris and Poland.[66] They assured him that they had achieved the resurrection of plants, though Digby admitted 'no industry of mine could effect it'.[67]

This alchemical science of resurrection, known as palingenesis, was based on the Doctrine of Signatures. In the medieval period this meant that the outward appearance of certain herbs and animals, for instance, had been deliberately shaped by God to indicate their harmony and sympathy with parts of the human body. Many herbal remedies were based on this principle. The alchemical scientists of the seventeenth century, influenced by Paracelsus, took the doctrine in a new direction by arguing that such sympathies were also inherent in the microcosmic, internal essences of all living things.[68] One could destroy and break down living matter through heat, reduce it to its elementary substances and then, through chemical processes, recreate the original form because its signature was encoded in its fundamental constituents. As one of its enthusiastic supporters, the Cartesian abbé de Vallemont, put it, 'when a Body is destroy'd, pull'd to pieces, and reduc'd into Ashes, we find again in the Salts, extracted from its Ashes, the Idea, the Image, and the Phantom of the same Body'.[69]

So, in the secrets of palingenesis lay the key to the existence of ghosts. It seemed to prove that people saw what they saw – an image of the dead. But they did not argue that it *was* the soul of the dead, but rather the simulacrum of the deceased encapsulated in the essential constituents of the body, and released as vapours and exhalations by the chemical breakdown of the putrefying corpse. The French chemist James Gaffarel, whose work, *Unheard-of Curiosities*, was translated into English in 1650 by the respected polymath and musician Edmund Chilmead, concluded from such experiments:

> The Ghosts of Dead Men, which are often seen to appear in Church-yards, are Naturall Effects, being only the Formes of the Bodies, which are buried in those places; or their Outward shapes, or Figures; and not the Souls of those Men, or any such like Apparition, caused by Evill Spirits.

He went on to point out that 'in Armies, where, by reason of their great numbers, many die, you shall see some such Ghosts very often, (especially after a Battell)'. The reason being that, as with the heating of plant ashes in a vial, the 'figures' of human bodies were 'raised up, partly by an Internall Heat, either of the Body, or of the Earth: or else by some Externall one, as that of the Sun, or of the Multitudes of the Living: or, by the Violent Noise, or Heat of great Guns, which puts the Aire into a Heat'.[70] De Vallemont agreed with Gaffarel's conclusion, but his acceptance of it would seem to contradict the conclusions he drew from Digby's experiments with crayfish, in which living physical matter was regenerated. Indeed the abbé salivated at the prospect of farming these tasty morsels by such means, affirming that they had 'an excellent Virtue to purifie the Blood'.[71] But such apparent inconsistencies could easily be argued away by the palingenesists. Thus Digby decided, 'I cannot allow Plants to have Life.' They had no 'principle of motion within them', he said. Consequently, though a plant's likeness could be reproduced via palingenesis, it was not a true resurrection because the plant 'never was at any time a determinate It, or Thing'.[72] In the great scheme of things it was recognised that plants were not

animals and crayfish were obviously not men, yet maybe future experimentation would reveal that the same laws of nature applied. De Vallemont speculated
that natural philosophers 'would at length carry their Experiments so far, as to
arrive at the Incomprehensible Mystery of the Resurrection'.[73]

He was wrong of course. The results of alchemical palingenesis were nothing
but wishful thinking shaped by what proved to be a false scientific framework.
Robert Boyle (1627–1691), the renowned experimental scientist and natural
philosopher, was initially intrigued but found the theory wanting. 'I much fear',
he wrote, 'that most of those that tell us that they have seen such plants ... have
in that discovery made as well use of their Imagination as of their Eyes.'[74] Still,
despite such an eminent rebuttal, those natural philosophers seeking arguments
to undermine the popular belief in ghosts during the late seventeenth and early
eighteenth centuries could not but help appropriate palingenesis to their cause.
John Webster referred to the experiments of Kircher and others as evidence
against direct spirit intervention in human affairs. It was 'not only possible, but
rational,' he decided, 'that animals as well as plants, have their Ideas or Figures
existing after the gross body or parts be destroyed, and so these apparitions are
but only those Astral shapes and figures'.[75] Likewise, at the end of the century,
the physician and occultist Ebenezer Sibly provided detailed instructions on
how to reproduce the 'simple spirit' of plants. The experiment demonstrated
that 'in the simple operations of nature many wonderful things are wrought,
which, upon a superficial view appear impossible, or else to be the work of
the devil'.[76]

Even if one accepted the possibility of palingenesis there were too many
limitations for it to succeed as a general explanation for ghost sightings. The
astral apparitions generated were physically linked to the corpses they mirrored,
and, therefore, could only be found in close proximity to the dead – as in
churchyards, crossroads and battlefields. Palingenesis could not explain haunted
houses and wandering ghosts, which made up the bulk of sightings over the
centuries. Neither could it account for spirits that could speak or had sentient
powers such as pointing or moving objects. The palingenesists over reached
themselves yet there was something admirable in their quest.

HAUNTING THE ENLIGHTENMENT

Writing in 1750, the physician and chemist Peter Shaw confidently observed
that 'Ghosts and Witches, at present, rarely make their Appearance. A better
Natural Philosophy has laid these Spirits, and quieted our Church-Yards; where
the Ghosts of the Deceased used to frolic and gambol, like Rats in a Cellar.'[77] Such

confidence was typical of the proponents of eighteenth-century rationalism. Around the same time, the writer William Shenstone stated with satisfaction that 'it is remarkable how much the belief of ghosts and apparitions of persons departed, has lost ground within these fifty years'. 'They have not been reported to have appeared these twenty years', he furthered.[78] They evidently knew little of the beliefs of the common people, and seemed to turn a deliberate blind eye to the continued belief in spirits amongst their social equals. It is true that by the eighteenth century the intellectual tide had turned against Neoplatonism and the conception of a spirit-infused universe. Several key aspects of Christian spiritualism, such as the reality of witchcraft, physical diabolic manifestations and the continuance of miracles, were difficult to incorporate into a materialist world. Rationalist scepticism was, however, by no means the clear victor. The emerging orthodoxy was subtler than an outright rejection of the long-held conceptions of divine revelation and satanic interference. The new mainstream view on witchcraft, for instance, was not that witchcraft was an impossibility, but rather that witches no longer existed. More to the point, ghosts weathered the changing intellectual climate remarkably well.

Ghosts may not have had the same explicit biblical justification as witchcraft, but the huge weight of historic evidence remained a powerful argument. Furthermore, reports of hauntings continued to pour forth from all social levels. As one anonymous clergyman wrote, 'almost every village in England can produce recent and undeniable proofs of these supernatural visitations, permitted by providence, for the discovery of truth; the exposition of some horrid crime, or as warnings to impious and guilty persons'.[79] So while the intellectual relevance of witchcraft withered, ghosts maintained their grip on educated thought throughout the scientific and philosophical transformations of the period. Scepticism remained a dirty word, and the public rejection of spirits could still attract a chorus of religious disapproval. Peter Shaw was evidently sensitive to this and felt the need to strike a note of caution. 'We of the present Age', he observed, 'should take Care lest, by hastily running from Superstition, we fall not at once into Scepticism and Irreligion.'[80]

While the concerns regarding the growth of true atheism were largely unfounded, those over deism were more justified. Most deists expounded the idea that God had detached himself from the world once he had created it, and henceforth had not interfered in human affairs. He had given humans the faculty of reason and therefore the means to comprehend the world, to understand their place in it and to find the path to true faith. The supposed miracles and supernatural happenings in the Bible could be explained away by science and reason. Deism was, then, an explicit affirmation of natural as opposed to providential religion. There was no place for heavenly or hellish spirit intermediaries. Ghosts, as deists such as John Trenchard and Thomas Gordon stated, were mere delusions brought on by dreams, opium, drink, disordered spleens and weak minds.[81] Such deistic anti-providential views had been floating around since the Reformation.[82] It was only during the late seventeenth and eighteenth centuries, however, that it became a distinct and flourishing force, due in part to the eroding authority of the Church of England, but also because it drew inspiration from the profound scientific and philosophical developments of the period.

Just as the perceived threat of the materialists had acted as a rallying point for those who saw the spirit world as a pillar supporting the edifice of Christianity, so several decades later deism provoked a resurgent defence of spirits against the perceived forces of unbelief, lending ghosts renewed theological respectability and purpose.[83] The clergyman and prolific pamphleteer William Assheton (1642–1711), writing in 1706, asserted: 'That there are Spirits and Incorporeal Beings, is no less certain than that there are Men. None but a Sadducee or an Atheist will pretend to deny it.' Another clergyman asserted that 'A person who looks upon the stories of ghosts and spectres as fabulous, must, I think, be an atheist or a deist.' True Christians could not deny the reality of such apparitions.[84] One ghost defender challenged the 'redoubtable philosophers to go through a church-yard after dark if you can'.[85] He doubted they could without experiencing a sense of fear. They would be forced to recognise the spiritual thread that connected the living and the dead, and their professed materialism would be exposed as mere bravado.

While the usual seventeenth-century defences continued to be trotted out, there was a move towards recognising the problems of anecdotal evidence, which reflected the increasing judicial caution regarding spectral evidence that had helped put an end to the witch trials. Glanvill's hotchpotch of stories became something of an embarrassment to the ghost cause. A sceptic writing in the *Gentleman's Magazine* in 1732 observed that the association of such esteemed names as Boyle and the Earl of Clarendon with hauntings generated doubts that conflicted with his adherence to Reason. However, Reason was restored 'by a whole Conclave of Ghosts met in the works of Glanvil and Moreton'.[86] The Independent minister Isaac Watts accepted that many of the accounts of ghosts presented in Glanvill's *Saducismus Triumphatus* and Baxter's *Certainty of the World of Spirits* were 'insufficient proof'. Yet he maintained that evidence of just one real ghost was required to prove that 'there is a State of separate Spirits'. William Assheton similarly made clear that 'even amongst Protestants, abundance of these Apparitions have been mere banter and Collusion', but held to the position that 'Angels have appeared, Therefore Human Souls may likewise appear.'[87] As the century progressed the evidence brought forward in defence of ghosts also became more selective, particularly with regard to the social status of informants. As the Rev. David Simpson remarked, 'the cry of superstition and credulity may be a sufficient answer to ninety nine in a hundred of the dreams and visions which are daily related'.[88] Still, despite such attempts at qualifying accounts of ghosts, the stark fact was that, with a couple of exceptions, those who continued to endorse ghost belief never saw a ghost themselves. One mid-century sceptic hammered the point home:

> the apparition is always seen, as it were at second hand. And if we are to select which we will choose to believe, and which discredit; what shall determine our faith and opinion; in stories equally attested, shall I say? Or rather equally not attested at all?[89]

By the late 1730s, attempts at maintaining a consensus between orthodox Anglican and evangelical tendencies had broken down, leading most significantly to the rise of Wesleyan Methodism. Ghosts ceased to act as ecumenical glue for factions within the Church of England, and consequently a further reposition regarding their reality took place. Just as ghost belief had been a signifier of Catholic 'superstition' during the Reformation, so now it marked out the evangelical tendency from sober, loyal Anglicans. Educated ghost belief became synonymous with pernicious religious enthusiasm, and to reject ghosts was a good way of allaying suspicions of having Methodist sympathies. As the influence of Methodism spread so did the propagandist Anglican accusations that the movement was responsible for fostering popular belief in witches, spirits and ghosts.

As is well known, John Wesley (1703–1791) and his followers were, indeed, devout believers in providence, diabolic possession, witchcraft and apparitions. In his *Journal*, which was published in instalments throughout his lifetime, he made several observations regarding ghosts. Considering his outspoken views on the spirit world, it is hardly surprising that he was repeatedly asked whether he had ever seen an apparition. His response to such enquiries was a weary

> No: nor did I ever see a murder. Yet I believe there is such a thing; yea, and that in one place or another, murder is committed every day. Therefore I cannot as a reasonable man deny the fact; although I never saw it, and perhaps never may. The testimony of unexceptionable witnesses fully convinces me both of one and the other.[90]

It was an argument expressed with the clarity and simplicity of a man skilled in popular communication. There was no need to resort to scriptural or philosophical authorities: he spoke plain common sense. Although portrayed as absurdly credulous by his detractors, Wesley earnestly wrestled with the problems of the evidence for ghosts. In the early 1760s he read Baxter's *Certainty of the World of Spirits* during a journey to London and wrote in his journal, 'It contains several well-attested accounts. But there are some which I cannot subscribe to. How hard is it, to keep the middle way! Not to believe too little, or too much!'[91] Ultimately ghosts could not be sacrificed to the materialists, and, like Isaac Watts, he settled on the position that just one verifiable account of communication with a spirit would be sufficient to tumble the philosophical 'castles in the air' of the deists and atheists.[92]

Despite the strong Methodist association with supernaturalism, Keith Thomas quite rightly warned that 'it would be wrong to associate the belief in ghosts with any particular denomination'.[93] Some Anglican clergymen were willing to out themselves, though tellingly they were usually of a strong Calvinist persuasion, such as the Rev. Augustus Toplady (1740–1778), vicar of Broad Hembury, Devon. In 1775 he preached that there was 'nothing absurd in the metaphysical Theory of Apparitions'. He admitted that the vast majority of reported instances were either untrue or delusions, but declared it was his 'stedfast and mature Belief' that disembodied spirits had and could appear to the living.[94] The Macclesfield clergyman David Simpson, whose opinion we have already read, was forced out of a couple of curacies because of his evangelism and friendship with Methodists.

Neither was debate regarding ghosts confined to the opposing camps of the Calvinists and materialists. Public figures from diverse walks of life also committed to print the reasons for their belief in ghosts, often as a means of signifying their religious and political alignments. One of the most influential writers of the early part of the century, the politician Joseph Addison (1672–1719), a man who was generally dismissive of 'vulgar' beliefs, felt that the rejection of ghosts was a step too close to the blasphemous presumption of believing humans knew as much as God the creator. Besides, the weight of historical evidence was sufficient enough to take their existence seriously. He argued:

> I think a Person who is thus terrified with the imagination of ghosts and spectres much more reasonable than one who, contrary to the reports of all historians sacred and prophane, ancient and modern, and to the traditions of all nations, thinks the appearance of spirits fabulous and groundless.[95]

That other crucial prop of ghost belief, scriptural authority, was cited by the actress and author Eliza Fowler Haywood (1693–1756):

> For my Part, while I have the Authority of Holy Writ, the Judgment of the
> Fathers, and the Opinion of the best and wisest of all Nations and Religions
> on my Side, I shall not be asham'd to avow my Belief that Apparitions of
> departed Souls are not merely traditional, nor ashamed of any Imputation
> our modern Philosophers may throw upon me for it.

Haywood's friend, the fashionable London fortune-teller Duncan Campbell (d.
1730) launched a more detailed and staunch defence of ghosts in which he
argued that there was nothing 'profane or irreligious' in believing in them.[96]

Someone who had ostensibly little vested interest in upholding ghost belief
was the botanist and apothecary Samuel Frederick Gray (1766–1828). In
the 1820s he published several respected works on pharmacy, but his first
publishing venture, a couple of decades before, was a book on ghosts. It
never appeared, and all that remains to tell us of this failed enterprise is a
pamphlet trying to raise a public subscription to fund its publication. We know
that Gray had planned to become a bookseller at one point, and so maybe
the book was a pragmatic money-making exercise to capitalise on the pubic
interest in ghosts. At any rate, Gray evidently planned to do more than just
provide the usual cobbled together collection of old stories. He intended to
rest his defence of the 'popular faith' in ghosts on social rather than religious
foundations. 'We know, from facts,' he stated, 'that vicious persons have been
frequently restrained from committing the most atrocious deeds, particularly
from imbruing their hands in blood, by a dread of the nocturnal appearance
of the injured person's Ghost.' Others 'of weak and vain minds' had likewise
been snatched from wickedness 'by real or fancied supernatural warnings.'
Gray argued, then, that ghost belief helped to uphold popular morality, and
so 'let us not hastily erase from the mind an opinion which, at the worst, is
perfectly harmless'.[97] Around the same time a similar defence of popular belief
was used with regard to the magical activities of cunning-folk. A pamphlet
biography of the Welsh cunning-man Mochyn Nant argued that if such people
did not exist, common people 'would act in open defiance of all Laws, both
human and divine'.[98] Such views, which went against the grain of 'civilised'
thought at the time, should, perhaps, be considered in the context of the anti-
authoritarianism engendered by the repressive political measures instituted
during the Napoleonic Wars.

Of all the intellectual voices that refused to laugh at ghosts, the most
influential was Dr Samuel Johnson. His most famous statement on the issue,
uttered in 1778, was in response to a woman who expressed incredulity on
the matter. With 'solemn vehemence' he replied, 'Yes, Madam: this is a question
which, after five thousand years, is yet undecided; a question, whether in

theology or philosophy, one of the most important that can come before the human understanding.'[99] By this time Johnson's views on the matter were inextricably linked, in public perception, with his involvement in that *cause célèbre* of mid-eighteenth-century England, the Cock Lane Ghost. The case was used as a rod with which to whip the ghost defenders. For the next century any suspected noisy ghost was witheringly dismissed as another Cock Lane. Johnson's reputation as a beacon of the Enlightenment suffered badly both during and after his lifetime. The poet Charles Churchill was not only quick off the mark in publishing the first part of his poem *The Ghost* to capitalise on the Cock Lane sensation, but mercilessly caricatured Johnson in the guise of the character Pomposo – the 'vain idol of a scribbling crowd'. The Scottish minister Donald MacNicol (1735–1802), whose work on the spurious ancient Gaelic *Poems of Ossian* had been criticised by Johnson, got his own back by mocking the doctor's 'superstitious' gullibility. 'I am told', he remarked with relish, 'he was one of those *wise* men who sat up whole nights, some years ago, repeating *paternosters* and other *exorcisms*, amidst a group of old women, to conjure the Cock-lane ghost.' Political rather than personal differences lay behind the Whig politician Arthur Browne's derision of Johnson's character. This was a man, mocked Browne, 'who considered the extorted confessions of insane old women as evidence of witchcraft, and made a serious enquiry into the truth of the tale of the Cock-lane Ghost'.[100]

When Boswell came to write his *Life of Samuel Johnson* he was inclined 'to disdain and treat with silent contempt' the numerous accusations of credulity levelled at his friend. But so widespread was the mistaken belief that Johnson had been taken in by the Cock Lane fraud that Boswell felt it necessary to provide a public rebuttal, pointing out that Johnson was instrumental in revealing the imposture. Providing further proof, he also recorded a conversation with his friend regarding a ghost seen by a young woman of Newcastle. John Wesley, who had recounted the case to Johnson, believed it was true, though his brother Charles did not, and neither did Johnson. He said of Wesley, 'he believes it; but not on sufficient authority. He did not take time enough to examine the girl.' No doubt he considered his own investigations in Cock Lane as a yardstick.[101]

Despite its notoriety and public familiarity Cock Lane was not a turning point in the debate over ghosts, just as the Tedworth Drummer made little obvious dent in spirit beliefs a century earlier. The exposure of frauds was no proof that ghosts did not exist. Believers could even put a positive spin on the case. If as much time and effort was given to investigating every instance of apparent spirit activity then a genuine case would eventually be confirmed beyond doubt. Neither should Samuel Johnson's detractors be taken as representative of educated opinion on the subject. The vast majority of educated people never produced books, poems and articles, or wrote letters to periodicals and newspapers. Maybe the historically silent majority were more inclined to side with Johnson's middle way than the evidence would suggest.

GHOSTS IN AN AGE OF REVOLUTION

In 1799 a tract on apparitions written by an anonymous divine included an address to the nation 'upon the pernicious and prevalent Doctrines of Atheism at this alarming Period'. It was a sign of the times that he managed to couple a defence of ghosts with a denunciation of Thomas Paine as a 'bane and pest of society'.[102] With the American and French Revolutions hovering like a spectre over England's ruling religious and secular elites, the last decades of the eighteenth century were a period of febrile political and religious activity. In such an atmosphere of uncertainty and instability many people sought comfort and guidance in the spiritual realm. It was a propitious time for mystical movements and prophets, such as Richard Brothers (1757–1824) and Joanna Southcott (1750–1814).[103] The renewed interest in all things spiritual and providential is also evident from the ubiquity of questions on the supernatural that were considered in that quintessential eighteenth-century forum of public discourse – the debating society.[104] Between 1789 and 1799 alone there were at least 33 debates in London regarding apparitions.[105] In October 1781, for example, the Coachmakers' Hall was the setting for a debate on the question, 'Is there any reality in the Doctrine of Apparitions?' Three years later, members of the Ciceronian Society considered 'Is the existence of Witches and Apparitions probable?' Debaters at the Christian Areopagus addressed the question, 'Does Reason or Revelation countenance a Belief in the Appearance of Ghosts and Apparitions?', while in November 1798, participants at the Westminster Forum deliberated, 'Is it true that any Ghosts or Departed spirits ever did appear to a Mortal in this World?' The substance of the debates is not easy to gauge from the sources. James Boswell, who recorded his attendance at a debate on the existence of apparitions at the Coachmakers' Hall in April 1781, provides a brief insight. He described the audience as numerous and containing some women. None of them were of the 'mere vulgar', he noted approvingly. As to the debate, 'they differed in opinion as to apparitions being seen in later ages. But I thought the opinion for was best supported, and Mr. Addison in the *Spectator* was brought as an authority.'[106]

While some debates centred on hoary precedents, others were sparked by recent occurrences, such as that at the Coachmakers' Hall in October 1789, which considered 'an Apparition lately appearing to a worthy Clergyman'.

The managers invited 'every person who can speak from Experience on this Occasion'. The apparition of a woman murdered in St Pancras sparked a series of debates on departed spirits in the spring of 1790. According to one advert, the ghost had 'not only frightened one Person to Death, but become the walking Terror of the whole neighbourhood'.[107] The majority of debates seem to have been refreshingly open-minded. An advertisement for a debate on ghosts at the Westminster Forum in January 1797 advised that

> it must receive the most ample investigation, from the number of Clerical and Literary Gentlemen by whom the institution is patronized. Many strange stories have been propagated concerning Apparitions, the Managers thus publicly declare, that they shall feel themselves gratified by the attendance of any person who can positively declare to the Audience, that they have either seen or conversed with a departed Spirit.[108]

At a debate at Capel-Court, in July 1790, regarding the reality of the apparitions of Julius Caesar and the prophet Samuel, a gentleman who had witnessed events at Cock Lane was present to 'communicate many valuable Particulars of that astonishing Transaction'.[109]

Some questions proposed for debate, however, were couched in typically sceptical fashion; the issue was not whether ghosts existed but the extent to which a belief in them was a mark of ignorance and credulity. Consider, for example, the following debate at the Westminster Forum in March 1790: 'Which is most absurd, a Belief in Apparitions, a Reliance on Dreams, or an implicit Faith in the Predictions of Judicial Astrology?' On such occasions those who believed in ghosts, astrology and the like were effectively appearing as defendants rather than engaging in an impartial debate. When the same question was considered for four weeks in a row at the City Debates, some of London's principal astrologers participated to defend their corner. The managers invited the occultist Ebenezer Sibly, author of the influential *A New and Complete Illustration of the Celestial Science of Astrology*, and the 'celebrated' astrologer Mrs Williams.[110] At the third meeting held on 19 April 1790, over 300 men voted for an adjournment of the debate. The final session, held the following week, attracted 'one of the most numerous and brilliant audiences ever remembered', and was attended by nobility, gentry and 'numbers of the first literary characters in the nation'.[111]

It is a testament to the influence of Dr Samuel Johnson that several years after his death his opinions on ghosts were the basis for at least two debates. One wonders what Boswell would have thought of the outcome of the Westminster Forum debate, in January 1788, on the question 'Was the Belief of the Existence of Apparitions by the late Doctor Johnson, an Impeachment of his Understanding?' By a small majority the audience decided that Johnson's 'belief in the existence of apparitions' was justified.[112] Although the recording of such outcomes is rare, it is significant that another sequence of similar debates, which focused on John Wesley's belief, ended in a similar resolution. The question, which was posed in response to recent press reports of the dispossession, in June 1788, of George Lukins by a group of Wesleyan ministers at Temple Church, Bristol,[113] and debated over at three evening meetings of the Capel Court Debating Society, was: 'Is the Rev. Mr. Wesley censurable for publicly maintaining the Existence of Witches, the Doctrine of Apparitions, and Demoniac Possessions?' At the first meeting 'an aged, venerable, and learned Methodist' gave accounts of several 'strange appearances', while a 'candid hearing' was also expected to be given to a female speaker who declared that she frequently conversed with an apparition. The debate 'terminated in Mr. Wesley's favour'.[114] The organisers of the memorable City Debate on apparitions and astrology of April 1790, pointed out in one of their adverts that, as several Dissenting ministers and those 'belonging to the Rev. Mr. Wesley's Communion, frequently attend these Debates, much important reasoning is expected on the Doctrine of Apparitions. The awful circumstance of an Apparition, related by the Rev. Mr. Wesley, shall be attended to.'[115]

PSYCHIC SCIENCE

Religion and philosophy had dominated the Enlightenment discourse over ghosts, but towards the end of the eighteenth century, science returned to the forefront of the debate. As we shall see in the next chapter, the pseudo-sciences that rose to prominence during the late eighteenth and early nineteenth centuries could be used to prove that ghosts were mere projections of the mind. Yet they were broad enough in their philosophical bases to allow for ghosts as external realities. The most influential of these pseudo-scientific developments was the concept of animal magnetism. Under certain conditions, adherents argued, mental and material impressions could be conducted through the medium of universal fluid. It was this conduction that explained magnetic attraction, the influence of the stars and electricity. However, the leading proponent of this theory, the Austrian Franz Mesmer (1734–1815), was primarily concerned with the medical implications of animal magnetism. If illnesses proceeded from the interruption or blockage of the universal fluid coursing through the human body, then it could also be cured by the application of magnets or through the sympathetic channelling of the vital forces between human bodies. The mesmerist was born.[116]

Many of the adherents of animal magnetism considered themselves as cutting-edge scientists, pushing forward the boundaries of rational knowledge. Through the exploration of the occult properties of nature, the foundations of the supernatural could be exploded. It was a reformulation of the enthusiastic scientific claims of those inspired by the heady amalgam of natural and Neoplatonic philosophies during the mid seventeenth century. The investigations of the mid-nineteenth century German chemist Baron Karl Von Reichenbach, for example, are reminiscent of those of Kenelm Digby. Reichenbach's conception of odic or vital force, which he thought permeated and radiated from nearly all material substances, was an obvious adaptation of animal magnetism. The odic force was invisible to most people, though its effects could be witnessed in manifestations of magnetic attraction, electricity, heat and light. Certain people were more sensitive to these vital emissions than others and could see the odic force radiating from objects at night. Bearing in mind that ghosts were rarely seen by more than one person at the same time, Reichenbach pondered whether ghosts were merely the natural vital effluence seen by odic-sensitive people. Fired up by his desire as a scientist to 'inflict a mortal wound on the monster, superstition', he decided to take one of his sensitives, Mlle Reichel, a woman who, he said, 'had the courage, unusual in her sex' to agree to accompany him to a cemetery on two dark nights. 'The result justified my expectation', he reported. 'She saw very soon a light, and perceived on one of the grave mounds, along its whole extent, a delicate, fiery, as it were, a breathing flame. The same thing was seen on another grave in a less degree.' The flames were about four feet high, and only appeared over new graves. This was proof that it was the vital forces released by decaying bodies that lay behind the churchyard ghost. He concluded with evident relish that 'I have, I trust, succeeded in tearing down one of the densest veils of darkened ignorance and human error.'[117]

Reichenbach's confidence in his ghost-busting theory was ill-founded, for the theory of animal magnetism that had inspired him also provided a crucial source of 'scientific' support for spiritualism. As one adherent put it, 'Mesmerism has been – humanly speaking – the corner-stone upon which the Temple of Spiritualism was upreared.'[118] Considering that the idea of animal magnetism was fundamentally a materialist reworking of the Neoplatonic notion of a world permeated and governed by spirits, it is no wonder then that it was eagerly adopted by those who continued to seek proof for the existence of ghosts. If all matter was infused with Mesmer's fluidic force then surely it also linked soul and body in life, and therefore could also explain communications with the afterlife. During the 1830s and 1840s, continental animal magnetists put the theory to the test and, sensationally, some claimed to have succeeded in contacting the spirits of the dead through trance or hypnotic states induced by magnetism.[119] In 1850, the same year that Reichenbach's magnum opus on odic force appeared in English, another translation, this time of the experiments of the Frenchman Louis Alphonse Cahagnet, was also published. Cahagnet claimed to have scientific proof of the existence of the afterlife. In his *Celestial Telegraph* he described how he had used eight somnambulists, that is people put into an ecstatic state by magnetism, as mediums. Through them contact was made with 36 souls. As Cahagnet explained, 'In the spiritual state the soul represents in man his whole form and each of his parts – his passions and pleasures, superiority, inferiority, and intelligence.' A spirit of the dead, 'individualized as on earth, has the recollection of its terrestrial existence, its family affections and friends, all which will be proved by psychological apparitions'.[120]

By 1850 the spiritualist movement had already caused a sensation across Europe and America. Initially communications were conducted via knocks, raps and the movement of tables, but as spiritualism developed so the supposed spirit manifestations became more elaborate and more physical. It is ironic that spiritualism soon came to rely on materialism for proof of its anti-materialist premise.[121] Spiritualists could explain the appearance of the spirits of the dead in seance rooms in terms of an ethereal materialisation of the primordial fluids attracted by the magnetic aura of the medium. If this was so, and such matter could be seen, touched and smelt, then logically it could also be scientifically analysed. The sceptics were constantly demanding proof, and with the first manifestations of ectoplasm it seemed that the very essence of ghosts was literally within grasp.[122] The term 'ectoplasm' was first used in cell biology in the 1880s to describe the viscid, white or translucent, semi-fluid substance that had been found to separate one cell from another. To Charles Richet, a French professor of physiology, the same substance seemed to constitute the streaming, fluid-like substance that emanated from the orifices and chests of mediums from the late nineteenth century onwards, particularly female ones, and sometimes apparently even formed into human faces and bodies. Ectoplasm was thought to be the solid essence of mesmeric fluidic forces, moulded by the sympathetic energy generated between the medium and the spirit world, allowing the dead to manifest themselves physically. Proof, at last, that ghosts had substance! This was something that had been argued back in the seventeenth century by the likes of Heydon, who saw ghosts as formulations of vaporous condensation and spiritual essences. But despite several decades of ectoplasmic emanations, close examination revealed them to be nothing more than mundane household items such as muslin, cheesecloth, gelatine, and frothy egg whites.

The Society for Psychical Research was at the forefront of the investigation of such medium-inspired evidence. There soon developed a general consensus amongst the SPR most influential members, such as Frank Podmore and Edmund Gurney, that ghosts were not the sentient souls of the dead returning to earth. As this view became increasingly apparent in the Society's publications, its spiritualist members began to leave, particularly in 1886 when a popular medium was denounced as a fraud in the pages of its journal.[123] What Podmore and his fellow investigators felt they *had* found some evidence for was the reality of wraiths – or the appearance of apparitions at the *moment of death*. As Frederic Myers explained in the introduction to the huge survey of apparitions conducted by Gurney and Podmore, cases of these 'phantasms of the living' represented an 'objective fact'. Even apparitions appearing several hours after apparent death were not necessarily the ghosts of the deceased, for 'the moment of actual death is a very uncertain thing'.[124] The body went through a process of dissolution during which it retained some psychic energy. Although Myers later came to be convinced that telepathic communications were possible between spiritual and material worlds, he suggested that some purposeless apparitions were formed from the residues of peoples' energy lingering after death – a visual psychic memory. This theory, with its echoes of Paracelsus's aerial spirits, palingenesis and odic force, has proved to have lasting currency. Less accepted was his curious suggestion that apparitions were the projections generated by the incoherent dreams of the dead.[125]

It is significant that the early psychical researchers tended to avoid the term 'ghost' or placed it in inverted commas. They preferred to talk of 'phantasms of the dead' or 'apparitions occurring after death'. As the biographer of Harry Price noted, the ghost hunter also 'disliked the word intensely, though he could not object to it in the name of the Ghost Club'. Other than the necessity of using it for publicity purposes, he preferred to talk instead of 'entities' or 'paranormal appearances'.[126] 'Earthbound spirit' is also used now. More recently, the term 'apparition' has also largely fallen out of usage in the SPR's *Journal* and *Proceedings*. For the same reason 'haunting' too is now also frequently placed in inverted commas in relevant academic literature.

'Ghost' carried too much historical baggage for those who sought to maintain an impartial, scientific, empirical position free of religious inference. Spiritualists did not talk of ghosts and their seances took place in enclosed, largely controllable environments that encouraged detailed if often flawed investigation. Poltergeists, even if unwelcome, were likewise housebound and generally performed to order. Ghosts came to be defined as all the other traditional apparitions that were not available for systematic observation. They appeared of their own volition and often outdoors. Their visits were infrequent or recorded only in legendary history.

Up until the advent of spiritualism and formal psychical investigation, the 'traditional' purposeful and memorial ghosts, with which this book is primarily concerned, had been integral to the debate about the spirit world. The modern spiritualist movement may have arisen from what was originally a typical case of noisy haunting, focused around adolescent girls (the Fox sisters of Hydesville, New York State), but it quickly broke from tradition. The spirit of the dead became 'a mobile spirit, free of earthly bonds, including the tragedy of its own death', and in the process a new necromantic religion was born.[127] Spiritualism was about the human desire to make contact with the dead, while much of the prior history of ghosts was about spirits seeking out the living and attempts to prevent or limit their earthly appearance. With spiritualism the tables were turned in more senses than one.

FIVE

All in the Mind

The debates over the reality of ghosts demonstrate how supernaturalism was equal to the forces of rationalism. For as long as it was commonly accepted that people really did see apparitions of the dead, whether they were products of diabolic manipulation, palingenesis or odic forces, then there was sufficient diagnostic confusion and inconsistency for the reality of ghosts to remain intellectually relevant. Over the centuries, however, there were critics who rejected the external reality of apparitions altogether and who insisted that they were merely internal figments of the imagination. This chapter, therefore, is concerned with the various explanations put forward for what people thought they saw and heard.

THE PLAY OF LIGHT AND SOUND

As numerous authors pointed out over the centuries, many ghost sightings could be put down to simple tricks of the light playing on the fertile imaginations of those fearful of the night. A ghost was nothing but the play of shadows, imbuing everyday physical features with a sense of movement and uncanny luminescence. A moonlit night was the perfect setting for the imagination to work this magic or mischief. Some saw beauty in the transformation it wrought. One eighteenth-century essayist recalled gazing at a pastoral mountain landscape as darkness descended and cogitating on how it was 'the time when the ghosts are supposed to make their appearance, and spirits visit the solitary dwellings of the dead'. But as the moon began to spread its silver rays over the scene he was possessed not with fear but awe at the beauty it cast, 'every object appeared more delicately shaded, and arrayed in softer charms'. It took a poetic soul and a rational mind to see the moonlit night in this way, he implied, and the essayist reflected 'on the excessive timidity that possesses many people's mind' to feel apprehension and terror at such a moment.[1] The eighteenth-century actress Eliza Haywood knew several such people who were of 'so timid a Nature, that they take every Shadow, which the Moon makes by her Shine on distant Objects, for a Ghost'. She recounted how a male friend took the churchyard test one moonlit night and fell into a fit after mistaking an old yew tree for the ghost of his brother who had died a year before.[2] The writer and actor Arthur Murphy (1727–1805) had similar churchyard experiences with some of his acquaintances. When 'the glimpses of the moon formed their own shadow upon the ground I could behold them suddenly stop and gaze at it with looks full of wildness and amazement'.[3] The moralising novelist Elizabeth Bonhôte (1744–1818) patronisingly portrayed the lower classes as being so cowed by superstition that they could barely step outdoors at night without being frightened near to death:

> After the sun has withdrawn his rays, though the bright beams of the moon illumine their paths, they see an imaginary ghost in every tree, gate, or stile; and when they retire to their apartments by themselves, are in a continual dread, lest their curtains should be undrawn by the hand of some visible or invisible spectre.[4]

Ghosts born of moonlit apprehension were created by the shedding of new light on familiar objects. Another origin of luminous deception imbued a light source with the semblance of sentient movement. A candle or lantern moving to and fro before the windows of a house or flitting along an alleyway at night, the dark rendering the candle's owner a strange, shadowy figure, could easily be mistaken for a spirit by timid individuals. One folklorist recorded that shepherds moving about the hills with a lantern at night during lambing time were sometimes mistaken for spirit lights.[5] Of a less innocent nature, Defoe recalled a hoax perpetrated by some Dorking schoolboys on the neighbours of an elderly lady who had recently died. One of the boys perambulated around her house and neighbouring fields at night with a lantern, leading locals to believe it was the spirit of the woman. 'It must be confess'd', said Defoe, 'that a dark Lanthorn, join'd with an Enthusiastick head, might prevail to make such a Sham take, with weak and bigoted People.'[6] The Yorkshire manufacturer and merchant Joseph Lawson (1821–1890) thought many ghost sightings derived either from such deception or from people wandering innocently at night with candles. He suggested, quite reasonably, that one of the consequences of the spread of gas was that the scope for such luminous deception was vanquished, as gas was a stationary source of domestic lighting.[7] Yet, under certain conditions, even gas lighting, the supposed destroyer of ghosts, could create its own apparitions. One night in October 1851 a couple of hundred people gathered outside an empty house in Northgate Street, Gloucester, after word got around that the pale ghost of a young girl had been seen at an open window at the top of the building. Two intrepid men entered the house to find the ghost but saw nothing. It eventually became apparent that the vision was nothing more than the light of a street lamp reflected by the window onto a whitewashed wall of the room. In 1872 a supposedly haunted house in Brixton Road, London, caused a great disturbance. There was a defective gas light in the house and every time it flickered a crowd of local boys raised the cry of 'Ghost!'[8]

Another moving light that caused much mystery, the ignis fatuus, described by one seventeenth-century dictionary as a 'flighty exhalation set on fire', was long cited as an explanation for some ghost sightings.[9] The Calvinist theologian William Fulke (1536/37–1589), the first English writer to discuss the supernatural interpretation and natural cause of the will-o'-the-wisp, stated that 'ignorant and superstitious fooles have thought [them] to be soules tormented in the fire of Purgatory'. He went on to suggest that 'the Devill hath used these lights (although they be naturally caused) as strong delusions to captive the minds of men with feare of the Popes Purgatory'.[10] It was not just the appearance of mysterious lights in the darkened countryside that generated the wealth of folklore surrounding the phenomenon; it was also because the light seemed to be sentient. As one seventeenth-century writer explained, it 'appears like unto a Candle, playing and moving to and fro the air'.[11] Numerous historical accounts record how the light followed or seemed deliberately to lead people into bogs, rivers and pits. Fulke observed how those so bothered 'will tell a great tale, how they have beene led about by a spirit in the likeness of Fire'.[12] Today the rational explanation for these lights is that they are caused by the combustion of natural gas produced by rotting organic material, usually in boggy or marshy places, though little research seems to have been done to confirm this. Some early modern naturalists suggested that the congregation of large numbers of glow-worms created the ignes fatui.[13] More orthodox interpretations, which were not so far from the modern explanation, concerned gaseous expulsions, such as the suggestion that they were caused by sulphurous exhalations from 'muddy Pools, Church-yards, and other putrid places'.[14] Fulke thought the flames might sometimes be caused by the ignition of 'glewish or oyly matter' in places such as churchyards where there was an 'abundance of such unctuous and fat matter'. The most accepted explanation, also suggested by Fulke, was that the violent movement of cold air created the flames. During the early eighteenth century this explanation was disseminated widely for the purpose of popular enlightenment in numerous editions of The Shepherd's Kalender.[15]

The folklore record shows that supernatural beliefs regarding the will-o'-the-wisp continued to be held in the late nineteenth and early twentieth centuries, with numerous informants recounting how they had been led astray at night by the lights. But widespread drainage of wetlands and bogs meant that by the twentieth century the *ignis fatuus* was a rare phenomenon in many areas of the country, yet industrialisation over the same period generated new gaseous ghosts. Strange lights were generated in mines by the leakage of natural gas. In Devon the Jack o' Lantern was thought to play over spots were veins of metal lay buried.[16] In 1804 *The Times* reported that a fiery spirit had reputedly plagued a farmhouse in the coalfields around Bilston, Staffordshire. The farmhouse had been built over an old coal-pit and an aperture in the cellar had long been used to dispose of household waste. One night the servant woman went down to the cellar and was frightened out of her wits by a blue flame bellowing forth from the hole. The mystery was solved when further investigation confirmed it was an ignition of mine gas, and as a consequence the farmer abandoned the property.[17]

As well as uncanny lights and reflections, the imaginations of the timid, childish or superstitious (in the words of the debunkers) were also provoked to feverish depths by strange noises in the night. These were often put down to nothing more than timbers and old furniture creaking and cracking as they expanded and contracted due to damp and dryness. Maybe they were the result of doors and windows rattling in the wind, or, in the last couple of centuries, water pipes and boilers gurgling, clanking and hissing. The spookiest nocturnal noises were those that suggested to fertile minds the deliberate movement of some unseen entity. Footsteps in the night or the sudden clatter of pots and pans, which no draught could have possibly disturbed, sent households into a panic. The rationalists' answer to such mysteries was simple – animals. Calmet commented on 'cats or owls, or even rats, which by making a noise frighten the master and domestics'.[18] A century later, Charles Ollier in his *Fallacy of Ghosts* singled out cats. They were, he suggested, 'prodigal agents in such matters, and there can be little doubt that the greater number of ominous noises which frighten sober people out of their senses are attributable to them'.[19] This was certainly true in the experience of Andrew Campbell, an actor at the Royal Dramatic College, Woking. In 1863 he described his experience of a haunting many years before, observing that 'anything which tends to allay the fears of superstition, particularly in the young, cannot but be approved'.[20]

Campbell's ghostly encounter occurred while staying at the Elizabethan manor house of a wealthy Hertfordshire farmer. One night, around midnight, the household was awoken by banging and crashing noises emanating from the kitchen and a sound of a heavy object being dragged across the floor. Armed with his blunderbuss, the farmer, along with his servants wielding pokers, went down and threw open the kitchen door. They were greeted with the sound of smashing glass and then silence. They found the floor littered with broken china and several panes of glass were broken. The house must be haunted, they thought. Several servants gave their notice to quit and the farmer's wife desired to leave. The rumpus was calmed when, several weeks later, Campbell discovered the real cause of the haunting. While walking along a path near the farm he came across the corpse of a cat with its head stuck in a saucepan. 'Had I not thus discovered the cause of all the alarm the house would have remained with the reputation of being haunted, and the children's children of the terrified farmer would have convinced other children that their grand-father's home was really a haunted one.'

CHILDHOOD STORIES

It was all very well detailing all the obvious natural causes for hauntings, but what made some people so timid in the first place? It was not only the uneducated and ignorant that started at shadows or refused to pass through churchyards at night. The answer seemed to stem from childhood influence. Some argued that moral, purposeful ghost stories could 'produce in youth, sentiments that will stimulate them to good and virtuous actions'. Andrew Baxter, writing in 1733, cautioned against telling children 'silly, idle relations' of ghosts, but warned, 'We ought not to tell them that all these things are groundless and absurd.'[21] Most eighteenth-century medical writers and edu-cationalists, however, saw exposure to them as mentally and socially damaging. Beliefs and impressions instilled in childhood were sometimes impossible to erase in adulthood. As Erasmus Darwin, a physician, natural philosopher and founder member of the Lunar Society explained, the 'false notions, which we receive in our early years ... affect all our future reasoning by their perpetual intrusions'.[22] Another physician warned that he could relate many instances where children who imbibed 'idle stories' of apparitions and haunted houses suffered a tragic fate in adult life, due to the timid nature it had instilled in them.[23] Such views harked back to the philosopher John Locke's warning, in his *Thoughts Concerning Education* (1693), that young, tender minds should be protected from 'Notions of Sprites and Goblins, or any fearful Apprehensions in the dark.' A couple of decades later Joseph Addison made a similar observation.[24] In Darwin's view, the only cure for childhood exposure to ghost stories was to increase the general knowledge of the laws of nature to 'counteract the fallacies of our senses'.[25] The more practical solution, of course, was not filling children's heads with fanciful stories in the first place. This was not as easy as it sounded, since servants rather than parents usually tended the infants of the educated and wealthy and were employed to keep them occupied. So the servants also had to be instructed. To this end *The Compleat Servant-Maid*, which was reprinted many times during the late seventeenth and eighteenth centuries, advised regarding the instruction of children:

> Neither terrify them into a Complyance to do any thing, by talking of Ghosts, Spirits, Hobgoblins, and such like ridiculous things, (which is a wicked Method too often put in Practice to the great Detriment of Children) for, comparatively speaking, as they are soft as Wax, the first Impression will be deep, and as they encrease in Years, they will retain it the stronger, and it will be almost impossible ever to root it out of their Minds.[26]

If blame was to be apportioned for the perpetuation of such pernicious fears, then it lay firmly with womankind. The *London Journal* stated in a note on ghosts in 1732, 'Mothers and grandmothers, aunts and nurses, begin the cheat.' In the same year the *Gentleman's Magazine* agreed: 'The Cheat is begun by Nurses with Stories of Bugbears, & c. from when we are gradually led to listen to the traditionary Accounts of local Ghosts.'[27] Elizabeth Bonhôte joined in the patriarchal attack, denouncing the 'ignorant nurse' and her foolish ghost stories, which 'neither time, good sense, or the united exertions of parental tenderness, or authority' could eradicate from children so damaged.[28] While female servants, usually uneducated and from the countryside, were singled out as the prime culprits in perpetuating irrational fears in the children of the expanding middling-sort in society, ultimately it was surely the responsibility of mothers to ensure their offspring were being properly tutored. The bookseller, translator and devoted family man Joseph Collyer asserted in his parenting guide that 'Mothers are the natural nurses of their children; and it is their business to tutor and mould minds as well as their bodies.' Consequently, they 'should be careful not to create groundless fears, by making the child afraid of being in the dark, and by telling him idle tales of ghosts'.[29] Such guides as *The Compleat Servant-Maid* were not meant to be read by their subject, then, but served as instructive reading for mistresses on how to ensure that their female servants behaved appropriately. A subtext to these concerns over the influence of female servants was that women could transmit their foibles and weaknesses to boys, potentially crippling their virility in later life. Reginald Scot thought that some men were prone to seeing ghosts due to a 'cowardlie nature and complexion, or from an effeminate and fond bringing up'.[30] One mid-eighteenth-century writer even personified 'foolish' ghost-beliefs as female, and beseeched 'pull the old Woman out of our Hearts', and thereby extinguish the absurd beliefs imbibed in childhood.[31]

The cause of adult timidity syndrome, as we might call it today, lay not only in childhood exposure to the scary tales of illiterate nurse maids. While books, periodicals and newspapers were seen as valuable conduits for providing the rational knowledge and spiritual strength to vanquish ghost belief, some types of literature were accused of perpetuating 'superstitious' fears. Thus the *Gentleman's Magazine*, in its 1732 discourse on ghosts, complained of the 'Suburbian Ghosts, rais'd by petty Printers, and Pamphleteers, and the Apparitions consequent to their Half-penny bloody Murders.'[32] During the early nineteenth century several educated men indulged in a bit of self-psychoanalysis to try and understand why they thought they had seen ghosts or had believed in them for so long, when they evidently did not exist. They found a resolution in their childhood reading material. Joseph Taylor, in his pamphlet on apparitions, confessed: 'in the early part of my life, having read many books in favour of Ghosts and Spectral Appearances, the recollection remained so strong in my mind, that, for years after, the dread of phantoms bore irresistible sway'.[33] But the formative effect of childhood reading was so powerful that its engrained influence could operate beyond the conscious rejection of ghosts. In the early 1820s, one man, who did not believe in ghosts and yet saw visions of a young woman he knew was dead, ascribed them to his overactive imagination. He had always been interested in the supernatural, he said, and thought his perusal of the *Tales of Wonder* and other ghost stories when a child shaped the hallucinations produced by his mind as an adult.[34]

The obvious strategy to undermine this second pernicious prop of infant timidity was to ensure that no such literature found its way into children's hands. The second approach, fully evident by the end of the eighteenth century, was to bypass the nurse completely and provide anti-ghost literature to be read by children. Women were at the forefront of this literary enterprise. The most famous works of the genre were the Cheap Repository Tracts produced for poor, rudimentary readers by the evangelical Hannah More, who was much concerned about the moral effect of ungodly, 'superstitious' popular literature.[35] Likewise, the educationalist Sarah Trimmer (1741–1810) provided a moral ghost story in her periodical *The Family Magazine*, which was produced 'To counteract the pernicious Tendency of immoral Books, &c. which have circulated of late Years among the inferior classes of People.' It consisted of a dialogue between Robert the ploughman and his sweetheart Betty. Betty loves reading about spirits and witches late at night and tells Robert about how she had been much frightened one night the previous week. As an owl screeched, the door creaked and the wind whistled down the chimney she thought she heard ghostly footsteps; all was explained by a dog scratching a piece of furniture. The dame who looks after her requests the parson to come and give her an instructive talk. He tells her that it was 'very wicked, as well as very foolish, to be afraid of ghosts' and orders her to burn all her story books, dream books and fortune-telling books. Robert agrees that the parson had, indeed, provided very good advice.[36]

Similar in vein, though much longer and clearly aimed at middle- rather than working-class readers, were the series of dialogues between several young ladies and a token young gentleman that formed Mary Weightman's The Friendly Monitor; Or, Dialogues for Youth against the Fear of Ghosts (1791). In their correspondence the reality of ghosts is debated with reference to excerpts from The Spectator and Bonhôte's The Parental Monitor. As Weightman stressed in her introduction, the book was 'professedly designed for the use and benefit of children, in assisting them to banish the tales of the nursery'. So too was a threepenny-bit pamphlet on the 'mischievous doctrine of ghosts', published several times at the beginning of the nineteenth century. This told the story of a Mr Howard and his four pretty offspring who are frightened by strange noises in their house. Careful investigation reveals a rational explanation, leading to the instructional observation: 'many things appear to us supernatural, merely from our want of properly inquiring into them; and the fears which generally seize us on these occasions, prevent our making a proper use of our senses'.[37]

MELANCHOLY

Those who started at shadows, saw ghosts in moonlit trees and jumped at the sound of nocturnal creaks were often diagnosed as suffering from melancholy, a mental affliction that may have had its origins in nursery fears and frights but afflicted people in adulthood. The symptoms – dejection, sadness, gloominess, introspection and haunting dreams – equate to a certain extent with what we now call depression, though the condition has to be understood in the context of the time rather than by modern comparisons. Although for much of the early modern period it was thought to arise from the fumes given off by corrupt, black blood rising to the brain, it was also understood and treated as a psychological condition.[38] Key symptoms of melancholia, which are not essential to the modern concept of depression, were hallucinations and visions. In a world in which spirits were thought to be pervasive it is no wonder that suffers complained of being plagued with devils, witches and ghosts. It was a standard argument proposed by early modern witchcraft sceptics like Reginald Scot and John Webster, that melancholy explained why some accused witches confessed to fantastic deeds and why some victims of witchcraft told extraordinary tales of spiritual malevolence.[39] Melancholiacs were not necessarily considered mad, however, though the condition could eventually lead to madness.

Robert Burton's *Anatomy of Melancholy* (1621) was hugely influential in defining, explaining and treating melancholia through the extensive compilation of thoughts on the matter from the ancient Greeks onwards. As a sufferer he was understanding and compassionate, advising from personal experience, 'Be not solitary, be not idle.' He described the development of melancholy in the sufferer as follows:

> At first his mind is troubled, he doth not attend what is said, if you tell him a tale, he cries at last, what said you? but in the end he mutters to himselfe, as old women doe many times, or old men when they sit alone, upon a sudden they whoop and hollow, or run away, and sweare they see or heare players, divels, hobgoblins, ghosts.

Ghosts, he further observed were 'ever in the minds' of the melancholic, and they met them at 'every turne'. Consequently he advised the friends and family of melancholics to avoid all tales of devils, spirits and ghosts when in their company.[40] Burton's citation of ghosts and spirits as symptomatic of the advanced stages of melancholy is attested to by the medical casebooks of a couple of his contemporaries who practised as astrologer-physicians. The London practitioner Simon Forman, whom Burton apparently consulted as a young man, dealt with numerous melancholiacs who complained of being troubled by spirits.[41] There was Susan Cuckston, for example, who 'in the 40th year of her age fell into a melancholy despair and was moch vexed & trobled in mind and possessed with a sprite for oftentimes the sprite wold speake & talke to her'. Another woman was 'haunted at night with a goste, or sprite contynually'.[42] The Buckinghamshire clergyman and physician Richard Napier was evidently considered a specialist in curing such mental disturbances. Many of his melancholic clients suffered from what he called 'strange fancies'. There was one who 'seeth many things which he seeth not', and the woman who was 'haunted, as she thinketh, with an ill spirit'.[43]

While a childhood disturbed by ghost stories was certainly thought to predispose one to suffering melancholy in adulthood, other factors were often thought to trigger the condition, such as anxiety brought on by religious enthusiasm, the fear of bewitchment, and grieving. Guilt was another cause that had strong associations with haunting. Thomas Hobbes, writing in 1656, explained how

For to some men, as well sleeping as waking, but especially to guilty men, and in the night, and in hallowed places, Fear alone, helped a little with the stories of such Apparitions, hath raised in their minds terrible Phantasmes, which have been, and are still deceiptfully received for things really true.[44]

This guilt-inspired melancholia helped explain why murderers sincerely thought the ghosts of their victims persecuted them. In a discussion on the issue Daniel Defoe observed that 'Conscience, indeed, is a frightful Apparition itself, and I make no Question but it oftentimes haunts an oppressing Criminal into Restitution.' In this sense, conscience made 'Ghosts walk, and departed Souls appear, when the Souls themselves know nothing of it.'[45]

The appearance of ghostly visions continued to torment the conscience of murderers during the nineteenth century. The potency of the tradition in affecting patterns of behaviour is well illustrated by the case of Thomas Bedworth, who, in 1815, was executed for the murder of Elizabeth Beesmore. Between the years 1804 and 1813 Bedworth had served in the navy and on his release from service found that his wife had been in a bigamous relationship and had three children during his long absence. In response, Bedworth bigamously married his wife's sister Elizabeth Beesmore and removed to London. The relationship soon turned sour and Bedworth slit her throat in a fit of jealousy. He fled northwards, passing through Hampstead, and slept in a hayfield in southern Hertfordshire. It was here that, according to his own confession, he was first tormented by 'the deep groaning of one, as in great agony, whose voice was exceedingly like that of the deceased, and he passed the remainder of the night in much disquietude and alarm'.[46] The next night he slept in a field near St Albans, where he heard the voice of Beesmore exclaim, 'Oh Bedworth! Bedworth! What have you done?' The next day, frightened and disorientated, he returned to London and spent the night in a sheep-pen at Smithfield Market. It was here that 'the murdered woman appeared to him with a dreadful noise, and bitter exclamations'. The next day, as he was walking up Highgate Hill, Beesmore's ghost appeared to him once more: 'she walked with him, side by side, until they reached the other side of the hill, and then taking the hand of the miserable man, place it upon her severed throat, groaned and mourned deeply!'[47] Bedworth fled northwards for several days, but haunted to distraction he eventually gave himself up in Coventry.[48] At the other end of the century, in 1887, a poacher named David Pilmore also gave himself up to police after seeing the ghost of a gamekeeper named Edward Copley he had shot dead during an affray at Badsworth, near Pontefract. Pilmore escaped, though a fellow poacher died while they were on the run and Pilmore buried his body in a wood. Pilmore hid himself in the wood for some time and then enlisted with the Royal Berkshire Regiment under an assumed name. It was while he was on sentry duty at Reading Barracks one night that he thought he saw Copley's ghost walk and in a state of shock immediately confessed his crime to another sentry. He was later sentenced to death at Leeds Assizes, but was subsequently reprieved.[49] As the literary historian Terry Castle perceptively commented, in such cases 'Providence now works at one remove, through the medium of individually psychology, but the end result is the same.'[50]

DREAMS AND NIGHTMARES

Terrible dreams may have been one of the symptoms of melancholy, but everyone, melancholic, mad or otherwise, were and are subjected to nocturnal visions. Dreams continue to perplex and fascinate us today, but in previous centuries their interpretation and significance was integral to fundamental issues of religion and philosophy.[51] Sleep was seen as an altered state of being on the boundary between life and death, and as such, an appropriate time for God, angels and the spirits of the dead to communicate. The Bible, particularly the Old Testament, supported the notion that dreams could be portentous. The biographies of medieval and post-Reformation Catholic saints are full of dream encounters with God and the angels. Even though many Reformation clergymen argued that the age of miracles was over and men should not expect to receive divine communications, dream visions lay at the heart of early modern radical Protestant movements. Through lay prophets, while asleep or in trance states, God rained down messages warning of divine sanction, personal and collective punishment, and ultimately the advent of the Apocalypse. English Puritan writings are littered with divine and demonic dream encounters. Dream books, popular across Europe, further reinforced the notion that dreams could be interpreted as omens within a secular as well as a religious framework of belief. Dream visions were, then, woven into the mental fabric of faith and the conception of life and afterlife. Even Descartes drew prophetic significance from several disturbing dreams he had as a young man. In one he was terrified by the appearance of several phantoms. He took them to be a warning from God regarding his sinful life, and he resolved to reform his behaviour subsequently.[52]

Ghosts were not usually seen as divine messengers – that role was usually reserved for angels, though it could be said that the interventionist saints in Catholic faith were technically the spirits of the dead. Yet there was no explicit biblical reason why, with God's permission, ghosts could not invite themselves into one's metaphysical world. But considering they usually appeared while people were conscious, there seemed little obvious reason why they should want to do so. Thomas Tryon believed he had an answer to this conundrum. 'Men in Dreams are nearer unto the condition of departed Souls than when awake;' he observed, 'and therefore they can with ease, and great familiarity discourse and reveal their minds unto them.' The reason why they could do so with greater ease was because it was very difficult for souls to garb themselves in aerial bodies, and the forces required to do so could only be generated when affection for the living and the urgency to communicate were 'wonderful strong and powerful'. For those spirits of the dead who had no murder to reveal or urgent information to impart, but merely wanted to maintain some affectionate relationship with their mortal loved ones, dreams provided a less arduous and gentler vehicle in which to manifest themselves in visible form.[53] The danger with such an interpretation of dream spirit communication was in assuming that what one saw or heard was a benign angel or the spirit of the dead when in fact it was the Devil himself. Sleep was also a state in which people's moral defences were at their weakest and the mind most vulnerable to nocturnal diabolic interference and deception. But for what purpose would the Devil want to mimic sympathetic ghostly visitations? This was certainly on Thomas Nashe's mind when he pondered, 'why in the likeness of one's father or mother, or kinsfolks, he oftentimes presents himself unto us'. He surmised that the only reason was that 'in those shapes which he supposeth most familiar unto us, and that we are inclined to with a natural kind of love, we will sooner harken to him than otherwise'.[54]

Tryon was writing at a time when, as we have seen, expressing ghost belief in some intellectual circles was akin to carrying a sign stating 'Down with Atheists and Deists'. Yet there was also increasing concern about the growth and influence of Enthusiastic, Nonconformist sects. They were accused of drawing upon and promoting dubious supernatural inspiration at a time when Anglican theology was slowly, painfully assuming a rationalist position. Tryon, for instance, was a former Baptist, who broke from the denomination after being enthused by the spiritualist, revelatory writings of the mystic Jakob Boehme. Partly because of the strong association of dream visions with the providential preaching of the likes of the Methodists and Moravians, during the early eighteenth century dream encounters with spiritual beings came to be pathologised by the medical fraternity.[55] Dreams were abnormal – even dangerous; a sign of mental disorder rather than divine inspiration.

The rationalisation of the dream experience was, in fact, as old as history. The early church fathers, such as Pope Gregory the Great (c. 540–604), cautioned against mistaking dreams brought about by bodily imbalance or an empty stomach for divine revelation.[56] So Thomas Nashe (1567–1601) was saying nothing controversial when he dismissed dreams as the 'bubbling scum or froth of the fancy', nothing more than 'the echo of our conceits in the day'.[57] Neither was Hobbes expressing anything particularly radical when he stated that the 'opinion that rude people have of fairies, ghosts and goblins' was born of their ignorant inability 'to distinguish dreams, and other strong fancies, from vision and sense'.[58] Natural disturbances of the stomach, mind and blood were also used to explain what people dreamed as well as why they dreamed. Hobbes suggested, for instance, that 'Cold doth in the same manner generate Feare in those that sleep, and causeth them to dream of Ghosts, and to have Phantasmes of horrour and danger.'[59] But to undermine completely the religious foundation of dream spirit communication required a fundamental rethink of the relationship between soul and body. To this end John Locke used dreams as part of his logical deconstruction of the principle that the soul was a sentient entity independent from the body. If that was the case, he enquired, why were dreams, 'for the most part, so frivolous and irrational'? Dreams, he suggested, were 'all made up of the waking Man's Ideas, though, for the most part, oddly put together'. If the soul was capable of acting independently while the body was at rest, why did it generate such nonsensical and incoherent thoughts?[60] To dream of ghosts was natural but to think one was in the presence of ghosts during sleep could only be rationalised in terms of mental disorder. This could be just a temporary condition engendered by sleep or it could be symptomatic of insanity.

A nightmare is now a synonym for a 'bad dream', but up until the last century it was used to describe a specific type of sleep disturbance involving paralysis, the sensation of a heavy weight on the chest, and vivid aural and visual hallucinations of a humanoid or animal presence. In his successful book on the *Philosophy of Sleep*, first published in 1830, the physician Robert Macnish described how he suffered from the condition: 'I have experienced the affection stealing upon me while in perfect possession of my faculties, and have undergone the greatest tortures, being haunted by spectres, hags, and every sort of phantom.'[61] The experience is known as sleep paralysis in modern medical terminology, and has been the subject of considerable international research in recent years.[62] This has shown that the phenomenon is triggered by the disturbance of rapid eye movement (REM) sleep episodes, and various estimates suggest that up to 20 per cent of the population may experience it at least once in their lives. Medical interest in the nightmare actually dates back to the ancient Greeks. The physician Galen (c. 129–216 AD), whose work dominated medical thought and understanding until the seventeenth century, provided a natural cause for this frightening experience, which in Greek was known as the *ephialtes*. But until the early twentieth century in popular culture the nightmare experience was also attributed to supernatural forces. Indeed, the term 'nightmare' derives from the ancient belief in the *mara*, a supernatural being that lay on people and suffocated them at night, just like the *incubus* of Roman mythology. People across Europe, while commonly aware of its natural causation, continued to explain it in terms of assaults by the Devil, witches, fairy-beings, vampires and ghosts. Today some reports of nocturnal alien visitations can be put down to the same experience.

In England, up until the twentieth century, witchcraft was the most common supernatural explanation for the experience. Witches were thought either to pay nocturnal visits themselves or to send evil spirits to oppress people in their sleep. Edmund Gardiner, in his *Phisicall and Approved Medicines* (1611) talked of 'this dreadfull griefe (which some being much deceived, thinking that it must onely proceede of witchcraft)'.[63] Because of the stereotypical image of the ugly old witch, the nightmare was described as 'hag-riding' in some parts of the country. In the area of Pudsey, Yorkshire, the experience was also called the 'bitch dowter'. As Joseph Lawson explained, sufferers 'saw a woman they knew well, as fair as every they saw anyone in their life, standing over them with a dagger or "whittle" (carving knife), threatening to murder them, whilst they could not stir hand or foot'.[64] As we have seen, molesting ghosts were uncommon, with violent behaviour usually being expressed through the throwing of objects and knockings. But as a modern comprehensive study of such supernatural assault traditions noted, the features of the nightmare were and are 'easily assimilated to accounts of haunting'.[65] Thomas Tryon observed regarding the nightmare that 'the Vulgar, when they are thus affected, conceit it some external thing comes and lies upon them, which they fancy to be some Ghost, or Hob-Goblin'.[66] This would seem to have been partly the case with Sara Rodes of Bolling, Yorkshire. In March 1649/50 she was plagued with the apparitions of local women both living and dead. Her mother deposed that one night she, Sara and her child lay in bed together, and 'after theire first sleepe' she awoke to find Sara quaking with fear. 'Mother,' she explained, 'Sikes wife [a suspected witch] came in att a hole att the bedd feete, and upon the bedd, and tooke me by the throate, and wold have put her fingers in my mowth, and wold needes choake me.' She said she was unable to speak because Sikes held her throat and pinned her down.[67]

It is possible that as popular fear of witches began to recede during the nineteenth century, ghosts may have become a more frequent explanation for sleep paralysis.[68] It would seem to have been an aspect of the experiential phenomena in the Sampford Ghost case, even if the haunting was undoubtedly a fraud. In the Rev. Colton's affidavit he mentioned that the occupants' sleep was disturbed by violent blows on their bodies from an invisible hand, and 'by a suffocating and almost inexpressible weight'.[69] It was certainly central to the haunting, in 1851, of the house of a gardener named John Clark and his family, of Weston-super-Mare, Somerset. One Sunday night in early June they and two lodgers heard strange noises like the rattling of chairs and tables. After this disturbing event all except Clark went back to sleep. As Clark recalled:

> he was wide awake, and heard footsteps coming up the stairs, and presently a man entered the room, and coming up to the bedside, placed his hands on Clark's face, drew down his arms, and grasped him very tight by his two hands; he held him in this situation for a short period, when the hands of the nocturnal visitor appeared to get gradually smaller, till they became as small as a young child's, when his hold relaxed, and the apparition disappeared ... it appeared to be a man about five feet six inches in height, with very black curly hair, and rather stout; that when he was holding him he placed his face very near his, and that he felt his breath very hot, as were also his hands. Clark says he tried to speak and move, but had no power to do either, but immediately his visitor left he jumped up in bed and gave an alarm.

Clark went to work the next morning, but found it difficult to get over the terror of his ghostly assault and fell seriously ill. A man named Tripp, who said he had lived in the house three years before, told Clark he too had seen the apparition nearly a dozen times, which was always heralded by the rattling of chairs and tables.[70]

Sleep paralysis could also explain the nocturnal torment of a man named Ingerson of Ramsey, Cambridgeshire, as reported in the *Cambridge Chronicle* in March 1844. This was almost certainly the tailor Jonathan Ingerson recorded in the 1851 census, and he would have been aged 36 at the time. Ingerson and his wife went to bed early one night and he woke up around twelve o'clock and heard the bedroom door open and shut and saw a women dressed in white enter. He was seized by the ghost, and, as he said, was 'nearly dragged out of bed'. Unable to budge the 'inanimate Ingerson', the ghostly woman then left angrily slamming the door shut on its way out. Nevertheless it returned again around four o'clock and attempted the same manoeuvre. The following night Ingerson asked a local Primitive Methodist preacher named Poole to sleep in their bedroom to ward of the tormenting ghost, which proved effective. The *Cambridge Chronicle* concluded, 'Such is the true version of this marvellous tale, a great portion of the inhabitants entirely believing it, shuddering with dread at the awful visitations experienced by Ingerson.'[71]

Following Galen's opinions on the subject, the early modern educated consensus was that the nightmare was merely the result of, variously, poor blood circulation, undigested vapours from the stomach oppressing the brain, or thick phlegm settling around the heart. Even James I dismissed supernatural causation. Still, the defence of the spirit world put up by the likes of Glanvill during the second half of the seventeenth century, and the related sensitivities regarding accusations of atheism meant that there remained some reluctance to completely dismiss the supernatural. One of the writers for the coffeehouse journal the *Athenean Mercury*, probably the Rev. Samuel Wesley, asserted that witches sometimes caused the nightmare. Even the highly respected physician Thomas Willis (1621–1675), a pioneering author on the brain and nervous system, and critic of the concept of possession, did not absolutely discount spirit involvement. 'The common people superstitiously believe, that this passion is indeed caused by the Devil, and that the evil spirits lying on them, procures that weight and oppression upon their heart', he observed. 'Though indeed we do grant, such a thing may be, but we suppose that this symptom proceeds oftenest from mere natural causes.'[72] By the early eighteenth century, though, popular educators identified the beliefs surrounding the nightmare experience as an unwelcome relic of 'superstition' perpetuating the pernicious belief in witches, spirits and ghosts. 'How many mistake the stagnation of their own Blood for being Hag-ridden?' complained Thomas Trenchard.[73] If the common people could be made to understand that nightmares were entirely natural and were given practical, natural cures to prevent attacks, then one more pillar holding up the 'temple of superstition' would be undermined. To this end, most of the numerous popular medical manuals produced during the eighteenth century had a section on the 'Incubus or Nightmare'. Some followed the advice of the influential physician Nicholas Culpeper (1616–1654), recommending as a good cure peony seeds taken just before bedtime and in the morning.[74] For regular sufferers the *Domestic Physician* suggested a combination of gentle purges, bleeding of the feet and the ingestion of powders of nitre and cinnabar. If that did not work one could always try Philip Woodman's disgusting concoction consisting of pigeon and peacock dung mixed with salt of amber. If the reader could not stomach that, then he also suggested the following: 'Take the Head of a dry'd Toad, and of a Swallow, and one Ounce of Male Peony Roots, cut into very small bits, put them all into a Black Silk Bag, and let it be hung about the Parties Neck.'[75] Preventative medicine was best, of course, and so the manuals warned sufferers not to indulge in heavy suppers or too much drink before bedtime, and not to sleep on their backs, all of which are recommended for sufferers today. William Buchan's highly successful and much reprinted *Domestic Medicine* further advised that 'deep thought, anxiety, or any thing that oppresses the mind, ought to be avoided'.[76] With this warning in mind we turn to the horrors of the conscious state.

HALLUCINATION

With the rise of psychiatry during the late eighteenth and early nineteenth centuries, and the development of more sophisticated categories of insanity, the medical fraternity paid more serious attention to people's claims to have seen visions of the dead. Such hallucinations were no longer easily dismissed as merely the products of dreams and religious enthusiasm, or ascribed to the now outmoded notion of melancholy. The medical fraternity began to move beyond explaining the symptoms and physical causes of apparitions. They increasingly sought to explore *why* the mind created such internal visions and to consider *what* people thought they saw. In the 1830s the physician and writer Robert Macnish, who had experienced his own fair share of visions, wondered,

> why should a ghost be dressed in red rather than blue, and why should it smile rather than grin? These are minutiae beyond the reach of investigation, a least in the present state of our knowledge.[77]

Hallucinations and dream experiences were normalised. It was recognised that the perfectly sane could experience visual and aural hallucinations, that disorders of perception were not necessarily disorders of the mind. Consciousness could be deceptive. The likes of the poet Coleridge and the novelist Walter Scott could talk freely of the apparitions they had seen without fear of being considered mad. Coleridge, who had an active interest in scientific discovery, when once asked if he believed in ghosts, replied, 'No, Madam; I have seen too many myself.'[78]

In England, the physician John Ferriar (1761–1815) was at the forefront of this movement towards medical normalisation. Informed by his work as physician at the 'lunatic' hospital attached to the Manchester Infirmary, Ferriar published *An Essay Towards a Theory of Apparitions* in 1813. He discussed how 'spectral delusions' were 'frequently experienced by healthy person' when strong impressions of the past stimulated the visual nerves. Other studies followed that repeated or developed Ferriar's views, most notably Samuel Hibbert's *Sketches of the Philosophy of Apparitions* (1824), in which he suggested that 'The objects of mental contemplation, may be seen as distinctly as external objects.'[79] These set the foundations for later studies, such as James Sully's psychological study of illusions, in which he discussed the 'Hallucinations of Normal Life'. As most ghosts were seen at night, Sully suggested that these 'visions' were the 'debris of dreams' lingering briefly during the first moment of waking consciousness. He concluded with satisfaction that this explained 'the genesis of ghosts, and of the reputation of haunted houses'.[80]

During the same period that early psychiatry was redefining the meaning of apparitions, dual advances were also being made in the science of optics and the physiology of the eye. These too were enthusiastically employed to explain away ghosts. While unconscious visions could be attributed purely to the workings of the mind, conscious, daytime apparitions demanded a consideration of the retina. The scientific investigator and populariser David Brewster (1781–1868) was particularly confident that the eye was the key to unlocking the phenomenon of ghosts, calling it 'the principal seat of the supernatural'.[81] In his *Letters on Natural Magic* (1832), Brewster brought together all the natural explanations that science could muster to explain away apparitions, with discourses on magic lanterns, the manipulation of mirrors, reflections and ventriloquism. More to the point, 'Letter III' included a lengthy account of the various aural and visual hallucinations of 'Mrs A', among them the vision of her deceased mother-in-law. There then followed an explanation of how such apparitions were caused by the projection of retinal images. According to Brewster, the 'mind's eye' was the 'body's eye', and the retina was the 'tablet' on which all visual impressions were created. The eye was an organ of ideas as well as the brain. So, ghosts were first and foremost physiological rather then mental creations. The idea that the eye could project retinal images transmitted by the brain was not founded on the strongest of medical foundations, even by the standards of knowledge on nerve function at the time.[82] What of the blind who were subjected to spectral illusions? Brewster admitted that 'it is not probable that we shall ever be able to understand the actual manner in which a person of sound mind beholds spectral apparitions in the broad light of day'.

Whatever the explanation, physiological or psychological, there still had to be some physical stimulation to trigger hallucinations of ghosts in the sane. There was no reason to discard the old medical explanations for temporary mental disorder, such as drink, drugs, intense ideas inspired by religion or literature, digestive or circulatory problems, and feverish illnesses. In the early nineteenth century John Alderson, senior physician at the Hull General Infirmary, set out to

> prove, that the belief in apparitions, ghosts, and spectres, is not only well founded, but these appearances are perfectly natural, arising from secondary physical causes, and depending on circumstances to which all nations, all mankind, are equally liable.[83]

To this end, he recounted a series of case studies from his years in medical practice, from which he argued that people experienced a variety of hallucinatory experiences that were similar to but not symptomatic of insanity, delirium, somnambulism or irrationality. There was the case of a man who had, on returning from America, suffered from severe headaches and a swollen throat, who began to experience vivid dreams. 'He had been hitherto, he said, an unbeliever in ghosts, but had certainly been tormented by spectres during the night when perfectly awake. He felt himself sane.'[84] Alderson agreed. Another patient suffering from what he called a 'nervous complaint', and who experienced ghostly visitations, was reluctant to admit to his visions for fear of being considered foolish or mad. When his wife left the room he unwillingly agreed when Alderson 'told him I knew he imagined he saw people in his room whom he did not wish to see, and others whom he knew to be dead'.[85]

However, the normalisation of ghost hallucination presented several conceptual and diagnostic problems. How did one know, for example, if conscious visions of the dead were products of an overactive but healthy mind, or symptomatic of incipient mental illness? In other words, what distinguished an unhealthy from a healthy apparition? It was clear that the authoress Catherine Crowe was suffering a bout of mental illness in February 1854 after being found naked, saying that spirits had told her she was invisible.[86] The conviction of being persecuted by ghosts certainly indicated an abnormal mental state. Other signs could also be found in the physical state of the dead as visualised in hallucinations. Seeing decomposing corpses was not normal. Take, for example, the 38-year-old woman admitted to Bethlem Asylum in 1796. She suffered from a persecution complex and delusions. She frequently saw at her bedside the ghost of a young man of whom she was fond and who had died some years before. He did not appear in his living state, though, but 'in a state of putrefaction, which left an abominable stench in her room'.[87] In another case a lawyer of 'good education and literary habits' had, during a severe chest infection in 1823, reported seeing on several occasions the vision of a young lady he knew, who had died two years before. He understood the apparition to be no more than a hallucination, and found the experience pleasing. Several years later, and now fully recovered, 'some circumstances occurred which produced in him great mental excitement'. Subsequently the apparition returned, but this time it was profoundly disturbing; her body assumed the form of a putrefied corpse he had seen dissected several years previously. He was plagued by the hallucination both day and night, and even when in company.[88]

For some educated commentators the move to normalise ghost hallucinations was a step too far. Psychiatrists or 'mad doctors' as they were derogatorily called, were widely criticised for blurring the boundaries between the objective and the subjective, between reason and madness. Concepts such as moral insanity – temporary episodes of madness in normal people triggered by external factors such as stress or drink – were widely condemned. It was becoming impossible to know who was mad and who was not. Society could not function if such uncertainties were to be accepted. Lines had to be drawn, and ghosts were used as markers. In 1848, for example, the writer Charles Ollier stated:

It may be laid down as a general maxim, that any one who thinks he has seen a ghost, may take the vision as a symptom that his bodily health is deranged … To see a ghost, is, *ipso facto*, to be a subject for the physician.[89]

It was in the courts and newspapers that reported on criminal trials though, that psychiatric concepts of hallucination were most publicly contested. Expressions of belief in witchcraft, magic and ghosts by an educated person were sometimes cited as evidence of insanity in murder trials and probate disputes.[90] In 1846, for instance, the will of William Thornhill was contested at the Derby assizes. It was alleged that Thornhill was a 'monomaniac'; in other words, someone suffering from an insanity characterised by a fixed delusion and obsessive preoccupation. In Thornhill's case this was exhibited by his views on supernatural agency. Devils, ghosts and angels were a favourite topic of conversation, and, as one witness testified, Thornhill believed 'that a man was a compound of spirit and body, and when the body dropped to the ground the spirit went somewhere, and he thought that sometimes the spirit assumed a form which became visible to the human eye'. He told another witness 'that the spirits of the departed could reassume the human form, but did so only upon extraordinary occasions'. When asked once if he had ever seen a 'bogle', he said no.[91] In 1890 the second husband of Elizabeth Webb, the widowed heiress to a large dairying business, contested her will on the grounds that she was delusional. As part of the evidence it was stated that she had once claimed she had been visited by the ghost of her first husband, and also that a fair-haired lady and her son appeared to her in a looking glass. As she experienced these 'delusions' some time after having made out her will, the jury found for the defendants.[92] Such attempts to use ghosts as the legal basis for claims of insanity rarely worked. Ghosts were too culturally pervasive to compartmentalise in medical terms and ultimately too widely believed in to pathologise. The surgeon Samuel Barnes testified, during a trial at the Exeter Assizes in March 1834, 'a belief of having seen apparitions is a proof of great weakness of mind, but not a proof of derangement; it arranges from weakness of intellect'.[93] Even that definition, a cautious conservative position for the time, would become redundant with the influence of spiritualism.

MAGICIANS AND 'BELLY SPEAKERS'

As David Brewster had shown in his *Letters on Natural Magic*, the mind could be manipulated not only by natural phenomena or internal impressions but also by deliberate manipulation of the external environment. There was nothing new in this observation though. Back in the late sixteenth century the witchcraft sceptic Reginald Scot had written a disquisition on the arts of legerdemain, illusion and trickery in order to undermine the belief in magic and spirit conjuration. In the following century the physician Thomas Ady did likewise. Furthermore, as we shall see in the chapter on 'ghost makers', early modern scientists also set out to mimic supposedly supernatural phenomena by the construction and use of automata and optical effects. In the age of the witch trials and capital laws against the practice of demonic magic there also existed, then, a tradition of practical and scientific debunking through the explanation and demonstration of supposedly miraculous phenomena. But it was only in the eighteenth century that stage magic and illusion was concertedly used in the service of popular enlightenment. By then the concept of witchcraft and diabolic intervention was intellectually on the wane. There was little risk of illusionists falling under authoritarian suspicion of the black arts, and therefore there was a greater freedom to practise what was often described as natural magic. The aim was not to deceive but to instruct and to expose the fallacy of 'superstition'. By the late eighteenth century most stage magicians, in both their acts, advertisements and publications, conscientiously espoused the Enlightenment cause. Philip Breslaw hoped, for instance, that his book of magic tricks, *Breslaw's Last Legacy: Or, the Magical Companion* (1784), would 'wipe many ill-grounded notions which ignorant people have imbibed'.[94] When the natural philosopher Joseph Priestley attempted a sensitive debunking of the Wesleys' supernatural explanations for the haunting of their Epworth home, he referred to Breslaw's powers of legerdemain. He suggested that it was understandable that those who saw his act and had no knowledge of his tricks 'would tell the story in such a manner as to imply a real miracle', but further explanation of his methods would show how mysterious phenomena could be 'produced in a natural way'.[95] Many stage magicians adopted the title 'Professor' to denote their role as educators and demonstrators of the rule of reason. Some described their acts as performances of 'experimental philosophy' or 'Mathematical Operations' rather than illusions or tricks.[96] Typical of the period was a show put on by John Mexville at the Lyceum in the Strand in May 1789, which was called 'Le Melange Amusant; Or, Undeceiving Exhibition'. This consisted of demonstrations of 'the modes of deceiving practised by Jugglers, Slight of Hand Men,

Fortune Tellers, and Natural Magicians', with the aim of preventing the public 'being dupes to sharpers and gamblers'.[97]

The changing status and rationale of stage magic and its role in debunking popular belief is well illustrated by the history of ventriloquism. Just as the eye could be deceived, so could the ear, and so the art of ventriloquism or 'belly speaking' had long been used to explain away spirits' communications.[98] Back in the late sixteenth century Reginald Scot had cited it as an explanation for the Witch of Endor's apparent success in making the spirit of the prophet Samuel speak. During the Cock Lane affair there was a strong suspicion amongst some that Elizabeth Parsons had used ventriloquism to generate the scratching and knocking noises through which the ghost supposedly communicated.[99] Yet in early modern England there was still considerable ambivalence at the time about the source of the ventriloquists' gift. Diabolic or spirit possession of the living was, after all, a significant component of numerous witchcraft accusations. One mid-seventeenth-century glossary hedged its bets and defined 'ventriloquist' in both a natural and supernatural sense as 'one that has an evil spirit speaking in his belly, or one that by use and practice can speake as it were out of his belly, not moving his lips'.[100] To underline the power of ventriloquism to generate a sense of spiritual presence we can turn to the fate of the merchant, concert promoter, bibliophile and occultist Thomas Britton (1644–1714). He apparently died after a friend, playing upon his belief in the spirit world, paid a ventriloquist to mimic the voice of God commanding him to get down on his knees and say the Lord's Prayer. Having obeyed the command he went home, took to his bed and died from the shock of the experience a few days later.[101]

A key text in promoting the rational force of ventriloquism was Jean-Baptiste de la Chapelle's large treatise Le Ventriloque, ou L'Engastrimythe, published in London and Paris in 1772, and subsequently translated into Dutch, Italian and Russian. La Chapelle explained away a large range of religious and magical aural phenomena from the Witch of Endor through to his own times, and highlighted the techniques and activities of ventriloquist hoaxers and charlatans and the folly of their dupes. La Chapelle recounted with particular pleasure the numerous tricks played by a consummate French ventriloquist, Monsieur Saint-Gille, including the time he mimicked the ghost of a dead monk. Sheltering in a monastery one day, during a thunderstorm, Saint-Gille found the brothers mourning the death of one of their order. While being shown his tomb, Saint-Gille threw his voice to make it sound as if the man's spirit was speaking from somewhere above them. The disembodied voice complained of the conditions in purgatory and reproached the friars for their lack of zeal in propelling his soul to Heaven. Chastened, the whole religious community was gathered to pray and say mass for his soul, with Saint-Gille amusing himself at their expense by providing a running commentary on their proceedings from the spirit of the dead man.[102] A similar prank was attributed to an English ventriloquist named Fitz-James, who made his name in Paris around 1800. While walking in a cemetery one day, he espied a family praying by a tomb. The mischievous ventriloquist threw his voice to make it seem as though the occupant of the tomb was speaking, thereby frightening the mourners out of their wits.[103]

There is only a little, anecdotal evidence regarding eighteenth-century professional ventriloquism in England, but it would seem that for much of the century practitioners of the art plied their trade at fairs, markets, race days and inns, pretty much as their counterparts had done in previous centuries. This was certainly the environment in which James Burne, or 'Shelford Tommy' as he was popularly known, performed, making quite a reputation for himself in and around Nottingham during the 1780s.[104] Towards the end of the century, however, it would seem that the ventriloquists gravitated towards the theatre stage. In July 1796, for instance, a notice in The Times announced the appearance of Thomas Askins at Sadler's Wells, describing him as the first 'possessor of that wonderful Power' to appear before a theatrical audience. He was back again in London for a long run in 1799.[105] His success in the capital made the one-legged Askins one of the most celebrated practitioners of the period. His real name was Thomas Haskey, from Walsall in Staffordshire. He lost his leg in the war with America, and on being discharged and given a pension he returned to Staffordshire, earning a little extra income from local gardeners by making holes with his wooden leg for planting potatoes. It was at this time that he first discovered his gift for ventriloquism and soon attracted a local reputation. There is no evidence as to how he came to the notice of London theatre managers, but he was so successful at Sadler's Wells that in 1796 he earned some £200.[106] The self-styled 'Rational Mystic' William Belcher met Askins just before his run at Sadler's Wells, and was told by the ventriloquist that his vocal skill was not of his own devising, claiming 'that the voice came a few years before of itself, and that it sometimes alarmed his wife in the night'. This led Belcher to describe Askins's ventriloqual voice as his 'familiar', for he knew 'not a more proper appellation'.[107]

Much of the ventriloquists' repertoire focused on showing the immobility of their mouths whilst singing, counting to 20 or the like. During Askins' performance of the latter feat a candle was held just in front of his lips for the benefit of the audience. Another favourite act, which allowed for more diversionary techniques to be employed, concerned the holding of a conversation with an imaginary person concealed some distance away, such as with a chimney sweep stuck up a chimney. Then there was the trick of making animals talk. One practitioner performed with a large dog whose jaw he would move with his hand to give the impression that it was speaking, while James Burne once frightened a servant girl by making a dead fish appear to say 'don't cut my head off' just as she was about to prepare it.[108] As to giving voice to inanimate objects, the ventriloquist's dummy, now a standard prop, only came into its own during the late eighteenth century, it would seem.[109] In England, amongst its earliest users was Burne, who had a wooden 'ill-shaped' doll that he kept in his pocket. Askins also employed a puppet, which he danced on his knee and held in his arms.[110]

To invest a puppet with the semblance of life was one thing, but to give the impression of communicating with the dead was another. As we have seen, it was an idle prank attributed to some ventriloquists, but it was another matter altogether to recreate such a trick in front of a formal audience. For obvious reasons no ventriloquist was going to use an actual cadaver as part of their act. Such a trick would have attracted immediate accusations of necromancy in the early modern period, while matters of taste kept such an idea suppressed in subsequent centuries, even in an era when public dissections were popular theatre. Still, one could easily create the impression of talking with the invisible spirits of the dead, as it was technically no different from creating conversations with chimney-bound sweeps. Around 1800, one celebrated conjuror told the Hull physician John Alderson that by burning a mix of antimony, sulphur and other chemicals in a confined room he could make a person 'fancy he saw spectres and apparitions; and that, by throwing his voice into a particular part of the room, he could make the person believe he was holding converse with spirits'.[111] As we shall see in the next chapter, coupling ventriloquism with magic lantern images also created a similar startling effect.

No ventriloquist was more determined in his pursuance of the Enlightenment mission that the Scottish magician John Rannie, who became the first and most celebrated ventriloquist in America.[112] Rannie began his first tour in Boston in 1801, while his younger brother James put on performances in New York City. In the spring of 1802 the brothers briefly joined forces before James decided to return to Britain. Over the next few years John built up his reputation touring up and down the eastern seaboard, even putting in a stint in the West Indies. Rannie advertised himself not just an entertainer but as a missionary of rationalism, whose aim was 'to remove the cobwebs of imposition from the eyes of ALL mankind' and 'to open the eyes of those who still foster an absurd belief in GHOSTS, WITCHES, CONJURATIONS, DEMONIACS, &c.'.[113] To that end the centrepiece of one of his acts was a demonstration of how the Witch of Endor used ventriloquism to fool Saul. In Boston, and no doubt elsewhere, this public debunking of a Bible ghost did not go down too well with some devout Protestants, and in his publicity material Rannie made much of the opposition he faced from benighted 'fanaticism'. His crusade received public support from the deistic journal *Prospect*, run by the blind polemicist Elihu Palmer.[114] Palmer had long waged a campaign against what he called 'supernatural theology'. In his book *Principles of Nature*, first published in New York in 1801, and later in several London editions, he remarked that 'the story of the witch of Endor is too contemptible for serious remark', and repeatedly mocked the belief in ghosts. Mankind was 'constantly insulted with a thousand incongruous and non-existent relations, such as ghosts, witches, and devils,' he said, 'which perpetually disturb the imagination, and draw the rational faculties into the vortex of fancy and fanaticism'.[115]

Another public advocate of both John Rannie's skills and his Enlightenment project was William Pinchbeck, author of the first exposition of stage magic printed in America, *The Expositor; Or, Many Mysteries Unravelled* (1805). In the same year he also published *Witchcraft or the Art of Fortune-Telling*, which was an exposé of the tricks of fortune-tellers and astrologers, whom he described as the deceivers of the 'weak and credulous'.[116] In *The Expositor* he laid out his aim to 'oppose the idea of supernatural agency in any production of man'. He announced:

> We may rationally conclude that superstition's baneful effects are these, – retarding the human capacity, operating dangerously on society, and destructive to the common interest of mankind.[117]

Pinchbeck, who described himself as a 'mechanic and a philosopher', was also a showman who had some success in 1798 touring the eastern states with a card-reading Learned Pig. Like the Rannies, he was a relatively recent immigrant from across the Atlantic. The Pinchbecks were a well-known family of eighteenth-century London inventors, clockmakers and automata makers. Christopher Pinchbeck (d. 1732) founded the business, setting up shop in Clerkenwell and then Fleet Street, while also displaying his wares at Bartholomew Fair in association with the famous juggler and conjuror Isaac Fawkes. He also did a successful sideline in gold trinkets made from his own alloy of copper and zinc, which was known as pinchbeck. Christopher's son, Edward, took over the shop while his other son, Christopher, set himself up in the same line of business and displayed mechanical wonders in a room above his shop. Christopher died in 1783 and his son-in-law, a tobacconist, ran the shop for a few years but auctioned off all the stock in 1788.[118]

During the 1820s and 1830s the debunking message was still being peddled by the illusionists. An advertisement for the celebrated English impressionist and ventriloquist William Love (1806–1867) was a classic of its kind. His entertainments, it was announced, were 'constructed with a view of creating an hour's amusement' but to

> the historical Student and Antiquarian, his productions cannot fail to prove a source of considerable interest and gratification, as they will satisfactorily elucidate the nature of the means which were resorted to in remote ages, to impose upon the superstitious multitudes.[119]

But the bold Enlightenment cause that had characterised the magician's *raison d'être* during the eighteenth and early nineteenth centuries had certainly become more discreet by the 1830s. A few decades later, however, stage magicians' re-engagement with the Enlightenment mission was reinvigorated by the rise of spiritualism.

From the 1860s onwards, spiritualist seances become more elaborate and more theatrical in their presentation. Mimicking the simple rappings or table-turning of early spiritualism was simple and dull fair for a paying audience. But as spiritualist performances become increasingly centred on spectacular physical as well as aural communication with the dead, the magicians could base whole shows on debunking the various forms of supposed spirit manifestation. There were apports, for example, which were objects that the spirits produced out of nowhere, such as the flowers and fruit that appeared at the seances of the celebrated medium Mrs Guppy. Slate-writing and musical spirits were easily reproduced by the magicians. In the 1870s the magicians were given further fuel by the vogue for physical materialisations of the dead. These were sometimes only disembodied hands seen and felt by the sitters, but some mediums were bold enough to introduce full materialisations, such as the spirit Lily called up by the medium Kate Cook. In fact as magic catalogues of the period show, mediums and magicians were borrowing from the same sources. For sale were such items as 'Luminous Materialist Ghosts and Forms', 'Rapping Hands' and 'etherialization' kits that enabled mediums and magicians 'to produce any number of spirit forms, in the perfect dark, which have the appearance of a fine, misty, luminous vapor'.[120]

Two London institutions in particular became centres for the public exposure of the mediums' tricks. The first to act as a base camp was the Royal Polytechnic Institute, founded at considerable expense by private investors in 1838 to promote the popular understanding of science and art.[121] Advertisements in the 1860s described it as 'the most liberal shilling's worth in London'.[122] To achieve its worthy aims the Institute's lecturers were also showmen, wrapping nuggets of scientific knowledge in visual and aural entertainment. Sometimes the science sold itself with lectures and displays on such cutting-edge wonders as electricity, photography, telephones and film. But the Institute's managers were constantly struggling to get the public through its doors, and so there was a heavy reliance on such entertainments as ventriloquial acts, magic lantern shows, dioramas, juggling and stage magic. The sensation caused by spiritualism provided an ideal vehicle for the popular scientific exposure of ghosts, spirits and mediums. During the mid 1870s the Polytechnic staged mock seances by its own 'Polytechnic Medium', which included a discourse on the

> conception of Ghosts and Spirits in the natural instinct of a non-material existence, various shapings of thought – Pre-Adamite Genii – Vampyres – Fetiches and Ghosts – The Churchyard Ghost – The modern materialised spirit.[123]

A decade before this, though, the Polytechnic lecturer 'Professor' James Matthews (d. 1880) was illustrating how spiritual materialisations could be faked in his magic shows. Throughout the 1860s and 1870s he divided his time working for the Polytechnic and Joseph Bland's Conjuring Repository in New Oxford Street, giving talks and demonstrations such as 'Conjuring Made Easy' and 'Illustrations of Modern Magic'.[124] In September 1864 Matthews went on a provincial tour with a show called 'Ancient and Modern Magic', and took with him the apparatus to stage a sensational new ghost illusion. As a surviving handbill announced: 'The Ghost! The Ghost!! The Ghost!!! See and Believe!!!'[125] The nature of the illusion and its cultural impact will be discussed in the next chapter, but suffice it to say for the moment that one of its inventors was Matthews's colleague, the chemist and illusionist John Henry Pepper (1821–1900).[126] In fact Pepper, who gave his name to the ghost illusion, was the most successful and well-known lecturer at the Polytechnic, and was its honorary director for two decades. Indeed, much of the Polytechnic's success during the 1860s was due to 'Pepper's Ghost'. In the spring of 1872 Pepper fell out with the management of the Polytechnic, however, and set up a 'Theatre of Popular Science and Entertainment' at the Egyptian Hall, as part of which he put on shows demonstrating that he could 'imitate any of the apparent miracles of spiritualism'. He nevertheless thought that there was 'something in it worthy of careful scientific investigation'.[127] Despite his high profile, Pepper's residence at the Egyptian Hall was a flop and he left Britain to tour the Unites States and Australia over the next decade.

During the late nineteenth century the Egyptian Hall in Piccadilly became the new centre for the ghost-busting magicians. Built in 1812 with its impressive facade based on an ancient Egyptian temple, it originally housed a museum of natural history. After a few years it became a general exhibition centre with its various lecture rooms and galleries rented out for painting exhibitions, concerts, and living exhibits such as Siamese twins and giants. In 1865 the ventriloquist and magician Colonel Stodare rented a room at the Hall and created quite a sensation presenting a recently developed illusion known as the Sphinx. There is no evidence that his act at the Hall contained any spirit debunking, and he died in 1866 aged only 35, but a few years before he had written a brief *Hand-book of Magic* in which he explained an illusion called 'palingenesy, or the art of reviving the dead', as well as how to 'make the image of a deceased person to appear'.[128] However, it was in 1873, a year after Pepper's show had failed there, that the Hall became the adopted home of spirit debunking, with the beginning of a long residency by the self-styled 'royal illusionists and anti-spiritualists' John Nevil Maskelyne and his partner George Alfred Cooke.[129] Their shows ran continuously until the demolition of the building in 1904, and consisted not only of straightforward magic displays but also anti-spiritualist farces such as 'Lady Daffodil Downy's Seance'.[130]

The early career of Maskelyne and Cooke was boosted, like others of the magical fraternity, by replicating the Davenports' famous spirit cabinet and exposing them as frauds. As young boys Ira and William Davenport lived in Rochester at the time the Fox sisters became big news. Several years later they began giving their own rather crude seances in darkened rooms. Around 1855, and still in their teens, they developed the idea of having themselves tied to chairs and shut in a wooden cabinet. Once the lights were turned down the usual inane spirit phenomena would then occur around the cabinet, such as objects being thrown around and tambourines being struck. The cabinet provided an idea cover for the boys to escape from the ropes with which they were tied, and slip discretely out of the box to perform the various spirit tricks before slipping their hands through the knotted ropes again. It was all very simple really, but the Davenports were amongst the first mediums to make the spirits perform rather than provide more sober communications through raps and knocks, while their youth and charm helped disarm audiences. After several years building up a reputation in America, the Davenports arrived in London in 1864 for an eventful though largely successful European tour. Their tricks were exposed several times, but as with other mediums, they still managed to pull in large audiences. Within weeks British magicians were putting on their own shows exposing the Davenport's techniques; advertisements for both nestling together in the London press. While the Davenports were giving their last London seance at the Hanover Square Rooms at the beginning of November, 'Professor' Redmond was putting on a show entitled 'The Brothers Davenport Challenged' at the London Pavilion Music Hall, Piccadilly. Meanwhile, not far away, at St James's Hall, the ubiquitous magician 'Professor' John Henry

Anderson, also known as the 'Wizard of the North', was holding his first public 'anti-spiritualistic seance'.[131]

The Polytechnic, the Egyptian Hall and their founding ethos – popular education through entertainment – were products of their era, and ill-suited to the cultural developments of the early twentieth century. In 1882 Quintin Hogg, a wealthy merchant and philanthropist, bought the Polytechnic, which was by then in poor financial state, and turned it into a successful but sober educational establishment with a strong religious emphasis.[132] In 1904 the Egyptian Hall, which had become popularly known as the 'Home of Mystery', was demolished, though Maskelyne continued his successful career performing elsewhere, teaming up for a while with the up-and-coming magician David Devant. The rise of the Music Hall helped to undermine 'scientific' entertainment; World War I understandably gave new impetus to the spiritualist movement, and between the world wars the populist newspapers and cinema helped to restore rather than undermine the presence of the supernatural.

* * *

Behind the attempts to explain ghost belief in terms of deception, delusion, hallucination and dreams lay the goal of vanquishing it. Ghosts were pernicious figments that had damaging social and personal consequences. Even the early psychiatrists, who stood up for the normality of ghost-*seeing* did not argue likewise for ghost-*belief*. During the twentieth century, however, belief once again achieved considerable intellectual currency. The social and cultural reasons for this will be examined at the end of this book, but this is the appropriate moment to mention the role of psychoanalysis in this process. In the writings on the subject by Freud and his adherents we can clearly see the influence of the various historical debates described in this chapter – melancholy, dream interpretation, nightmares, hallucination, and formative childhood experience. What the early-twentieth-century psychoanalysts, heavily influenced by anthro- pological studies, added to the debate was a clearer sense of the universality of ghosts' psychological function and the cultural reasons for belief in them. They also left aside the question of their reality. As Jung wrote, accounts of ghosts should be taken 'for what they are, *psychic facts*', and the analyst should not 'pooh-pooh them because they do no fit into our scheme of things'.[133]

Freud briefly considered the meaning of ghosts in his studies on dreams, taboos and bereavement, but he never gave concerted attention to the subject despite recognising their cultural and psychological significance.[134] In *Totem and Taboo* (1913), for instance, he suggested that ghost belief was generated by the repression of disturbing and conflicting feelings of hostility and affection towards the dead. One of Freud's pupils, Ernest Jones, developed the idea, arguing that dreams of the dead, along with nightmares, related to childhood parental conflict, in particular the expression of repressed death wishes and guilt over incestuous relations.[135] It was left to others, though, to explore the broader cultural and psychological significance of ghosts. Those studying the psychology of child-rearing in non-Western societies found Freudian conflict theory particularly insightful. In the 1950s John Whiting argued, from his study of the Kwoma of New Guinea, that a preoccupation with parental ghosts was linked with anxieties caused by the lengthy or frequent absence of parents. As another psychologist observed, 'It follows from this that in societies where someone is always around and prepared to gratify a child's need immediately, fear of ghosts ought to be low.'[136] One could update the point and consider the impact of parenting trends in modern England, where in many families both parents now work. Freudian psychoanalytical explanations for ghosts, and those developed by Jungians for that matter, may have had little direct influence on public understanding, but twentieth-century psychiatry, through its absorption by the creative mass media, did contribute to a growing sense of the reasonableness of believing in ghosts.

Part Three

Representation

Six

Imitating the Dead

As long as ghost-beliefs have been recorded, there have been instances of those who have attempted to simulate hauntings. The next chapter will examine the history of projection as a means of reproducing ghosts, but now I want to consider the ways in which and reasons why, over the centuries, people have dressed up as ghosts or mimicked the stereotypical activities of malevolent spirits. Even the most devout believers in ghosts over the centuries recognised that many hauntings were frauds. Puzzled by the uniformity of the manifestations adopted by several famous hoaxers, such as the Cock Lane culprits, Andrew Lang pondered, 'Do impostors and credulous persons deliberately "get up" the subject in rare old books? Is there a method of imposture handed down by one generation of bad little girls to another?'[1] It is a provoking question, but also an easy one to answer. The manifestation and activities of ghosts were so integral to the oral and literary culture of the last 500 years that there was no need to research and revise how ghosts appeared and what they did. It was their familiarity that made hoaxes successful. Ghost hoaxers, whether running about the streets, hovering over graveyards or disturbing bedrooms, were performing for an audience. That was the whole point. So, as we shall see in a later chapter, it was necessary to perform according to the audiences' expectations, perceptions and understanding of ghosts. Otherwise a hoax, just like a play, would fail.

REFORMATION PROPAGANDA

In the Reformation propaganda war no opportunity was spared to heap humiliation and calumnies on the Catholic clergy. Anti-Catholic popular literature was full of images of monks defecating demons, indulging in gluttony and sexual depravity. If the propagandists were to be believed, then after wallowing in vice, monks and priests liked nothing better for recreation and personal enrichment than mimicking the spirits of the dead. They were

165

portrayed as masters of ghost deception, following in the footsteps of the duplicitous pagan priests of the ancient world. The evangelical Protestant John Bale (1495–1563), a former Carmelite friar, denounced his erstwhile brethren for their tricks and necromancy in making the dead supposedly speak. Reginald Scot, in demolishing the reality of the raising of Samuel, said he 'could cite a hundred papistical and cozening practises, as difficult as this and as cleanly handled'. Samuel Harsnett, a future Archbishop of York, in a searing attack on 'Popish Impostures', execrated the Catholic priesthood who 'worke their wonders, making Images to speake, vaults to sound, trunks to carry tales, Churchyards to swarme, houses to rush, rumble, and clatter with chaynes, high-waies, old graves, pittes, and woods ends to be haunted'. As to the exact nature of these supposed deceits, Sir John Melton described how 'Scab-shin Fryers' placed accomplices in specially made vaults under the tombs of rich men so that when members of the family came to pray for the souls of the deceased, 'they should heare a dreadfull voice under the Sepulchre'. The ventriloquial voices of the dead would tell mourning families that they should give over their property to the local monastery to ease the passage of their souls to heaven. If an incident recounted by the humanist Catholic theologian Erasmus, and later printed by Lavater, is to be believed, the priesthood indeed possessed a genius for such deceptions He described how on Easter eve a priest placed candles on the backs of some crabs and let them scrabble around the graves in a churchyard to simulate the souls of those in purgatory hovering above their corpses.[2]

The clergyman John Gee (1595/96–1639) provided a lengthy account of the papist deception apparently perpetrated on one Mary Boucher of London around 1621. Mary was in the service of a recusant lady, who together with three Jesuits, planned to convert her to Catholicism and have her 'Nunnified'. One of the strategies they employed was to present Mary with the apparition of her godmother. To this end a 'gastly ghost, walking in a sheet knit upon the head, came unto her where shee lay in her bed'.[3] The pale and wan spirit touched Mary with 'a hand cold as earth or iron' and said 'shee was come from Purgatory, where she had long endured torture and torment'. She wanted to help Mary avoid the same fate by urging her to reject the Protestant faith. 'By all meanes see that you tell my children what you have seene, and how their Mother appeared unto you, and what counsel she hath given you.'[4] The apparition appeared one more time urging Mary to become a nun. When her mother got to hear of the stratagems being employed to convert her daughter she managed to rescue her from the snare of popery. Gee claimed to have visited Mary sometime later to verify the story. Whether Gee's account is to be trusted is another matter. He had good reason to be publishing anti-Catholic ghost stories. He himself was under suspicion of being in the service of Rome. He certainly mixed with Catholics in London and was present at a terrible disaster on 26 October 1623 when a building near the French embassy collapsed during Catholic evensong, killing nearly 100 people.[5] Following the publicity surrounding the event, Gee, who saw his escape as a 'spiritual deliverance', made amends for his apostasy by publishing a lengthy exposé of Catholic proselytising activities in England. By producing a second pamphlet focusing on the Boucher apparitions Gee had an eye on the popular appeal of the subject, seeing it as providing a good vehicle for spreading word of his renewed enthusiasm for Anglicanism.

Suspicions of Catholic machinations were even raised during the Cock Lane affair, with one pamphleteer remarking that he was 'sometimes almost tempted to suspect; that those constant Dabblers in puddle Waters, the JESUITS, may be at the Bottom of this Affair, as they were in that of the Boy of Bilston'.[6] But there is little clear and conclusive evidence that Catholic priests really were busy faking ghosts and other supernatural phenomena in early modern England. Reginald Scot referred briefly to two cases of priests having been caught simulating 'walking spirits' at Canterbury in 1573 and Rye in 1577.[7] Suspicions of Catholic activity were raised regarding a case of haunting in Minehead in 1637.[8] Otherwise there is not much to work on other than accusations and rumours. The Catholic clergy were certainly active in some parts of the country, such as Lancashire, practising and advertising exorcism as a propaganda exercise. The trial of the Samlesbury witches in 1612 revealed that the accusations of witchcraft made by a 14-year-old girl, Grace Sowerbuts, had apparently been inspired and shaped by the 'subtil practise and conspiracie of a Seminarie Priest' named Thomson in order to convert local people. It was 'a bloudy practice, fit for a Romanist', said the clergyman Richard Bernard a few years later.[9] The Boy of Bilson (Bilston), referred to above, was another such case exposed in 1620–21. The twelve-year-old William Perry, whose parents were Roman Catholics, exhibited all the classic signs of possession, vomiting pins and the like, and several recusant priests were requested to exorcise him. The Bishop of Lichfield and Coventry, Thomas Morton, caught the boy faking, and suspected the whole case was a propaganda ploy by priests in the region to promote Catholicism.[10] To what extent his suspicions were justified is difficult to gauge. All that can be said with certainty is that accusations of Catholic fakery and supernatural deception far outweighed any actual evidence of such practices. On this note, we shall move on to firmer evidential ground.

LOOKING THE PART

As we have already seen, ventriloquism and illusion could be used to simulate certain types of haunting, but these required either natural ability or acquired skills. For the average person the easiest and most successful way to fake a ghost was to don a white sheet. Reginald Scot remarked in 1584 that 'one knave in a white sheet hath cozened and abused many thousands that way'.[11] To show the venerable nature of the ruse let us begin with a story by that scathing critic of papal corruption, Erasmus. He had spent a year at Oxford in 1499 and then stayed at Cambridge University between 1509 and 1513, and it is possible that real events inspired him to set his story of a ghost hoax at a farm near London.[12] His colloquy, entitled 'The Exorcism: Or, The Apparition', tells of a local prankster named Pool who raises a rumour in the neighbourhood that a tormented soul haunts a local bridge, and can be heard emitting 'hideous Howlings'. He then suggests to a local village priest that, 'as he was a Holy, and a Learned Person, he would do his best toward Relieving of a poor Soul out of that terrible Affliction'. The priest attempts several exorcisms at the bridge, and each time Pool, with the help of some accomplices, stages a series of elaborate pantomimes to convince the priest he is in communication with not only the tormented ghost but also the Devil, who roars 'This Soul is mine, and you have no Power over it.' Pool gets his son-in-law to play the ghost. He 'wraps up himself in a Sheet, like a Corps, with a live Coal in a Shell that shew'd through the Linnen, as if something were a burning'.[13] The priest is thoroughly taken in by the hoax, and, turning the usual Protestant accusation of priestly deception on its head, Erasmus pokes fun at clerical credulity. That such an elaborate hoax on the clergy was not beyond the realms of possibility in the period is evident from a court case in 1605/06. It concerned the accusation of John Mountford, Rector of Radwinter, Essex, that the church clerk and others had tried to force him out of his incumbency. He said that by some 'devise or sleight', they

> did procure fearfull & uglie shapes & formes of evill spirittes or divilles sundrie tymes by day & night to haunt and walke about the church & churchyard visiblie to be seene, sometimes in the shape of a man, sometimes of a dogg, catt or such like.

Invisible blows also buffeted those who ventured into the church and churchyard. The jury found the defendant not guilty.[14]

Most hoaxes were neither so elaborate nor conspiratorial, and merely consisted of individuals prowling around in a white sheet emitting groans.

They were most commonly perpetrated in urban areas where the streets and churchyards, even at night, provided a large and captive audience. In 1761, residents around Westminster Abbey and St John's churchyard, Millbank, got up a subscription of five guineas as a reward for any person or persons that captured a ghost impersonator that was terrorising the neighbourhood and frightening the 'weak minded'. The servant of a local gentleman was duly caught wrapped in a white sheet with the corners hanging over his head.[15] One night in April 1804 a ghost was pursued through the streets around St Paul's churchyard, London, until it found itself cornered, rather fittingly, in a dead end. It turned out to be a man who had dressed in a white muslin robe and whitened his legs with chalk. He was brought before an alderman and it was considered that the man was mentally deranged. It is not clear whether this was a conclusion drawn from his general behaviour or because only an idiot would perform such a prank after the Hammersmith shooting a few months earlier.[16]

In October 1830 consternation was caused in Angel Street, Bedford, after a ghostly figure was seen peering into windows. The following week a local newspaper cleared up the spooky mystery:

> The other night a foolish fellow walked about New Town, covered with a white sheet, and a mask on. We would caution him against a repetition of such folly, or a punishment may await him that he little dreams of.[17]

This warning proved uncomfortably true for the ghost impersonator who terrified the village of Handsworth in December 1844. A posse of six men beat him so badly he required hospital treatment. Another prankster who tormented a village on the outskirts of Shrewsbury in February 1888 narrowly avoided a similar fate. Some 50 villagers armed with sticks caught him, and they only released him on the condition that he donated £5 to the Salop Infirmary.[18] Apprehending a ghost hoaxer was not always so easy in urban areas. For a couple of weeks in September 1885 the police in Derby were inundated with complaints about several young men dressed in white sheets roaming the streets at night frightening local women and children. When a soldier caught one of the hoaxers, an errand boy named Christopher Burrows, aged around 16, he threw off his sheet and brandished a pistol at his captor.[19]

To create a ghost scare one did not even need a sheet. Appearing in white clothing at night was sometimes sufficient to terrify people. The 'Camberwell Ghost' Joseph Munday, aged 43, was imprisoned in 1872 for loitering and making 'menaces and gestures'. He had frightened numerous people, particularly local children. One victim was a young girl named Eyre who described how she was walking along Cator Street, Peckham, when Munday 'darted out, threw open his coat, to display a white slop [smock], and threw up his arms and uttered some strange sounds'.[20] One night in May 1830, an unfeeling prankster, on seeing a woman named Marshall and her friends keeping vigil over the grave of her infant in St Philip's churchyard, Birmingham, stripped to his shirt, put on a white night cap and 'made a sudden dart to the spot where they were assembled'. The women fled in terror except for the mourning mother, who, determined to fend off a possible resurrectionist, seized hold of the ghost and called for the assistance of a watchman, who had him arrested.[21]

SPRING-HEELED JACK

A notorious and vicious ghost prankster, who plagued the outskirts of London in late 1837 and early 1838, generated the enduring legend of Spring-Heeled Jack thanks to copycats and his subsequent portrayal in popular sensational literature.[22] The affair began when reports circulated in London and outlying villages in Hertfordshire of a frightening figure dressed in a large cloak that revealed itself variously in the form of a ghost, a devil or a hairy beast. The apparition primarily targeted women and on several occasions apparently tore their dresses with claws. On 8 January the Lord Mayor made public the details of an anonymous letter he had received from a Peckham resident stating that several women from villages on the outskirts of London had been severely frightened, to the extent of becoming insane, after being assailed by the 'spectre'. 'This affair has now been going on for some time,' said the author, 'and, strange to say, the papers are still silent on the subject.' However, she (for the letter was presumed to have been written by a woman) intimated that the spectre was the prank of a man from the 'higher ranks of life' who made a wager that he would visit several villages near London in three different guises – that of a ghost, a bear and the Devil – in order to cause a sensation. The Mayor treated the letter with inappropriate light-heartedness and said that 'as the terrible vision had not entered the city, he could not take cognisance of its iniquities'.[23] However, following the publication of the letter and the Mayor's response in The Times and other newspapers, the Mayor received letters from other concerned residents detailing further outrages by the 'Peckham Ghost'. Thomas Lott, of Bow Lane, said that the scoundrel had been active in the neighbourhood of his Hornsea residence, 'where if I catch Mr. Ghost on any part of my premises, I shall administer that to his substantial part that if ever he reappears it shall be only his serial essence, or as a ghost in fact'. An inhabitant of Stockwell wrote to say that several people in Stockwell, Brixton, Camberwell and Vauxhall had been frightened into fits, some to death, and expressed the hope that the Mayor would 'not think lightly of this matter'. A Middlesex magistrate related how a former servant of his had recently informed him that the female population of Hammersmith feared to go out after dark for fear of being molested by the ghost or monster. He promised to enquire into the affair and apprehend the 'miscreants' who were 'undoubtedly working real mischief'. Another letter-writer expressed similar concerns regarding events in Lewisham, Blackheath and St John's Wood.[24] Despite such correspondence the Mayor continued to express scepticism about the severity of the effects on the female population, and was not inclined to launch a full-scale manhunt or ghost hunt.

By mid February the ghost had been given the name of 'Spring-Heeled Jack' by some and an urban legend was born. Rumours of further attacks circulated in and around London, though those who doubted the existence of the ghastly attacker had to revise their opinion when confronted with news of the terrifying assault on Jane Alsop, the 18-year-old daughter of a wealthy gentleman who lived in an isolated spot between the villages of Bow and Old Ford. At about a quarter to nine one night in mid February someone violently rang the bell, and when Jane opened the door she was confronted by a man in a large cloak. He identified himself as a policeman and said 'For God's sake, bring me a light, for we have caught Spring-heeled Jack.' When she gave him a candle he lit it and threw open his cloak, presenting 'a most hideous and frightful appearance'. He was dressed in some garb that Alsop described as resembling a white oilskin. He also wore some sort of helmet through which he 'vomited forth a quantity of blue and white flame from his mouth'. He grabbed her, clawing at her dress, neck and arms until she was pulled from his grasp by one of her sisters. Members of her family cried for help and the attacker ran off. The police launched an investigation and Mr Alsop offered a reward of ten guineas for the capture of the ghost impersonator.[25]

On the 22 February, PC Lea reported that, from what he had found out, the same person 'had been in the neighbourhood for nearly a month past, frightening men as well as women; and had, on one occasion, narrowly escaped apprehension'. Lea also believed that a number of young men were assuming ghostly guises in imitation.[26] By the beginning of March two men had been charged with the Alsop outrage: one was a master bricklayer named Payne and the other a carpenter named Milbank. Both of them were in the vicinity after having been shooting. Suspicion was focused most on Milbank who was wearing a white shooting jacket and a white hat that night. However, after two days of hearings at Lambeth Street police court, the presiding magistrate came to the conclusion that despite the fact that Milbank claimed to be so drunk that night that he could not remember anything, he was innocent and the charges were dropped. It would seem that no one was ever prosecuted for the Alsop assault.[27] A few weeks later, however, two crude imitators were arrested: a youth named Daniel Granville, who was caught in Kentish Town wearing a mask with blue glazed paper coming out of the mouth, and James Painter, who was fined for dressing up in a bearded mask and sheet and frightening people in Kilburn.[28] For a month or so the press continued to attribute strange sightings and assaults, which had little connection to the original attacks, to the now legendary Spring-Heeled Jack. On the 14 April, for example, the *Brighton Gazette* reported that 'he had found his way to the Sussex coast', a gardener in Brighton having seen a bear-like creature run along a wall topped with broken glass, which then jumped down and chased the frightened man before scaling the wall and escaping.[29]

SOUNDING THE PART

The decision on what hoax strategy to adopt depended on the environment in which the hoaxer wished to or had to operate, due to constraints of time or social and physical access. The white sheet technique was most appropriate for the rural outdoors and urban streets. It was more difficult to effect successfully indoors unless buildings were unoccupied. The white-sheet was usually only employed in occupied houses for criminal purposes. Otherwise the best strategy to create hauntings in confined spaces was to simulate auditory or noisy ghosts, which people did not necessarily expect to be accompanied by any visual apparitions. The spectral voice, for example, could be achieved by ventriloquism, but there were other simple tricks that could be employed. In the 1580s Pierre Le Loyer cited a French case where a long hollow reed or cane was secretly placed through a wall near the bed of a woman, and from another room her manservant spoke into it at night mimicking the voice of her dead husband. The same ruse was apparently used around 1603 to deceive a widowed gentlewoman of Cannington, Somerset, into giving her estate to a 'special friend' rather than her son. As a high court heard in 1605, the culprit used a ladder to climb up to her bedroom window one night. He wore a mask and a frightful wig and held a dark lantern in one hand. Seeing his victim was asleep he 'did putt the one end of the cane upon her pillow close to her eare, & puttinge the other end to his mouth did throw the said cane with a counterfeit voice'. He whispered that he was the Devil and would carry her off to hell if she did not do as he said.[30] The vocal haunting of the Hartt family home in Orford Hill, Norwich, in 1826, was rather less sophisticated. It was the work of a servant boy who gained surreptitious access to the attic from an unoccupied house next door. He scared the inmates by calling out in an ominous voice, 'Beware! Leave off your wicked life, Hartt!! Read your Bible.' After several nights the boy was obviously getting rather desperate in his hideaway, as the ghost was once heard moaning 'Bread and butter – ham, bread and butter – blow my guts, I am so hungry!' A thorough investigation by a Sheriff's officer led to his arrest. The Bury *Gazette* expressed its 'sincere hope the magistrate will make him suffer for his fun'.[31]

Basic poltergeist phenomena such as knocking and rapping on walls were fairly easy to orchestrate by a variety of subterfuges and with the help of accomplices. The cause of a haunting that shook a house in Somerset during the eighteenth century was revealed to be a large boy who broke into an abandoned adjoining property and jumped up and down on a large central beam that ran through both houses.[32] The confession of a twelve-year-old girl named Baker, the daughter of a working man, who in 1857 was sentenced to 14 days in Wandsworth gaol for criminal damage, revealed a simple technique for simulating the ghostly movement of objects. She tied a strand of her long hair round the article she wished to disturb and tugged on it, thereby making it appear as if it had been moved by an invisible hand.[33] As several cases discussed shortly will show, stone-throwing was a particularly satisfying and relatively easy manifestation to emulate. Lavater related the case of a novice friar whose faith in spirits was tested by his colleagues. They began by throwing stones into his chamber at night, before one of them entered draped in a white sheet.[34] In most instances stone-throwing led to rumours of a haunting, but it would seem that on some occasions, as with the white-sheet wearers, hoaxers were inspired by an existing ghost scare. Such would seem to be the case regarding an 'extraordinary outrage' in Pimlico in October 1823. For a couple of weeks the neighbourhood had been alarmed by reports that a ghost had been seen in nearby fields. Then the stones started to rain down on houses in Elizabeth Place, Queen Street, with nearly all the windows in several properties being smashed.[35] In many instances, particularly of the stone-throwing type, the culprit was never caught, thereby providing confirmation to some in the neighbourhood that the activities were, indeed, of a spiritual origin.

Sheet-wearing was a typically male form of ghost hoax mostly perpetrated by young men, while the simulation of obstreperous ghosts or poltergeist activity appealed more to young females. This gender distinction is in part explained by the social spaces in which young men and women were to be found. In rural villages and small towns in particular, it was socially unacceptable for young women to roam the streets and fields unaccompanied at night, and therefore it was more difficult for them to play the visual apparition without being detected. Young housebound women could more easily mimic domestic-centred poltergeist activity.

SERVANTS

With regard to the social status of hoaxers, servants had long been criticised not only for instilling ghost belief into the minds of their young charges, but also for plaguing their employers with ghostly phenomena. Writing 75 years after the haunting of the Wesley's Epworth home, Joseph Priestley believed that 'it was a trick of the servants, assisted by some of their neighbours'.[36] In a sermon attacking the popular belief in ghosts delivered in 1818, James Plumptre, vicar of Great Gransden, Huntingdonshire, blamed the fear of ghosts in part on 'frauds by wicked servants'.[37] Although these were unsubstantiated accusations, the historical record does indeed confirm that servants were more responsible for orchestrating hoaxes than any other occupational group. Young female servants predominated. In December 1825, for example, a servant girl named Anne Page was sentenced to pay £5 damages for smashing the windows of several new houses in Hanover Street, Newington. Many people in the neighbourhood had believed that a ghost was responsible for the stones, brickbats, lumps of coal and old shoes that were thrown at houses between eight and eleven o'clock at night. The local constable and several watchmen failed to find a spirit, but her employer Mr Grensell eventually caught Page in the act. He had been sitting at tea with friends one evening when a lump of coal was thrown through the window, breaking the pane. He ran downstairs and into the street where he was informed by a passer-by that the thrower had disappeared into the kitchen of his own house. Grensell found Page there in an agitated state. She admitted 'she was the person that had been mistaken for a ghost'. In court she remained silent and like a typical teenage 'affected sullenness'. Unable to pay the £5 she was committed to Brixton prison for a month.[38] In May 1878 a 14-year-old servant girl was prosecuted for a series of mysterious disturbances at the farm of John Shattock, of Goathurst, Somerset. Great alarm was caused in the village by the noisy haunting of Shattock's house. For two weeks loud knocking was heard at the front and back doors of the property, furniture and crockery were moved around, a pig trough was inexplicably found at the front door, and a straw rick was set on fire. Several policemen and villagers took turn to stand guard for several nights.[39] It was understandable that Shattock wished to get to the bottom of the troubles quickly as ten years earlier his thatched house and farm buildings had burned to the ground. Fortunately his property was insured, but no doubt suspicions would have arisen if history repeated itself.[40] The district superintendent of police was finally called in to investigate and concluded that the servant girl Ann Kidner, who had only been recently hired, was responsible. Kidner protested her innocence in court, and because no witnesses had actually seen her perform any of the acts of mischief she was discharged on the grounds of insufficient evidence. Prosecuting stone-throwers was similarly difficult. A servant girl named Maria Herbert, aged about 16, was eventually arrested for the 1823 Pimlico stone-throwing. The Marlborough Street magistrate who presided over the case had little doubt about her guilt, but because her uncle was adamant that she was innocent, and it was suspected that other children were involved, he had to discharge her.[41]

WHY?

There were numerous reasons for perpetrating a ghost hoax. Some were no more than pranks inspired by a sense of mischievous fun. Joseph Priestley suggested that the servants he accused of orchestrating the Epworth phenomena meant nothing 'by it, besides puzzling the family and amusing themselves'.[42] This was, perhaps, the mild-mannered, wishful thinking of a middle-class employer of servants. In August 1886 a rare female sheet-wearer, who flitted in and around Park Street, Yeovil, at midnight, causing much panic, said she did it merely to 'frighten the children'.[43] There were deeper motives behind some pranks. It would appear that the hoaxer behind the Hammersmith ghost scare of January 1804 acted out of petty revenge. Shortly after the shooting of Thomas Milward, a shoemaker named Graham was brought before the Hammersmith magistrates' office and admitted that he was the original ghost. He told the sitting magistrate, Mr Hill, how he had been annoyed by his apprentices frightening his young children with ghost stories, and in order to get his own back he wrapped himself in a blanket one night and appeared before them as they passed homewards. And so the ghost panic was born.[44] One of the more unusual motives, if the hoaxers were to be believed, was to enlighten the 'superstitious'. In August 1815 the 16-year-old James Cainess, the son of 'a respectable man', told a Holborn magistrate that he had been employed to imitate a ghost 'with a view to undeceive, than to impose upon the credulous multitude'. His mysterious employer had, he said, paid him liberally to investigate a ghost that had supposedly been sighted in St Andrew's churchyard, Holborn, causing hundreds of the 'lower orders' to gather nightly. Cainess found that the ghost was nothing more than the light of the moon shining unusually brightly upon a tombstone. His employer then asked him to 'keep up the joke'. So Cainess dressed in a white jacket and trousers, and with a white cotton cap on his head, skipped around the graveyard one night emitting hysterical laughter and sepulchral groans, until the police dragged him to the ground and arrested him.[45] Twenty-four years later, magistrates heard a similar story from another young man, a French polisher named William Livins. He was charged with trespassing in Christchurch burial ground, Blackfriars, and disturbing the peace. For several weeks in October and November 1839, large crowds had gathered around the railings of the burial ground following rumours of a ghost. Livins testified:

> I was returning from work, and seeing a crowd outside the church I inquired what was the matter, and was told that there was a ghost there. I laughed at the absurdity of the thing, and to show the people that there was no foundation for such a report, I got over into the burial-ground, and went up to the spot where his ghostship was said generally to make his appearance, and was in the act of quitting the place when the policeman pinned me.[46]

Many hoaxes, particularly those mimicking noisy hauntings, were, as has been mentioned, the work of adolescent girls. On the surface we find familiar teenage reasons for malicious behaviour. The Baker girl mentioned earlier, who was jailed for smashing her parents' crockery, glass and furniture, explained that she played the trick because they had forbidden her to go out. She was described by a local clergyman as 'a very bad girl, exceedingly idle and dirty, and fond of wandering the streets to get into bad company'.[47] One feels more compassion for a 16-year-old servant named Betty Perry, who was responsible for a noisy haunting that plagued a house in Limekiln Street, Dover, in December 1839. On being caught she denied being responsible but eventually confessed. She said that she had caused the mischief because she was frightened of being left alone and thought that the attention she generated would keep the family at home. She was subsequently discharged.[48]

Although the disturbances they produced might have been similar, there is an important distinction between the cases of Baker and Perry: one concerned tensions within the family group, while the other was a manifestation of emotional problems created by the servant–employer relationship. Psychological, anthropological and historical studies of adolescent possession and poltergeist activity focus almost exclusively on their meaning in terms of interpersonal conflict within kin groups. In this respect, sceptics who believe all such phenomena are hoaxes share common ground with those who have seen poltergeists as manifestations of psychic energy generated by troubled pubescent or hormonally charged minds. Either way, the phenomena are usually interpreted as the product of domestic violence, repressed hostility between children and parents, or sexual frustration resulting from over-protective or suffocating parents. What the examples of nineteenth-century ghost hoaxes shows, is that from an historical perspective we also need to develop a better understanding of how and why relationships between young, female servants and employers also manifested themselves in the simulation of supernatural activity. One recognises the insecurities and frustrations that must have been a common experience for young servants like Betty Perry. They were removed from their families and familiar environments at a formative age, and had to live with strangers and negotiate the inequalities and sexual politics between masters and servants. Betty found expression for her emotional state through a form of displacement activity that enabled the release of pent up frustration through vandalism, while at the same time attracting the attention she obviously craved.

It is no coincidence that these servant girls fit the profile for those who most often claimed to be possessed by witches and devils in early modern England, and who have more recently been at the centre of obsession or poltergeist activity.[49] Gauld and Cornell's analysis of nearly 200 English and North American poltergeist cases where there was an obvious individual focus for manifestations, revealed that nearly three-quarters were female and 78 per cent under the age of 20. The evidence from Brazilian studies suggests a similar pattern.[50] Both possession and poltergeist activity can be read as ways in which adolescents can and did transform the supernatural into domestic power, radically altering the dynamics of household relationships.[51] From a historical perspective we can see how, as a social and psychological strategy, possession became less pertinent and potent by the nineteenth century as the currency of diabolic intervention weakened both intellectually and in popular culture. The concept of ghost infestation, by contrast, continued as a vibrant and widespread belief. It is no wonder, therefore, that it continued to be exploited by frustrated youths, who helped perpetuate fear and anxiety about ghosts across all social levels.

Some young women and men simulated ghosts to deflect attention away from themselves. Lovers had good reason to keep prying eyes and ears otherwise occupied. Calmet described how some ghosts were 'but a contrivance of young people to carry on, by this means, an amorous intrigue'.[52] Rumours of the haunting of an unoccupied house in Aylesbury market square in 1834 were revealed to be based on nothing more than some boisterous love-makers.[53] In September 1817, a Mrs Water, of Hampstead, wrote to her nephew regarding the haunting of her cottage. Unusual noises emanated from around the property and her maids said they had seen a white figure in the garden. The nephew suspected human agency and so he and a friend hid in the shrubbery and kept a vigil. Around one o'clock in the morning, a pale, shrouded figure entered the garden from an adjoining field and proceeded to rattle the window shutters and doors. The mystery was revealed when one of the servant maids appeared and embraced the ghost. Water's nephew and his friend emerged to interrupt the amorous ghost, causing the maid to disappear back inside and her lover to hide in a pigsty. Setting fire to the straw in the sty flushed him out, and his identity was revealed to be that of a young gentleman residing with his parents in the vicinity.[54]

The servant girl Harriet King's motives for disturbing her master's house in Ashford Road, Maidstone, in the winter of 1859, were of a less innocent nature. She confessed to having generated a haunting scare over a period of weeks by ringing the doorbell and shaking doors in the house in order to provide a cover for her side-career as a prostitute. As some of her clients came in the evening she needed some means of creating a diversion at a time when the whole household was in.[55] Similar suspicions arose during a case of assault heard by a Marylebone magistrate in October 1839. A Tottenham Court Road pawnbroker named Franklin had a great deal of trouble with a servant maid who said she had seen a ghost in his house. Such was her fear of it, she had nearly broken her neck rushing downstairs after one sighting. Franklin and his wife did not believe the ghost story and accused another housemaid, Maria Rogers, of letting a young man into the house while they were away, despite his strict instructions not to admit anybody. In her defence Rogers told Franklin that the nursery maid had also seen the ghost of a man in the drawing room. However, on being questioned about this, the nursery maid said the man she saw was no ghost but flesh and blood. She had also seen two decidedly non-spiritual young gentlemen with Maria in the kitchen that same night.[56]

CRIME

Suspicions that criminals were behind many supposed hauntings were voiced repeatedly over the centuries. The eighteenth-century Benedictine Abbot Augustin Calmet observed, for example, that they often turned out

> to be a thievish or dissolute servant, who conceals his thefts and debaucheries, by counterfeiting a ghost. Sometimes it proves to be a company of coiners, who have got possession of the vaults of an old mansion, and frighten away everyone from it.[57]

Newspapers and the authorities frequently suspected that criminals were behind some nineteenth-century urban ghost scares. Thomas Lott thought the person behind the Peckham ghost scare of 1838 was no aristocratic prankster, but

> some determined thief who visits houses in the absence of the heads of families, and who seeks by this method of at once paralysing the energies of the servants to obtain and escape with his booty on easy terms.[58]

When, in the same year, a ghost in the form of a tall white figure with big red eyes, was apparently seen in an empty house in Stafford Street, Liverpool, the police suspected thieves were using the property, though a search revealed no sign of them.[59] Literary fiction, particularly from the eighteenth century onwards, also played with the scenario of criminals creating hauntings as smokescreens for their activities. The late-sixteenth-century *Scoggins Jestes*, for instance, tells of how Scoggin, while in Rome, lodged in the house of a wealthy widow, whom a young gentleman planned to lighten of her money. In the evenings the man 'came into her house & lapped himselfe in a white sheete, counterfetting a spirit, thinking she would run her wayes, and leave her money to his disposing'. The women saw behind the ruse and employed Scoggin to teach the impostors a lesson. When the fake ghost next appeared, Scoggin 'basted him on both sides with a cudgell'.[60] That such suspicions and fictional scenarios were not merely the product of middle-class fears and literary fantasies is amply proven by the annals of crime.

Let us begin this trawl of the criminal employment of ghosts with those who had the audacity to blame their thefts on the spirit world. The notorious thief, highwayman and one-time cunning-man, Thomas Wilmot, who was hanged in 1670, apparently played the ghost to make off with a table-full of gambling money. He was staying in a gentleman's house said to be haunted by the ghost of his grandfather's barber, who slit his throat due to his unrequited love for a chambermaid. The scheming Wilmot offered to lay the ghost. So one night as the gentleman and his friends were playing cards and dice downstairs, Wilmot, who was meant to be grappling with the spirit, 'rubbed over his Face with the White of the Wall, and then tying a Knot at one End, to place directly on his Head, he converted himself with a Sheet'. Then with a shaving razor bloodied by nicking a finger, he descended the stairs and appeared in front of the gentlemen. When they saw him they cried, 'The Ghost! The Ghost!' and ran off in all directions, leaving Wilmot to empty the table. The following morning they fell into a Dispute about a Spirit's taking Money; some of them, who were well read in the History of Apparitions, affirming that a Ghost never meddled with any Thing, but often discover'd hidden Treasures for the Advantage of others.

Sometime later he used his reputation as a conjurer to defraud an elderly gentleman who believed his house was haunted. As part of the ghost-laying ritual he required the old man to be blindfolded and lie down silently in a circle drawn on the floor. Meanwhile Wilmot went upstairs and made love to the man's wife who was party to the whole fraud.[61] That blaming a theft on a ghost was not unique to Wilmot's devious mind is evident from a case of pilfering heard by a magistrate at Hatton Garden police court in 1836. The defendant, a girl who stole a pair of tortoiseshell spectacles and other items from a neighbouring lodger, initially denied the crime and told the police that a ghost had stolen the things: 'she saw an apparition all in white open the door of the room from which the property was taken, and having bundled up the articles vanish with them through the window'. Seeing that her ghost alibi failed to have the desired impact, she later changed her story, saying instead that she saw several angels fly in the room and one of them put on the spectacles and disappeared. The magistrate proved not to be as open-minded as Wilmot's seventeenth-century gentlemen acquaintances.[62]

A more sinister criminal strategy was to exploit the belief in ghosts to extort or extract money from people. In 1621, for instance, one Henry Church was prosecuted for employing several London magicians to scare his new wife into making over her inheritance to him 'by delusory shewes and apparitions & voices in goastly and fearfull manner'.[63] A detailed illustration of how devious extortioners could slowly but surely gain influence over their victims is provided by the trial, in 1810, of Margaret Conners, who stood accused of robbing her fellow lodger Mary Anderson. Conners, aged 25, began her ruse by pretending to practise strange magical rituals. For several nights in July she placed the poker and tongs crosswise under their bed. She cut out rings and other shapes from a piece of white cloth and put them in the fire, and then filled a teacup with sand and planted a sprig of southernwood in it, around which she placed figures cut out of paper. She also gave Mary some broth in which she placed some powder. All this was designed to give the impression that Conners had magical powers, though the ostensible purpose of the rituals is not apparent from the records. In any event, on the evening of 9 August, as the two young women were sitting at the table, a knife was thrown at Mary by some unknown force, which Conners explained was the spirit of her husband. Conners made play of giving some bread and cheese to the spirit and asked Mary to look at the wall. She did not see a man, however, 'but the figure of a lamb, about the size of a large cat'. When they went to bed, Conners told Mary to look at another part of the wall, where she 'saw faintly the figure of a man with something white over his shoulders'. Conners said the spirit wanted something from her box, which she kept by the side of the bed. When Mary asked what, Conners replied that she should take every item out and the spirit would take what he desired that night. Mary, much frightened, emptied her box and the next morning found all her possessions had gone. She subsequently saw Conners wearing some of her missing garments, and when she confronted her, Conners said 'that these apparitions told her that she must wear my clothes or else I should be tortured'. Weeks later, Mary realised that she had been duped and informed the police.[64]

Thieves also donned the classic white sheet as a diversionary ruse. No one did this better than the master thief Arthur Chambers, who was executed for an unrelated crime in 1706. Passing himself off as a man of fortune he took expensive lodgings at a house in Soho Square. One day he told his landlord that his brother had recently died and had requested in his will to be buried in Westminster Abbey. Would the landlord do him the great favour of allowing the coffin to be kept at his house overnight before being carried to the funeral? He agreed and the next day Chambers hired a hearse and arranged for his accomplices to deliver a fine coffin to his landlord's door that evening. Unbeknown to the landlord and the rest of the household, Chambers had secreted himself in the coffin. He was wrapped in a winding sheet and had rubbed flour into his face. After the household save the maid had gone to bed, Chambers arose in his ghostly guise and descended downstairs where he confronted her. She screamed 'A Ghost, a Ghost!', and ran upstairs to her master's chamber. He chided her for being foolish but when Chambers ascended to appear before he and his wife, all three were transfixed with fear. Chambers then quickly ran back down and opened the front door to his accomplices who proceeded to make off with several hundred pounds worth of goods.[65]

In the nineteenth century the urban police and the press suspected that pickpockets instigated some of the ghost hunts that occurred on the streets. They would certainly have found rich pickings amongst the thronging crowds whose attentions were diverted by their quest. A ghost sensation at St Andrew's church, Holborn, in 1815, drew such large crowds that 'the light fingered gentry had become so numerous and successful, that it required the utmost vigilance of the police to prevent these disgraceful proceedings'.[66] Twenty years later the *Manchester Guardian*, reporting on a ghost sensation in the town, observed that 'hundreds of people congregated near the spot, including many pickpockets, who are ever quick at discovering a crowd, and who would ply their vocation undismayed by the presence of a hundred ghosts'.[67] However, few of those arrested at ghost hunts were specifically charged with orchestrating such a criminal diversion. When a magistrate accused William Livins of doing as much to attract crowds outside Christchurch burial ground in 1839, his father appeared in his defence and was adamant his son had not played the trick 'for the purpose of giving thieves an opportunity of robbing'.[68]

Ghost simulation could also be used to keep people off the street and cloistered in their homes at night while criminals went about their business outside. The nineteenth-century Sussex folklorist Charlotte Latham attributed many hauntings in the county to the work of smugglers, who wandered the countryside at night with blue lights to ensure people stayed in doors. One smuggler apparently confessed to the police how his gang had attempted to frighten away the occupants of a house in Rottingdean that lay close to one of their tunnels. At night they rolled barrels of spirits up the passage causing the occupants of the house to hear ghostly rumblings emanating from the ground. The house soon attracted a reputation for being haunted. Latham suggested that the success of the Preventive Service – armed police and naval officers whose job was to patrol the coastline – had 'laid many ghosts in Sussex'.[69] In 1804 a correspondent to the *Morning Chronicle* noted that a few years before, a smuggling gang on the Welsh coast travelled around in a hearse drawn by the simulated ghosts of six headless white horses in order to frighten off customs officers.[70] The great early British film comedian Will Hay included a similar idea in *Ask a Policeman* (1939), in which smugglers frighten away villagers with a phantom coach and headless driver.

Poachers also stood accused of similar tactics to keep the countryside clear of people at night. In early 1834 the west Yorkshire village of Collingham and surrounding area were thrown into considerable disquiet by the mysterious haunting of a large plantation situated on the brow of a hill between the village and Thorp Arch. Loud moans and groans regularly resonated from in and around the wood between nine and ten o'clock at night. Villagers speculated that it was the troubled spirit of a blacksmith and poacher who had recently died. The local turnpike-keepers were so frightened that they refused to man their gates. Such was the disruption and perturbation caused by the supposed haunting that the local magistrates launched an investigation. The ghost turned out to be a member of a poaching gang with a speaking trumpet, who positioned himself at strategic points, such as under a bridge, while his comrades got on with their depredations.[71] In a similar vein, the eighteenth-century bookseller James Lackington recalled how, in his Somerset youth, a white apparition was repeatedly seen taking poultry from various premises. Despite the depredations people were too afraid to go near it, all except one man who suspected foul play. On seeing the ghost climbing over his wall he knocked it down and found that it was a female neighbour wearing a shroud.[72]

THE HOUSING MARKET

In 1732 the *Gentleman's Magazine* noted that the reason for some hoaxes was 'to sink the Rents of a House, which an Ousted Tenant has a Mind to retake'. The following decade Eliza Haywood, a devout believer in ghosts, also recognised that 'Houses have been reported to be haunted out of Malice to those who own'd them'.[73] The historical record would seem to bear out these claims. Pity the poor landlord lumbered with a haunted property. Consider the dilemma facing one Mrs Jervis of Regent Street, Poplar, in 1818. For three years a property she owned close by had been plagued by a noisy ghost, which drew sensation-seeking crowds. So widespread was the knowledge of its haunted status that she could not find any tenant to take possession of it. Exasperated by the financial consequences she requested the Shadwell magistrates to investigate. Several constables were ordered to occupy the house but they were apparently unable to apprehend the culprit.[74] A few years later, in 1825, the landlord who built several new properties in Hampton Street, Walworth, had no problem enticing respectable tenants. However, the activities of a mysterious stone-thrower, which were attributed by some locals to the work of a ghost, threatened his financial security. He believed the culprit was motivated by complaints that had been made that the new buildings were an eyesore. Consequently he asked for a summons against a young woman whom he suspected was involved. The following month, when Anne Page targeted several houses in Hanover Street, Newington, the landlord affected complained to the local magistrates that the ghost rumours 'had such an influence over the minds of many of his tenants' that they were threatening to leave the properties.[75]

One can also understand tenants' concern about living in a haunted property. They were often frightened, discomforted by both the often destructive mani-festations and the crowds of onlookers, yet were contractually or financially required to remain. In February 1834 the *Bristol Journal* reported that four men had recently applied to the town's magistrates to see if they could get out of a tenancy agreement as their rooms were haunted. They had consulted a lawyer who said he could not advise them, so they then resorted to the magistracy. While lying in bed one of the men's daughters said she saw the ghost of a woman with light hair and grey eyes. She wore a cap with lace strings and the girl felt a draft of air as the ghost passed by her bed. Another of the men saw the ghosts of two women, one in mourning clothes. All four claimed to have seen a strange blue light. The magistrates could do little, and merely tried to persuade the men that such things as ghosts were highly improbable. One of the men countered by citing John Wesley as an esteemed authority on the reality of the spirit world.[76]

While in the above cases it was tenants and landlords that were victimised, there is a long history of the cynical exploitation of ghosts in the housing market. In his list of natural explanations for haunted houses, Calmet stated:

> now, it is a tenant who wishes to decry the house in which he resides, to hinder others from coming who would take his place ... or a farmer who desires to retain his farm, and wishes to prevent others from coming to offer more for it.[77]

That this ruse was not just the product of a suspicious mind comes from the autobiography of the German-born American showman Andrew Oehler. In his youth, in the mid 1790s, he worked as a tailor's apprentice near Lausanne. The owner of the mansion his master rented wanted to sell it off, but Oehler's master could not afford the price. To help him out, Oehler came up with a scheme to make people believe the place was haunted. To this end he manufactured groans, clankings and other eerie noises when prospective buyers came to see the property. The mansion soon acquired a reputation and the owner ended up having to sell it to the tailor for a much lower price.[78] Back on English territory, in 1830 an empty house in Grange Road, Bermondsey, was reported to be haunted in the neighbourhood, causing large crowds to gather outside. The owner of the house, an eccentric clergyman, having recently died, it was suspected that an interested party wished to prevent the property from being let.[79] Suspicions were also raised when, in 1947, a request was made to the Luton Assessment Committee that the rateable value of a property be reduced because its worth had been lessened by its reputation for being haunted by the ghosts of two murdered eighteenth-century lovers.[80]

TRAGIC CONSEQUENCES

As we saw in the first chapter, death could ensue from seeing an apparition and from being mistaken for a ghost. It should come as no surprise, then, that hoaxes also occasionally ended in tragedy. In December 1830 George Gillett was tried for manslaughter at the Old Bailey for frightening to death an 81-year-old woman named Mary Steers of Twickenham. One afternoon Gillett, who lived in the same building, climbed onto the roof and, unseen by Steers, began to throw bricks and mortar onto her landing in imitation of a stone-throwing ghost. A few minutes later he wrapped himself from head to toe in a white sheet, walked into Steers's room and sat down by the fire. He then took out a hatchet from under the sheet and in an eerie voice intoned that he was going to chop off her head. Steers took up the fire tongs in defence and shouted for help. Gillett left the room only to reappear shortly after and reveal his identity. Nevertheless, Steers was so agitated by his ghostly appearance that she fell ill, saying at one point, 'I knew I should never get over it – that fright has killed me.' She died just over two weeks after the incident. Gillett was found not guilty, as it could not be proved that the fright he gave her was the direct cause of her death.[81]

A similar case was also heard at the inquest on the body of Robert Mitchell, of Alfreton, Derbyshire, in December 1856. Mitchell, an agricultural labourer aged 15, used to fetch milk from a farm at Roby Fields where his father was employed to dig some drainage channels. The path he took had the reputation of being haunted. Mitchell was in the habit of stopping for a chat with two young farm labourers named John Percival and Isaac Hudson, aged 22 and 15 respectively. On the evening of 22 December, the three lads, the farmer, Mr Day, and his wife, sat for nearly two hours talking about ghosts, and Percival and Hudson described some mysterious knockings that had recently frightened them. Later the two young men secretly agreed to scare Mitchell as he made his way home in the dark. Percival went off to find a white tablecloth while Hudson accompanied Mitchell some of the way home through the fields. As they approached a stile, Percival suddenly appeared uttering a moaning noise. Hudson ran off in feigned fright leaving Mitchell in a state of terror that failed to subside once Percival had thrown off the tablecloth to reveal the hoax. Mitchell arrived home in a highly excited and exhausted state, looking pale and frightened. He could not eat and the next day had to be taken home from work and placed in bed, where he began to rave and vomit before expiring. A doctor gave the opinion that he died from shock to the nervous system and Percival was arrested. He spent nearly three months in Derby gaol awaiting trial at the assizes. The jury found him not guilty of manslaughter, but the judge, Lord Campbell, warned him 'never again to indulge in practical jokes'.[82]

*   *   *

Despite such sad cases, the history of hoax hauntings provides a healthy corrective to the view, repeated over the centuries, that the minds of the uneducated and the poor were weighed down with nocturnal fears and foreboding regarding the appearance of the dead. While criminals, lovers and property speculators obviously benefited from general apprehensions regarding ghosts, the crowds drawn to urban hauntings and the many hoaxes perpetrated by the working classes counter the patronising eighteenth-century portrayals of labourers too frightened to leave their houses at night or frequent churchyards after dark. The numerous cases of adolescent servant girls mimicking noisy ghosts also rectify the long-held view that women and children were the most credulous sections of society. As with the activities of some working-class female spiritualists, we find cultural assumptions and social relations being subverted, with servant girls playing on the gullibility of their masters and the young putting one over on their elders. By playing ghosts, hoaxers may have helped perpetuate ghost-belief by maintaining the currency of stereotypical manifestations, but at the same time they also challenged perceptions of who were the haunted in society.

SEVEN

Projecting Ghosts

Previous chapters have examined how ghost hoaxers went about their business, and the range of explanations for ghosts as illusions and realities based on different interpretations of religion, human perception, emotion and intelligence. But there is also another history of alternative reality, not of ghosts who proved to be hallucinations or flesh and blood, but external projections – visions that had no substance and yet were real, which could trick the eye and tease the critical faculties. I am talking of the science and art of producing ghostly images; in essence the long and shadowy history of modern photography and motion pictures. Although, as we shall see, some have projected the history of ghost making back into the ancient world, the story really begins in the fecund and heady world of Renaissance science and occultism.

SMOKE AND MIRRORS

How to create an image of a ghost that could be seen and yet was intangible? That had the translucent or opaque quality that clearly distinguished the spirits of the dead from the living? Well, as early as the 1530s, the occult philosopher Cornelius Agrippa had observed that mirrors or 'looking-glasses' could be used to create such images:

> By the artificialness of some certain Looking-glasses, may be produced at a distance in the Aire, beside the Looking-glasses, what images we please; which when ignorant men see, they think they see the appearances of spirits, or souls; when indeed they are nothing else but semblances kin to themselves, and without life.[1]

A couple of decades later, Jean Pena, a mathematics professor in Paris, also wrote how concave mirrors could 'Cheat the eye of a man and make him believe that

187

what he sees in the air are the spirits of the dead.'[2] It was one thing to create such aerial reflections when meteorological conditions were right, but another to bring them down to earth, to manipulate their movement and provide a sense of proximity, whilst still concealing the connection between ghost maker and apparition. To achieve this heightened illusion of projected realism early scientists turned to the camera obscura. This consisted of a darkened box fitted with a convex lens, into which external light was admitted, and images of external objects were consequently projected onto a white surface in a darkened space. Renaissance astronomers had used such a device to see images of the sun and eclipses, and it has also been claimed that artists of the period used it to produce life-like portraits. The problem with the camera obscura was that the image was projected upside down – ghosts doing headstands would have been more baffling than convincing. By the late sixteenth century, however, with the development of more sophisticated lenses, and the use of a mirror to ensure the image was projected the right way up, the Italian occultist and scientist Giambattista della Porta (1540–1615) was putting on displays for friends using actors and scenery in one room which he then projected into an adjoining room. As he wrote of his display of hunting scenes, the audience could not 'tell whether they be true or delusions'.[3] By the early seventeenth century entrepreneurial showmen were already making use of the camera obscura, and the supernatural was a dominant theme in their displays. A Belgian Jesuit complained in a learned treatise on optics that such 'tricksters' pretended they had magic powers and boasted 'of making the ghosts of the devil appear from Hell'. At the sight of them, some in the audience 'begin to turn pale, while others, terrified of what is to come, begin to perspire'.[4] Not surprisingly considering the 'war' against witches and magical practitioners across Europe at the time, and the Reformation disputes over ghosts, the projection of such supernatural imagery was seen by some as socially and morally pernicious.

There are no such accounts of similar shows in England at the time, but there is little doubt they were being put on in London. One reason for saying as much was the presence in the capital of the influential inventor and telescope maker Cornelius Drebbel (1572–1633). Drebbel was a showman as well as a scientist, entertaining wealthy backers and their coteries, the Prince of Wales among them, with his inventions, of which the most famous were a submarine, wind machine and a perpetual motion machine. He also put on magic shows and created special effects for court masques.[5] A skilled manipulator of lenses and mirrors, he had a reputation for producing surprising lighting effects. In a letter written around 1608 or 1609 he talked of 'a new invention, which I have found by means of optics, with which I can do wonderfully ingenious things'. It is likely that it was some sort of adaptation of the camera obscura involving a magnification device. With it he could give the illusion

> as if the earth opens and the spirits rise up from it, first in the form of a cloud and then changing themselves into such a shape as I think fit ... Nay, I make the giants, such as they existed in former ages, to seem to rise up from the earth, twenty, thirty feet tall, moving and stirring so wonderfully and perfectly as if the parts of their bodies seem to live in a natural way.[6]

Although the camera obscura could produce wondrous representations of moving images, a major limitation was that it required bright natural light to ensure successful projection. Furthermore, creating living scenes and props was an expensive exercise. So the next big step forward in the science of ghost making, which occurred during the mid seventeenth century, was the development of an instrument that generated and intensified its own light source. In a darkened room such a device could project images painted on glass slides onto a white background. The hoaxer's favourite guise, the white sheet, proved to be an ideal surface. This projection box soon came to be known as the 'magic lantern', and its creation has often been attributed to the Jesuit priest and inventor Athanasius Kircher (1602–1680). Kircher was a scientist in the Drebbel mould, famous in his own lifetime for his machines powered by hydraulics and magnets, and his illusions created by mirrors and the camera obscura. These he displayed in his own museum in Rome and in spectacles he put on for European monarchs and aristocrats.[7] Kircher was certainly instrumental in disseminating the secret of the magic lantern due to the description of it in the second edition of his *Ars Magna Lucis et Umbrae*, or *The Great Art of Light and Shadow* (1671). It would seem, however, that its original developer was the great Dutch scientist and astronomer Christiaan Huygens, discoverer of the rings of Saturn, though the matter is disputed.[8] The attribution is based on educated speculation because Huygens wrote little about his lantern projector, and he evidently considered it an embarrassing trifle compared to his other ground-breaking studies. That Huygens was the inventor is suggested by a letter from a Father Guisony to Huygens in 1660, in which he recounted how Kircher was putting on magnet tricks at the College of Rome, commenting that 'if he had the invention of the Lantern, he would truly be terrifying the cardinals with ghosts'.[9] The evidence suggests that it was only acquaintances of Huygens who were familiar with the lantern, and it was after his visit to England in 1661 that one of his correspondents, the London optical instrument maker Richard Reeves, began to put on projection displays. Samuel Pepys recorded in his diary how, on one of Reeves's visits to his house, 'He did also bring a lanthorne with pictures in glasse, to make strange things appear on a wall, very pretty.'[10]

From the beginning, the magic lantern, this creator of artificial life, was more commonly associated with the portrayal of death and demons, playing on the fear of audiences cloistered in darkened rooms. Indeed an acquaintance of Huygens, a Parisian engineer, appropriately called it a 'lantern of fright'.[11] Skeletons and devils were amongst the most popular images for slides. Kircher included them in his shows, while Huygens's 1659 sketch for an animated sequence of lantern slides depicting skeletons was inspired by Holbein's masterpiece 'The Dance of Death'.[12] Thomas Rasmussen Walgenstein (1627–1681), who conducted magic lantern tours across Europe, displayed the figure of death to the King of Denmark during one show, which 'inspired horror among those surrounding the king'.[13] In Nuremburg a former monk and optical instrument maker, Johann Griendel, put on lantern shows depicting hell and ghosts, as well as paradise and village weddings.[14] A French traveller who saw one of his displays during the early 1670s wrote:

real Phantoms and Ghosts are now no longer sensible of the other World. I know divers Persons of great courage who have chang'd pale at the sight of these Sports and of these Magical Artifices.

Such was the dread inspired by these projections, he continued, 'I was apt to believe that there never was in the World a greater Magician than he.'[15] That the same associations were made in England is evident from Daniel Defoe's observation, in his History of the Devil, that the magic lantern was

an optic machine, by the means of which are represented, on a wall in the dark, many phantasms, and terrible appearances, but no devil in all this; only that they are taken for the effects of magic, by those that are not acquainted with the secret.[16]

During the mid eighteenth century Edme-Gilles Guyot entertained and scared French audiences with a further elaboration, casting the ghostly images onto a dense cloud of smoke, thereby giving a sense of depth to the illusion which was lacking from static projections onto a flat surface. In the following decade Johann Schröpfer, a Leipzig coffeehouse proprietor and founder of his own Masonic lodge, created extraordinary smoke-projection effects with his Gespenstermacher or 'ghost maker'. Schröpfer differed from the other men mentioned above in that he used his ghost maker to make people believe he really was able to call up the spirits of the dead. He conducted seances in a room draped in black for his Masonic colleagues and other visitors, in which the spirit raising was accompanied by terrifying bangs, screams and whistles created with the help of his wife and a team of assistants. He also learned the art of ventriloquism in order to give the impression that his spirits spoke. It is possible that soporifics and other drugs were burned in the smoke filled seance room to further befuddle those present.[17] Instructions on how to emulate Guyot's technique were also available in English by the early 1770s. In his book *Rational Recreations*, which was first published in 1774 and went through several editions, William Hooper included a section on how 'to produce the appearance of a phantom' by projecting onto a cloud of smoke produced by throwing incense onto hot coals.[18] Intriguingly, though, there is little evidence that magic lanternists followed Hooper's instructions and thrilled English audiences with cloud lantern shows.

In the seventeenth century the ability of magic lantern operators to conjure up such spirit images led to the blurring of the boundaries between theatre, necromancy and natural magic. The relationship between illusion and demonic magic was subtle and problematic both for its practitioners and for those trying to make sense of the extraordinary effects they produced.[19] Only God, remember, could perform miracles, while the Devil, whose knowledge of the hidden or occult secrets of nature was second only to God, worked through illusion and deception to produce marvels – the same arts employed by early modern showmen scientists. It was not much of a step, therefore, for magic lantern operators to fall under suspicion of performing true spirit conjurations, which in turn could lead to accusations of diabolism. Huygens, for example, had to allay the fears of his father, Constantin, who had met Drebbel in London in 1622. In a letter to his father Huygens wrote: 'It made me smile that in your last, it pleased you to warn me against the magic of Drebbel, and to accuse him of being a sorcerer.'[20] The French Cartesian abbé de Vallemont explained in the 1690s:

> The magic lantern is an Optical machine, & which one calls Magical, without doubt because of its prodigious effects, & the ghosts, & the frightening monsters that it shows, & which is attributed to magic by people who do not know the secret.[21]

To avoid attracting suspicions of satanic inspiration it was necessary for the inventors to overcome their understandable reluctance to reveal the secrets of their machines. Even with his high profile, Kircher was careful to explain the workings of his amazing contraptions. In his autobiography he recalled having to put on a 'theatrical performance' in the German town of Mainz:

as they saw some things that went beyond common knowledge, the legates who witnessed the performance were so excited to great admiration that some of them accused me of the crimes of Magic ... I was obliged to expose the mechanisms.[22]

Although basically a tool for creating visual entertainments, the magic lantern was also employed in the service of religious rationalism, as part of a wider campaign to discredit the supernatural phenomena of the 'superstitious' ancient pagans. Kircher gave over a good part of his museum to machines that demystified the pagan mysteries of Egyptian magic. He had a statue of a multi-breasted goddess, for example, which sprayed milk from its nipples. More controversially, the magic lantern was appropriated to explain the story of the Witch of Endor's raising of Samuel's spirit, this time from a visual rather than an aural point of view. As early as the mid sixteenth century Jean Pena suggested that the ghost of Samuel was nothing but an illusion created by using mirrors.[23] In the late seventeenth century those seeking to forge a more rationalist, scientific framework for Christianity found in magic lantern projections further graphic proof that man could conjure up realistic images of the dead, and must have done so in the past.[24]

The impulse to reveal the mysteries of the ghost-making lantern helped the proliferation of their manufacture, and during the eighteenth century a new breed of humble, itinerant magic lantern showmen made a living tramping the byways of Europe with their equipment strapped to their backs. In England these itinerant lanternists or 'gallantee men', as they were also known, were predominantly Italian like many other circus folk and street entertainers at the time. An elderly contributor to the *Penny Magazine* in 1845 recalled his youthful memories of these characters:

they were the first foreigners we ever saw ... The designs on their slips of glass were for the most part exceedingly grotesque: and their own personal appearance was scarcely less so in our young eyes.[25]

The shows were usually put on in the long winter months and during the summer the foreign gallantee men would return to the continent while others would switch to other acts that could be conducted out of doors. One old street showman interviewed by Henry Mayhew recalled how during the summer he travelled round the fairs and races with a performing bear and monkey, but a month before Christmas went with a galantee show of a magic lantern. We showed it on a white sheet, or on the ceiling, big or little, in the houses of the gentlefolk, and the schools where there was a breaking-up.[26]

PHANTASMAGORIA

As the eighteenth century drew to a close it would appear from the London press that the magic lantern's reputation as the king of ghost makers had been usurped by a new mirror illusion. In 1799, 'Magical and Extraordinary Mirrors' were put on display in Oxford Street, which produced 'admirable Apparitions, in answer to certain questions asked by the spectator' and displayed images of celebrated men of the age 'living or dead'.[27] But across the channel a new version of the magic lantern was lifting ghost making onto a whole new level.

Up to this point the link between the lanternist, his lantern and the image – in other words, between the living and the apparitions of the dead – was usually obvious even in a blacked out room. The use of screens or mirrors could be used to deflect the audience's attention from the lantern, but it was the development of back projection onto a screen that gave the lantern ghost independence from its master and an apparent life of its own. Moving the lantern backward and forwards in synchronisation with an adjustable diaphragm built into the lantern's optical tube produced the startling effect of ghosts lunging towards the audience and then receding. Simple movement had been achieved early in the century by moving one slide over the top of another. The effect was pretty basic, though, such as making the sails move on a windmill or the eyes of a face to roll. This new development made fluid motion possible, and ghosts could be made to rise from the ground and seemingly glide in the air around and above the audience.

An elusive German named Paul Philidor, who would later adopt the surname de Philipsthal, put on the first recorded back-projection lantern display. Press notices confirm that he was putting on ghost shows in Berlin in 1789 and in Vienna over the next couple of years.[28] In 1792 he removed to Paris and in December placed an advert in a Parisian daily newspaper announcing that his amazing 'Phantasmagoria' produced 'the apparition of Spectres and evocation of Shades'. The show received rave reviews in the press and the crowds flocked to see the extraordinary visions that scarily approached and retreated from view in the darkness. Despite his success, Philidor's shows seem to have terminated rather abruptly in April 1793. The reason for his sudden disappearance can be inferred from a report that he mocked the French Revolutionary leaders in his show by portraying them as Devils. It would appear that around the same time Philidor obtained a passport for England; and with this last tantalising piece of information the historian loses sight of this influential ghost maker for several years.[29]

Although Philidor was the originator of the moving back-projection 'Phantasmagoria', the man who inspired its international success and consequent cultural significance was Étienne-Gaspard Robertson (1763–1837).[30] Born in Liège, Belgium, Robertson had initially trained for the priesthood but his interest in scientific experimentation and art, coupled with a spirit of adventure, led him to become first a teacher and then a scientific showman in Paris. Although Robertson, who wrote a two-volume memoir of his life, never mentioned having seen Philidor's short-lived but memorable Phantasmagoria, he was certainly inspired by it. Robertson was evidently keen to erase Philidor from the history of the magic lantern, for when he applied for a patent for his own 'Fantascope' he described his apparatus as 'a perfection of Kircher's magic lantern'. Robertson had certainly been experimenting with magic lanterns for many years before he put on his first public display using moving back projection in January 1798, which he tellingly called the 'Fantasmagorie'. Robertson promised his audience 'apparitions of Spectres, Ghosts and Revenants, as they must and could have appeared throughout history, in every place and in every nation'. It must be said that although Robertson arrogantly claimed for himself the invention of the phantasmagoria, he did innovate and improve the experience by using a brighter light source and creating a more translucent screen that merged into the darkness, thereby enhancing the luminosity and integrity of the apparitions projected.

It was in 1801 that the first phantasmagoria shows were staged in England, when Philidor, now called Philipsthal, emerged from years of obscurity to appear at the Lyceum Theatre in London.[31] The *Britannic Magazine* reported that 'With the aid of his broken English, and a most sublime interpreter, he indeed converts his shadows rapidly into substantial English guineas.'[32] Others were also quick to cash in on the popularity of the new magic lantern show. By the winter, Monsieur St Clair had also arrived from the continent with his 'Phantasmagoria; Or, Supernatural Appearances'.[33] He seems to have come to some sort of arrangement with *The Times*, since his London shows were frequently praised in editorial puffs. On 5 January 1802, for example, in a digest of 'news' the paper noted how St Clair had 'astonished audiences', stating that his 'supernatural appearances' were 'of a more surprising nature, in point of ghostly effect, than were ever witnessed in the world before'.[34] A couple of weeks later it further reported that this wonderful man ... is in the true sense of the word, if not a Dealer, a Manager of Spirits; every shape and every form appearing to view at his magic touch, in the most surprising and miraculous manner.[35]

The following year Mark Lonsdale, presumably one and the same as the author of several Drury Lane musical farces during the 1780s and 1790s, displayed his 'Spectrographia, or Phantomimic Illusions'. He had a stint at the London Lyceum, an advert for which was emphatic that it was 'no servile tedious imitation of the phantasmagoria'. It was nevertheless based on a 'representation of Traditional Ghosts and Supernatural Appearances ... accompanied by such amusing Relations and explanatory Details, as naturally attach themselves to the subject'. Amongst the ghosts portrayed were those of Julius Caesar appearing to Brutus, and a meeting with a churchyard ghost. Considering the competition in London, the likes of Philipsthal and St Clair were also quick to tour the provincial theatres, with phantasmagoria shows being put on in Bath, Bristol, Gloucester and Liverpool in 1802.[36] In the year of the Hammersmith ghost shooting, further competition emerged to capitalise on the spectre craze. The German conjuror Moritz appeared at the King's Arms, Cornhill, while in 1805 the well-known comedian Jack Bologna entered the fray with his 'Phantascopia'.[37] Bologna was one of the first Europeans to cash in on the American market, showing his phantasmagorical 'Apparitions of the Dead or Absent' in New York in the autumn of 1803. Another comic, William Bates, gave the first display in Boston the following year and shows sprang up in other towns in the northeastern states in ensuing years, mixing ghosts with projected portraits of American presidents.[38]

In 1805 the magic lantern ghost shows in London came under attack with the arrival of the German opticians and showmen Schirmer and Scholl. They held public demonstrations of the phantasmagoria in which they allowed the audience behind the scenes to reveal how the projection was created. This was a hard-nosed business decision, for it was used as a taster to a projection display using their own invention, the ergascopia, which they had toured around central and Eastern Europe since the 1790s. They challenged

all the Artists of the Universe to imitate their Performances in this Science. They flatter themselves to prove to an enlightened English public the great difference between their natural phantoms and those that have been produced by Mr. Philipsthal, and others, through a Magic Lanthorn.

The magic lantern ghosts were, they said, 'dull and lifeless, compared to the Ergascopic or living and acting Apparitions'. With the magic lantern, they justifiably asserted, 'it is absolutely impossible to introduce real life or natural motions and expressions in those dull mechanic figures', whereas the ergascopia displayed 'graceful acting apparitions, not to be distinguished from real life.'[39] Their *pièce de résistance* was a scene, in which a treasure seeker, with a spade in one hand and a real burning candle in another, appears in the distance and walks towards the audience. He then puts his lantern on the ground and begins to dig, looking around fearfully. A spirit suddenly emerges from the hole, lights a candle and waves it about in front of the audience before it vanishes. Judging from this description, and Schirmer and Scholl's contempt for the magic lantern, their 'masterpiece of optical illusion', would appear to have been a sophisticated camera obscura projection or some device involving mirrors and lenses akin to the catadioptrical phantasmagoria described by David Brewster in 1832. Brewster echoed Schirmer and Scholl's critique of the magic lantern's shortcomings, observing that

> to perfect the art of representing phantasms, the objects must be living ones, and in place of chalky ill-drawn figures mimicking humanity by the most absurd gesticulations, we shall have phantasms, of the most perfect delineation.[40]

The shock and awe of the phantasmagoria was bound to wear off after a few years and new developments were needed to keep thrill-seeking audiences interested. One innovation was to give the illusion that the spirits raised by the lantern also spoke. Sound effects and ghostly voices had long been used to heighten the atmosphere in projection displays, but not to provide synchronised speech. Johann Schröpfer may have been the first to marry the phantasmagoria with that other popular form of illusion of the time – ventriloquism, but it was Robertson who first used it in public exhibitions. He employed the talented practitioner of the belly-speaking art Fitz-James. As we have seen, he was no stranger to resurrecting the voices of the dead. The partnership seems to have initially prospered, but in 1802 Fitz-James was lured by an offer to perform in London, and engineered a bust-up with Robertson. In retaliation Robertson replaced his performance with a flea circus. Around the same time a conjuror and ventriloquist named Mr Comte set up his own competing talking phantasmagoria in Paris, which borrowed heavily from Robertson's show.[41] Andrew Oehler was particularly ingenious in creating synchronised speech by marrying ghost projection onto smoke with a technique borrowed from the Invisible Girl illusion, which was one of the most celebrated attractions of the early nineteenth century. In his memoirs he explained how he had a tube placed through an adjoining room that matched the spot where the ghost's mouth would be seen by the audience. An assistant spoke through the tube and, as Oehler explained, the speech 'coming out of the end of the tube, drives the smoke a little apart, and makes an appearance like the moving of the lips of a person when he speaks.'[42]

Lantern ghost shows were presented as more than just entertainment; they were an enlightenment instrument for exploding the belief in spirits – a triumphant force of science over 'superstition'. In Revolutionary anti-clerical France, Philidor opened his performance with a rationalist speech:

> I shall show you no spirits, because there are none, but I shall produce before you simulacra and pictures such as spirits are supposed to be, in the dreams of the imagination or in the lies of charlatans.[43]

In an account of a visit to Philipsthal's show in London, the chemist and inventor William Nicholson (1753–1815), was critical of the lighting and poor quality of the slides, but appreciated 'the attempt to explain the rational object or purpose of the exhibition ... unfortunately for the audiences his English was unintelligible'.[44] Robertson claimed he was supported by the Revolutionary Central Bureau 'to destroy the enchanted world that owes its existence solely to the magic wand of fanaticism'. He was, he stated, a physicist and an optician, not 'a magician, a necromancer, in an age in which all marvels have succumbed to human reason'.[45] Adverts in the London press for St Clair's phantasmagoria underlined that it was 'intended to do away with the superstitious idea of ghosts and spectres by unmasking the artifices practised by certain pretended magicians on the minds of the weak and credulous'.[46] One of the first phantasmagoric displays in America, in 1803, was advertised as exposing the fallacy of ghost beliefs and aimed to 'destroy the absurd opinions which prevailed in the last ages'.[47] Yet as one academic has pointed out, everything 'was done, quite shamelessly, to intensify the supernatural effect'.[48] Consider, for example, a newspaper advert for Philipsthal's phantasmagoria display at the Lyceum in the Strand in October 1801. This show of 'spectrology', it stated, 'claims the merit of unmasking artful impostors and pretended exorcists, and of opening the eyes of those who still foster an absurd belief in Ghosts', yet at the same time the advert emphasised the verisimilitude of the experience. Philipsthal, it boasted, 'will, by his skill in Physics, produce the Phantoms or Apparitions of the dead or absent, in a way more complete and illusive than has ever been offered to the eye on a public Theatre'.[49]

By the end of the eighteenth century the once delicate margin between the practice of natural and demonic magic, which had exposed ghost illusionists to accusations of satanism, had, in intellectual terms, become a concrete boundary. After an ardent and, at times vitriolic period of debate during the late seventeenth and early eighteenth centuries, an intellectual consensus slowly emerged that the age of miracles was definitely over, that both God and the Devil had withdrawn from earthly affairs. Although the old view of imminent satanic threat was by no means rejected wholesale, the intellectual environment of the eighteenth century was such that magic lanternists were free to mimic the demonic magician for theatrical effect without risking accusations of dabbling in the Black Arts. Consider, for instance, the following account of a *Gespenstermacher*'s performance in Leipzig in 1784:

> The supposed magus leads the assembly of the curious into a room whose floor is covered with black cloth and in which is an altar painted black with two flaming torches and a skull or a funerary urn. The magus draws a circle in the sand around the table or altar, and begs the spectators not to step outside the circle. He begins his conjuration by reading from a book and burns resiny mastic for good spirits, stinking things for bad. At a stroke the lights go out of themselves, with a loud detonation. At that moment, the conjured spirit appears.[50]

Most exponents of the phantasmagoria did not go so far; they may no longer have need feared being tainted with diabolism, but they still attracted accusations of promoting 'superstition' amongst the uneducated. Yet numerous lanternists still resorted to depictions of necromancy as a promotional gimmick. A common illustration in advertisements for phantasmagoria shows portrayed an appropriately attired magician standing in a magical circle conjuring spirits. Thus a poster produced for Philipsthal's stint at the Lyceum shows a gowned magician, wand in one hand, incense burner in the other, standing within a magical circle with a skull and candles, conjuring up the shrouded figure of a female ghost. Twenty-five years later the playbill for a show by the illusionist and lanternist M. Henry at the Theatre Royal, Haymarket, contained a similar but slightly updated engraving.[51] The inspiration for these images was a woodcut that, for several centuries, adorned popular publications telling the story of the notorious Dr Faustus, which depicted him in a magical circle conjuring the Devil.

While it was safe to play the necromancer in enlightenment Europe and America, one had to be careful elsewhere. The German-born adventurer and showman Andrew Oehler deeply regretted putting on an awesome Robertson-like ghost show in Mexico City in 1806. In a room bedecked with black tapestry and skeletons, he set a large altar on top of which he placed a skull. A brazier of burning coals stood beyond it. His influential guests, who included the

Governor of Mexico City and senior government leaders, were led into the sepulchral room where Oehler announced that he was going to raise a departed spirit. He asked members of the audience if there was someone in particular they would like him to summon. One man said he would like to see his late father once more. Oehler then uttered some incantations, placed some chemicals on the brazier and stepped aside as a thick pall of smoke arose. Then, by means of a hidden magic lantern beam projected via an angled mirror, a venerable face appeared in the smoke and began to speak. As Oehler recalled:

> in an authoritative voice [I] demanded of him to tell from whence he came; whether from the dismal and deep! The infernal pit! Or from the happy regions of the endless felicity above! He immediately told us he came from above.

Shortly after the vision faded and the room was suddenly lit up. As the audience left, the mood was uncharacteristically subdued. In the early hours of the morning Oehler was arrested by soldiers, charged with raising spirits, and imprisoned in a deep pit. He was kept there for several months and fed on bread and water. He was only released after a Spanish marquis, who was evidently familiar with the phantasmagoria, heard of his plight and explained to the authorities that he was no diabolic magician but a scientific illusionist. The Governor apologetically explained that he had been imprisoned to placate 'the clamours of the Spanish monks and friars'. Oehler returned to New Jersey and vowed never to act the conjuror again.[52]

THE ST JAMES'S PARK GHOST

In January 1804, a few days after the Hammersmith ghost tragedy, at a time when the popularity and influence of phantasmagoria shows were at their peak, another sensational ghost appeared to strike fear into the capital's population. The Hammersmith ghost had quickly proven to be a mix of hoax and mistaken identity, but the St James's Park was more perplexing. As we shall see, considering the probity of the witnesses, the usual explanations for seeing apparitions did not seem to apply. Perhaps the magic lantern could shed some revealing light.

On Friday 13 January 1804, The Times reported that a soldier in the Coldstream Guards stationed in St James's Park had, a few nights before, seen the ghost of a headless woman wandering the place between one and two o'clock in the morning. Only a few days before, when reporting on the shooting of the

Hammersmith 'ghost', *The Times* had assumed that the panic was the result of the 'Christmas tricks' of 'some very silly and thoughtless person' walking around in a ghost disguise. Because a Coldstream Guard said he saw one, however, *The Times* took the sighting more seriously, especially when the soldier asserted he was 'sure it was not a person dressed up in a white sheet'. The soldier was so shocked by his experience that he had to be taken to hospital the next day. A couple of nights later a comrade, a hardened war veteran, when on guard at the same spot, also saw the headless women enter the park from the end of Queen Street. He described later how he was so frightened his jaw locked and he was unable to demand 'Who comes there?' He deserted his post and subsequently fell into fits and joined the first soldier in hospital. Several others saw it walk over the park, paling before vanishing. *The Times* ended its report with the equivocal statement: 'it is an undoubted fact, that two sentinels have been sent there [hospital] from the effects of fright, whatever may have been the real cause of it'.

To corroborate its story, though not out of any sense of supporting the reality of the ghost, on the Monday *The Times* printed a signed declaration by one of the soldiers who had seen the ghost, which it obtained from the adjutant of the Coldstream Regiment:

> I do solemnly declare, that, whilst on guard at the Recruit House, on or about the 3rd instant, about half past one o'clock in the morning, I perceived the figure of a woman, without a head, rise from the earth, at the distance of about three feet before me. I was so alarmed at the circumstance, that I had not power to speak to it, which was my wish to have done; but I distinctly observed that the figure was dressed in a red striped gown with red spots between each stripe, and that part of the dress and figure appeared to me to be enveloped in a cloud.
>
> In about the space of two seconds, whilst my eyes were fixed on the object, it vanished from my sight. I was perfectly sober and collected at the time, and, being in great trepidation, called to the next sentinel, who met me about half way, and to whom I communicated the strange sight I had seen.
>
> Signed GEORGE JONES,
> Of Lieutenant-Colonel Taylor's Company of Coldstream Guards.

Another guard, Richard Donkin, also signed a declaration recounting the strange noises and eerie feeble voice he heard emanating from an uninhabited house near the haunted spot.[53] On 16 January, Jones was also taken to Bow Street magistrates' court where Sir Richard Ford questioned him as to what he had seen. Jones repeated his belief that he had encountered a ghost.[54]

What to make of it all? Jones was questioned as to 'whether his imagination had received any impressions from reading any dismal story'. He replied in the negative. A correspondent to the *Morning Chronicle* suggested that it was a trick played by someone clad in white with black crape around his head: 'if the night be moderately dark … Argus himself would not be able to discern the head, though all the rest of the person would be visible.' 'I think, Mr Editor, I have hit the right nail on the head', he smugly concluded.[55] An investigation launched by *The Times* reached a different conclusion. The paper found that the ghost had been created by 'an application of the Phantasmagoria' by two Westminster School scholars, who had set their equipment up in an empty house near the Bird Cage Walk where the headless woman had been seen.[56] This explanation seems, at first, rather far-fetched. Still, it is possible that it really was an elaborate lantern hoax. Consider, for instance, George Jones's statement that the ghost appeared 'to be enveloped in a cloud'. Anyway, if the St James's Park ghost was created by a phantasmagoria it was a classic example of the way in which new technology could be used to enforce the belief in ghosts as well as debunk it. So impressive was the ghostly vision seen by the guards that they were prepared to state publicly, on oath, a belief in ghosts, at a time when the most appropriate media response was to scoff.

SPIRIT PHOTOGRAPHY

Histories of spirit photography usually begin in the 1860s as an aspect of the story of spiritualism. An American jewellery engraver and amateur photographer named William Mumler is regularly credited as the first person to produce a photograph of a spirit – that of his young female cousin, who had died twelve years before. He published the photograph in 1862 and the media sensation it provoked inspired him to give up engraving and set himself up as a 'Spirit Photographic Medium'.[57] In Boston and then New York, he prospered by servicing a clientele desperate for comforting confirmation that the spirits of their deceased loved ones hovered around as guardian angels. But Mumler's thriving career was interrupted in 1869 when he was charged with fraud. He was acquitted due to lack of evidence, despite it being proven that one of the supposed spirits photographed was actually still alive.[58] His defence was predicated on the supposition that the spirits of the dead *did* appear to the living, and therefore there was no reason for Mumler to fake his photographs. Despite 400 years of theological and rationalist explanations for the impossibility of the Witch of Endor's powers, the spirit of Samuel was once again raised by Mumler's lawyers in the service of their client. As part of their defence case they cited the Bible story, and speculated, rather absurdly, that if a camera had existed at the time it would have captured the image of the prophet.

Spiritualist photography was surprisingly late to appear in England, with the first examples emerging from the studio of Frederick Hudson in 1872.[59] In March that year the celebrated medium Elizabeth Guppy and her husband, who was an amateur photographer, posed for Hudson. To their amazement, when the photographs were developed a veiled figure, more material and less translucent than Mumler's ghosts, was perceptible behind Mr Guppy. Shortly after, on Elizabeth Guppy's suggestion, the painting medium Georgina Houghton began a series of sittings with Hudson during which various spirit manifestations were captured on film, including the ghost of a rabbit. Houghton and Hudson were quick to realise the commercial prospects of these sensational photographs and had large numbers of reproductions printed, which were sold via retail outlets. Others soon jumped on the bandwagon, even though exposés of how such images could be faked were swiftly published in a spiritualist magazine and a photographic periodical.[60] In 1875 the young French spirit photographer Edouard Buguet, who had opened a studio in Baker Street the previous year, was prosecuted for fraud in Paris. Buguet made a full confession which was widely reported in the French and English press. He described how he simulated the spirits by making a preliminary photographic exposure of a wooden doll wrapped in gauze, to which he attached photographs of faces stuck on cardboard, of which police found some 240 examples.[61]

Yet despite the understandable preoccupation with spiritualism, ghost photography has more innocent origins in the early history of photographic experimentation. In the 1850s an amateur photographer had produced ghostly images by photographing one person behind a plate-glass window and another in front. The result was an image showing a faint figure reflected through the glass encountering the substantial figure of the person standing in front.[62] But another basic technique was to prove more impressive. The long exposure times, often hours, required by the earliest cameras meant that people or animals that moved out of shot at some point would appear as a vague, transparent image on the glass plate. It was Sir David Brewster who recognised in the early 1850s that this exposure problem could be used to *deliberately* create ghostly images. He came across the idea after seeing a calotype (the name for Fox Talbot's patented paper coated with a film of silver iodide) of York Minster, taken in 1844, in which a boy had sat on the steps of the Minster for a while during the long exposure and consequently appeared as a translucent ghostly figure on the plate.

In 1856 Brewster published *The Stereoscope*, which provided an account of his lenticular stereoscopic device that gave depth to an image by viewing two photographs of the same scene taken from slightly different angles. While Brewster dedicated its application 'to the fine and useful arts and to education', he also advertised its ghostly entertainment value. He suggested:

> For the purpose of amusement the photographer might carry us even into the realms of the supernatural. His art enables him to give a spiritual appearance to one or more of his figures, and to exhibit them as 'thin air' amid the sold realities of the stereoscopic picture.[63]

Brewster's idea was quickly taken up by the London Stereoscopic Company, which had been set up in the district of Cheapside in 1854. In 1857 the company created quite a sensation with a series of images entitled 'The Ghost in the Stereoscope', which had the added novelty of being tinted with colour. The first in the series was probably 'Ghost in the Stereoscope, affrightening the Rustic Gamblers', which was promoted as producing ghost effects 'the most marvellous ever produced'. 'The ghost is quite spiritual,' the advert boasted, 'material objects being visible through his body.'[64] In December another advert in the press, entitled 'A Ghost', pronounced that it was 'causing the utmost wonder and excitement throughout London, as the immense crowds in Cheapside fully testify'.[65] This was probably no idle boast. As has already been recounted, thousands turned out in 1874 just to see a paper ghost pinned to a tree in Westminster. The company soon produced new ghost scenes and, not unexpectedly, considering their success, imitations soon proliferated to take commercial advantage of the interest in ghost pictures. In the winter of 1857 the company had to take out adverts warning that pirate ghost slides were being circulated and if caught, their producers would be prosecuted. They reminded the public that the genuine ghost pictures were endorsed with the words 'kindly suggested by Sir David Brewster'.[66]

The stereoscopic ghosts, whether legitimate or pirated, were starkly different to the 'naturalistic' ghosts of accidental exposure from which Brewster got his idea. They were theatrical snapshots portraying stereotypical, shrouded visitants, arms raised portentously before their shocked audience. There was no devious attempt to deceive. Brewster, as we saw in a previous chapter, was an influential debunker of magical beliefs through scientific demonstration, and so, considering their debt to him, the Stereoscopic Company, ended their adverts for 'A Ghost' with the proviso that 'This slide for obvious reasons, is largely purchased by parents and schools.' This was a breathtakingly disingenuous statement. There was no obvious educational value in the photographs, no provisos about the folly of believing in ghosts. Indeed they pandered explicitly to the popular thirst for supernatural sensation just as the phantasmagoria had originally done. No doubt amongst the crowds who came to gawp at the photographs on display at the Company's Cheapside premises, expressions of wonder, humour and scepticism mixed with discussion on the reality of ghosts and tales told of recent sightings.

The origin and development of spirit photography from the 1860s onwards was, in contrast, all about deception, about the struggle to provide and exploit physical proof of the truth of spiritualism. Considering the Society for Psychical Research, stage magicians and photographers regularly debunked photographs and demanded more credible evidence, it is strange indeed that by the end of the nineteenth century spirit photographs had became cruder and less convincing. Instead of refining and developing the filmic appearance of ghostly translucence, achievable through long exposure and double exposure, spirit photographers produced what clearly looked like cut and paste superimpositions. Instead of shadowy figures hovering in the background, clearly-defined disembodied faces, obviously cut out of photographs or magazines, appeared in front of or crowding around the sitter. The effect was hardly convincing and sometimes absurdly comical.[67] The reason for this seeming lack of care or sophistication may be related to two profound developments in image making. As we shall see later in this chapter, in 1897 audiences were treated to the portrayal of ghosts in the first motion pictures. Furthermore, two years earlier the discovery of X-rays revealed images of the human body otherwise hidden to the eye. Science, not magic, had truly rendered the invisible visible, and X-ray images quickly caught the public imagination. As an article published in 1896 observed, X-ray photographs were 'repeated in every lecture-room; they are caricatured in comic prints; hits are manufactured out of them at the theatres'.[68] Spirit photography could not compete with these developments, either in terms of visual sensation or in providing demonstrable proof that the photographic plate could capture the invisible. As a consequence, spirit photographers began to produce images primarily for the spiritualist community rather than catering for popular interest. Adhering to popular perceptions of how a ghost should look became less of a consideration, while many spiritualists' critical faculties were impaired by their profound desire for physical proof of the spirit world.

A PATENT GHOST

By the 1840s public interest in magic lantern ghost shows had waned. No doubt the stereoscopic ghosts of the 1850s stole some of their limelight, but the lanterns themselves lost their mystique, having become cheap and easily available. Once the monopoly of scientific instrument makers, they were now being sold widely through retail outlets. In his memoirs Robertson remarked that London opticians had manufactured and sold several thousand 'ghost machines' across Europe.[69] When the London stationers Joseph Nowill and Joseph Burch had their shop burgled in 1817, one of the magic lanterns stolen was valued at a mere five shillings, only two shillings more than a box of dominoes.[70] Middle-class consumers were targeted with advertisements on how to buy and operate lanterns as family amusements. In 1861 'Professor' John Henry Pepper described in clear terms in his *Scientific Amusements for Young People* how to make a camera obscura and operate a magic lantern. Four years later the prestigious London scientific-instrument makers Henry Negretti and Joseph Zambra published a pamphlet on the operation of their magic lanterns that included a section on 'spectral effects, ghosts described, and how to produce them'. In the same year another publication, by 'a mere phantom', also advised on how to buy and use a magic lantern.[71] The profits of the gallantee men were consequently sorely squeezed. No wonder the old showman interviewed by Henry Mayhew grumbled that his show brought in very little: 'When we started, magic lanterns wasn't so common; but we can't keep hold of a good thing in these times.'[72]

By the mid nineteenth century there had also been a definite shift in emphasis from the magic lantern as ghost maker to the magic lantern as sober educational tool. The trend is certainly detectable in advertisements. In 1793 the London magic lantern manufacturer Scott advertised his wares as 'a pleasing Family Amusement' and used the modern-sounding slogan 'A cheerful House should never be without one'. More to the point, each lantern was sold with twelve slides on which were painted '40 grotesque figures'. By the 1830s, however, adverts were more in line with that of the globemakers Messrs Harris and Son. Their 'improved Phantasmagoria Lantern' would not only 'prove a source of rational amusement, but be the means of instructing young people in several branches of useful knowledge'.[73] In a similar vein, in 1825, the optician R. Ebsworth also advertised astronomical slides to accompany his *Popular Treatise* on the subject.[74] During the 1840s and 1850s Pepper's Royal Polytechnic Institution played a significant role in demonstrating the pedagogic value of the magic lantern, and by the mid nineteenth century numerous churchmen had joined the band of enthusiastic lanternists, using slides to give morally-improving illustrated lectures in Sunday schools and halls. A perusal of the catalogues of several major dealers in slides during the second half of the nineteenth century shows that religion, temperance and education constituted the bulk of slide topics.[75] The subject of ghosts was also desensationalised and appropriated for this educational mission. In 1891 the *Pall Mall Gazette* noted,

'Lectures on Ghosts and Witches are getting in demand', and recommended as a good example a lecture, *Gossip about Ghosts*, written by a former chemistry lecturer at the Royal Polytechnic Institution, George Tweedie. It was illustrated with 50 lantern slides, and sold by and available for loan from 'all opticians and lantern outfitters'. The lecture began:

> Spook hunting has recently become as fashionable as Slumming was a few years since, and although I fancy the nett result of it all will be to leave matters pretty much where they were before; the believer continuing to believe, and the scoffer continuing to scoff, it will not be altogether an unprofitable labour if I venture to place before you a summary of what has been recorded of ghostly phenomena.

Amongst the slides and stories were the Hammersmith ghost, 'The Drummer Ghost', the ghost of Julius Caesar, Saul and the Witch of Endor, and the 'Ghost that warned Villiers'. Tweedie's lecture concluded with the observation that the 'average healthy man, properly educated, temperate in all things, goes through the world untroubled by any such phantasms as we have seen to-night'.[76]

Let us return back to the mid nineteenth century once again, for just as it seemed as if the phantasmagoria ghost show was on its way out, a far superior ghost-making technique was developed, which combined the fluidity of real movement achievable using the camera obscura with the sense of translucence and opacity provided by the magic lantern. Furthermore, the image produced did not appear on a screen, thereby creating a three-dimensional effect, and could interact and respond to people in a stage environment. In 1863 it came to be known as 'Pepper's Ghost', after John Henry Pepper, but the origins of the invention lay with a retired Liverpool engineer Henry Dircks (1806–1873).[77] At a scientific conference in 1858 Dircks had used a model to demonstrate how, depending on the strength of the light source, glass could be both transparent and reflect images at the same time. By placing a sheet of glass at the front of a stage, hidden from the audience, and illuminating an actor in front of it with powerful limelight, an image of the actor could be projected onto the stage. Think of how, when a train goes through a tunnel, the images of those sitting on the other side of the carriage appear in the window as though they are external to the train. As one unimpressed witness to Pepper's illusion observed, 'The Metropolitan Railway affords excellent opportunities of observing ghosts of the interior of the carriage in the external atmosphere.'[78] Dirks tried to interest several theatres with his 'Dircksian Phantasmagoria' but the logistics put them off, as major structural changes to the auditorium would have to have been made to ensure that the ghost actor was not visible to the audience and that all the audience could view the illusion. Dircks tinkered with his invention over the next few years but it was only when he teamed up with Pepper that a viable model was found, though Dircks was later embittered by what he perceived as Pepper's appropriation of the invention. Pepper's solution was to have a pit constructed at the front of the stage in which the actor reclined at 45 degrees with his or her image being projected onto a glass sheet that was also positioned at the same angle. It was not long before a magician named Silvester improved the system by reflecting the projection off an angled mirror, thereby allowing the ghost actor to stand upright. By using screens it was also possible to create the startling illusion of headless ghosts or disembodied body parts. Of course it was necessary for the ghost actor and the actors on stage interacting with the apparition to carefully rehearse their choreography, a skilled job in itself.

When it was first shown to the public in 1863 the ghost was a sensation amongst all sections of the public. In May the Prince and Princess of Wales visited the Polytechnic and were given a demonstration of how the illusion worked. Six months later the Royal family were drawn to the Windsor Theatre, for the first time since the days of George III, to see an evening of short dramas constructed around the illusion, including one called *My Uncle's Ghost*.[79] In 1864 a racehorse called Pepper's Ghost appeared at Ascot and other major races. The ballad writers, ever quick to exploit and excite public interest, also immortalised the illusion. One example ran:

> At Music Halls, Theatres too,
> This 'Patent Ghost' they show,
> The Goblin novelty to view,
> Some thousands nightly go;
> For such a sight they gladly pay,
> In order just to boast,
> To all their 'country cousins' – they –
> Have seen a perfect Ghost.[80]

Another good indicator of its cultural impact, in London at least, was that cabmen adopted the name to describe those customers who were in the habit of vanishing before paying their fare. One such character was the jobbing actor and fraudster Henry Horace Linguarde. The nickname was doubly appropriate as Linguarde made a modest living as a Pepper's Ghost actor wandering between provincial theatres. When he was prosecuted for various cases of non-payment in the winter of 1864, his lawyer claimed he was 'labouring, like the ghost he was in the habit of representing, under an ethereal, spiritualised hallucination'.

The jury saw through this defence, however, and Pepper's Ghost was sentenced to twelve months' hard labour.[81]

Dircks and Pepper knew that theatres and music halls would lose no time in mimicking the Ghost and wisely took out a patent. Six music hall and theatre owners challenged the patent on the grounds that they had already been using a similar illusion, but the Lord Chancellor dismissed the case and questioned the veracity of the witnesses' accounts of their pre-Pepper ghosts. Dircks and Pepper's case was also boosted by supportive letters from Michael Faraday and David Brewster. Yet the ruling against the music-hall men may have been harsh, for the Dutch-born Parisian conjuror Henri Robin, an expositor and entertainer in the Pepper mould, claimed he had been putting on plate-glass ghost projections or 'Living Phantasmagoria' as early as 1847. He had demonstrated the illusion during tours of England in the early 1850s and at the Egyptian Hall in 1861. Although Robin's 'Living Phantasmagoria' was evidently not as sophisticated as Pepper's Ghost, the basics, as described by Robin, were similar enough to prevent Dircks and Pepper from obtaining royalties for the use of their illusion in France.[82] The Ghost proved more profitable across the Atlantic. In early 1863 the American barnstorming showman Harry Watkins had seen a performance at the Polytechnic whilst on tour in England, and immediately snapped up the American rights to the illusion. As a vehicle to display the illusion he chose a mediocre melodrama called *True to the Last*, concerning a villain tormented by the ghosts of his victims. It was first shown in a New York theatre in August 1863, and although the play got stinking reviews, the Ghost ensured it ran profitably for nearly two months.[83]

The presentation of the Ghost at the Polytechnic was moulded in Pepper's tried and tested fashion. Its employment in brief dramas, such as Dickens's short story *The Haunted Man*, provided the entertainment while accompanying lectures on optics and illusion got across the didactic message about the folly of ghost beliefs and supposed spiritualist manifestations. Mockery was also employed. Amongst the entertainments put on in the 1860s were such 'laughable spectral sketches' as *The Haunted House* and *The Spectre Barber*.[84] However, not all were convinced by Pepper's balancing act. An anonymous correspondent to *The Times* complained of the Polytechnic's ghost shows that 'Mysteries in professed conjuring shops are to be expected and tolerated, but in establishments designed for instruction, and recommended to public attention on that ground, they are entirely out of place.'[85] Furthermore, it is clear from Dircks's account of his invention that he had little intention or interest in using his ghost illusion to educate. He thought it 'a safe prediction, that the belief in ghosts will never die', and rather then expend futile effort trying to undermine it, he desired rather to provide a more authentic simulation of a ghost to heighten theatrical sensation.[86]

GHOST SHOWS TO EARLY CINEMA

As we shall see in the next chapter, Pepper's Ghost continued to pull in audiences at the Polytechnic, the Egyptian Hall and regional theatres for a couple of decades, but it proved a more enduring attraction for the itinerant showmen who travelled around the fairs of provincial England. Amongst the more unusual job descriptions to be found in the censuses must be 'Ghost showman' and 'traveller with ghost show', which were the occupations of one Richard Bennett and George King in 1881. During the last 25 years of the nineteenth century numerous such shows toured the country, the most notable being Wall's 'Grand Phantascope', 'Captain Payne's Ghost Show', 'Wallser's Ghost Illusion', and Bidall's wonderfully titled 'Phantaspectra Ghostodrama'.[87] Heindrick Hudson's 'The Spectre Buccaneer, and His Ghostly Surroundings' advertised that his 'entirely new and marvellous Ghost walks and talks with the audience, dances, takes himself to pieces, hangs himself upon the wall, &c.'.[88] Such showmen usually pitched at fairs and races or hired out venues in towns. Still, any convenient open space would do, as we find from the prosecution of William Wallser in January 1876 for keeping a place of public music and dancing without a license. Wallser, who came from a well-known family of travelling showmen, had set up his caravans on the site of two demolished houses in Old Street, Shoreditch. He placed the two caravans one in front of the other and covered the space in between with canvas. The caravan facing the street contained a steam organ, which played to attract punters, who were charged one penny each. Under the canvas a Pepper's Ghost display was put on with an organ and triangle accompaniment. The show lasted about 20 minutes and consisted of the apparition of a headless man who has his head restored to its rightful place, followed by dancing female figures.[89]

The most reputed of all ghost showmen was Randall Williams (1846–1898), whose parents had made a living performing conjuring tricks and hawking knick-knacks at fairs around Wales.[90] The young Randall felt cramped by his parents' Welsh tours, and ran away to expand his horizons by working as an assistant to showmen around England. Once he had saved up enough money, he set up his own conjuring and illusion booth. Around 1863 he attended a display of Pepper's Ghost at a venue in Manchester, and from his front-seat position managed to carefully observe how the trick was done. Showing the enterprise, astuteness and flair that later led him to entitle himself, justifiably, as the 'King of Showmen', Williams decided to devise his own version of the trick and made it the centrepiece of his travelling spectacle. So lucrative was his new show that Williams was later able to splash out £500 on a new and impressive gilded show frontage. As he recalled shortly before his death, 'ever since the ghost business has been the mainstay of my show'.[91] By the mid 1890s, however, it would seem that Pepper's Ghost was no longer the crowd-puller it had once been, and so one can imagine the enthusiasm and relief with which ghost showmen like Williams greeted the advent of the motion picture.

In the first few years of English cinema, beginning in 1895, most films were made by setting the camera in one position and filming familiar moving objects such as people, boats and trains – essentially capturing mundane actuality. Depicting lifelike movement was the initial novelty of the cinema, coupled with the desire for people to see themselves or the familiar environment around them. For both these reasons films of workers pouring out of factories were amongst the most popular. The film would then be processed as quickly as possible and shown in the local vicinity to crowds of people wanting to see images of themselves flickering on the screen. Editing, which is the key to the magic of modern cinema, only developed in the early twentieth century, but before then several film-makers had innovated by creating brief cinematic fantasies using stop motion, stage illusion techniques and camera trickery developed from spirit photography.[92]

Considering that most of the earliest cinematographers had been magicians, magic lanternists or ghost showmen, it is no surprise to find that, when it came to exploiting the new visual medium, they reprised not only tried and tested techniques but also familiar subject matter.[93] The French trick-film pioneer George Méliès's introductory prospectus of 1897 advertised that he specialised 'mainly in fantastic or artistic scenes', which, he observed, differed 'entirely from the customary views supplied by the cinematograph – street scenes or scenes of everyday life'.[94] Amongst them were The Vanishing Lady, in which a woman is transformed into a skeleton, and the self-explanatory The Haunted Castle (1897). Over the next few years ghosts made further appearances in a handful of his films, such as Spanish Inquisition (1900), in which the appearance of the ghost of a torture victim leads to the satisfying death of an executioner as he swings at the apparition with an axe and falls into a fire. The Jewellery Robbery (1903) concerns another vengeful spirit, this time that of a woman who has been killed by a burglar, wrapped in a sheet and thrown into a trunk. The woman's ghost, along with several companions, confuses and panics the burglar until the police arrive. The same year he also made Le Revenant, shown in England as The Apparition, or Mr. Jones' Comical Experiences with a Ghost, in which the movement of furniture and candles by an invisible force plagues hotel guests. The ghost then manifests itself, changing from transparent to opaque form.

Méliès (1861–1938), the son of a shoe manufacturer, became captivated with stage magic during a year's work experience in a London shoe and corset shop. He was a regular at the Egyptian Hall, and back in France, several years later, bought the Théâtre Robert-Houdin, in which he put on magic shows and lantern projections. Inspired by the Lumière brothers' première of the ciné-matographe in December 1895, but rebuffed by the brothers when he asked to purchase one of their machines, he travelled to England to purchase similar equipment from one Robert W. Paul and used it to devise his own camera and projector. Just over three months after the Lumière brothers' première, Méliès had set up the world's first permanent cinema at the Théâtre Robert-Houdin.

His equally pioneering English contemporary in the field of film illusion was the Brighton-based George Albert Smith (1864–1959).[95] In his teenage years Smith had made a living doing seaside shows involving hypnotism and mind-reading. Evidently a skilled showman, even in his youth, his techniques were well known and had long been practised by stage magicians. His hypnotism act, for example, followed the same pattern as modern ones in which stooges, apparently randomly picked from the audience, were employed to say and do stupid things while supposedly under the influence. Thanks to numerous positive reviews in Brighton newspapers, in 1882 he made the acquaintance of one of the founders of the Society for Psychical Research, Edmund Gurney, and became his private secretary until Gurney's death in 1888. Smith continued to work for the SPR until 1892 when he moved back to Brighton and took over running the St Ann's Well pleasure gardens. He successfully built up the business, adding baboons, trapeze artists, a gypsy fortune-teller, photography and magic lantern shows. Motion pictures were to be another attraction.[96] In 1898 he produced a series of one-minute films, and it is no surprise, considering his background, that the subject matter was predominantly supernatural. One of them was the ghost scene from *The Corsican Brothers*, an old stage favourite based on a Dumas novel, for which Smith used his own patented double-exposure technique.[97] Another was the comedy *Photographing a Ghost*, in which two men carry a large box marked 'ghost' into a photographer's studio. When the box is opened the transparent ghost of a 'swell' steps out. It plays merry with the photographer who tries to strike it with a chair. In the end the ghost disappears through the floor, perhaps in imitation of a theatrical trapdoor exit. *The Mesmerist, Or Body and Soul* also used double exposure to show the transparent spirit of a young girl, under mesmeric influence, leave her body, walk around the room, and then return.

Sadly none of Smith's spirit films have survived, but those of the influential English trick-film-making partnership of the aforementioned Robert W. Paul (1869–1943) and Walter Booth (1869–1938) have done. They were an ideal partnership with Paul, the producer, being a scientific instrument maker, just like his seventeenth-century lanternist predecessors, while the director Booth was an illusionist, who had worked as a magician at the Egyptian Hall. Their signature ghost film was The Haunted Curiosity Shop (1901), an impressive single-shot picture lasting just under two minutes, in which a shopkeeper is plagued by the floating head of an Egyptian mummy that turns into a blacked-up woman, which he manages to shut in a wardrobe. A faint ghost then appears in front of the wardrobe. When the shopkeeper opens the wardrobe again, out comes an ancient Egyptian who then turns into a skeleton. More antics then follow with some dwarves. The same year they also produced Scrooge; Or Marley's Ghost, the topic of a popular lantern slide and now the earliest film rendition of Dickens's story, in which Paul and Booth had Marley's ghost dressed in the traditional white sheet posing in the fashion of the stereoscopic photographs. They also produced a ghost in their medieval extravaganza The Magic Sword, which also featured witches, ogres, a fairy and a magic cauldron.[98] The third of the early English ghost-film producers, though working a few years later, was Cecil Hepworth (1874–1953), whose father Thomas had been a successful magic lanternist and author of several books on the subject. In Hepworth's The Ghost's Holiday (1907) some spirits are seen rising from their churchyard graves and holding a ball at a hotel. Five years later he produced Ghosts, in which two men dress up as ghosts to frighten each other.

It was not only English and French film-makers who exploited the fascination with ghosts. Early American studios also appealed to the popular interest in the supernatural. Like Smith and Méliès, the American film pioneer Thomas Edison and his Manufacturing Company resorted to ghostly scenarios in their early films. In 1900, for example, they produced Uncle Josh in a Spooky Hotel. With a running time of just over a minute, this comedy consists of a shrouded ghost that appears behind Josh and slaps him as he talks to his landlord. Josh retaliates, thinking the landlord has hit him. The ghost then reappears to slap the landlord, who hits back at Josh. The film ends with both of them seeing the ghost and running out of the room.[99]

Looking through the content of all these pre-World War I films, familiar themes emerge, which is not surprising considering the derivative nature of early film fiction. When ghosts were portrayed as realities their role was usually to enact revenge upon murderers, following the venerable tradition of ghosts in literature and popular culture. In the 1914 American production Ghost of the Mine, for example, a murderer is brought to justice by the ghost of a young girl he has killed. Another earlier film, *Remorse* (1906), produced by the Pathé brothers, concerns a servant who murders his rich master to steal his sack of gold. The servant hides the body in a haystack, but the ghost of the master suddenly appears. The frightened servant tries to stab it with a fork but it disappears. More ghosts appear in and around the house to torment the murderer until the Grim Reaper arrives to serve justice. But as films grew longer and more driven by plot, ghostly visions were increasingly portrayed as frauds perpetrated for criminal purposes. The setting was nearly always a haunted building. The English film *Miss Simpkin's Boarders; The Incident of the Curate and the Ghost* (1910) concerned boarding house residents chasing a ghost who is actually a burglar in disguise. The folly of their quest is highlighted when they end up capturing by mistake a curate who has gone for a glass of water. A popular American drama, *The Ghost Breaker* (1914), co-directed by Cecil B. De Mille, and remade in 1922 and 1940, was based around the bogus haunting of a Spanish castle to aid the stealing of hidden treasure.

Considering the ongoing controversy surround spiritualism at the time, it is surprising how little early cinema engaged with the subject – particularly in view of the important role photography played in the debate. In 1900, Edison's Manufacturing Company had produced the comedy *A Visit to the Spiritualist*, in which a country 'hayseed' is mesmerised by a spiritualist and sees ghosts and goblins. Two years later Méliès produced *The Cabinet Trick of the Davenport Brothers*. But it was another decade before cinematic drama tackled the subject. In 1913 the actor and film-maker Douglas Payne produced *Spiritualism Exposed*, in which a London medium tries to defraud an heiress by pretending she has spirit communications. The American production *Bogus Ghost* (1916) similarly concerned a woman who is thought to have been drowned. She is alive, however, and pretends to be a spirit to convince the clients of a fraudulent medium. The upsurge in spiritualism during World War I generated a few sympathetic film portrayals, such as *The Greatest Question* (1919), in which the spirit of a soldier appears to his mother, but any sympathetic rapprochement with spiritualism was short-lived.[100] Through the 1920s and 1930s the portrayal of spirits was used to highlight the folly of believing such things, as exemplified by the unmasking of a fake spiritualist by a gang of children in *Shivering Spooks* (1926).

With much of the output of the early studios being highly derivative in subject matter, early cinema's most original contribution to the portrayal of ghosts in fiction was in comedy. As the next chapter will show, up until the advent of motion pictures, ghosts generally appeared in plays and novels as mysterious, blood-curdling or portentous entities. There were a few exceptions, such as their use in early eighteenth century satires, and in a couple of Pepper's Ghost sketches, but, otherwise, fictional ghosts were overwhelmingly portrayed as realities serving dramatic and often sensational purposes. While the early trick-films used ghosts in humorous situations, the emphasis was still on impressing the audience with the illusion. It was the silent slapstick comedies that created a new, enduring ghost genre. English films like Miss Simpkin's Boarders and Hepworth's Ghosts created the template of mistaken identities and hoaxers, but it was Hollywood's silent film industry, particularly Hal Roach's studio, which turned the ghost into a favourite comedy standard.

The principal gag was based on the comedian mistaking someone for a ghost because he or she is covered in some white substance. So in Buster Keaton's The Goat (1921), Keaton's character is frightened by a construction worker covered in mortar, while in Laurel and Hardy's early talkie The Live Ghost (1934) the duo are terrified by a drunken sailor who has fallen into some whitewash. The classic white sheet was not forgotten. In Neighbors (1920), Keaton is mistaken for a ghost as he hides under a sheet while trying to evade a cop. In Laurel and Hardy's Habeas Corpus (1928) the pair are hired to steal bodies from a graveyard, with much of the action centring around a detective draped in a white sheet who runs through the churchyard, and then hides in and rises from the grave being opened by Stan. Ghosts were also used to set up the great sight gag of the comedian's hair standing on end. Laurel and Hardy employed this, but one of its earliest outings was in Harold Lloyd's haunted house comedy Haunted Spooks (1920). There was, of course, nothing new in these various depictions. They were replicating actual experience. As we have seen in previous chapters, people did go around town and countryside dressed in white sheets to frighten people, sometimes literally to death. People really were mistaken for ghosts because they were wearing white clothing, and once again the consequences for those concerned were by no means humorous. Played out on the screen, however, the very same situations were meant to be farcical: only nincompoops and ignoramuses, albeit sympathetic ones, could possibly be fooled, and the audience were meant to laugh at their fright. As a consequence the slapstick ghost robbed the white sheet of its power to scare. Many millions today believe that the spirits of the dead walk the earth, but surely few people, if confronted with a white sheet on a dark night, would seriously cry 'Ghost!' Laurel and Hardy helped put paid to that.

*   *   *

The comedy stars of the silent film era are all dead, of course, but the fact that they live on in their films highlights why the history of projection has had an equivocal relationship with ghosts. Writing in 1887, Joseph Lawson stated with satisfaction that Professor Pepper's Ghost had helped to extinguish the last remnants of ghost belief by showing people that it was 'impossible to distinguish the genuine from the manufactured.'[101] His confidence was misplaced, as was that of earlier magic lanternists. Ghost-belief was vibrant in the towns and cities where the population was most exposed to the magic lantern and Pepper's Ghost. If anything, it may have stimulated urbanites to go out into the streets and try and see the real thing for themselves. Ghost projection opened up new realms of possibility. In a sense, by creating realistic ghosts, scientific endeavour reduced the gap between reality and belief. Film, in particular, helped cement this perception. As well as being an imaginative tool for simulating spirits, it also captured the actual dead for posterity and brought them back to life over and over again. They looked directly at the audience through the camera lens and even talked to them. They may not have been ghosts, but if the dead could break the fourth wall of cinema then, despite the objections of physics, it seemed less implausible to the human imagination that they could also travel through the fourth dimension.

EIGHT

Treading the Boards
and Under the Covers

The historical experience of haunting cannot be properly understood without considering the fictional portrayal of ghosts over the centuries. Fiction, whether presented on the page or on the stage, both reflected and shaped popular perceptions about ghosts. For much of the period under discussion the majority of people were illiterate, and most people never visited a theatre, but the influence of plays, pamphlet accounts, ballads and novels reached beyond the theatre audiences and those who could read. It is difficult to tease apart the patterns of influence between the media, belief and public perception in the past, but we must be sensitive to the reciprocity between them. It is certainly the case that playwrights, novelists and balladeers pandered to general preconceptions to ensure audience recognition. Ghosts behaved in certain ways, and to depart too far from popular preconceptions was to risk failure in attempting to recreate the haunted experience. Yet, in the process, stereotypical ghostly traits were reinforced in popular belief and action. Many of the hauntings discussed in this book can be seen as forms of popular or street theatre, which in their manifestation or deliberate staging, were influenced by contemporary literature and visual entertainment. It is likely, for instance, that the depiction of ghosts in white sheets on stage and in literature helped to perpetuate the use of this disguise by hoaxers. Those witnessing a hoax were often participating in the drama rather than being passive spectators. They had to construct their own plots, and literary and theatrical as well as oral traditions shaped how they made sense of what they saw and heard. The fictional portrayal of ghosts dates back to classical antiquity, but its influence on the English public begins with the rise of print culture.

THE ELIZABETHAN STAGE

The ghost was a central figure in the development of Elizabethan drama, though the interest had surprisingly little to do with the Reformation preoccupation

216

with purgatory.[1] Ghosts certainly inhabited late medieval metrical tragedies, where they were guided from the depths of hell and acted as witnesses to marvellous journeys,[2] but it was the tragedians of Ancient Greece and Rome who most influenced Elizabethan dramatists. The flourishing of Renaissance humanism during the early sixteenth century, and the re-engagement with the literature of the ancients, led to the emulation and development of classical intellectual thought and artistic creativity. Since ghosts played an important role in the cultures of death and the afterlife in pagan Rome and Greece, they were well represented in classical tragedy.[3] The plays of the philosopher Lucius Annaeus Seneca (4 BC–65 AD) are generally agreed to have been the most influential texts on Elizabethan theatre. Yet he was by no means an original dramatist. His plays were essentially variations of those by the great Greek tragedians of the fifth century BC – Aeschylus and Euripides. It was Aeschylus who first used ghosts as dramatic, vengeful interventionists in human affairs, while one of Euripides' lasting contributions was the concept of the prologue ghost, a literary device where a ghost sets the scene of a play and introduces the main characters. Seneca combined both ghostly roles in his tragedies.[4] The strength of his influence on Elizabethan drama was due less to his originality and more to the availability of his works in translation. English versions of his two plays that employed ghost characters, *Thyestes* and *Agamemnon*, had first been translated into English in the 1560s, but it was the collected edition of his translated works published in 1581 that proved most influential.[5]

A few English plays employed ghosts in benign roles, such as George Peele's *Old Wives' Tale*, in which the grateful ghost of poor Jack, whose body the local churchmen have refused to bury, appears to aid the gentleman, Eumenides, who offered to pay for his burial.[6] However, most of the dramatic ghosts of the late Elizabethan period were vengeful bloody spirits in the Senecan fashion. Thomas Kyd's *The Spanish Tragedie*, which concerns a Spanish gentleman's descent into madness following the murder of his son and his eventual revenge on his killers, which may have been staged as early as the late 1580s, set the trend, with the ghost acting as a commentator on the unfolding events. Elsewhere ghosts commonly appeared on stage shrieking 'Revenge!' before retiring out of sight; or, in the case of the anonymously-authored *Locrine*, the slightly more expansive 'Revenge, revenge for blood' and 'Vindicta, vindicta'. In fact, such was the ubiquity of these limited, formulaic ghostly exclamations in plays of the period that they inevitably attracted mocking criticism in some literary quarters. The author and physician Thomas Lodge, having seen a pre-Shakespearean version of *Hamlet* in 1596, objected to 'the ghost which cried so miserally at ye Theator, like an oisterwife, Hamlet, revenge'.[7] The comedy *A Warning for Fair Women* (1599) also lamented:

> Then, too, a filthy whining ghost,
> Lapt in some foul sheet, or a leather pilch,
> Comes screaming like a pig half sticked,
> And cries, Vindicta! – Revenge, Revenge![8]

The most famous stage ghosts of the period were, of course, those penned by Shakespeare. It is intriguing why he had such enthusiasm for theatrical ghosts when they evidently held relatively little interest for those other major dramatists of the age, Christopher Marlowe and Ben Jonson. Perhaps it was his greater affinity with the popular drama and beliefs of the period. As Stephen Greenblatt has observed, 'What there is again and again in Shakespeare, far more than in any of his contemporaries, is a sense that ghosts, real or imagined, are good theater.'[9] The range of his dramatic use of ghosts was also more sophisticated than the many Senecan clones. He invested the vengeful ghost 'with a new dignity and endowed it with a new purpose'.[10] It is the depth and resonance of the ghost scenes in *Richard III*, *Hamlet*, *Macbeth* and *Julius Caesar* which ensured their enduring appeal to audiences of all tastes and social levels across the centuries and across a range of media.

Much has been written about Shakespeare's ghosts over the last 300 years, with the opinions expressed reflecting broader, changing cultural debates regarding their reality. One area of discussion, which has recently attracted considerable attention, has been the extent to which Shakespeare's ghosts are purgatorial in conception. Do they tell us much about his religious views and, indeed, those of a society still mentally negotiating the transformations wrought by the Reformation? Not much it would seem. But the most enduring and contentious issue historically has been whether Shakespeare intended his ghosts to be subjective or objective; in other words, figments or realities. The debate began in earnest during the mid eighteenth century. From the perspective of the 'enlightened' critic, Shakespeare could only be taken seriously if his ghosts were mere projections of disturbed or guilty minds. To have ghosts wandering the stage portraying a reality was too absurd to merit serious contemplation. The views of the writer and actor Arthur Murphy (1727–1805) were representative of this early psychological school of literary interpretation. In Murphy's opinion, 'Shakespeare seems to have selected his *Hamlet* chiefly to shew the horrors and gloomy sights that continually crowd upon the mind of a weak or melancholy person.' Thus the ghost scene in Macbeth was 'one of the strongest proofs that a GHOST or APPARITION proceeds either from GUILT or FEAR or is a mixture of both'.[11] By the Victorian period the general consensus was that Shakespeare's ghosts were intended to be nothing more than hallucinations or subjective mental projections. In other words, Shakespeare used ghosts as a means of representing physically the mental states of characters. As Alfred Roffe wrote in 1851, in his philosophical discourse on the subject, 'Most of Shakespeare's admirers doubtless imagine that such an intellect as his, could never have given credence to a ghost.'[12]

By the late nineteenth century the pervasive influence of spiritualism across the arts had generated something of a backlash against the materialist and psychological inspiration ascribed to Shakespeare's use of ghosts. In 1884 Oscar Wilde deemed it necessary to point out to a journalist that 'in Shakespeare's day ghosts were not shadowy, subjective conceptions, but beings of flesh and blood, only beings living on the other side of the border of life'.[13] A full-blooded psychical as opposed to psychological interpretation was proffered in 1925 by the American Theosophist Louis William Rogers (1859–1953). Rather than merely reiterating the point that in Elizabethan England many educated people believed in ghosts, Rogers drew support for a literal reading of the ghost scenes by citing 'reliable scientific testimony' affirming the spirit world provided by the likes of William Crookes. The 'public is at last putting prejudice aside', he was relieved to say, and so people could appreciate Shakespeare's ghosts at face value.[14] In academic circles too, the arrogant Enlightenment assumptions regarding Shakespeare's intentions came under attack. In 1907 Elmer Edgar Stoll wrote an article for an American literary journal in which he criticised the 'common, even universal' subjective approach to Shakespeare's use of ghosts adopted by those who taught or wrote about the playwright. Stoll argued that nearly all the ghosts were meant to be interpreted and viewed as objective realities; they were themselves 'both meaning and fact'.[15]

Getting back to Elizabethan and early Stuart theatre, how were ghosts portrayed on stage? Could one tell who was a ghost just from looking at the actor? Or was knowledge of the plot necessary? To a certain extent theatre managers and playwrights appealed to the popular conceptions of how ghosts manifested themselves. There are certainly some references to the wearing of white sheets, for example,[16] though white clothing was also used to represent virgins and shepherds. But equally, traditional stage garb for those playing ghosts were pilches, which were warm garments made of dressed furry leather worn in cold weather.[17] This Eskimo-like apparel was presumably symbolic of the coldness of the dead. Cadaverous paleness was also an integral characteristic of the stage ghost. Though little is known about the use of stage make-up at the time, it is clear that flour was used to whiten the faces of actors playing 'mealy' ghosts, just as it was nearly two centuries later.[18] In the more sophisticated playhouses of the period, stage trapdoors were employed to make the denizens of the underworld rise, and it is likely that smoke was used to make the entrance more otherworldly.

Ghosts, no matter whether benign or evil, did not ascend from below stage solely for supernatural effect, there was also an important symbolic reason. The theatre represented a microcosm of the universe, most obviously demonstrated by Shakespeare's Globe, with the stage acting as the plane of human existence, while the area below stage equated with the infernal region where witches and devils were at home and the realm of purgatory where the souls of the dead were punished. The space above the stage represented the heavens from whence angels and the gods of the ancients descend to the stage to communicate with messages for the living.[19] Yet, while stage managers and playwrights were obviously conscious of and influenced by this spatial cosmic symbolism, they were by no means bound by it. Regarding the appearance of ghosts on stage, from a purely theatrical point of view it was best to employ the trap entrance sparingly, as its overuse lessened its dramatic effectiveness. The movement of some stage ghosts were also better served by entering and exiting via the sides of the stage or, as in Hamlet, through the arras or rear stage curtains, which could serve to represent the battlements through which the ghost of the king is seen to disappear.[20]

There is some debate about whether thunderous sound effects were commonly used. As well as heightening the sense of drama, such an accompaniment would have served the practical purpose of drowning out the sound of the winches and pulleys used to hoist and lower the traps. One late eighteenth-century critic complained of the 'squeaking trap-doors' whenever ghosts appeared, and recommended they walk on and off to avoid such cacophonous intrusion.[21] What there is certainly no evidence for in the Elizabethan period is the use of music to evoke a sense of the eerie.[22] One of the earliest references to ghostly mood music is in Thomas Goffe's The Raging Turke (1631) where there is a direction for 'solemne Musicke' at the appearance of several spirits who gather around the bed of the main character.

Whatever their apparel, whether white sheets, pilches, a bloody shirt, or armour as in Hamlet, ghosts generally had to walk in a certain way, sometimes described as gliding but always slowly and silently.[23] Quick and nimble ghosts had no place in tragedy. The critics were ever sensitive about this. A waspish review of Hamlet at Drury Lane in 1822 complained, 'Mr. Cooper played the ghost with too much elasticity of movement: from his mode of entering the room ... he might really have passed for the ghost of a dancing master.'[24] As to special effects, we saw in the previous chapter that people like Cornelius Drebbel were employed to provide sensational lighting and illusory effects for aristocratic masques. John Dee constructed an impressive automated scarabeus, which appeared to fly, for a staging of a comedy by Aristophanes. On the continent Jesuit theatre productions were particularly well known for their use of mechanical effects.[25] There is no evidence, however, of the camera obscura or other mirror effects being used to create ghostly images on the English stage. A bit of smoke, pilches, mealy skin and a trap door entrance was the most audiences could expect.

FROM SHAKESPEARE TO DRYDEN

The influence of Senecan tragedy continued to dominate the theatre during the early seventeenth century, and the success of Shakespeare's ghosts no doubt further spurred other dramatists to exploit the spirit world. George Chapman's *The Revenge of Bussy D'Ambois* (1613), for example, concerned yet another murdered family member urging his kin to exact revenge on his killers, while Fulke Greville's posthumously published *Alaham, a Tragedy* (1633) was constructed around a prologue ghost. It has been suggested that stage ghosts began to lose their voices around this time, with their stage presence increasingly limited to a mime of pointing, beckoning and head shaking.[26] This is certainly the case in the plays of several renowned playwrights. Webster's *The White Devil* (1612) contains the silent ghost of Isabella, while in Philip Massinger's *The Unnaturall Combat*, written during the 1620s, there is a lengthy dialogue with frustrating ghosts who respond with 'several gestures' and then answer 'still by signes' before exiting.[27] Yet a perusal of the work of lesser-known and anonymous playwrights, based on classical scenarios, reveals that numerous talkative ghosts continued to tramp Jacobean stages. The ghost of Caesar in *The Tragedie of Caesar and Pompey* (1607) holds a lengthy conversation with Brutus, while the three ghosts at the centre of John Stephens's *Cynthia's Revenge* (1613) are models of loquacity.

Theatres were suppressed during Cromwell's Puritan Republic, and when their doors opened again on the return of monarchy in 1660, dramatic playwrights increasingly turned their backs on ghostly characters. The *farceurs* were in the ascendant and quick to mock earnest portrayals of the supernatural. Ghosts were increasingly revealed as the product of mistaken identity or mischievous design – with hilarious consequences. Pilches were consigned to history as white sheets proved more appropriate and convenient garb for situation comedy. In the anonymously-written farce *The Ghost: Or the Woman Wears the Breeches* (1653), for example, one of the characters dons a sheet to play a wrathful spirit, and is asked:

> Were't though the Ghost and thing that cheated us?
> Thank this white sheet and this disguise, I was;
> Nay, tremble not, I am no Ghost.[28]

In Thomas Shadwell's comedy *Epsom-Wells*, a gentleman is robbed by thieves who dump him in a churchyard, tie his hands behind his back and put a white sheet over him to frighten away potential rescuers. John Vanbrugh's *The Relapse* (1697) contains a scene in which one of the characters is unnecessarily frightened: 'I thought verily I had seen a Ghost and 'twas nothing but the white Curtain, with a black Hood pinn'd up against it.' In more absurdist vein is the character in Peter Motteux's *The Novelty* (1697) who is plagued by a supposed ghost dressed in a shroud. To defend himself from its next ghastly visit he gropes in the dark for a dagger and instead grabs a sausage – 'I'll venture to keep that for my Breakfast! But I think I feel my Pistol, I'll keep him off with that.'[29]

Nevertheless, despite the increasing tendency to portray stage ghosts as frauds and fancies of the imagination, the public evidently continued to appreciate the appearance of 'real' ghosts in old-style tragedies. Nathaniel Lee included the novelty of singing ghosts in the successful staging of his rhyming drama the *Rival Queens* (1677), and vengeful and warning ghosts in his Roman play *Nero* (1674).[30] In the latter, Lee, like many of his colleagues, played safe by setting the appearance of ghosts in the ancient past and generated deliberate ambiguity about their reality by having them appear to the lead characters at moments of insanity or love-induced anxiety. The only Restoration playwright to exploit unabashedly the popular appeal of ghosts was John Dryden (1631–1700), who employed them in a variety of innovative ways and settings, though always comfortably in historical contexts. He had the cheek, for example, to have the ghost of Shakespeare speak the prologue in his stage adaptation of *Troilus and Cressida*. His rhyming historical drama *The Indian Emperour*, first staged in 1665, which concerned the conquest of Mexico, contained a scene in which two ghosts rise up through a trapdoor, stand still and silent on stage, and point accusingly at King Montezuma. Next his murdered queen ascends, a dagger in her breast, at the sight of which Montezuma exclaims:

> I feel my Hair grow stiff, my Eye-balls rowl,
> This is the only form could shake my Soul.

The queen's ghost proceeds to give a long speech about how she awaits his spirit after his death, and then returns below the stage.[31] When, a few years later, Dryden returned to the same setting in *Almanzor and Almahide: Or, the Conquest of Granada by the Spaniards* he created an even more loquacious female ghost, this time the mother of Almanzor. Instead of rising from the ground, however, she appears standing in a doorway. The portrayal of the ghost of Laius, King of Thebes, in Dryden's musical version of *Oedipus: A Tragedy*, was, in Walter Scott's admiring view, only paralleled by Shakespeare's spirit creations.

As the stage directions show, Laius's ghost is first heard groaning beneath the stage in traditional fashion, accompanied by a peel of thunder and flashes of lightening. Later, the stage is darkened then suddenly illuminated as he arises in a chariot, with the ghosts of three of his men behind him. Later he appears less impressively, however, to do a bit of the usual pointing before vanishing with a clap of thunder.

Dryden was the creator of some of the most talkative ghosts on stage of the period, and he was well aware of their audience appeal. In an epilogue he once wrote:

> Their treat is what your Pallats relish most,
> Charm! Song! And Show! a Murder and a Ghost!
> We know not what you can desire or hope,
> To please you more, but burning of a Pope.[32]

Their prominence in his work inevitably attracted criticism from some quarters, most notably George Villiers (1628–1687), the Duke of Buckingham, who mocked Dryden's work in his enduring, co-written satire on heroic drama, *The Rehearsal* (1671). One passage of dialogue in the play runs as follows:

Smith: How comes this song in here? For, methinks, there is no great occasion for it.

Bayes: Alack, Sir, you know nothing: you must ever interlard your Playes with Songs, Ghosts and Dances.[33]

In 1672 Dryden responded to such criticisms, observing that 'Some men think they have raised a great argument against the use of spectres and magic in heroic poetry, by saying they are unnatural.' He countered, quite reasonably, by arguing that, 'an heroic poet is not tied to a bare representation of what is true, or exceeding probable; but that he may let himself loose to visionary objects and to the representation of such things'.[34]

While the portrayal of ghosts in plays became increasingly contested from an intellectual and artistic point of view during the late seventeenth century, popular literature embraced the ghost with even greater enthusiasm than ever before.[35] An early eighteenth-century correspondent to *The Spectator* grumbled about the many distracting noises emanating from the streets of London, amongst them

> the publication of full and true accounts of houses haunted, ghosts appearing, &c. which the orators (perhaps half a dozen at a time in a street) harangue us with (every three steps) as loud as lungs will let them.[36]

Referring to the haunting of their Epworth home, Samuel Wesley wrote to one of his sons that 'It would make a glorious penny book for Jack Dunton.'[37] As the examples of broadsides, ballads and pamphlets I have cited in previous chapters show, ghosts were nearly always portrayed as either purposeful and/or diabolically malicious. The reality of ghosts was upheld, reflecting the position of Glanvill and his ilk rather than the Anglican orthodoxy of the time. One pamphlet concluded its account with the statement, 'By this we may see and admire the power and Justice of an Almighty God', while another warned 'let it be your real Example, and thereby so moderate your Deeds and Actions in this life, that hereafter, in the World to come, we may enjoy Peace and Rest'.[38] In terms of audience reach, the producers of such literature were probably more effective in arguing the religious significance of the existence of ghosts than the contemporary efforts of Glanvill, Baxter and Sinclair.

The format of popular ghost literature was also used to spread political propaganda. During the Civil War and Restoration numerous pamphlets appeared professing to contain valedictory dialogues with the ghosts of Charles I or Cromwell.[39] Another flood of such literature poured from the presses during the crisis of the Stuart monarchy between 1678 and 1683, caused by attempts to prevent the Catholic James II from acceding to the English throne. Both Whigs and Tories (particularly Whigs) exploited a range of prophetic phenomena such as comets, astrological conjunctions and the apparitions of armies in the air, to bolster the righteousness of their cause.[40] Those involved in the Popish Plot proved particularly ripe for ghost imagery, with titles like *A Dialogue Between Doctor Titus and Bedlow's Ghost* (1684), which referred to William Bedlow (Bedloe) and Titus Oates, two of the conspirators who alleged they had uncovered a Catholic plot to murder Charles II.[41] The pretender to the throne the Duke of Monmouth also inspired pamphlets, such as the royalist broadside in which a ghost appears to the Duke and says 'Like Samuel at the Necromantick Call, I rise to tell thee, God has left thee, Saul.'[42] While the title pages of such political squibs aped those of the entertaining and moralistic popular accounts of ghosts, the contents rarely had any exciting narrative content, and were more akin to the dialogues and satirical verses of plays of the period.

ENLIGHTENMENT AND ENTERTAINMENT

Joseph Addison observed in 1711:

there is nothing which delights and terrifies our English Theatre so much as a Ghost, especially when he appears in a bloody Shirt. A Spectre has very often saved a Play, though he has done nothing but stalked across the Stage, or rose through a Cleft of it, and sunk again without speaking one Word.[43]

He may have had Dryden in mind, but in the early years of the century of Enlightenment the hammy tragedy had by no means been banished from the stage. Shrouded ghosts arose and sank as usual in the likes of Roger Boyle Orrery's *The Tragedy of King Saul*, Aaron Hill's *Elfrid*, and Benjamin Griffin's *Injured Virtue*.[44] Ironically, a ghost did not save Addison's own comedy, *The Drummer: Or, the Haunted House*, based on the Tedworth case of 1662. It folded in 1715 after only three nights. The play was not advertised as Addison's and he was so embarrassed by its poor reception that he kept his authorship a secret. It was only after his death in 1719 that his good friend and co-writer of *The Spectator* Richard Steele republished the play and defended its qualities.[45] Although it was published several times in English as well as in German, Italian and French over the next three decades, it was the Cock Lane sensation that helped resurrect the play on stage and sparked off a brief revival of entertaining as opposed to portentous stage ghosts. To cash in on interest in Cock Lane a ghost scene was added to a royal performance of the pantomime *Apollo and Daphne* at Covent Garden, while at Drury Lane *The Farmer's Return* was staged in which the eponymous farmer travels to London to see a famed ghost and returns home to mock the credulity of the city-dwellers.[46] As one literary historian has observed, the urban setting of the Cock Lane haunting provided a refreshing, humorous inversion of the usual literary stereotype of the credulous country bumpkin, and this seems to have tickled the fancy of fashionable theatregoers.[47]

Yet for much of the eighteenth century, stage ghosts were largely confined to appearances in classical tragedies and Shakespeare. When playwrights used them in contemporary compositions they risked swift ridicule. Henry Fielding warned:

> The only supernatural agents which can in any manner be allowed to us moderns, are ghosts; but of these I would advise an author to be extremely sparing. These are indeed, like arsenic, and other dangerous drugs in physic, to be used with utmost caution; nor would I advise the introduction of them at all in those works, or by those authors, to which, or to whom, a horselaugh in the reader would be any great prejudice or mortification.[48]

The *Hamlet*-inspired ghost scene in Benjamin Martyn's *Timoleon* (1730), which concerned the eponymous fourth-century BC Greek general, may have helped it achieve modest success, but it also attracted considerable ridicule.[49] The satirist James Miller was quick to mock Martyn:

Be sure to introduce a Ghost or – God;
Make Monsters, Fiends, Heav'n, Hell, at once engage,
For all are pleas'd to see a well-fill'd stage.[50]

By the mid eighteenth century, ghosts were far more comfortably at home in burlesques that mocked both classical and Shakespearean traditions. George Alexander Stevens was one author who took heed. In his comedic *Distress upon Distress: Or, Tragedy in True Taste* (1752), for instance, there is a brief scene in which a ghost carrying a candle walks into the bedroom of the character Arietta as she sleeps in a chair. The ghost's portentous speech is interrupted in untimely fashion, and the effect is rather like a Spike Milligan limerick:

In dismal Ditty, doleful sounding Verse,
I'm sent thy Fall, Arietta, to rehearse.

A bell then tolls:

But hark, the Bellman summons me away,
If I had Time, I had much more to say.[51]

In more sophisticated satirical vein was John Gay's *The What D'Ye Call It: A Tragi-Comi-Pastoral Farce* (1715). In this play within a play five ghosts appear to three justices of the peace in order to denounce the harsh sentencing that created them. The first two are the ghosts of men pressed into military service by the justices and who subsequently died. The third is the lover of one of the men, who hanged herself after hearing of his death. The fourth is the ghost of an embryo who explains to the justices:

I was begot before my Mother married,
Who whipt by you, of me poor Child miscarried.

The final ghost is the bastard-bearing mother who died after receiving the whipping. Gay has the ghosts behaving in the formulaic fashion, pointing fingers and dolefully shaking their heads, to which one of the justices, Sir Roger, responds, 'Why do you shake your mealy heads at me?' The scene ends with one of the ghosts dismally singing a ditty about goblins and fairies while the rest dance around the frightened justices who swiftly take their leave.[52] Gay's preface to the play consists of a mock elucidation and defence of the many criticisms laid against it, including the absurdity of a talking embryo's ghost. Such a thing was, for example, 'very improper to the dignity of Tragedy, and were never introduc'd by the Antients'. After the preface there follows a dialogue between the various actors staging the play, in which the preoccupation of tragedians with ghosts is further ridiculed. Thus the actor, Sir Roger, enters and demands:

I will have a Ghost; nay, I will have a Competence of Ghosts. What, shall our Neighbours think we are not able to make a Ghost? A play without a Ghost is like, is like, – igad it is like nothing.[53]

By the mid eighteenth century the idea of representing ghosts on stage was considered by intellectuals as crude in its enactment and a distraction from the dialogue: they detracted from the theatrical experience. In 1752, for example, the writer and satirist Bonnell Thornton (1725–1768) grumbled that he would like to 'confine all dumb ghosts beneath trap-doors'.[54] Only the portrayal of the ghost in Hamlet was still tolerable to critics, in part because it was traditionally dressed in armour, in part because it spoke, and also because the drama was set comfortably in the past. To present ghosts in a contemporary setting was an abomination, for ghosts were, as one critic said, 'a bold violation of probability', therefore laughable and consequently inappropriate in serious theatre. Critics recommended that the sense of fear and awe of seeing a supposed ghost should be transmitted via the physical response of the actor. As one later critic advised, 'An actor might make the presence of the perturbed spirit visible by his actions, – by the eye of terror, – the agitation, – the changed countenance, – the sunken voice.'[55] No one at the time did this better than the famed actor David Garrick (1717–1779), whose pose of shock and fear in the ghost scenes in Hamlet and Richard III was immortalised in paintings and engravings.[56] Yet even Garrick was not immune to a bit of stage gimmickry. To add a further level of sensation to his performance he employed a hairdresser to construct a mechanical wig, which he could manipulate to make its hair stand on end when Hamlet first sees the ghost. The effect apparently was the cause of much astonishment amongst the audience.[57] Not everyone was in thrall to the Garrick 'start'. It was criticised by some for being too artificial. When Boswell once asked Dr Johnson, 'Would not you, sir, start as Mr. Garrick does, if you saw a ghost?', Johnson replied, 'I hope not. If I did, I should frighten the ghost.'[58]

The full force of Enlightenment criticism was insufficient to keep ghosts off stage for long. They rose again en masse in the late eighteenth century. The expansion of non-licensed theatres, which catered for the broader tastes of a more socially diverse audience, certainly boosted the popularity of fictional ghosts. But by the nineteenth century the contentiousness of educated debate regarding the supernatural had diffused to a considerable degree, giving the theatres licence to further subvert witches and ghosts by turning them into popular subjects for light entertainment. In 1787 the Theatre Royal in Haymarket ran the light-hearted *The Ghost; Or, the Man Bewitched*, while ten years later the Theatre Royal Drury Lane had a long-running hit with *The Scotch Ghost; Or, Little Fanny's Love.*[59] In 1793 the King's Theatre, Haymarket, put on a revival of the farce *The Ghost*, and the following year Sadler's Wells unveiled a new musical entertainment called *The Village Ghost* written by the actor and theatre manager Charles Isaac Mungo Dibdin, which was staged again in 1801. In the same year Sadler's Wells put on *Mother Shipton's Ghost.*[60] The showman Philip Astley's establishments also periodically included ghost musicals in its line-up of equestrianism, tight-rope walking, conjuring and tumbling. In 1790 Astley's Royal Grove put on a musical piece called *The Sham Ghost; Or, the Miller Outwitted*, but his biggest ghost success came in 1804 with the comedy *Ghost and No Ghost; Or, the Haunted Village*, the popularity of which was no doubt boosted by the Hammersmith ghost sensation in the same year. It proved to have a healthy stage life, being put on as late as 1812.[61]

Another important boost to the cultural currency of ghosts was the rise of the Gothic novel, which played to an entirely different range of senses to the musicals and burlesques, but no doubt still appealed to much the same audience. The gothic impulse was to enhance the reality of haunting through the evocation of scene, environment and period. The settings were usually medieval, continental and Catholic; obviously nearer in time than the previous preoccupation with pagan ancient Rome and Greece, but still comfortably distant enough to portray ghosts as fictional realities. Castles, storms, murders and persecuted maidens provided the appropriate atmosphere and context for purposeful ghosts to play their role. Horace Walpole's *Castle of Otranto* (1764) set the pattern of the gothic novel, and he revelled in presenting the supernatural as real. Ghosts were used to frighten and shock, walking out of pictures, prowling in monkish guise. But not all who followed in his footsteps shared his liberating use of ghosts. In the preface to the second edition of her medieval gothic tale *The Old English Baron* (1778), Clara Reed expressed her disapproval. She said she was prepared to allow 'of the appearance of a ghost', but it, and other magical elements, 'must keep within certain limits of credibility', otherwise the novel would excite laughter rather than the imagination.[62] That other famous female gothic novelist, Ann Radcliffe, author of *The Mysteries of Udolpho* (1794), took an even more stiff, rationalist view on the portrayal of ghosts. While quite skilful in building up atmosphere and playing with the plot potential of supernatural forces, she determinedly ensured that natural explanations were eventually revealed for all the apparent spiritual manifestations. Those critics who supported Radcliffe's 'explained supernatural' approach naturally condemned the real ghost in Madame de Genlis's *The Knights of the Swan: Or, the Court of Charlemagne*, which appeared two years later. De Genlis was well aware of the reception it would receive, writing in a footnote, 'This spectre will undoubtedly provoke criticism.' In her defence she proffered the usual excuse – 'This ghost is made to appear in an age in which this mighty engine of terror was consecrated by universal belief.' Then, in a refreshing 'what the hell' moment, asserted that if it had the same 'effect on the passions' on her readership as the manuscript did on her friends, then she should 'assuredly be acquitted'.[63] While Radcliffe's work was popular in its day, the greater appeal of 'real' ghosts to the senses and enjoyment of the reading public was apparent when Matthew Lewis's *The Monk* appeared in 1796. Lewis delighted in cranking up the shock value of the occult, and the gothic gauge is turned up to the maximum as the reader follows the decent into iniquity of the eponymous Capuchin monk Ambrosio, one of whose more benign actions is laying a ghost in the Red Sea. With the help of the magic lantern the ghost, of the Bleeding Nun, which is the subject of a side story in *The Monk*, also went on to achieve iconic status.

Gothic novels were ripe for mockery by those who gained no thrills from the suspension of belief. The poet Mary Alcock (d. 1798) made fun of the clichéd content of their plots and characters in 'A Receipt for Writing a Novel', in which she listed all the necessary ingredients, including the advice:

> A cruel father some prepare
> To drag her by her flaxen hair;
> Some raise a storm, and some a ghost,
> Take either, which may please you most.[64]

Others, in contrast, expressed concern about the social and psychological effects of Gothic literature. In his discussion on the content of nightmare hallucinations, the physician Robert Macnish described how, if someone had been reading *The Monk* or *The Mysteries of Udolpho* and experienced an attack of the nightmare,

> it will be aggravated into sevenfold horror by the spectral phantoms with which our minds have been thereby filled. We will enter into all the fearful mysteries of these writings, which, instead of being mitigated by slumber, acquire an intensity which they never could have possessed in the waking state. The apparitions of murdered victims … will stalk before us; we are surrounded by sheeted ghosts, which glare upon us … our companions are the dead.[65]

The gothic transferred to the stage during the 1790s, though Enlightenment sensitivities ensured that the portrayal of 'real' ghosts continued to be confined to distant historical contexts. When the playwright James Boaden staged his successful gothic drama *Fontainville Forest* in 1794, he set it in the early fifteenth century. This and the fact the ghost was purposeful and had a couple of words to say, was deemed by Boaden to justify its inclusion. The critics were not convinced, but the audiences were thrilled.[66] Such was the intellectual distaste for stage ghosts that it was a praiseworthy event when, in 1794, the actor and producer John Philip Kemble, after years of playing Macbeth alongside an actor as Banquo's ghost, took the bold step of declaiming to thin air. The audiences were less happy with the innovation.[67] While the theatre public evidently liked their ghosts to be corporeal rather than imaginary, there must also have been disappointment and ennui at their formulaic representation. The response of Partridge, Tom Jones's companion in Henry Fielding's eponymous novel, to seeing the ghost in Hamlet was: 'Though I can't say I ever actually saw a ghost in my life, yet I am certain that I should know one, if I saw him, better than that comes to.'[68] As we have seen, to encounter a person in a white sheet on one's way home at night was enough to frighten people to death, but to see the same effect on stage or a man dressed in armour rise from a creaking trapdoor was another matter altogether.

In the 1770s the artist and later spiritual healer Philippe Jacques de Loutherbourg (1740–1812) transformed the art of stage-setting with the sophisticated use of lighting and scenery, but it took a couple of decades for the new techniques to be applied to the by now jaded stage ghost.[69] The rejuvenating vehicle was Matthew Lewis's 1797 hit gothic play at Drury Lane, *The Castle Spectre*, which soon transferred to provincial theatres such as the Theatre Royal, Bristol.[70] Boaden had taken pains to ensure that the staging of his ghost impressed, but the quality of the scenery in *The Castle Spectre*, which was based on Conway Castle in North Wales, and the skilled lighting effects were something new. Set in the medieval period as usual, the play told the stale old story of wicked Earl Osmond who has murdered Lady Evalina, the mother of his niece Angela, whom he intends to betroth, despite the fact that she is in love with Earl Percy. Evalina's ghost, a silent character, appears to her daughter twice, and on the last occasion her appearance causes a diversionary fright enabling Angela to stab evil Osmond.

The Drury Lane manager, sensitive to the newspaper critics, had initially urged Lewis to confine the 'Ghost to the Greenroom', but Lewis knew what would bring in the audiences and decided to turn Lady Evelina's appearances into theatrical highlights using dramatic musical accompaniment and flashes of light. The effect was impressive, with one magazine reviewer observing 'that the silence and the gestures of the ghost operate very forcibly on the audience'.[71] Yet the play received the expected critical mauling, in part because of the quality of the writing and plotting, but also because of Lewis's emphasis on ghost spectacle at a time when critics urged that such representations should be expunged from serious theatre. The play was accused of being a one-trick event with audiences flocking not for the drama but for the sensational appearance of Lady Evelina's ghost, though this is somewhat belied by the fact that the book of The Castle Spectre was also a bestseller.[72] One reviewer of the play was led to express his disdain for British theatregoers' love of stage trickery and scenery: 'ghosts, gliding in their winding sheets, are what interest and convulse a modern audience', he spat with disgust.[73] It was the duty of the theatre critics to tow the line regarding the portrayal of 'superstition' as real, but then as now, the paying public evidently had different views. The Castle Spectre made more than £15,000 in its first season.[74] It is not easy to determine the composition of theatre audiences at this time, but it is likely that educated artisans were an important constituency. These were the same people who attended debating societies and who, as we saw in a previous chapter, gave majority verdicts in favour of Dr Johnson's and Wesley's views on ghosts.

FROM GOTHIC TO MELODRAMA

In 1801 The Times grumbled about 'the ghosts that of late have infested the stage'. Three years later, in its brief report of an apparition observed in Cambridge, it dryly commented that the case would, 'probably, become the subject of a new play or novel for the delight and terror of the Spectre-loving circles'.[75] Interest at the time was fuelled, in part, by the popularity of the magic lantern and camera obscura ghost shows, and more obviously by the success of The Castle Spectre. The influence of the latter is evident from the subsequent ubiquity of the term 'spectre' in literature. Lewis's hit play continued to be staged throughout much of the nineteenth century, appealing to the tastes of an expanding theatregoing public. A reviewer of a performance at Drury Lane at Easter 1823 called it 'that pink of holyday plays'. 'A ghost at Easter, is worth a million', he said. 'The school-girls of fourteen were absolutely transfixed … not one of them will venture, for the next six weeks, to look in the glass with her night-cap on.'[76] The avenging ghost of the murdered became a requisite element of any self-respecting early-nineteenth-century gothic melodrama. Lewis used the device again in Adelmorn the Outlaw (1801), and others ploughed the same theatrical furrow, though with more vocal ghosts. There was The Gamblers, Or the Murderers at the Desolate Cottage, staged at the Coburg Theatre in 1823, which involved the story of two inseparable friends, one of whom is murdered on the way to his marriage ceremony. His ghost appears to his friend to reveal the murder plot. The actor playing the ghost was on stage for much the play, even travelling in a cabriolet.[77] A similar plot formed the basis of C.P. Thompson's *The Shade* (1829). There was also Milner's *Alonzo the Brave, Or the Spectre Bride* (1826).[78] Away from the theatres, melodramatic ghosts proved equally popular in the plays put on by touring companies at fairs around the country. The famous early-nineteenth-century touring showman John Richardson (1766–1836) knew well their value. They were just as essential to the success of his shows as fight and death scenes. On one occasion, when a play was going badly, Richardson asked for the leading man to improvise. The fact that the audience had just seen him die on stage was no obstacle. Richardson exclaimed with satisfaction, 'Then the piece is saved – on with his ghost!'[79]

Just as the seventeenth- and early-eighteenth-century vogue for tragedian ghosts attracted mocking critics, so the early-nineteenth-century gothic ghost was a natural target for the numerous farces and burlesques of the period. There was *The Earls of Hammersmith, Or the Cellar Spectre* (1811) in which the traditional role of the dumb stage ghost was mocked. The silent spirit of a footman unrolls a scroll bearing the warning 'WED NOT LADY MARGARET, SHE IS YOUR GRANDMOTHER.'[80] These humorous send-ups of the ghost melodrama proved enduringly popular, combining special effects with humour, providing thrills as well as giggles. Thus, after *The Castle Spectre*, the most popular ghost play of the first half of the nineteenth century was William Moncrieff's farce *The Spectre Bridegroom, Or a Ghost in Spite of Himself* (1821). From the 1820s this played at theatres across the country. At The Theatre in Leeds, for example, it ran regularly from the 1820s to the 1840s.[81]

By mid century, gothic melodramas had gone out of theatrical fashion in the capital if not in the provinces. When *The Castle Spectre* was staged at Sadler's Wells theatre in 1863 *The Times* observed that it represented 'a class of drama that has now entirely vanished from the London stage'. The play had become a curiosity, serving as an insight into 'the sort of thing that more than sixty years ago excited the sympathies and caused the terror of the many'.[82] The paper also contrasted the portrayal of the classic white-shrouded ghost of Lady Evalina with the 'modern' representation of Louis dei Franchi's ghost in *The Corsican Brothers*. Indeed, by the 1860s dei Franchi had supplanted Lady Evalina as the melodramatic stage ghost supreme.

Fabian and Louis dei Franchi were the telepathic, separated Siamese twins in Dion Boucicault's stage adaptation of Alexandre Dumas's novel *Les frères corse* (1844), which was first shown at the Princess Theatre in 1852. Central to the plot is that when Louis is killed in a duel he appears in spirit form to show his brother and mother a vision of his terrible fate. Fabian swears to revenge his death. The play ends with the sensational appearance of Louis's ghost gliding across the stage. The part of the two brothers was originally played by the great Shakespearean actor Charles Kean, and in his tight trousers and white shirt he was, perhaps, the first sexy ghost to haunt the stage. Indeed one satirical burlesque written by James Robinson Planché shortly after Kean's successful run had a ghost, Richcraft, wearing the dress of Louis dei Franchi. When he appears to his brother, the latter asks:

> Be thou my brother, or a fiend they send us?
> Bringing with thee an air from the Princess's,
> In the most questionable of un-dresses.[83]

Whether Kean's tight-trousered ghost heightened Queen Victoria's appreciation of the play we do not know, but she went to see it on no less than eight occasions.

Meanwhile, on the classical stage, the denunciations of portraying Shakespearean ghosts continued, with Banquo's silent spirit in Macbeth attracting the most opprobrium. At a Covent Garden performance of the play in 1807 the audience hissed disapprovingly when he made his appearance. It was a 'stage-barbarism' said one reviewer.[84] Four years later another staging of the play led The Times critic to call upon 'every man who has an idea of dramatic propriety' to 'protest against Banquo's Ghost'. 'These observations have been made innumerable times,' he complained, 'and we scarcely hope any good from them.' Representing the ghost was, as the critic observed, 'a mere trick for the galleries'.[85] By 'the galleries' he meant the 'credulous ghost-believing public' or working classes; they were one and the same thing to snobbish theatre critics. The unpalatable fact for middle-class patrons was that the working classes were frequenting the patent theatres, such as Drury Lane and Covent Garden, in increasing numbers, particularly after 1830 when admission prices in most London theatres dropped significantly.[86] It was in part, therefore, financial concerns that kept Banquo's ghost on stage.

The urban working classes of nineteenth-century England, even the illiterate, were far more familiar with the works of Shakespeare than might be supposed. Some were taught to read from his plays, Mechanics' Institutes put on recitations, while burlesques of his work were popular in working-class theatres. For some, particularly radicals such as the Chartists and the early labour movement, knowledge and understanding of his works was an important badge of cultural pride as well as providing the tools for developing oratorical skills.[87] For many, though, Shakespearean plays were nothing more than sources of theatrical entertainment and there were certain things they liked and disliked about them. The nature of these popular tastes were well encapsulated by a London costermonger interviewed by the journalist Henry Mayhew:

> Of Hamlet we can make neither end nor side and nine out of ten of us – ay, far more than that – would like it to be confined to the ghost scenes, and the funeral, and the killing off at last. Macbeth would be better liked, if it was only the witches and the fighting.[88]

Like an echo of Addison's comment nearly a century and a half earlier, it would seem that it was the ghosts that helped to maintain Shakespeare's popularity. There was, though, some disquiet about this popular exposure to the bard. The Rev. James Plumptre, who was known for his morally-improving and expurgated versions of plays, complained in 1818 that much of the prevailing belief in ghosts was 'owing to his [Shakespeare's] representations which still keep possession of the stage'.[89]

During the first half of the nineteenth century, traditional popular literary formats such as ballads and broadsides continued to circulate in town and country. Henry Mayhew noted that a ballad of the Cock Lane ghost was still being sold on the streets of London nearly a century after the affair.[90] The burgeoning music halls provided a new forum for the ghost song. At the Princess Theatre, Leeds, in April 1852, two comedic songs, sung by a Mr Grainger, were part of the evening's entertainment. One was called 'Hamlet's Ghost' and the other was the locally-inspired 'The Holbeck Ghost'.[91] Broadsides with titles such as Apparition of a Ghost to a Miller to Discover a Hidden Murder maintained the old narrative style of the seventeenth and eighteenth centuries.[92] The publisher William Hone even resurrected the old political ghost squib for one of his satirical attacks on the Prince Regent, entitled, The Appearance of an Apparition to James Sympson of Huddersfield in Yorkshire, an Elderly Broad-cloth Weaver, Commanding Him to Do Strange Things in Pall Mall. One of the tasks was to peep into the Regent's closet, where he saw, amongst other things, 'the heads of a divorce, a French clock, and some Roman fiddle-strings'.[93]

Yet gothic and melodramatic influences also seeped into urban street literature. The title of the broadside An Account of the Dreadful Apparition that Appeared Last Night to Henry —— in This Street, sounds like the old-style ghost pamphlets, but it is set in a castle rather than the London streets, and the narrative is pure gothic.[94] The change can also be seen in popular literature recording recent murder cases. In the autumn of 1860 an eight-page penny pamphlet concerning a sensational Stepney murder trial was printed with the title The Terrible, Unearthly, Soul-stirring Narrative of the Dark, Midnight, Agonising Wanderings, and

Fearful Prognostications of the Supposed Spirit or Ghost of Jas. Mullins. James Mullins was a 50-year-old Irish plasterer and former government spy who was hanged for the murder of a widow named Mary Emsley. The newspapers assiduously reported the case without a whiff of a ghost being mentioned. The pamphlet trumped the press by announcing that it not only contained the last words of Mullins to his priest but also his tormented spirit's subsequent appearance: 'The Haunted Confessional! The Haunted Grave! The Satanical Apparition! The Fearful Thrilling Declaration!'[95] However, the broadsides and trial pamphlets were on their last legs by the 1860s. They could not compete with the rapidly expanding daily newspapers and local weekly press. The newspaper editors also exploited the attractions of a good ghost story, and the broadside publishers sometimes lifted accounts straight from the regional papers.[96] The only edge the broadside producers had was that they could depict ghosts as startling realities, when the newspapers generally maintained a mocking or distant tone. But unlike in the theatre, ghosts were ultimately unable to save the old literary formats.

SPECTACLE

Victorian audiences increasingly wanted spectacle, and this drove forward innovations in theatrical technology. With the profusion of working and lower-middle-class playhouses in London and other urban centres from the 1830s onwards, the need to retain customers was greater than ever before. Ghosts had to be portrayed more realistically – or perhaps that should read more *artistically*. Henry Dircks recalled how as a child in the early nineteenth century he had been in awe of the ghost in a staging of *Hamlet* but certainly not because of its appearance: 'I was more struck with the language and unearthly eloquence of the spectre ... I did not for a moment suppose it had retired to any neighbouring churchyard.'[97] Public expectations put theatre producers under increasing pressure to redress the yawning gap between prose and visual presentation. The white sheets and mealy faces were sloughed, and more clever lighting techniques were used to provide an aura of ghostliness. The traditional, clunking trapdoor entrance also went out of vogue in some theatres. 'The rising of the ghosts through stage-traps was always a clumsy contrivance,' remarked *The Times* in 1814, 'and we are glad to see it laid aside.'[98] At Drury Lane, ghosts were now made to appear behind gauze or tissue to give an ethereal air. *The Times* was particularly approving of the ghosts in a Covent Garden staging of *Richard III*, which entered from the wings 'within a sort of aërial mist, which gives the whole scene a fine effect'.[99] The acting profession did not lament the slow demise of the trap. Considerable skill and concentration were required to work it safely and effectively, and that was not always evident. The actor John Palmer (1744–1798) nearly died in 1778 when the trap was lowered too quickly while he played Banquo's ghost at the Haymarket Theatre.[100] Numerous theatres kept their traps however, and the need to present ghosts in new exciting ways led to technical innovations such as the impressive Corsican trap or ghost slide, developed for the gradual gliding materialisation of the spirit of Louis dei Franchi in *The Corsican Brothers*.[101]

Lighting was crucial, of course, to the successful portrayal of ghosts, but once again variety and innovation was required to keep audiences interested. A reviewer of the melodrama *The Gamblers, Or the Murderers at the Desolate Cottage* wearily remarked that, 'as must always be the case where a ghost has nearly the entire possession of the stage, a great deal of brimstone [is] consumed in the flashes of fire'.[102] Coloured lighting, which developed in the early nineteenth century, helped to create more atmosphere. Different hues were created by burning chemicals in iron pans or boxes which were ignited in the wings of the theatre at appropriate moments. Red fire was naturally used for the appearance of the Devil and villains, while blue fire was used for the appearance of ghosts.[103] This was in keeping with the long-standing belief that candles burned blue when spirits were present.

The most profound development in theatrical lighting was the move from candles and oil lamps to gaslights. Drury Lane, the Lyceum and Covent Garden were the first to switch in 1817, though some theatres, particularly in the provinces, took several decades to make the change. The change from candle to the brilliant illumination of gaslights created a significantly different viewing experience from some parts of the theatre, particularly the boxes, highlighting the physicality of the actors more and their facial expressions less.[104] The gaslight glare and consequent reduction of shadows was bound to emphasise the size and deportment of ghosts, as well as the manner of their entry and dress. Back in 1794, during rehearsal for *Fontainville Forest*, Boaden dismissed the original actor playing the ghost, in part because he was a short stocky man; he replaced him with a more characteristically lean-looking actor. It is possible that it was the altered viewing conditions created by gas illumination that led to complaints of inappropriately-sized ghosts during the early nineteenth century. In September 1817, for example, a reviewer of *Hamlet* at Covent Garden complained that the 'ghost is the most substantial we ever saw. He does not look like one that has "peaked or pined" long.'[105] Reviewing a rendition of Hamlet at Drury Lane six years later, *The Times* theatre critic was relieved to see the actor James Wallack playing the ghost, as he was 'the first ghost of any "moderate compass" which we have seen for many years. Hitherto fat pursy spirits have been all the rage.'[106] There was a practical as well as an artistic reason for not employing substantial ghosts, as Mr Banks, co-lessee of the Liverpool and Manchester Theatres, found to his personal discomfort. For many years during the early nineteenth century, Banks, 'a remarkably large, fat man', enjoyed playing the ghost in Hamlet. He was evidently accomplished in the role, but on one occasion elicited much mirth from the audience of the Manchester Theatre when his large stomach got wedged in the trapdoor entrance as he descended. The machinery ground to a halt and several stagehands were required to lift him out. Banks, recognising the humorous circumstances of his plight, could not resist a belly laugh himself.[107]

Stage plays certainly influenced the content of phantasmagoria shows. A poster for a spectrology show at the Taunton Theatre in 1802/03, for example, advertised slides of Hamlet's Ghost and the Bleeding Nun from The Monk.[108] In fact the latter was one of the most popular magic lantern slides at the time. Somewhat surprisingly, however, magic lanterns made little impact on the presentation of theatre ghosts. This was primarily because it was difficult to incorporate projections with live action in front of the screen without ruining the effect of both. One of its few successful stage employments was its use, in 1826, to provide a moving background projection of the phantom ship in a popular production of The Flying Dutchman.[109] It has been argued, nevertheless, that the lantern shows seeped deep into the artistic psyche, with 'phantasma-goric logic', that is a sequence of connecting mental images, influencing, for example, the writings of Charles Dickens. It is represented most obviously in Ebenezer Scrooge's succession of ghostly visitations in A Christmas Carol, and also in the similar festive scenario involving the cantankerous grave-digger Gabriel Grub in Pickwick Papers. Grub is shown the error of his ways one Christmas Eve by a goblin who conjures up a serious of instructive visions.[110]

Pepper's Ghost overcame the theatrical limitations of the magic lantern and one might have expected it to revolutionise the portrayal of stage ghosts. No longer would playwrights, actors and theatre managers have to agonise over how to evoke the requisite sense of awe and wonder at the appearance of a ghost. But it was rarely used in plays other than tableaux, dramatised readings of short stories such as Dickens's The Haunted Man and the Ghosts' Bargain, or brief enactments such as Hamlet meeting the ghost. However, in 1863, two full-length dramas at the popular working-class Britannia Theatre, Hoxton, were quickly written to exploit Pepper's Ghost. One was called The Widow and Orphans, and the other, Faith, Hope and Charity, by the Britannia's resident playwright Colin Henry Hazlewood (1823–75), concerned the ghost of a clergyman's wife who returns to haunt her murderer.[111] Although Hazlewood became well-known for his adaptation of Lady Audley's Secret, Faith, Hope and Charity proved to be one of his most successful self-penned plays and ran constantly throughout 1863 and regularly in subsequent years. In 1879 the ghost in the play was still said to be proving 'a great attraction' at the Britannia.[112] Henry Dircks expressed his pride at the economic boost his invention had given to the theatre world:

> Plays, once dead, re-animated by 'The Ghost' – institutions once not over-burdened with wealth, now enriched – advertisers wondering at the rush of advertising ghosts – then the many actors, lecturers, lime-light operators, printers, artists, 'The Ghost' gives employment to?[113]

For most theatres, however, the huge sheet of glass that was required to produce the effect was costly, created too many restrictions on the movement of actors, scenery and props, and also blocked the sound of any actors behind it.[114] The risks involved were highlighted in a prosecution brought against the Lancashire and Yorkshire Railway Company by a producer at the Theatre Royal, Newcastle. Like a number of other provincial theatre managers, the producer's son, Alfred Davis, manager of a theatre in Cheltenham, had been quick to capitalise on the popularity of Pepper's Ghost, and in the autumn of 1863 had toured a production of The Castle Spectre in which Lady Evalina's ghost was produced by the Dircks and Pepper technique. In early November Davis's father desired to put on the show at the Theatre Royal and requested his son to send the necessary equipment, including a huge ten-by-eight-foot sheet of glass. A rival music hall in Newcastle had just put on its own Pepper's Ghost and Davis was anxious to have his up and running as quickly as possible. Unfortunately, when the glass arrived it was found to have broken into several pieces. Davis desperately tried to obtain another sheet but only succeeded in finding one unsatisfactorily smaller, which reduced the number of people in the auditorium who could view the illusion properly. Consequently the public response was poor and Davis lost out to his rival. It was a financial disaster, with estimated losses of £100, £37 of which had gone in payment for the rights to put on the patented illusion for twelve months.[115] Because of such hazards and complications, for the rest of the century, producers continued to rely on lights, flashes, make-up and traps to create ghost illusions. In Shakespearean theatre, though, the ghost became increasingly invisible. As one theatre historian characterised the development of the nineteenth-century staging of Caesar's ghost in Julius Caesar: 'Trapwork – gauzes –nothing at all!'[116]

The most enduring dramatic use of Pepper's Ghost was in the touring ghost shows that set up at fairs and circuses around the country during the last few decades of the nineteenth century. These often put on 15- or 20-minute extracts of ghost scenes from well-known literature. A practical reason for the shortness of the plays was the sweltering conditions endured by the ghost actor. The blazing gaslights needed to produce an effective projection meant that the lower stage quickly became insufferably hot, and actors used to call it the oven or O.V.[117] Nevertheless, 15 or 20 minutes was also a commercially optimum period to have a good turnover of customers. Furthermore, it was a suitable length to enact ghost scenes from the best-selling literature of the time such as *The Corsican Brothers*. Representative was the Spectral Opera Company's tour of the south coast in 1884, which advertised extracts from *Uncle Tom's Cabin* and *A Christmas Carol*.[118] The latter needs no explanation, as it remains an iconic ghost story. The relevant passage in Stowe's bestselling *Uncle Tom's Cabin*, first published in England in 1853, was a chapter entitled 'An Authentic Ghost Story'. This recounted how the slave-owning plantation proprietor Simon Legree is badly frightened one night in his bed by a tall figure in a white sheet whispering 'Come! Come! Come!' The scene had the perfect ingredients for a Pepper's Ghost vignette. Early film-makers followed in the footsteps of the ghost showmen by picking out scenes from well-known literature such as *A Christmas Carol* and *The Corsican Brothers*. Shakespeare's ghosts were reproduced on screen with varying degrees of success. A 1911 film version of *Richard III*, lasting just under half an hour, has been described as representing 'pre-1914 stage adaptations at their worst'.[119] Symptomatic of its dreadfulness was the ghost scene in which no attempt was made to use the standard ghost-making technique of the double exposure. Instead the ghosts appear in rapid succession of jump cuts creating an unintentionally comedic rush of gesticulating spirits. Far more effective was the gliding, translucent double-exposure ghost in Cecil Hepworth's production of *Hamlet* (1913), which readers can see for themselves via the British Film Institute website.[120]

*   *   *

While recognising the significant literary and theatrical influence on public belief and perception, neither medium fully represented ghost tradition. There was a preoccupation with the hoaxer and the purposeful ghost. The noisy spirit and the self-absorbed, memorial ghost rarely figured. There are pragmatic reasons why. The former usually remained an invisible presence difficult to dramatise on stage, thought its manifestations obviously made good copy as real-life drama. The latter did not usually interact with the living and therefore was usually only fit for fleeting appearances rather than central casting. In this sense, then, there was a significant gap between legend, experience and fiction.

While over the centuries theatre producers strove to produce more realistic ghosts, and writers struggled to generate through prose the sense of awe and fear inspired by hauntings, there was a subtext to much of their creative endeavours. The quest for realism in fictional representation, like ghost projection, could serve as an act of sensory exorcism, making people cast aside their preconceptions of reality. From the opposite spectrum, the comic or light-hearted portrayal of ghosts could lead to their reality being laughed out of existence or rendered innocuous. As *The Times* remarked of Astley's 1804 extravaganza *Ghost or No Ghost*,

> we really are of opinion, from the uncommon applause given to this sprite, by a crowded audience every evening, that Hobgoblins and Apparitions will in time lose their powerful influence even with the most timid.[121]

Yet the fact that ghost-belief remained pervasive over the centuries shows that people could cope easily with multiple realities when it came to the existence of ghosts.

Here is a true and perfect Relation from the Faulcon at the

Banke-fide; of the ftrange and wonderful aperition of one Mr. *Powel* a Baker lately deceafed, and of his appearing in feveral fhapes, both at Noon-day and at night, with the feveral fpeeches which paft between the fpirit of Mr. *Powel* and his Maid *Jone* and divers Learned men, who went to alay him and the manner of his appearing to them in the Garden upon their making a circle, and burning of wax Candels and Jenniper wood, laftly how it vanifhed.   The tune of, *Chevy Chafe*.

S Trange news, ftrange news, I here have write
  come liften and I le tell,
The ftrangeft news that ever yet
within our age befell.
And I le repeat it word by word
to let the Nation know,
The mighty wonders of the Lord,
which he to them doth fhew.

For near upon fix moneths ago,
there was a Baker eyed,
Clo e by the Faulcon many know,
which is on Southwarke fide.
His body after buryed was,
in earth for to remain,
But not long fence it came to pafs,
that his Spirit rofe again.

And walked up and down the place,
where he before did dwell,
And lookt moft Ghaftul in his face,
that hundreds there can tell.
And ratling throw the houfe would he,
afrighting people that.
He fometimes like a Goat would be,
and fometimes like a Catt.

He into feveral fhaps would turn,
with dolful voyces then

He'd like a flame of fire burn,
ftraight to a man agen.
This houfe be conftant haunted that,
at midnight and noone-day
And fometimes feemed like a Catt,
which fcar'd his Son away.

Then none within this houfe did dwell,
but one poor fervant Maid
Which very often did perceive,
this ghaftul Ghoft fhe faid.
Whofe pale and dreadful glemering light,
reduc't her to a fear
For making of the bed one night,
it to her did appear.

She then beholding of his face,
poor foul it made her quake
And fhe lay trembling in the place,
that every joynt did fhake.
He up and down the Chamber ran,
his hands abroad were fpread
His Nofe was waxed pale and wan,
his eyes funk in his head.

At which the Maid cry'd out O Lord,
I heartily do pray
That by the power of thy word,
chafe this fame fiend away.

Plate 1

Here is A True and Perfect Relation from the Faulcon at the Banke-side; of the strange and wonderful aperition of one Mr. Powel, a baker lately deceased. By permission of the Bodleian Library, University of Oxford. Shelfmark: Wood 401 (183).

Plate 2

Laying a Ghost! Richard Newton after George Montard Woodward (1792). By permission of the Trustees of the British Museum.

Plate 3

The Ghosts; Or Mrs. Duffy and Mrs. Cruckshanks. Written by T. Dibidin, Esq. (1805). The image mocks the St James's Park ghost sensation of the previous year (see Chapter 7). By permission of the Bodleian Library, University of Oxford. Shelfmark: Harding B 10 (37).

Edward Kelly a Magician, raising the Ghost of a Person lately deceased, in the Church Yard of Walton le dale, Lancaster.

Plate 4

Edward Kelley raising a ghost. From [Robert Cross Smith], *The Astrologer of the Nineteenth Century* (London, 1825). Author's collection.

Plate 5
The Hammersmith Ghost. Engraving 1804. By permission of the Wellcome Library, London.

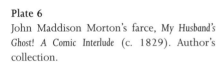

Plate 6
John Maddison Morton's farce, My Husband's Ghost! A Comic Interlude (c. 1829). Author's collection.

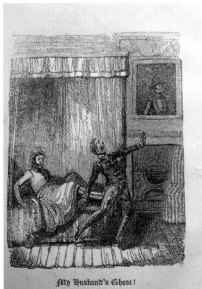

MY HUSBAND'S GHOST!

A COMIC INTERLUDE,

In One Act,

BY JOHN MADDISON MORTON, ESQ.

PRINTED FROM THE ACTING COPY, WITH REMARKS,
BIOGRAPHICAL AND CRITICAL, BY D.—G.

To which are added,

A DESCRIPTION OF THE COSTUME,—CAST OF THE CHARACTERS,—
ENTRANCES AND EXITS,—RELATIVE POSITIONS OF THE
PERFORMERS ON THE STAGE, AND THE WHOLE
OF THE STAGE BUSINESS,

As performed at the

THEATRES ROYAL, LONDON.

EMBELLISHED WITH A FINE ENGRAVING,

From a Drawing taken in the Theatre by MR. R. CRUIKSHANK.

LONDON:
JOHN CUMBERLAND, 2, CUMBERLAND TERRACE,
CAMDEN NEW TOWN.

David Garrick as Hamlet.

Plate 7
David Garrick as Hamlet, adopting his trademark pose at seeing the ghost. Author's collection.

Plates 8a and 8b

Ghost-making machines. An example of a magic lantern (top) and the phantasmagoria (bottom), as represented in David Brewster's *Letters on Natural Magic* (first published 1832). Author's collection.

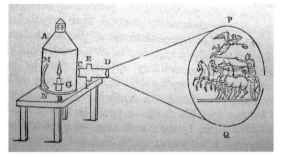

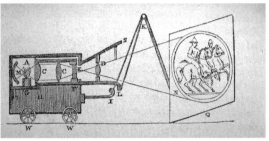

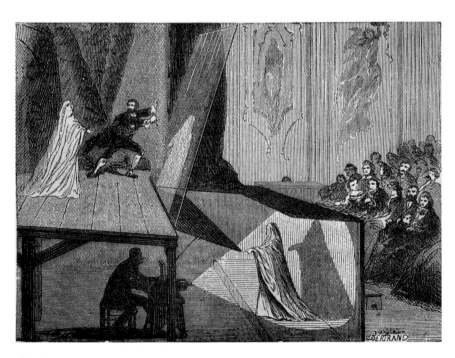

Plate 9

Pepper's Ghost Illusion. From Jean Eugène Robert-Houdin, *The Secrets of Stage Conjuring* (London, 1881). By permission of the British Library.

Plate 10

The Haunted Lane. A double exposure stereoscope ghost card (1889). Courtesy of the Library of Congress, Prints & Photographs Division, LC-USZ62-49314.

Plate 11

The Widow's Mite. A double exposure stereoscope ghost card (c. 1876). Courtesy of the Library of Congress, Prints & Photographs Division, LC-USZ62-68335.

Plate 12

A poster advertising William Wallser's well-known Ghost Show (c. 1874). Evanion Collection, Evan 2778. By permission of the British Library.

The Future for Ghosts

The extraordinary fact about the history of ghosts is that it is not a story of decline, unlike that of those related supernatural beings witches and fairies. Indeed, the future looks bright for ghosts. In 2003 a MORI poll found that 38 per cent of the British population believed in ghosts and that 19 per cent of the population had seen, felt or heard one. The following year, 42 per cent of people interviewed by ICM said they believed in ghosts, while a Populus poll in 2005 found a slightly lower figure of 34 per cent.[1] In fact, since the 1950s, opinion polls have shown a consistent rise in ghost-belief amongst the British. In 1950 a Gallup survey revealed that only 10 per cent of people thought ghosts existed and only 2 per cent said they had seen one. Not long after, research by the sociologist Geoffrey Gorer revealed that 17 per cent expressed a belief. Averages taken from Gallup polls since then show that 19 per cent of people in the 1970s said they believed in ghosts, rising to 28 per cent in the 1980s and 31 per cent in the first half of the 1990s.[2] The increase in ghost-belief appears even more startling when measured against other supernatural concepts that were widely held in the past. In the 1970s only 11 per cent of people said they believed in black magic – a figure that changes only 1 or 2 per cent in the polls up until 2005. Likewise, belief in lucky charms over the last 30 years has varied little from the 17 per cent of believers found in Gallup polls during the 1970s.[3] As to other entities, in 1950 Gorer found that around a fifth of the population thought the Devil existed, a percentage that fluctuates by only a few percentage points up until the present day, when a recent survey found that 29 per cent believed in the Devil.[4] In 2005 only 3 per cent of people believed in vampires.[5] Only angels, which are essentially the spirits of the dead, attract similar levels of belief as ghosts in present-day Britain.[6] Why should ghosts have become *more* believable than the Devil in modern British society?

To answer this we need to question what these opinion polls are actually telling us. Considering all the evidence presented in this book for the vibrancy of ghost-belief in Victorian England, it seems highly unlikely that after just a few decades it had dwindled to the extent that only one-tenth of the population believed in them. What the polls reveal, then, is that since the 1940s people have become less embarrassed about *expressing* their belief in ghosts. In other words, ghost-belief has become more socially acceptable. Historians have

241

only recently begun to study the nature and extent of supernatural beliefs in the inter-war period. The work that has been done shows that spiritualism as a practice and as an organised religion had become firmly established in English society amongst all social levels, and that the newspapers, which were becoming increasingly socially influential, were less sneering and dismissive of supernatural phenomena and ideas like astrology.[7] But certain sections of society were more uncomfortable than others about the way their beliefs might be perceived. It is significant that Gorer's survey in the early 1950s indicated that ghost-belief was slightly higher among the poor and the upper middle class.[8] In the inter-war period it would seem that it was sections of society in between these two groups that felt most uncomfortable about the issue. In 1934 Ernest Bennett observed that

> In some middle-class circles it is generally not considered good form to mention ghosts except in a jocular way; and many devout Christians who anticipate, with some assurance, eternal happiness hereafter, regard any mention of disembodied spirits as an unpleasant and depressing topic.[9]

It is understandable that recently emancipated middle-class women, with their increasing political and social influence, would feel sensitive about giving ammunition to a patronising male establishment by expressing a belief that, as we have seen, had long been used to highlight the credulity of womankind. Another section of society that was also sensitive about maintaining a rationalist public reputation was the politically-conscious working class. It was common for nineteenth-century working-class radicals and politicians to mention the 'superstitions' and supernatural fears of their youth as a means of highlighting how far they had come socially and intellectually. Gorer found that those most sceptical about ghosts and religion in the early 1950s were prosperous working-class men.[10]

In attempting to understand further why ghost-belief, and its expression, is so vibrant in modern England, it is useful to compare the British poll findings with those of other countries, in this instance America and France.[11] Considering that America is the most religious country in the Western world, it is not surprising that an opinion poll in 2003 found that 51 per cent of Americans believed in ghosts and 68 per cent believed in the Devil. Turning to France with its strong Catholic tradition, the results are more unexpected. A poll conducted in 2000 found that only 13 per cent believed in ghosts. The comparative lack of belief in ghosts in France does not, however, signify a general scepticism regarding the paranormal; 35 per cent of the French population believed in predictive dreams compared to 25 per cent in England, while 42 per cent and 40 per cent respectively believed in telepathy.

These polls reveal a fascinating reversal of the centuries-old propagandist representation of ghost-belief in Catholic and Protestant faiths. After 500 years of Protestantism and its orthodox doctrinal rejection of ghosts, we find ghost-belief much higher in England and predominantly Protestant America (although the growth of the Hispanic population is changing this fact) than in Catholic countries. The historical trends that lie behind these figures are a subject for their own book, but they demand some consideration in order to contextualise the English experience. Regarding the USA, the fact that half of the population believes in ghosts is understandable considering the influence of evangelical, providential Protestant churches amongst both Caucasians and African-Americans. We have seen how in England during the eighteenth and nineteenth centuries Methodism and spiritualist sects similarly sought to uphold the age of miracles. As to France, it must be pointed out that the Catholic church has long downplayed the concept of purgatory, and the clergy have had little need to promote ghosts for propaganda purposes since the seventeenth century. It is a reasonable extrapolation, therefore, that by the twentieth century ghost-belief would be no more common in Catholic countries than in Protestant ones.

The low level of ghost-belief in modern France is surprising nevertheless. There is a doctrinal reason for it. In Catholic countries ghosts are not the only representatives of the dead. The saints continue to fulfil a potent, influential role in popular worship and belief. While claims that Marian apparitions, for instance, have increased in Catholic countries during the twentieth century is difficult to prove, there has certainly been little significant diminution in such saintly manifestations.[12] With saints acting as regular, celestial intercessionary figures, the relevance of ghosts is reduced. That is not to say that ghosts are still not an important aspect of Catholic popular religious belief. There are many accounts of their various manifestations, similar to those in England, in nineteenth-century ethnographic sources.[13] But in modern French society the saints have retained more relevance as healers and divine intermediaries for the devout. It could be argued, furthermore, that over two centuries of revolutionary secularism and anti-clericalism in education has also reduced the relevance of ghosts in popular culture. This has been reinforced further in recent decades by the comparative lack of serious interest shown in ghosts and the paranormal by popular scientific magazines and newspapers.[14] In England the Protestant Reformation was largely successful in eradicating the worship of saints, and reducing the relevance of angels in popular religion as well. Ghosts remained the sole manifest representatives of the afterlife for most Anglicans. As such, they retained a greater historical hold on the religious consciousness of the laity, in a country where religion has never been entirely divorced from politics and education. Also, in contrast with France, the popular press has shown a much greater preoccupation with the reality of ghosts, thereby perpetuating the currency of the issue in popular culture.

The issue of ghost-belief in twentieth-century England cannot be fully understood without also considering the secularisation debate.[15] There is no doubt that participation in organised religion has dwindled massively over the last century, and in the last 50 years in particular. Only a small percentage of the population now attends church once a week. Since 1900 the number of Anglican clergy has halved, while the number of Methodist clergy fell from 4,700 to 2,500 between 1950 and 1995.[16] Whether this means that religious belief has dwindled concomitantly is another matter. Some sociologists point to surveys that show a continuance of belief in basic religious principles that contrasts with the data regarding participation in organised religion. Belief in God has hovered at around 70 per cent or more for much of the last 50 years, and in the 2001 census a non-compulsory question on religious persuasion revealed that nearly 78 per cent of people in England and Wales consider themselves Christians. The percentage of people believing in the afterlife has remained consistent at 40–50 per cent since the war; 65 per cent of people today say they pray at least once a year, while only around 12 per cent of the population describe themselves as atheists.[17] One sociologist has described this continuing expression of religious identity as representing 'believing without belonging'. Others argue that these poll findings reflect residual sentiments and that the level of belief will surely decrease before long. There may be signs of this in polls over the last five years in which the percentage of those believing in God has dropped to 60–65 per cent.

There is no doubt, though, that religious belief has become more individualistic, flexible and pluralistic, no longer tied to institutions or denominations. The continued vibrancy of the belief in ghosts is, perhaps, an example of this. They act as transferable anchors of spirituality. One can renounce one's Christian faith and become a Muslim or a Neo-pagan and retain the same belief in the return of the dead while abandoning all other Christian tenets. The population's increasing openness about ghosts could also be a direct consequence of the weakening influence of the Protestant churches and the doctrinal conformity they imposed. A poll from 1947 revealed that 'a considerable proportion' of those who said they had seen or heard a ghost were not members of any church. In the 1980s a survey of religious belief in rural England came up with the similarly significant finding that only 19 per cent of active members of the Anglican church expressed a belief in ghosts, compared to 29 per cent of the wider population.[18]

Industrialisation and urbanisation have usually been cited as key factors in the process of secularisation. If one subscribes to the secularisation thesis then it would be expected that ghost-belief would decline, not only because of waning religious influence but also as a result of the population's divorce from traditional geographies of haunting and the darkness of the nocturnal countryside. One academic folklorist has argued that for this reason, in Finland, 'Belief in ghosts was dispelled not by logical reasoning but rather as a by product of the changes brought about by industrialisation and urbanisation.'[19] This may well be true for a country that only underwent major industrialisation during the twentieth century, but as this book demonstrates, ghost-belief was vibrant in rapidly urbanising Victorian England.[20] Gorer had his preconceptions challenged when he was surprised to find that ghost-belief was 'nearly as frequent in the metropolises as in the villages'.[21]

Some Anglican clergy, recognising the waning of the church's influence and aware of the continued social currency of ghost-belief, have realised that re-engagement with the popular experience of haunting is one small way of maintaining their relevancy in society. In 1974 the ordained Anglican John Richards, secretary of the Bishop of Exeter's Study Group on Exorcism, commented:

> Had I, even in the nineteen sixties, ventured to suggest that exorcism should be a small but real part of the Church's ministry of healing, most opinion – even informed opinion – would have dismissed the suggestion as medieval superstition.[22]

For Richards, 'ghosts proper' manifested themselves because they sought spiritual solace from the living before departing and finding their rest in God. He cited two cases in which the needs of ghosts had been met through prayer. 'It is a pity', he commented, 'that the whole subject of praying for the dead is abhorrent to some Christians.'[23] Several clergymen have tapped into the zeitgeist in recent decades and sought to publicise their role in aiding restless souls and conduct prayers and readings to clear haunted houses of ghosts or 'earthbound spirits'. In 1970 the Rev. Donald Omand, rector of Chideock, recounted his exploits in *Experiences of a Present-day Exorcist*, which had a foreword written by the Bishop of Portsmouth. A few years later, Dom Robert Petitpierre, an Anglican monk described as a 'leading Church of England authority on ghosts', included a chapter on 'helping departed spirits' in his *Exorcising Devils*. In 1990, J. Aelwyn Roberts repeated the success of Omand's book with his catchily-titled *Holy Ghostbuster: A Parson's Encounters with the Paranormal*.[24] Roberts remarked how, during his years of training at theological college after World War I, 'no lecturer or demonstrator uttered a single word on how to deal with ghosts'. He 'often wondered why ghosts at that time were not part of the curriculum', particularly as there was so much popular interest in them.[25]

Yet the issue of ghost-belief continues to have a place in theological discourse as well as in pastoral care. In a recent article, two academic theologians presented a written report of a playful debate, or theological 'divertissement', they had with colleagues on the question of the existence of ghosts. Although sceptical themselves, the general conclusion of the debate was that 'room exists within theology for a diversity of opinions concerning ghosts, and for the deployment of other, non-theological forms of argument'. They did not, however, consider ghosts to be a matter of significant dogmatic consequence. Nevertheless, they recognised that the offering of prayers was pertinent in situations of 'ghostly infestation', for even if no ghosts were involved, the prayers themselves could have a cathartic healing effect on the psychologically disordered.[26]

Belief in ghosts is not dependent on religion of course. Many ghost-believers today do not consider ghosts to be the souls of the dead, but rather psychic imprints on the atmosphere, residual energy forces left behind by those who died while in a violent emotional state. Seeking answers for their social currency in terms of church doctrine and secularisation can, therefore, take us only so far. While the Bible is rarely cited in modern popular discourse as proof of the existence of ghosts, that other old, twin argument, the sheer number of cases recorded over millennia and from different cultures, continues to be seen as a valid defence. In 1939 the Dean of St Paul's, the Very Rev. W.R. Matthews, remarked that 'it has always seemed to me difficult to resist the weight of evidence that apparitions have formed a part of human experience through the centuries'.[27] The idea that all those thousands of witnesses over the years were mistaken, defrauded or delusional seems as improbable to some people today as the concept of ghosts does to others.

There is no doubt that the media has also played its part in maintaining the cultural relevancy of ghosts. They continue to inspire the imagination of novelists, particularly of the horror genre, while the continued popularity of Victorian and Edwardian ghost stories demonstrate the enduring attraction of ghosts in historical as well as contemporary settings. Radio and television have brought the literary ghost stories of the likes of M.R. James to new audiences. The BBC has produced versions of James's wonderfully spooky tales again and again over the last 50 years.[28]

In recent decades, cinema has usually presented ghosts as realities, and reprised the character of the purposeful ghost, morally bound to rectifying injustice, or the ghost who desires to make one last gesture of love to the bereaved.[29] With regard to the physical representation of ghosts, even stylised, computer-generated spooks retain elements of traditional characteristics. The white, luminescent ghosts in films like *Casper* (1995) (based on a 1940s cartoon) are reminiscent of the formless winding-sheet apparitions of the past and the tradition of the ghostly will-o'-the-wisp. Motion pictures have, furthermore, given greater cultural presence to distinctly literary types of ghost, such as the comedy ghost, with its origins on the Restoration stage, and the genre of romantic film ghosts, which was strong in the late 1930s and 1940s and emerged again in the 1990s. As to the development of new cinematic genres, the most significant has been the concept of the community of ghosts portrayed in films like *Ghost* (1990) and *Truly Madly Deeply* (1991).[30] In the past, whether in tradition, legend, fiction or experience, ghosts were hardly ever depicted communicating with each other, so the idea of a society of ghosts certainly marks a significant departure.

British television's contribution to the cultural relevance of ghosts has been most evident in the field of children's programming and populist documentaries. Eighteenth-century educators must be turning in their graves at the way in which television has presented ghosts as realities in children's programmes. During the late 1970s and early 1980s there was the BBC's long-running *Rentaghost*, about a trio of ghosts, each from a different period of history (as their costumes clearly indicated), who attempted to engage in various forms of employment in the world of the living.[31] ITV's similar contribution to the genre of collaborative ghosts, *The Ghosts of Motley Hall*, concerned a group of spirits determined to ward off property investors from buying their dilapidated dwelling. For a more mature audience, there was the detective duo of *Randall & Hopkirk (Deceased)*, which ran for one series in 1969–70, and was recently remade. There are numerous other examples of the use of ghosts in television light entertainment over the decades, and also in spine-tingling dramas, but these programmes will, perhaps, be amongst the most familiar to readers. They show how relaxed society in general has become about portraying their reality. Unlike violence and sex, there is no need to put warnings stating 'the next programme contains graphic scenes of the dead, which may offend religious and emotional sensibilities'. We can laugh at ghosts and with them, whether we believe in them or not.

Moving from escapist fare to the documentary tradition, British television has consistently presented the debate over ghosts in an impartial way, with both sceptics and believers given equal opportunity to put their case. There was no determined enlightenment debunking in evidence, no mission to push a rationalist agenda. Indicative was ITV's 1955 programme *The Unexplained*. 'The clanking chain and the moan in the night! Natural or supernatural?', went the blurb in the *TV Times*. The subtitle encapsulated the equivocal approach

– 'The Inexplicable is explained ... Perhaps!' In 1962 the ITV series *About Religion* broadcast a documentary investigating ghosts and apparitions, providing dramatic re-enactments while in an accompanying studio discussion the Rev. W.R. Matthews appeared to discuss the possibility of the dead returning to the living.[32] The public service broadcasts of the BBC followed a similar format in programmes such as the 1967 BBC2 documentary *Two Steps in the Dark*. This concerned the ghostly manifestations that occurred in a London photographer's studio. During the war an airman had apparently murdered a woman and child next door. The renowned psychologist Hans Eysenck presented the sceptical position while Dr George Owen was willing to admit psychic forces might have been at work. A review in *The Times* began, 'Whatever we think about ghosts few can have remained unimpressed last night.'[33]

In recent years the personal computer, which has had an increasingly profound impact on the way we think, what we know and how we interact with others, has provided another platform for ghosts to imprint themselves on our consciousness. As we have seen in the last two chapters, history shows a recurring link between ghosts and emergent communication technologies, such as the telegraph, photography and film. They were all seen by some as holding out the possibility of bridging the gap between the living and the dead, between the corporeal and the disembodied. Recent children's fiction, such as Margaret J. Anderson's *The Ghost Inside the Monitor* (1990), has held out the same possibility for the present technological age, with computers acting as mediums through which children communicate with and befriend the spirits of the dead.[34] Moving from the virtual to the real, computer technology has provided new formats for recording the visual and aural manifestation of ghosts, in other words archiving the intangible. The internet not only acts as a new conduit for the dissemination of old and new ghost legends, it has also enabled the formation of new communities of believers, who can share, swap and debate their experiences. The internet has further enabled a new generation of ghost hunters to present their investigations to the public, establish reputations and construct their own multi-media experiences of the spirit world.[35] Cyberspace has become part of the geography of haunting.

The fact that ghosts remain a significant aspect of modern culture and belief does not mean that perceptions of their manifestation have remained unchanged. Some developments indicative of broader social, economic and lifestyle changes have already been mentioned in this book, such as the diminution of the liminal landscape in modern urban society. The countryside has been disenchanted, and ghosts, in legend or experience, are rarely seen these days groaning at crossroads, pacing bridges or lingering by pools. Yet, at the same time, some aspects of tradition and experience have translated into new forms rather than disappeared in response to societal developments. An obvious example of this is the way in which changing transport technologies have entered the experiential tradition of ghosts. From the mid twentieth century onwards the legendary currency of phantom coaches and horsemen went into decline, but in the same period reports of ghostly cars, often described as vintage, in other words from a definable previous era, began to appear with increasing frequency. They memorialised the places where, either in reality or subsequent legendary explanation, cars and their drivers met with a terrible accident.[36] The same period also saw the rise of the phantom hitchhiker, a modern legend that reworks old themes. Sometimes they are the ghosts of young women run over or involved in a crash on the way to a wedding or a dance. They re-enact their last moments, suddenly appearing in the road or walking out in front of cars, leading drivers to swerve dangerously or believe they have run over someone. Other phantom hitchhikers are classic warning ghosts, appearing on a dangerous bend to help people avoid their own fate.[37] These twentieth-century roadside ghosts are folkloric signifiers of the increasing cultural importance of the car over the last 50 years, and the psychological significance of the car crash as a modern tragedy. One wonders if the recent ritual practice of planting memorial crosses and laying flowers at the locations of fatal accidents will also act as focal points for the generation of new hauntings. If so, they would be poignant successors to those commemorations of roadside tragedy in centuries past – the gibbet and crossroads ghosts.

* * *

Ghosts have confounded centuries of criticism. Modern science's attempt to exorcise them has foundered, just like Reformation theology, Enlightenment philosophy and Victorian mass education in previous centuries. Whichever way you look at it, sociologically, psychologically, culturally, as long as people believe in ghosts they will continue to exist. Neither science nor religion can exorcise beliefs generated by personal experience, and to be haunted by the dead would seem to be a part of the human condition. Our dreams and reveries constantly conjure up images of the departed. They pervade our consciousness. Even if we do not believe in them, they are still with us in what we watch, read and hear; they are engrained in our language. We may be living longer, but that gives us more time to think about death, more opportunity for our preconceptions and beliefs to be challenged as our ultimate fate draws closer. Perhaps there is a subconscious fear that if we lay the belief in ghosts we will lose an element of our humanity. Some of us evidently need ghosts to live as much as they require us to die.

Notes

INTRODUCTION

1. *The Papers of Joseph Addison* (Edinburgh, 1790), vol. 3, p. 280.
2. Anthony Hilliar, *A Brief and Merry History of Great Britain* (Dublin, 1730), p. 15.
3. C.G. Jung, 'Foreword', in Aniela Jaffé, *Apparitions and Precognition* (New York, 1963), p. vi.
4. Rev. W.P. Witcutt, 'Notes on Warwickshire Folklore', *Folklore* 55, 2 (1944) 72.
5. Peter Underwood, *The A–Z of British Ghosts* (London, 1992), p. 9.
6. James I and VI, *Dæmonologie* (Edinburgh, 1597), p. 60.
7. For a useful discussion of the early origins of the various European terms for ghosts see Claude Lecouteux, *Fantômes et Revenants au Moyen Âge* (Paris, 1996), pp. 129–37.
8. James I and VI, *Dæmonologie*, p. 57; Ludwig Lavater, *Of Ghostes and Spirites Walking by Nyght* (London, 1572), pp. 1, 3.
9. Henry Guerlac, 'The Word Spectrum: A Lexicographic Note with a Query', *Isis* 56, 2 (1965) 206–7.
10. Éva Pócs, *Between the Living and the Dead* (Budapest, 1999), p. 38. For an example of its use in England see Owen Davies, *Witchcraft, Magic and Culture 1736–1951* (Manchester, 1999), p. 189.
11. Gillian Bennett, *Alas, Poor Ghost! Traditions of Belief in Story and Discourse* (Logan, 1999), p. 17.
12. There is a considerable amount of academic discussion on the meaning of 'haunting' from literary, psychological and sociological perspectives. See, for example, Julian Wolfreys, *Victorian Hauntings: Spectrality, Gothic, the Uncanny and Literature* (Basingstoke, 2002); Avery F. Gordon, *Ghostly Matters: Haunting and the Sociological Imagination* (Minneapolis and London, 1997).
13. See Lizanne Henderson and Edward J. Cowan, *Scottish Fairy Belief* (East Linton, 2001), pp. 19–20; Emma Wilby, *Cunning-Folk and Familiar Spirits* (Brighton, 2005), p. 18.
14. Carole G. Silver, *Strange and Secret Peoples: Fairies and Victorian Consciousness* (Oxford, 1999), pp. 42–3; Diane Purkiss, *Troublesome Things: A History of Fairies and Fairy Stories* (London, [2000] 2001), pp. 86, 133.
15. K.M. Briggs, *The Fairies in Tradition and Literature* (London, 1967), pp. 141–2.
16. J.C. Atkinson, *Forty Years in a Moorland Parish* (London, 1891), pp. 219–20, 230.
17. QS/Ba 2/74. An illuminating study of the case is provided in Laura Gowing, 'The Haunting of Susan Lay: Servants and Mistresses in Seventeenth-Century England', *Gender & History* 14, 2 (2002) 183–201.
18. John Aubrey, *Miscellanies* (London, 1696), pp. 62–4.
19. Joseph Glanvill, *Saducismus Triumphatus* (London, 1681), pp. 238–41.
20. Malcolm Gaskill, *Crime and Mentalities in Early Modern England* (Cambridge, 2000), pp. 231–2; West Yorkshire Archive Service QS 1/7/2/8/11.
21. *Great News from Middle-Row in Holborn: Or, a True Relation of a Dreadful Ghost* (London, 1679); *A New Ballad of the Midwives Ghost* (London, 1680).
22. Essex Record Office, Q/SR 187/53.
23. *The Times*, 6 July 1858; *The Times*, 10 January 1862. See also Owen Davies, *Murder, Magic, Madness: The Victorian Trials of Dove and the Wizard* (London, 2005), p. 192.

24. Aubrey, *Miscellanies*, pp. 66–7. See Jo Bath and John Newton, '"Sensible Proof of Spirits": Ghost Belief During the Later Seventeenth Century', *Folklore* 117 (2006) 3–4.

25. Norfolk Record Office, PD 9/1.

26. *The Times*, 7 July 1829.

27. Andrew Lang, *Cock Lane and Common-Sense*, 2nd edition (London, 1896), pp. 95, 138. See also Lang, 'Protest of a Psycho-Folklorist', *Folklore* 6, 3 (1895) 236–48.

28. Glanvill, *Saducismus*; George Sinclair, *Satan's Invisible World Discovered* (Edinburgh, 1685); Richard Baxter, *The Certainty of the World of Spirits* (London, 1691); Richard Bovet, *Pandæmonium. Or the Devil's Cloyster* (London, 1684).

29. The two best overviews are in Gillian Bennett, *Traditions of Belief: Women and the Supernatural* (London, 1987) and R.C. Finucane, *Appearances of the Dead: A Cultural History of Ghosts* (London, 1982), reprinted under the title, *Ghosts: Appearances of the Dead and Cultural Transformation* (Amherst, 1996). Rather less impressive but worth noting is Eric Maple's breezy survey, *The Realm of Ghosts* (London, 1964).

30. For example, Jean-Claude Schmitt, *Ghosts in the Middle Ages* (Chicago, 1998); Peter Marshall, *Beliefs and the Dead in Reformation England* (Oxford, 2002); John Newton (ed.), *Early Modern Ghosts* (Durham, 2002); Frederick Valletta, *Witchcraft, Magic and Superstition in England, 1640–1670* (Aldershot, 2000), ch. 4. The discussion on ghosts in Keith Thomas's *Religion and the Decline of Magic* (London, 1971) remains a valuable source of information and ideas. Peter Maxwell-Stuart's *Ghosts: A History of Phantoms, Ghouls, and Other Spirits of the Dead* (Stroud, 2006) has just been published. I also look forward to the forthcoming publication of Sasha Handley's PhD research on English ghost stories 1660–1800, *Visions of an Unseen World: Ghost Beliefs and Ghost Stories in Eighteenth-Century England* (2007), and Peter Marshall's case study, *Mother Leakey and the Bishop: A Ghost Story* (2007).

CHAPTER 1

1. C.S. Burne, 'Ghost Invisible to First-Born Son', *Folklore* 19, 3 (1908) 342; Francis Grose, *A Provincial Glossary, with a Collection of Local Proverbs, and Popular Superstitions* (London, 1787), p. 11.

2. Ruth L. Tongue, 'Odds and Ends of Somerset Folklore', *Folklore* 69, 1 (1958) 43.

3. Schmitt, *Ghosts*, pp. 63, 130; Finucane, *Ghosts*, p. 84.

4. Henry Swainson Cowper, *Hawkshead* (London, 1899), p. 332. It is worth noting, in the light of the strength of the Nordic murdered child-ghost tradition, that considerable Viking settlement occurred in the Lake District during the late eighth century.

5. Ludwik Stomma, *Campagnes insolites: Paysannerie polonaise et myths européens* (Paris, 1986), pp. 93–4, 174; Owen Davies, 'The Nightmare Experience, Sleep Paralysis, and Witchcraft Accusations', *Folklore* 114 (2003) 194; Juha Pentikainen, *The Nordic Dead-Child Tradition*, FFC 202 (Helsinki, 1968).

6. Pentikainen, *Nordic Dead-Child*, p. 355.

7. For a comparative study of Irish and French unbaptised child spirit legends see Anne O'Connor, *The Blessed and the Damned: Sinful Women and Unbaptised Children in Irish Folklore* (Oxford, 1005).

8. Peter Marshall, 'Old Mother Leakey and the Golden Chain: Context and Meaning in an Early Stuart Haunting', in John Newton (ed.), *Early Modern Ghosts* (Durham, 2002), p. 98.

9. QS/Ba 2/74. Gowing, 'The Haunting of Susan Lay', 183; *A Strange and Wonderfull Discovery of a Horrid and Cruel Murther* (London, 1662), p. 4.

10. Schmitt, *Ghosts*, p. 174.

11. Pócs, *Between the Living and the Dead*, p. 30; Mall Hiiemäe, 'Soul's Visiting Time in the Estonian Folk Calendar', 'Traditional Folk Belief Today: Conference dedicated to the 90th anniversary of Oskar Loorits', available online via <www.folklore.ee/folklore>.

12. Ronald Hutton, *The Rise and Fall of Merry England* (Oxford, 1994), pp. 106–7; Hutton, *The Stations of the Sun* (Oxford, 1996), ch. 36.

13. See Marshall, *Beliefs and the Dead*, pp. 14–15.

14. See Hutton, *Stations of the Sun*, ch. 37; Nicholas Rogers, *Halloween: From Pagan Ritual to Party Night* (Oxford, 2002), chs 2 and 3.

15. Cited in Schmitt, *Ghosts*, p. 178.

16. *Anti-Canidia; Or, Superstition Detected and Exposed* (London, 1762), p. 22.

17. Thomas Nashe, *The Unfortunate Traveller and Other Works*, ed. J.B. Steane (London, 1972), p. 210.

18. Henry More, *The Immortality of the Soul* (London, 1659), p. 291.

19. *Aristotle's New Book of Problems*, 6th edition (London, 1725), p. 124.

20. Henry Bourne, *Antiquitates Vulgares* (Newcastle, 1725), p. 41.

21. Joseph Hammond, *A Cornish Parish: Being an Account of St. Austell* (London, 1897), p. 360.

22. *New Lights from the World of Darkness; or the Midnight Messenger* (London, 1800), p. 4.

23. *Strange and Wonderfull Discovery of a Horrid and Cruel Murther*, p. 4.

24. Cowper, *Hawkshead: Experiences of the Paranormal* (London. 2002), p. 328.

25. Evans, *Seeing Ghosts*, p. 88.

26. Hammond, *A Cornish Parish*, p. 360.

27. Baxter, *The Certainty of the World of Spirits*, p. 138.

28. Henry Penfold, 'Superstitions connected with Illness, Burial, and Death in East Cumberland', *Transactions of the Cumberland and Westmorland Antiquarian and Archaeological Society* 7, N.S. (1907) 60–1.

29. See William Wells Newell, 'The Ignis Fatuus, its Character and Legendary Origin', *Journal of American Folklore* 17, 64 (1904) 39–60.

30. See, for example, Ruth Tongue, *Somerset Folklore* (London, 1965), pp. 93–4; Grace E. Hadow, 'Scraps of English Folklore, IX (Suffolk)', *Folklore* 35, 4 (1924), 355; Charlotte Latham, 'Some West Sussex Superstitions Lingering in 1868', *Folk-Lore Record* 1 (1878), 53; Ethel Rudkin, 'Will o' the Wisp', *Folklore* 49, 1 (1938) 46–8.

31. Sabine Baring-Gould, *Further Reminiscences, 1864–1844* (London, 1925), p. 122.

32. Eric Robinson and David Powell (eds), *John Clare by Himself* (Ashington and Manchester, 1996), p. 251.

33. Grose, *A Provincial Glossary*, pp. 9–10.

34. Robinson and Powell, *John Clare by Himself*, p. 251.

35. David Cressy, *Birth, Marriage and Death: Ritual, Religion, and the Life-Cycle in Tudor and Stuart England* (Oxford, 1997), pp. 428–32; Ruth Richardson, *Death, Dissection and the Destitute* (London, 1988), pp. 20–1.

36. Aubrey, *Miscellanies*, pp. 67–8.

37. See Schmitt, *Ghosts*, p. 16, plates 4, 5 and 6.

38. See, for example, *A New Ballad of the Midwives Ghost* (London, 1680); *A Godly Warning for all Maidens* (London, c. 1670); *The Lunatick Lover; Or, the Young-Man's Call to Grim King of Ghosts* (London, c. 1670); *Here is a True and Perfect Relation from the Faulcon* (London, 1661).

39. *News of the World*, 14 December 1851.

40. *The Times*, 7 November 1836.

41. This account is based on reports in the *Morning Chronicle*, 6, 9 and 10 January 1804; *The Times*, 6 and 14 January, 18 July 1804; *Old Bailey Proceedings Online* (<www.oldbaileyonline.org>, 2005), January 1804, trial of Francis Smith (t18040111–79).

42. *Morning Chronicle*, 10 January 1804.

43. *The Demon of Marleborough. Or, More News from Wilt-Shire* (1675), preface; Sinclair, *Satan's Invisible World*, pp. 102, 128.

44. Grose, *A Provincial Glossary*, p. 10.

45. Schmitt, *Ghosts*, p. 204; Finucane, *Ghosts*, p. 82.

46. Finucane, *Ghosts*, pp. 200–1.

47. Thomas Lacquer, 'Bodies, Death, and Pauper Funerals', *Representations* 1 (1983) 112.

48. Ethel H. Rudkin, 'Lincolnshire Folklore', *Folklore* 44, 2 (1933) 213.

49. Cowper, *Hawkshead*, p. 333; W.E.T. Morgan, 'A Few Folk- and Other Stories', *Transactions of the Woolhope Naturalists' Field Club* (1924–26), 101.

50. L.H. Hayward, 'Shropshire Folklore of Yesterday and To-Day', *Folklore* 49 (1938) 239.

51. Rudkin, 'Lincolnshire Folklore', 209.

52. Jane C. Beck, 'The White Lady of Great Britain and Ireland', *Folklore* 81, 4 (1970) 305.

53. Confirmed by Schmitt, *Ghosts*, p. 202; Evans, *Seeing Ghosts*, p. 25.

54. Finucane, *Ghosts*, p. 82.

55. Percy Manning, 'Stray Notes on Oxfordshire Folklore', *Folklore* 14 (1903) 65. For another example see Andrew Lang, *Dreams and Ghosts* (London, 1897), p. 137.

56. Reprinted in *The Times*, 22 January 1834.

57. J.O. Halliwell (ed.), *A Chronicle of the First Thirteen Years of the Reign of King Edward the Fourth. By John Warkworth* (London, 1839), p. 24.

58. Baxter, *Certainty of the World of Spirits*, pp. 37, 58.

59. *The St James's Surprizing and Afrightful Apparition* (London, 1722).

60. Atkinson, *Forty Years in a Moorland Parish*, p. 216.

61. Morgan, 'A Few Folk- and Other Stories', p. 100.

62. D. Felton, *Haunted Greece and Rome: Ghost Stories from Classical Antiquity* (Austin, 1999), p. 105, n.94.

63. Andrew Reynolds, 'Executions and Hard Anglo-Saxon Justice', *British Archaeology* 31 (1998).

64. Edith Oliver and Margaret Edwards, *Moonrakings: A Little Book of Wiltshire Stories* (Warminster, n.d.), pp. 82–3; Boys Firmin, *An Illustrated Guide to Crowborough* (Brighton and London, [1890] 1905), p. 153.

65. Baxter, *Certainty of the World of Spirits*, p. 58; Charlotte Latham, 'Some West Sussex Superstitions Lingering in 1868', *Folk-Lore Record* 1 (1878) 20.

66. See Philip C. Almond, *Heaven and Hell in Enlightenment England* (Cambridge, 1994), pp. 131–6.

67. Jaffé, *Apparitions*, p. 137.

68. Theo Brown, *The Fate of the Dead* (Ipswich, 1979), p. 41.

69. See, for example, Celia Green and Charles McCreery, *Apparitions* (London, 1705), pp. 118–22; Evans, *Seeing Ghosts*, pp. 92–3.

70. Bennett, *Alas, Poor Ghost!*, pp. 98–114.

71. *True Relation of the Horrid Ghost of a Woman* (London, 1673), p. 7.

72. Daniel Defoe, *The Political History of the Devil* (London, 1726), pp. 367–70. For other, similar candle beliefs see Steve Roud, *The Penguin Guide to the Superstitions of Britain and Ireland* (London, 2003), p. 57.

73. Alexander H. Krappe, 'Spirit-Sighted Animals', *Folklore* 54, 4 (1943) 391–401.

74. Baxter, *Certainty of the World of Spirits*, p. 37; Grose, *A Provincial Glossary*, p. 11; Cowper, *Hawkshead*, p. 330.

75. Baxter, *Certainty of the World of Spirits*, p. 30. In Estonian ghost tradition olfactory ghosts are also rare and mostly smell of decay; see Eha Viluoja, 'Manifestations of the Revenant in Estonian Folk Tradition', *Folklore. Electronic Journal of Folklore* 2 (1996) section 4.

76. Aubrey, *Miscellanies*, p. 67.

77. See Constance Classen, 'Heaven's Scent: The Odour of Sanctity in Christian Tradition', *Journal of Religion and Culture* 4, 2 (1990) 87–92.

78. Wilkie Collins, *The Haunted Hotel* (London, 1878), ch. 19. On literary smelly ghosts see Lawrence Andrew Cooper Jr., 'Gothic Realities: The Emergence of Cultural Forms Through Representations of the Unreal', PhD thesis, Princeton University, 2005, pp. 198–201.

79. Green and McCreery, *Apparitions*, p. 80.

80. Douglas J. Davies, *Death, Ritual and Belief*, second edition (London and New York, 2002), pp. 172, 179; Bennett, *Alas, Poor Ghost!*, p. 106.

81. Ella Mary Leather, *The Folk-Lore of Herefordshire* (Hereford, [1912] 1992), p. 35.

82. Oliver and Edwards, *Moonrakings*, p. 71.

83. *Liverpool Albion*; reprinted in *The Times*, 17 November 1847.

84. Glanvill, *Saducismus*, pp. 97, 98.

85. Glanvill, *Saducismus*, pp. 97, 98; Manning, 'Stray Notes on Oxfordshire Folklore', 71; Finucane, *Ghosts*, p. 197.

86. John U. Powell, 'Folklore Notes from South-West Wilts', *Folklore* 12, 1 (1901) 73.

87. Grose, *A Provincial Glossary*, pp. 11, 12.

88. Green and McCreery, *Apparitions*, p. 95.

89. Glanvill, *Saducismus*, p. 269.

90. Ebenezer Sibly, *A New and Complete Illustration of the Occult Sciences* (London, 1792), p. 1096.

91. Schmitt, *Ghosts*, p. 201.

92. *Aristotle's New Book of Problems*, p. 123.

93. Catherine Crowe, *The Night Side of Nature: Or, Ghosts & Ghost Seers*, 3rd edition (London, 1852), p. 214.

94. Glanvill, *Saducismus*, p. 287.

95. *True Relation of the Horrid Ghost of a Woman*, p. 6; Glanvill, *Saducismus*, pp. 287, 239.

96. Joseph Priestley, *Original Letters, by the Rev. John Wesley, and his Friends* (Birmingham, 1791), p. 146.

97. University Library Cambridge, MS Add7621/354.

98. Paul Chambers, *Sex and Paranormal* (London, [1999] 2003), pp. 11–29; Davies, 'The Nightmare Experience', 190–3.

99. The point is well made by Jo Bath, '"In the Divell's likenesse": interpretation and confusion in popular ghost belief', in Newton, *Early Modern Ghosts*, pp. 73–4.

100. On the German history of the word and concept see Harry Price, *Poltergeist Over England* (London, 1945), pp. 1–3; Annekatrin Puhle, 'Ghosts, Apparitions and Poltergeist Incidents in Germany Between 1700–1900', *Journal of the Society for Psychical Research* 63 (1999) 303–4. For a detailed survey of poltergeist phenomena see Alan Gauld and A.D. Cornell, *Poltergeists* (London, 1979).

101. Lang, Cock Lane and Common-Sense, pp. 142–3.

102. Lithobolia: Or, the Stone-Throwing Devil (London, 1698).

103. Baxter, Certainty of the World of Spirits, p. 42.

104. John Beaumont, An Historical, Physiological and Theological Treatise of Spirits (London, 1705), p. 306.

105. Reprinted in The Times, 26 April 1821.

106. The Life and Death of Mr. Vavasor Powell (London, 1671), p. 8.

107. Eugene Crowell, Spirit World: Its Inhabitants, Nature and Philosophy (Boston, 1879), pp. 184–5.

108. Thomas Hobbes, Leviathan (London, 1651), p. 374.

109. Anti-Canidia, p. 22.

110. Saturday Review, 19 July 1856, 268–9.

111. Editor's notes, Occult Review 3 (1906) 114.

112. Crowe, The Night Side of Nature, p. 216.

113. Alfred Roffe, An Essay upon the Ghost-Belief of Shakespeare (London, 1851), p. 21.

114. Occult Review 3 (1906) 317.

115. Ernest Bennett, Apparitions andd Haunted Houses: A Survey of Evidence (London, 1939), p. 349; Green and McCreery, Apparitions, pp. 192–6. Cats and dogs also predominate in Estonian ghost tradition; see Viluoja, 'Manifestations of the Revenant'.

116. Herts Guardian, 24 March 1877.

117. See, for example, Elliott O'Donnell, Animal Ghosts: Or, Animal Hauntings and the Hereafter (London, 1913), chs 4 and 5.

118. Davies, Death, Ritual and Belief, p. 188.

119. Keith Thomas, Man and the Natural World: Changing Attitudes in England 1500–1800 (London, 1983), pp. 138–41. More generally see Rod Preece, Brute Souls, Happy Beasts, and Evolution: The Historical Status of Animals (Vancouver, 2005).

120. See Peter Harrison, 'Descartes on Animals', Philosophical Quarterly 42, 167 (1992) 219–27; Wallace Shugg, 'The Cartesian Beast-Machine in English Literature (1663–1750)', Journal of the History of Ideas 29, 2 (1968) 279–92.

121. Herts and Essex Observer, 12 January 1878.

122. See Jeremy Harte, 'Black Dog Studies'; Simon Sherwood 'A Psychological Approach to Black Dogs'; and Jennifer Westwood 'Friend or Foe? Norfolk Traditions of Shuck', all in Bob Trubshaw (ed.), Explore Phantom Black Dogs (Loughborough, 2005); Theo Brown, 'The Black Dog in Devon', Transactions of the Devonshire Association 91 (1959) 38–44.

123. See Alexandra Walsham, Providence in Early Modern England (Oxford, 1999), pp. 186–94.

124. Richard Boulton, A Compleat History of Magick, Sorcery, and Witchcraft (London, 1715–1716), vol. 1, p. 46; Glanvill, Saducismus (1681), p. 136.

125. Harte, 'Black Dog Studies', pp. 16–18.

126. Thomas Gordon, The Humourist: Being Essays Upon Several Subjects (London, 1720), pp. 84–7.

127. Anti-Canidia, p. 22.

128. Narrative of the Demon of Spraiton, in a Letter from a Person of Quality in the County of Devon (London, 1683), p. 5; Bovet, Pandæmonium, pp. 187–8; Sad and Wonderful Newes from the Faulcon at the Bank Side (London, 1661), p. 3; Strange and Wonderful News from Lincolnshire. Or, a Dreadful Account of a Most Inhumane and Bloody Murther (London, 1679), p. 4.

129. Robert Hunt, Popular Romances of the West of England, 3rd edition (Felinfach, [1881] 1990), p. 351; Penfold, 'Superstitions connected with Illness', 59; Manning, 'Stray Notes on Oxfordshire Folklore', 65.

130. Leather, Folk-lore, p. 35; James Obelkevich, Religion and Rural Society: South Lindsey, 1825–1875 (Oxford, 1976), p. 282.

131. Samuel Bamford, *Early Days* (London, 1849), p. 30.

132. Mabel Peacock, 'Folklore of Lincolnshire', *Folklore* 12 (1901) 172. See also *Notes & Queries* 4, 99 (1851) 212.

133. Schmitt, *Ghosts*, p. 196.

134. Christabel F. Fiske, 'Animals in Early English Ecclesiastical Literature, 650–1500', *Proceedings of the Modern Language Association of America* 28, 3 (1913) 368–87.

135. Owen Davies, 'Angels in elite and popular magic, 1650–1790', in Alexandra Walsham and Peter Marshall (eds), *Angels in the Early Modern World* (Cambridge, 2006), p. 300.

136. On familiars see James Sharpe, *Instruments of Darkness: Witchcraft in England 1550–1750* (London, 1996), pp. 71–4; Davies, *Witchcraft, Magic and Culture*, pp. 181–4; James A. Serpell, 'Guardian Spirits or Demonic Pets: The Concept of the Witch's Familiar in Early Modern England, 1530–1712', in Angela Creager and William Chester Jordan (eds), *The Animal/Human Boundary: Historical Perspectives* (Rochester, 2002), pp. 157–90; Wilby, *Cunning-Folk and Familiar Spirits*. More generally on the influence of the puritan emphasis on the Devil see Darren Oldridge, *The Devil in Early-Modern England* (Stroud, 2000).

137. Schmitt, *Ghosts*, p. 172.

138. Eamon Duffy, *The Stripping of the Altars: Traditional Religion in England 1400–1580* (New Haven and London, 1992), p. 369.

139. Reginald Scot, *The Discoverie of Witchcraft* (London, 1584) (1651 edition), p. 105.

140. Sibly, *New and Complete Illustration of the Occult Sciences*, p. 1095.

141. *The Rest-less Ghost: Or, Wonderful News from Northamptonshire, and Southwark* (London, 1675), p. 5.

142. Hayward, 'Shropshire Folklore of Yesterday and To-Day', 240–1.

143. A.R. Wright, 'Presidential Address: The Folklore of the Past and Present', *Folklore* 38, 1 (1927) 32.

144. Bamford, *Early Days*, p. 29.

145. Roy Palmer, *The Folklore of Shropshire* (Almeley, 2004), pp. 133, 134. See also Paul Devereux, *Haunted Land* (London, 2001), pp. 154–5.

146. See Daniel Woolf, *The Social Circulation of the Past: English Historical Culture 1500–1730* (Oxford, 2003), esp. ch. 9.

147. L.V. Grinsell, *Folklore of Prehistoric Sites in Britain* (Newton Abbot, 1976); Adam Fox, *Oral and Literate Culture in England 1500–1700* (Oxford, 2000), pp. 238–42.

148. Fox, *Oral and Literate Culture*, pp. 243–51; M.A. Courtney, *Cornish Feasts and Folklore* (London, 1890), p. 74; K.M. Briggs, 'Historical Traditions in English Folk-Tales', *Folklore* 75, 4 (1964) 231. On the Alfred celebration see Paul Readman, 'The Place of the Past in English Culture, c. 1890–1914', *Past & Present* 186 (2005) 147–201.

149. See Woolf, *Social Circulation of the Past*, p. 385; Fox, *Oral and Literate Culture*, pp. 255–7; Alan Smith, 'The Image of Cromwell in Folklore and Tradition', *Folklore* 79, 1 (1968) 17–39.

150. W.S. Lach-Szyrma, 'Folk-Lore Traditions of Historical Events', *Folk-Lore Record* 3, 2 (1880) 157–8.

151. Thomas Babington Macaulay, *The History of England from the Accession of James II*, vol. 1, ch. 5.

152. Valerie Chancellor, *History For Their Masters* (Bath, 1970), pp. 105–7, 53. See also, Rosemary Mitchell, *Picturing the Past: English History in Text and Image 1830–1870* (Oxford, 2000).

153. Cowper, *Hawkshead*, p. 326.

154. Jennifer Westwood and Jacqueline Simpson, *The Lore of the Land* (London, 2005), p. 269; J. and P. Loader, *Tales of Lulworth in Olden Days* (1932); cited in M.M. Banks, 'Phantoms in Dorset', *Folklore* 54, 4 (1943) 402.

155. E. Gillespy, *A Disquisition upon the Criminal Laws; Shewing the Necessity of Altering and Amending Them* (Northampton, 1793), p. 34.

156. For an in-depth analysis of the passage see James E. Harding, 'A Spirit Deception in Job 4:15? Interpretive Indeterminacy and Eliphaz's Vision', *Biblical Interpretation* 13, 2 (2005) 137–66.

157. *An Account of Some Imaginary Apparitions, the Effects of Fear or Fraud* (Dunbar, c. 1792), p. 7.

158. James Lackington, *Memoirs of the Forty-Five First Years of the Life of James Lackington*, 8th edition (London, [1791] 1794), p. 35.

159. Jones uses the expression 'felt not her/his cloaths about her/him' repeatedly; Edmund Jones, *A Relation of Apparitions of Spirits* (1780), pp. 3, 33, 37, 77, 78.

160. *Northampton Mercury*, 22 January 1814. Thanks to Mark Fox for this reference.

161. *Somerset County Herald*, 20 January 1894.

162. *Bristol Mirror*; reprinted in *The Times*, 24 March 1841.

CHAPTER 2

1. Atkinson, *Forty Years in a Moorland Parish*, p. 215. For biographical information see the *New Dictionary of National Biography* (henceforth *New DNB*).

2. See, for example, the essays in Hilda Ellis Davidson (ed.), *Boundaries and Thresholds* (Stroud, 1993); Bob Trubshaw, *Explore Mythology* (Loughborough, 2003); Nyree Finlay, 'Outside of Life: Traditions of Infant Burial in Ireland from Cillin to Cist', *World Archaeology* 31, 3 (2000) 407–22.

3. See Reimund Kvideland and Henning K. Sehmsdorf (eds), *Scandinavian Folk Belief and Legend* (Minneapolis and London, 1988), pp. 118–21.

4. Bovet, *Pandæmonium*, pp. 180, 187–8.

5. Jeremy Harte, 'Haunted Roads', *The Ley Hunter* 121 (1994) 1–7.

6. John Glyde, *Folklore and Customs of Norfolk (being Extracts from 'The Norfolk Garland')* Wakefield, [1872] 1973), p. 64.

7. T.C. Lethbridge, *Ghost and Ghoul* (London, 1961); T.C. Lethbridge, *Ghost and Divining-Rod* (London, 1963).

8. Robert Roberts, *A Ragged Schooling: Growing up in the Classic Slum* (Manchester 1976), cited in Jenny Hazelgrove, *Spiritualism and British Society Between the Wars* (Manchester, 2000), p. 28.

9. A similar observation has been made in relation to modern Estonian hauntings; see Ülo Valk, 'Ghostly Possession and Real Estate: The Dead in Contemporary Estonian Folklore', *Journal of Folklore Research* 43, 1 (2006) 49.

10. *The Times*, 16 August 1866.

11. John Heydon, *The Harmony of the World* (London, 1662), p. 180.

12. Baxter, *Certainty of the World of Spirits*, p. 31.

13. Powell, 'Folklore Notes from South-West Wilts', 73.

14. James Carr, *Annals and Stories of Colne and Neighbourhood* (Manchester, 1878), pp. 199–200.

15. Joseph Lawson, *Progress in Pudsey* (Stanningley, 1887), p. 68.

16. Morgan, 'A Few Folk- and Other Stories', p. 100; Hayward, 'Shropshire Folklore of Yesterday and To-Day', *Folklore* 49 (1938) 240. For some further examples see Janet Bord, *Footprints in Stone: Imprints of Giants, Heroes, Holy People, Devils, Monsters and Supernatural Beings* (Loughborough, 2004), pp. 143–6.

17. Henry Mayhew, *London Labour and the London Poor* (London, [1851] 1967), vol. 1, p. 411.

18. Cited in Thomas, *Religion and the Decline of Magic*, p. 707.

19. J.W., *A Full and Compleat History of the Lives, Robberies, and Murders, of all the Most Notorious Highwaymen* (London, c. 1742), p. 85.

20. The point is well made in Carol Banks, '"Shadow and Substance": Ghost, Mere Fantasy or Visionary Experience?', in Newton, *Early Modern Ghosts*, p. 39.

21. See Mark Jenner, 'Death, Decomposition and Dechristianisation? Public Health and Church Burial in Eighteenth-Century England', *English Historical Review* 120 (2005) 615–32.

22. See, for example, Schmitt, *Ghosts*, pp. 182–4; T.P. Magoun, 'Football in Medieval England and in Middle-English Literature', *American Historical Review* 35, 1 (1929) 39; F.G. Emmison, *Elizabethan Life: Disorder* (Chelmsford, 1970), pp. 111–23. On people's contemporary relationship with burial grounds see Doris Francis, Leonie Kellaher and Georgina Neophytou, *The Secret Cemetery* (Oxford, 2005).

23. Scot, *Discoverie*, book xv, ch. 39.

24. Marshall, *Beliefs and the Dead*, p. 255.

25. Nashe, *The Unfortunate Traveller*, p. 212.

26. *Surrey Advertiser*, 13 September 1875.

27. *The Times*, 24 April 1841.

28. Essex Record Office, D/7 1/1/111/19.

29. Oliver and Edwards, *Moonrakings*, p. 71.

30. *Annual Register*, 5th edition (1775), p. 130. For further examples and discussion see Michael Macdonald and Terence R. Murphy, *Sleepless Souls: Suicide in Early Modern England* (Oxford, 1990), pp. 48–9, 212–13; Robert Halliday, 'Criminal Graves and Rural Crossroads', *British Archaeology* 25 (1997).

31. *Notes & Queries* 4, 99 (1851) 212.

32. Henry Fielding, *The History of Tom Jones* (Dublin [1749] 1759), vol. 2, pp. 29–30.

33. Charles Moore, *A Full Inquiry into the Subject of Suicide* (London, 1790), vol. 1, p. 316.

34. 'Notes on English Folklore', *Folklore* 28, 3 (1917) 313; F.B. Kettlewell, 'Trinkum-Trinkums' *of Fifty Years* (Taunton, 1927), p. 52.

35. Rudkin, 'Lincolnshire Folklore', 212–13; Chas. W. Whistler, 'An Historical Ghost', *Folklore* 19, 3 (1908) 342–3.

36. For a general global study of the folklore of crossroads see Martin Puhvel, *The Crossroads in Folklore and Myth* (New York, 1989).

37. Briggs, 'Historical Traditions', 232.

38. On the practice of gibbeting see V.A.C. Gattrell, *The Hanging Tree: Execution and the English People* (Oxford, 1884), pp. 267–9. Richardson, *Death, Dissection and the Destitute*, pp. 35–6; Albert Hartshorne, *Hanging in Chains* (London, 1891); Nicola Whyte, 'The Deviant Dead in the Norfolk Landscape', *Landscapes* 4, 1 (2003) 24–39.

39. For examples see Whyte, 'The Deviant Dead'.

40. *The Times*, 28 March 1856.

41. Charles Dickens, *Great Expectations*, ch. 1. See Steven Connor, 'Forgeries: The Metallurgy of *Great Expectations*' (2005), <www.bbk.ac.uk/english/skc/forgeries/forgeries.pdf>.

42. Cowper, *Hawkshead*, p. 326.

43. Grose, *A Provincial Glossary*, p. 14.

44. *The Times*, 17 March 1806.

45. See Vladimir Jankovic, 'The Politics of Sky Battles in Early Hanoverian Britain', *Journal of British Studies* 41 (2002) 429–59, esp. 432–3.

46. The New Yeares Wonder. Being a Most Certaine and True Relation of the Disturbed Inhabitants of Kenton (London, 1643); A Great Wonder in Heaven: Shewing the Late Apparitions and Prodigious Noyses of War and Battels (London, 1642).

47. Bennett, Apparitions, pp. 284–7. See also Westwood and Simpson, Lore, pp. 133, 538.

48. David Clarke, The Angel of Mons: Phantom Soldiers and Ghostly Guardians (Chichester, 2004), pp. 192–3.

49. Daniel Defoe, An Essay on the History and Reality of Apparitions (London, 1727), pp. 376, 379.

50. Leather, Folk-lore of Herefordshire, pp. 34–5.

51. Somerset County Herald, 21 December 1867.

52. J.B. Partridge, 'Cotswold Place-Lore and Customs', Folklore 23, 3 (1912) 342.

53. J.S. Lucas, 'The Hoard of Anglo-Saxon Coins Found at Chancton Farm, Sussex', Sussex Archaeological Collections 20 (1868) 212–14; cited in Jacqueline Simpson, 'Legends of Chanctonbury Ring', Folklore 80, 2 (1969) 129.

54. The Female Ghost: Being a Strange and Wonderful Discovery of an Iron Chestful of Money (London, 1705). Thanks to Janice Turner for bringing this to my attention.

55. Authentic Narrative of the Mysterious Warnings, Relative to the Hidden Treasure at Limehouse (London, 1821), p. 8.

56. The Times, 11 April 1871.

57. Defoe, History and Reality of Apparitions, p. 379.

58. Hadow, 'Scraps of English Folklore', 355.

59. Partridge, 'Cotswold Place-Lore', 335.

60. James Raine (ed.), Depositions from the Castle of York (Durham, 1861) , pp. 161–2. See also Stephen Greenblatt, 'The Touch of the Real', Representations 59 (1997) 22–4.

61. Samuel Bamford, Early Days (London, 1849), pp. 27–8.

62. Charles James Billson, County Folklore: Leicestershire and Rutland (London, 1895), p. 44; Rudkin, 'Lincolnshire Folklore', 209. See also L.F. Newman and E.M. Wilson, 'Folklore Survivals in the Southern "Lake Counties" and in Essex: A Comparison and Contrast', Folklore 63, 2 (1952) 101.

63. Charlotte Burne, Shropshire Folklore: A Sheaf of Gleanings (London, 1883), p. 108.

64. Whitehaven Herald; reprinted in The Times, 1 March 1843.

65. The Times, 30 November 1863; 2 March, 22 March and 8 April 1864.

66. New Lights from the World of Darkness, p. 44.

67. Thomas Tonkin, 'Natural History', MS, pp. 10–11, cited in A.K. Hamilton Jenkin, Cornwall and the Cornish (London, 1933), p. 247.

68. See for example Hammond, A Cornish Parish, pp. 359–60.

69. Margaret Ringwood, 'Some Customs and Beliefs of Durham Miners', Folklore 68, 3 (1957) 423–4. On similar Welsh miners' beliefs see Robin Gwyndaf, 'The Past in the Present: Folk Beliefs in Welsh Oral Tradition', Fabula 35 (1994) 257–8.

70. The Times, 23 October 1867.

71. Thomas Salmon, Modern History: Or, the Present State of All Nations (London, 1732), vol. 15, pp. 354, 356.

72. Charles Mackay, Extraordinary Popular Delusions and the Madness of Crowds (New York [1841] 1932), p. 593.

73. Court Journal; reprinted in The Times, 10 September 1863.

74. The Times, 23 August 1834.

75. The Times, 17 August 1851.

76. Lackington, Memoirs, p. 31.

77. *The Times*, 1 August 1868.
78. S.C. Williams, *Religious Belief and Popular Culture in Southwark c. 1880–1939* (Oxford, 1999), p. 80.
79. See <www.visitdoncaster.co.uk/Tourism/historical/HistDelight/Epworth.asp>.
80. David Inglis and Mary Holmes, 'Highland and Other Haunts: Ghosts in Scottish Tourism', *Annals of Tourism Research* 30, 1 (2003) 57–61.
81. Inglis and Holmes, 'Highland and Other Haunts', 55–6.
82. *The Times*, 23 and 28 September 1936.
83. William H. Salter, *Zoar, or the Evidence for Psychical Research Concerning Survival* (London, 1961), ch. 5; an online version is available at <www.survivalafterdeath.org>.
84. See, for example, Jack Hallam, *Haunted Inns of England* (London, 1972); Richard Jones, *Haunted Inns of Britain and Ireland* (London, 2004); Roger Long, *Reputedly Haunted Inns of the Chilterns and Thames Valley* (Fontwell, 1993).
85. Thomas Burke, *The English Inn* (London, 1930), ch. 4.
86. William Lilly, *William Lilly's History of his Life and Times* (London, [1715] 1822), pp. 32–4.
87. *Great News from Middle-Row in Holborn. Or, a True Relation of a Dreadful Ghost; A New Ballad of the Midwives Ghost*.
88. Quoted in 'Parsons, Elizabeth', *New DNB*.
89. *Chesterfield Courier*, reprinted in *The Times*, 26 June 1834. The identity of the landlord is confirmed by entries in local trade directories; see <www.wirksworth.org.uk/79-PUBS.htm>.
90. Eric Partridge, *A Dictionary of Historical Slang*, abridged by Jacqueline Simpson (London, 1972).
91. *The Times*, 5 June 1869.
92. June Lewis-Jones, *Folklore of the Cotswolds* (Stroud, 2003), p. 71; Wally Barnes, *Ghosts, Mysteries and Legends of Warrington* (Wigan, 1991); *Barnet & Potters Bar Times*, 29 October 2003 (see <www.barnettimes.co.uk/features/newsfeatures/display.var.427935.0.a_popular_haunt_with_lots_of_ghosts.php>); <www.visityork.org/media/factsheets/twenty.asp>.
93. Underwood, *The A–Z of British Ghosts*, pp. 185–6.

CHAPTER 3

1. On early definitions of the word in the Christian era see Lecouteux, *Fantômes*, pp. 75–6.
2. Daniel Ogden, *Greek and Roman Necromancy* (Princeton and Oxford, 2001), p. xxii. See also H.J. Rose, 'Ghost Ritual in Aeschylus', *Harvard Theological Review* 43, 4 (1950) 257–80.
3. *The Times*, 30 and 31 March 1857.
4. See K.A.D. Smelik, 'The Witch of Endor: I Samuel 28 in Rabbinic and Christian Exegesis till 800 A.D.', *Vigiliae Christianae* 33, 2 (1979) 160–79; Valerie I.J. Flint, *The Rise of Magic in Early Medieval Europe* (Princeton, 1991), pp. 50–5; Steven Connor, *Dumbstruck: A Cultural History of Ventriloquism* (Oxford, 2000), ch. 3. On Augustine's views on ghosts generally see Schmitt, *Ghosts*, pp. 17–22; Finucane, *Ghosts*, pp. 36–7.
5. Joseph W. Trigg, 'Eustathius of Antioch's Attack on Origen: What is at Issue in an Ancient Controversy?', *Journal of Religion* 75, 2 (1995) 224.
6. Schmitt, *Ghosts*, pp. 15–16; Edward Peters, *The Magician, the Witch and the Law* (Hassocks, 1978), p. 69; Charles Zika, 'Endor, Witch of', in Richard Golden (ed.), *Encyclopedia of Witchcraft: The Western Tradition* (Santa Barbara, 2006), vol. 2, pp. 308–10.

7. Scot, *Discoverie* (1651 edition), p. 103.

8. Thomas Ady, *A Candle in the Dark* (London, 1655), p. 148.

9. Thomas Cooper, *The Mystery of Witch-Craft* (London, 1617), p. 154.

10. John Edwards, *A Farther Enquiry into Several Remarkable Texts of the Old and New Testament* ((London, 1692), p. 320.

11. James I and VI, *Dæmonologie*, preface.

12. *Henry Cornelius Agrippa's Fourth Book of Occult Philosophy* (London, 1655), p. 91.

13. Cornelius Agrippa, *Three Books of Occult Philosophy*, trans. J.F. (London, 1651), pp. 488, 489.

14. Agrippa, *Three Books of Occult Philosophy*, p. 491.

15. Richard Kieckhefer contextualises the usage of this broad definition of necromancy in his *Magic in the Middle Ages* (Cambridge, 1889).

16. Glanvill, *Saducismus*, p. 43.

17. On their scrying activities see Deborah E. Harkness, 'Shows in the Showstone: A Theater of Alchemy and Apocalypse in the Angel Conversations of John Dee (1527–1608/9)', *Renaissance Quarterly* 49, 4 (1996) 707–37. For a good general account of Dee see Benjamin Woolley, *The Queen's Conjuror: The Life and Magic of Dr Dee* (London, 2001).

18. John Weever, *Ancient Funerall Monuments* (London, 1631), p. 46.

19. Wharton's story is well told in J. Kent Clark, *Goodwin Wharton* (Oxford, 1984). Wharton's meeting with Geoffrey is related on pp. 35–6.

20. See Roy Porter, 'The Diary of a Madman, Seventeenth-Century Style: Goodwin Wharton, MP and Communer with the Fairy World', *Psychological Medicine* 16, 3 (1986) 503–13.

21. See Paul Barber, *Vampires, Burial, and Death: Folklore and Reality* (New Haven and London, 1988). For examples of ritual decapitation from the Scandinavian sagas see Lecouteux, *Fantômes*, pp. 101–2.

22. Per Sörlin, *'Wicked Arts': Witchcraft and Magic Trials in Southern Sweden 1635–1754* (Leiden, Boston, Köln, 1999), pp. 37, 85; David Lederer, 'Living with the Dead: Ghosts in Early Modern Bavaria', in Kathryn A. Edwards (ed.), *Werewolves, Witches, and Wandering Spirits: Traditional Belief and Folklore in Early Modern Europe* (Kirksville, 2002), pp. 37–8.

23. Weever, *Ancient Funerall Monuments*, p. 22. See also MacDonald and Murphy, *Sleepless Souls*, p. 48.

24. Alison Taylor, 'Burial with the Romans', *British Archaeology* 69 (2003) 14–19; Alison Taylor, *Burial Practice in Early England* (Stroud, 2001); Reynolds, 'Executions and Hard Anglo-Saxon Justice'; Mary McMahon, 'Early Medieval Settlement and Burial Outside the Enclosed Town: Evidence from Archaeological Excavations at Bride Street, Dublin', *Proceedings of the Royal Irish Academy* 102 (2002) 81.

25. Leather, *Folk-Lore*, p. 35; Tongue, 'Odds and Ends of Somerset Folklore', 44.

26. *The Times*, 16 September 1834.

27. Erasmus, *Twenty-Two Select Colloquies* (London, 1689), pp. 188–9.

28. It should be noted that there was also considerable debate amongst early modern Catholic theologians about the probity of exorcism. See, for example, Sarah Ferber, *Demonic Possession and Exorcism in Early Modern France* (London, 2004), pp. 85–8.

29. *Constitutions and Canons Ecclesiastical* (London, 1678), p. 33.

30. James I and VI, *Dæmonologie* (1603), p. 59.

31. See Thomas, *Religion and the Decline of Magic*, pp. 575–85; Sharpe, *Instruments of Darkness*, pp. 190–211; Oldridge, *The Devil*, pp. 129–33.

32. Jones, *A Relation of Apparitions*, p. 45.

33. *Strange and Wonderful News from London-Wall* (London, 1674), p. 4.
34. Bourne, *Antiquitates Vulgares*, p. 90.
35. Atkinson, *Forty Years*, p. 59.
36. Carr, *Annals and Stories of Colne*, pp. 198–200; Newman and Wilson, 'Folklore Survivals in the Southern "Lake Counties"', 101.
37. *Notes & Queries* 2, 55 (1850) 404.
38. Manning, 'Stray Notes', 67–9.
39. Stuart Piggott, 'Berkshire Mummers' Plays and Other Folklore', *Folklore* 39, 3 (1928) 280–1; Geoffrey Gomme, 'Scraps of English Folklore, V', *Folklore* 21, 2 (1910) 222. See also K.E. Kissack, 'A Curious Form of Exorcism', *Folklore* 68, 1 (1957) 296–7.
40. Brown, *Fate of the Dead*, pp. 27–8, 42–3; William Bottrell, *Stories and Folk-Lore of West Cornwall*, 3rd series (Felinfach, [1880] 1996), p. 153.
41. Essex Record Office QS/Ba 2/74; Gowing, 'The Haunting of Susan Lay', 183–4.
42. Addison, *The Drummer*, p. 22.
43. Grose, *A Provincial Glossary*, pp. 15–16.
44. Powell, 'Folklore Notes from South-West Wilts', 74; Kettlewell, 'Trinkum-Trinkums', p. 51.
45. Thomas Bond, *Topographical and Historical Sketches of the Boroughs of East and West Looe* (London, 1823), pp. 154–5; Brown, *Fate of the Dead*, pp. 33–4; Courtney, *Cornish Feasts*, pp. 98–9.
46. Kettlewell, 'Trinkum-Trinkums', p. 51.
47. Courtney, *Cornish Feasts*, p. 95.
48. Richard Polwhele, *Traditions and Recollections, Domestic, Clerical and Literary* (London, 1826), p. 605.
49. Hamilton Jenkin, *Cornwall and the Cornish*, p. 236.
50. Timothy Tangherlini, '"Who Ya Gonna Call?" Ministers and the Mediation of Ghostly Threat in Danish Legend Tradition', *Western Folklore* 57 (1998) 153–78.
51. *Strange and Wonderful News from Lincolnshire. Or, a Dreadful Account of a Most Inhumane and Bloody Murther*, p. 4.
52. *Sad and Wonderful Newes from the Faulcon at the Bank Side*, p. 4. The case was also turned into a ballad, *Here is a True and Perfect Relation from the Faulcon* (London, 1661).
53. *Full and True Account of a Strange Apparition, that Two Months Last Past hath Frequently Appeared and Haunted the House of Mr. S—ge* (London, 1685).
54. *Whip for the Devil; Or, the Roman Conjurer* (London, 1683), pp. 92–3.
55. *Whip for the Devil*, p. 94.
56. See Michael Hunter, 'New Light on the "Drummer of Tedworth": Conflicting Narratives of Witchcraft in Restoration England', *Historical Research* 78 (2005) 311–53; Price, *Poltergeist over England*, ch. 5.
57. Glanvill, *Saducismus*, p. 109.
58. Cited in Hunter, 'New Light on the "Drummer of Tedworth"', 328.
59. Glanvill, *Saducismus*, p. 98.
60. Cited in Hunter, 'New Light on the "Drummer of Tedworth"', 345.
61. *An Extract of the Rev. Mr. John Wesley's Journal, from May 14, 1768, to Sept. 1, 1770* (London, 1790), p. 6.
62. See Oliver Goldsmith, *The Mystery Revealed, Containing a Series of Transactions and Authentic Memorials Respecting the Supposed Cock Lane Ghost* (1762); Douglas Grant, *The Cock Lane Ghost* (London, 1965); E.J. Clery, *The Rise of Supernatural Fiction, 1762–1800* (Cambridge, 1999), ch. 1; Paul Chambers, *The Cock Lane Ghost: Murder, Sex and Haunting in Dr. Johnson's London* (Stroud, 2006).
63. John Rayner, *A Digest of the Law Concerning Libels* (London, 1765), p. 84.

64. 'Parsons, Elizabeth', New DNB.

65. For biographical details see the New DNB.

66. Cited in Grant, The Cock Lane Ghost, p. 52.

67. John Douglas, The Criterion: Or, Miracles Examined with a View to Expose the Pretensions of Pagans and Papists (London, 1754).

68. Seasonable Present to the Renowned Society of Ghost-Mongers (London, 1762), p. 9. A version of this text also appeared in the Gentleman's Magazine (February 1762), 82–84.

69. Grant, The Cock Lane Ghost, 114.

70. An Authentic, Candid and Circumstantial Narrative of the Astonishing Transactions at Stockwell (London, 1772), pp. 5, 23.

71. Taunton Courier; 23 August 1810.

72. Taunton Courier, 23 August 1810. A transcription of the letter can be found at <www.sampford-peverell.co.uk/history/ghost/letter1.html>.

73. C.C. Colton, Sampford Ghost. A Plain and Authentic Narrative of Those Extraordinary Occurrences (Tiverton, 1810).

74. See The Times, 27 August 1810, 1 September, 22 September 1810 and 18 October 1810.

75. John Marriott, Sampford Ghost!!! A Full Account of the Conspiracy at Sampford Peverell (Taunton, 1810); on Moon see Davies, Cunning-Folk, p. 47.

76. J.F.C. Harrison, The Second Coming: Popular Millenarianism 1780–1850 (London, 1979), p. 105.

77. William Vowles, The Question of Apparitions and Supernatural Voices Considered (Tiverton, 1814), pp. 25, 35.

78. On the influence of Mesmer and animal magnetism see Robert Darnton, Mesmerism and the End of the Enlightenment in France (Cambridge, Mass., 1968); Fred Kaplan, '"The Mesmeric Mania": The Early Victorians and Animal Magnetism', Journal of the History of Ideas 35, 4 (1974) 691–702; Diethard Sawicki, Leben mit den Toten: Geisterglauben und die Entstehung des Spiritismus in Deutschland 1770–1900 (Paderborn, 2002).

79. The Times, 26 June 1841.

80. Vetus, Wesley's Ghost (London and Manchester, 1846). See also Scrutator, Wesley's Ghost, and Whitfield's Apparition (London, 1846); Sigma, The Ghost of John Wesley Mourning over the Decrease of Members in the Methodist Church (London, 1872).

81. Robert Young, The Entranced Female: Or, the Remarkable Disclosures of a Lady Concerning Another World (London, 1841).

82. William Reid Clanny, A Faithful Record of the Miraculous Case of Mary Jobson (Newcastle, 1841).

83. Edmund Procter, Joseph Procter's son, had extracts from his father's diary published in the Journal of the Society for Psychical Research 5 (1891–92) 331–52. These were reprinted in Price, Poltergeist over England, ch. 15. The quote is from p. 173.

84. Crowe, The Night Side of Nature, p. 336.

85. Philo-veritas, Modern Miracles Condemned by Reason and Scripture (London, c. 1843).

86. See <www.theghostclubsociety.co.uk>; Guiley, Encyclopedia of Ghosts and Spirits, pp. 151–3.

87. Court Journal; reprinted in The Times, 10 September 1863.

88. On the Phasmatological Society see Charles Oman, 'The Old Oxford Phasmatological Society', Journal of the Society for Psychical Research 33 (1946) 208–9; Janet Oppenheim, The Other World: Spiritualism and Psychic Research in England, 1850–1914 (Cambridge, 1985), p. 123.

89. Cited in Oppenheim, The Other World, p. 77.

90. W.F. Barrett et al., 'First Report of the Committee on Haunted Houses', Proceedings of the Society for Psychical Research 1 (1883) 101–11.

91. See, for example, Alan Gauld, *The Founders of Psychical Research* (London, 1968); Andrew MacKenzie, *Hauntings and Apparitions* (London, 1982), pp. 1–40.

92. See Oppenheim, *The Other World*, pp. 33–4.

93. *Somerset County Herald*, 13 June 1868.

94. *Somerset County Herald*, 25 July 1868.

95. *Pulman's Weekly News*, 21 July 1868. See also the editions for 28 July and 4 August 1868.

96. *Somerset County Herald*, 8 August 1868. For similar examples of reportage see Davies, *Witchcraft, Magic and Culture*, pp. 35–9.

97. Reprinted in *The Times*, 25 October 1852.

98. *The Times*, 6 July 1874.

99. *The Times*, 12 September 1853.

100. *Manchester Guardian*, 19 October 1835.

101. *Norwich Mercury*; reprinted in *The Times*, 16 October 1845.

102. See Robert D. Storch, '"Please to Remember the Fifth of November": Conflict, Solidarity and Public Order in Southern England, 1815–1900', in Robert D. Storch (ed.), *Popular Culture and Custom in Nineteenth-Century England* (London, 1982), p. 76; Nigel Goose and Owen Davies, 'Magic, Custom and Local Culture in Hertfordshire 1823–1914: An Exercise in Nominal Record Linkage', *Local Population Studies* 71 (2003) 75–81.

103. Robert D. Storch, 'The Policeman as Domestic Missionary: Urban Discipline and Popular Culture in Northern England, 1850–1880', *Journal of Social History* 9, 4 (1976) 495.

104. *News of the World*, 17 August 1851.

105. *The Times*, 27 May 1865.

106. See, for example, Rober D. Storch, 'The Plague of the Blue Locusts: Police Reform and Popular Resistance in Northern England, 1840–57', *International Review of Social History* 20 (1975) 61–91; A. Croll, 'Street Disorder, Surveillance and Shame: Regulating Behaviour in the Public Spaces of the Late Victorian British Town', *Social History* 24 (1999) 250–68.

107. *The Times*, 21 December 1826.

108. *The Sun*; reprinted in *The Times*, 23 September 1828; *The Times*, 13 October 1842.

109. *The Times*, 1 June 1867.

110. *The Times*, 11 October 1882.

111. *The Times*, 6 July 1876.

112. John R. Gillis, 'The Evolution of Juvenile Delinquency in England 1890–1914', *Past & Present* 67 (1975) 104.

113. *Maidstone Journal*; reprinted in *The Times*, 20 December 1859.

114. *Somerset County Herald*, 2 February 1861.

115. *The Times*, 6 July 1874.

116. See Julia Briggs, *Night Visitors: The Rise and Fall of the English Ghost Story* (London, 1977), pp. 63–5.

117. See *The Times*, 27 February, 10 and 11 March 1936.

118. Harry Price, *The Most Haunted House in England* (London, 1940); Harry Price, *The End of Borley Rectory* (London, 1946); Colin Wilson, *Poltergeist!: A Study in Destructive Haunting* (London, 1981), pp. 287–96.

119. *The Times*, 25 May 1937.

120. See, for example, Peter Underwood and Paul Tabori, *The Ghosts of Borley: Annals of the Haunted Rectory* (Newton Abbot, 1973).

121. Wilson, *Poltergeist!*, p. 296.

122. Wilson, *Poltergeist!*, pp. 296–314; <www.survivalafterdeath.org>.

123. My thanks to Anne Tucker (Paynter's daughter) for this information. See also Jason Semmens, '"Whyler Pystry": A Breviate of the Life and Folklore-Collecting Practices of William Henry Paynter of Callington, Cornwall', *Folklore* 116, 1 (2005) 75–94.

124. Peter Underwood, *No Common Task: The Autobiography of a Ghost-Hunter* (1983).

125. Anthony D. Cornell, *Investigating the Paranormal* (New York, 2001); Loyd Auerbach, *Ghost Hunting: How to Investigate the Paranormal* (Berkeley, 2003); Richard Southall, *How to be a Ghost Hunter* (St. Paul, 2003); Derek Acorah, *Ghost Hunting with Derek Acorah* (London, 2005).

126. The development of this mediumistic role becomes apparent in the inter-war years. See Hazelgrove, *Spiritualism*, p. 31.

127. E.J. Dingwall, Kathleen M. Goldney and Trevor H. Hall, *The Haunting of Borley Rectory: A Critical Survey of the Evidence* (London, 1956).

128. For good overviews of recent developments in psychical research see Ian S. Baker, '"Do Ghosts Exist?" A Summary of Parapsychological Research into Apparitional Experiences', in Newton, *Early Modern Ghosts*, pp. 109–25; W.G. Roll and M.A. Persinger, 'Investigations of Poltergeists and Haunts: A Review and Interpretation', in J. Houran and R. Lange (eds), *Hauntings and Poltergeists: Multidisciplinary Perspectives* (Jefferson, 2001), pp. 123–63; P.A. McCue, 'Theories of Haunting: A Critical Overview', *Journal of the Society for Psychical Research* 66 (2002) 1–21.

129. Richard Wiseman, Caroline Watt, Paul Stevens, Emma Greening and Ciarán O'Keeffe, 'An Investigation into Alleged "Hauntings"', *British Journal of Psychology* 94 (2003) 195–211; Jason J. Braithwaite and Maurice Townsend, 'Sleeping With the Entity – A Quantative Magnetic Investigation of an English Castle's Reputedly "Haunted" Bedroom', *European Journal of Parapsychology* 20, 1 (2005) 65–78.

CHAPTER 4

1. On this topic see Nancy Caciola, 'Wraiths, Revenants and Ritual in Medieval Culture', *Past & Present* 152 (1996) 3–45; Jacqueline Simpson, 'Repentant Soul or Walking Corpse? Debatable Apparitions in Medieval England', *Folklore* 114 (2003) 389–402; Barber, *Vampires, Burial, and Death*; Schmitt, *Ghosts*; Darren Oldridge, *Strange Histories* (London, 2004), ch. 4.

2. Caciola, 'Wraiths, Revenants and Ritual', 15–20; Lecouteux, *Fantômes*, pp. 91–111; N.K. Chadwick, 'Norse Ghosts (A Study in the Draugr and the Haugbui), *Folklore* 57, 2 (1946) 50–65.

3. James I and VI, *Dæmonologie*, p. 58.

4. André Valladier, *La Saincte Philosophie de l'ame* (Paris, 1614); cited in Clark, *Thinking with Demons: The Idea of Witchcraft in Early Modern Europe* (Oxford, 1997), p. 172.

5. This account of Richard's views is based on J.S.W. Helt, 'The "Dead who Walk": Materiality, Liminality and the Supernatural World in François Richard's "Of False Revenants"', *Mortality* 5, 1 (2000) 7–17.

6. Thomas Tryon, *A Treatise of Dreams and Visions* (London, 1689), p. 24.

7. William of Newburgh, *Historia rerum Anglicarum*; extracts reprinted in Andrew Joynes, *Medieval Ghost Stories* (Woodbridge, 2001), pp. 97–102.

8. Caciola, 'Wraiths, Revenants and Ritual', p. 22.

9. See Schmitt, *Ghosts*, pp. 142–7; Simpson, 'Repentant Soul or Walking Corpse?', 394–5.

10. For an impressive analysis of ghost belief and the English Reformation see Marshall, *Beliefs and the Dead*, ch. 6; Finucane, *Ghosts*, ch. 4.

11. *Calendar of State Papers, Domestic Series, Elizabeth,* 1581–1590 (London, 1865), p. 226; Thomas, *Religion and the Decline of Magic,* p. 707; 'Henry Caesar', *New DNB.*

12. See Marshall, *Beliefs and the Dead,* pp. 245–6.

13. Scot, *Discoverie,* (1651 edition), p. 334.

14. Robert Hunter West, *The Invisible World: A Study of Pneumatology in Elizabethan Drama* (Athens, Georgia, 1939), p. 53.

15. The point is well made in Marshall, *Beliefs and the Dead,* p. 233. For discussion on continental ghost treatises see Clark, 'The Reformation of the Eyes: Apparitions and Optics in Sixteenth- and Seventeenth-Century Europe', *Journal of Religious History* 27 (2003) 143–60; Finucane, *Ghosts,* ch. 4.

16. Bruce Gordon, 'Malevolent Ghosts and Ministering Angels: Apparitions and Pastoral Care in the Swiss Reformation', in Bruce Gordon and Peter Marshall (eds), *The Place of the Dead: Death and Remembrance in Late Medieval and Early Modern Europe* (Cambridge, 2000), pp. 95–100.

17. Noel Taillepied, *A Treatise of Ghosts,* trans. Montague Summers (London, 1933), p. 66.

18. Pierre Le Loyer, *A Treatise of Specters* (London, 1605), 'The Epistle Dedicatrie'.

19. Sharpe, *Instruments of Darkness,* p. 108.

20. See Thomas, *Religion and the Decline of Magic,* pp. 706–7.

21. 'Randall Hutchins' *Of Specters* (ca. 1593)', translated from the Latin by Virgil B. Heltzel and Clyde Murley, *Huntingdon Library Quarterly* 11 (1947–48) 407–29.

22. 'Randall Hutchins' *Of Specters',* 410, 412.

23. 'Randall Hutchins' *Of Specters',* 423, 426.

24. See Norman T. Burns, *Christian Mortalism from Tyndale to Milton* (Cambridge, Mass., 1972); Almond, *Heaven and Hell in Enlightenment England,* ch. 2; J.F. Maclear, 'Anne Hutchinson and the Mortalist Heresy', *New England Quarterly* 54, 1 (1981) 74–103.

25. Isaac Watts, *An Essay Toward the Proof of a Separate State of Souls Between Death and the Resurrection* (London, 1732), pp. 57–8.

26. Joseph Glanvill, *Essays on Several Important Subjects in Philosophy and Religion* (London, 1676), p. 45.

27. *The Strange Witch at Greenwich (Ghost, Spirit, or Hobgoblin) Haunting a Wench* (London, 1650), p. 15.

28. Marshall, *Beliefs and the Dead,* p. 264.

29. The point is well made in Gillian Bennett, 'Ghost and Witch in the Sixteenth and Seventeenth Centuries', *Folklore* 97, 1 (1986) 3–14.

30. Glanvill, *Saducismus,* p. 226.

31. Baxter, *Certainty of the World of Spirits,* p. 61.

32. Michael Hunter and Annabel Gregory (eds), *An Astrological Diary of the Seventeenth Century: Samuel Jeake of Rye 1652–1699* (Oxford, 1988), p. 117.

33. Robert Burton, *The Anatomy of Melancholy* (London, 1621), p. 66.

34. John Cotta, *The Trial of Witch-Craft Shewing the True and Right Methode of the Discovery* (London, 1616), p. 38.

35. See Clark, *Thinking with Demons,* p. 185.

36. John Flavell, *Pneumatologia, a Treatise of the Soul of Man* (London, 1685), pp. 267, 271–2.

37. John Webster, *The Displaying of Supposed Witchcraft* (London, 1677), p. 312.

38. Webster, *Displaying of Supposed Witchcraft,* pp. 298, 297, 300.

39. Webster, *Displaying of Supposed Witchcraft,* p. 312.

40. Defoe, *History and Reality of Apparitions* (1727), p. 99. See also Bourne, *Antiquitates Vulgares,* pp. 40–1. For detailed discussion of Defoe's views on apparitions see Rodney M. Baine,

Daniel Defoe and the Supernatural (Athens, Georgia, 1968); George Starr, 'Why Defoe Probably Did Not Write *The Apparition of Mrs.Veal*', *Eighteenth-Century Fiction* 15, 3–4 (2003) 421–51; Jayne Elizabeth Lewis, 'Spectral Currencies in the Air of Reality: *A Journal of the Plague Year* and the *History of Apparitions*', *Representations* 87 (2004) 82–101.

41. Hobbes, *Leviathan*, pp. 7, 53, 374; Thomas Hobbes, *Elements of Philosophy, the First Section, Concerning Body* (London, 1656), p. 299.

42. See Michael Hunter, 'The Problem of "Atheism" in Early Modern England', *Transactions of the Royal Historical Society* 35 (1985) 135–57. More generally see Michael Hunter and David Wootton (eds), *Atheism from the Reformation to the Enlightenment* (Oxford, 1992).

43. Thomas, *Religion and the Decline of Magic*, pp. 198–200

44. Baxter, *Certainty of theWorld of Spirits*, p. 17.

45. Glanvill, *Saducismus*, F3v. See Almond, *Heaven and Hell in Enlightenment England*, pp. 34–5.

46. Thomas Bromhall, *A Treatise of Specters* (London, 1658), p. 343.

47. *Narrative of the Demon of Spraiton, in a Letter from a Person of Quality in the County of Devon* (London, 1683), p. 1.

48. *Narrative of the Demon of Spraiton, in a Letter from a Person of Quality in the County of Devon*, p. 1.

49. See Sharpe, *Instruments of Darkness*, ch. 11; Charles Webster, *From Paracelsus to Newton: Magic and the Making of Modern Science* (Cambridge, 1982), ch. 4.

50. Glanvill, *Saducismus*, pp. A2r, A2v, 100.

51. Patrick Curry's entry for Heydon in the *New DNB*. See also Curry, *Prophecy and Power: Astrology in Early Modern England* (Oxford, 1989), pp. 47–9.

52. Heydon, *The Harmony of theWorld*, p. 182.

53. *Mr Culpeper's Ghost, Giving Seasonable Advice to the Lovers of His Writing* (London, 1656), p. A3r; Heydon, *The Harmony of theWorld*, p. 182.

54. Heydon, *The Harmony of theWorld*, ch. 14.

55. Han van Ruler, 'Minds, Forms, and Spirits: The Nature of Cartesian Disenchantment', *Journal of the History of Ideas* 61, 3 (2000) 384–6. In a similar vein, Cartesian principles were also used to prove the efficacy of dowsing. See Michael R. Lynn, 'Divining the Enlightenment: Public Opinion and Popular Science in Old Regime France', *Isis* 92, 1 (2001) 34–54.

56. See Andrew Fix, 'Angels, Devils, and Evil Spirits in Seventeenth-Century Thought: Balthasar Bekker and the Collegiants', *Journal of the History of Ideas* 50 (1989) 527–47; Andrew Fix, *Fallen Angels: Balthasar Bekker, Spirit Belief, and Confessionalism in the Seventeenth Century Dutch Republic* (Dordrecht and London, 1999).

57. G.J. Stronks, 'The Signficance of Balthasar Bekker's The Enchanted World', in Marijke Gijswijt-Hofstra and Willem Frijhoff, *Witchcraft in the Netherlands from the Fourteenth to the Twentieth Century* (Rotterdam, 1991), pp. 149–156.

58. John Beaumont, *An Historical, Physiological and Theological Treatise of Spirits, Apparitions, Witchcrafts, and Other Magical Practices* (London, 1705), p. 348. On Beaumont's life see the *New DNB*.

59. John Beaumont, *Gleaning of Antiquities* (London, 1724), p. 191.

60. Beaumont, *Gleaning of Antiquities*, p. 192.

61. See Brian Levack, 'The Decline and End of Witchcraft Prosecutions', in Marijke Gijswijt-Hofstra, Brian Levack and Roy Porter, *Witchcraft and Magic in Europe*, pp. 38–40.

62. Kenelme Digby, *A Discourse Concerning theVegetation of Plants* (London, 1661), p. 89.

63. Digby, *A Discourse*, pp. 83–5.

64. See Jacques Marx, 'Alchimie et Palingénésie', *Isis* 62 (1971) 274–89; Allen G. Debus, 'A Further Note on Palingenesis: The Account of Ebenezer Sibly in the Illustration of

Astrology (1792)', *Isis* 64 (1973) 226–30; François Secret, 'Palingenesis, Alchemy and Metempyschosis in Renaissance Medicine', *Ambix* 26, 2 (1979) 81–92.

65. Pierre le Lorrain de Vallemont, *Curiosities of Nature and Art in Husbandry and Gardening* (London, 1707), p. 349. First published in French in 1703.

66. On Davisson see the *New DNB*.

67. Digby, *A Discourse*, p. 75.

68. On the debates between the followers of Paracelsian and the more orthodox Galenic system of medicine see, for example, Allen George Debus, *The French Paracelsians: The Chemical Challenge to Medical and Scientific Tradition in Early Modern France* (Cambridge, 2002).

69. De Vallemont, *Curiosities*, p. 325.

70. James Gaffarel, *Unheard-of Curiosities: Concerning the Talismanical Sculpture of the Persians, the Horoscope of the Patriarkes, and the Reading of the Stars*, trans. Edmund Chilmead (London, 1650), pp. 138–9.

71. De Vallemont, *Curiosities*, p. 350.

72. Digby, *A Discourse*, pp. 80–1.

73. De Vallemont, *Curiosities*, p. 348.

74. Robert Boyle, *Certain Physiological Essays and Other Tracts Written at Distant Times* (London, 1669), p. 82.

75. Webster, *Displaying of Supposed Witchcraft*, p. 319.

76. Sibly, *A New and Complete Illustration of the Occult Sciences*, p. 1114.

77. Peter Shaw, *The Reflector: Representing Human Affairs, As They Are* (London, 1750), p. 142.

78. William Shenstone, *The Works in Verse and Prose, of William Shenstone Esq* (London, 1764), vol. 2, pp. 68, 72.

79. *The History of Apparitions, Ghosts, Spirits or Spectres* (London, 1762), p. iv.

80. Shaw, *The Reflector*, p. 143.

81. John Trenchard, *The Natural History of Superstition* (London, 1709), p. 23; Gordon, *The Humourist*, p. 79.

82. Walsham, *Providence in Early Modern England*, pp. 29–30.

83. Thomas, *Religion and the Decline of Magic*, pp. 705–6; Sasha Handley, 'Reclaiming Ghosts in 1690s England', in Kate Cooper and Jeremy Gregory (eds), *Signs, Wonders, Miracles: Representations of Divine Power in the Life of the Church* (Woodbridge, 2005), pp. 345–56; Bath and Newton, '"Sensible Proof of Spirits"', 6–9.

84. William Assheton, *The Possibility of Apparitions* (London, 1706), p. 3; *The History of Apparitions, Ghosts, Spirits or Spectres*, p. iii.

85. *Apparitions, Supernatural Occurrences, Demonstrative of the Soul's Immortality* (London, 1799), p. 10.

86. *Gentleman's Magazine*, 22 (1732) 1002. Moreton referred to Andrew Moreton, pseudonym of Daniel Defoe, author of *The Secrets of the Invisible World Disclos'd* (London, 1729).

87. Watts, *An Essay Toward the Proof of a Separate State of Souls*, p. 57; Assheton, *The Possibility of Apparitions*, pp. 13–14.

88. David Simpson, *A Discourse on Dreams and Night-Visions* (Macclesfield, 1791), p. 89.

89. *Anti-Canidia*, pp. 20–1.

90. John Wesley, *An Extract of the Rev. Mr. John Wesley's Journal, from May 14, 1768, to Sept. 1, 1770* (London, 1790), p. 6.

91. John Wesley, *An Extract of the Rev. Mr. John Wesley's Journal, from October 29, 1762, to May 25, 1765* (Bristol, 1768), p. 103.

92. Wesley, *An Extract ... from May 14, 1768, to Sept. 1, 1770*, p. 5.

93. Thomas, *Religion and the Decline of Magic*, p. 708. See also Starr, 'Why Defoe Probably Did Not Write' 431–2.

94. Augustus Toplady, *Joy in Heaven. And the Creed of Devils. With a Word Concerning Apparitions* (London, 1788), pp. 62, 63.

95. *The Spectator*, 2nd edition (London, 1713), vol. 2, p. 103.

96. Eliza Fowler Haywood, *The Female Spectator* (London, 1745), p. 282; Duncan Campbell, *Secret Memoirs of the Late Mr. Duncan Campbel* (London, 1732), ch. 10.

97. Samuel Frederic Gray, *Phantasmatophaneia; Or, Anecdotes of Ghosts and Apparitions* (c. 1797). On Gray's life see the *NewDNB*.

98. *The Conjuror of Ruabon* (Ellesmere, c. 1820), p. 8. For another expression of the same sentiment see also *The Life and Mysterious Transactions of Richard Morris, Esq.* (London, 1799), pp. 19, 4, 39.

99. James Boswell, *The Life of Samuel Johnson* (Dublin, 1792), vol. 3, p. 28.

100. Charles Churchill, *The Ghost* (London, 1762), p. 49; Donald MacNicol, *Remarks on Dr. Samuel Johnson's Journey to the Hebrides* (London, 1779), p. 198; Arthur Browne, *Miscellaneous Sketches* (London, 1798), vol. 1, p. 72.

101. Boswell, *The Life of Samuel Johnson*, vol. 1, pp. 337–8; vol. 3, p. 27.

102. *Apparitions, Supernatural Occurrences, Demonstrative of the Soul's Immortality*, p. 24.

103. See Clark Garrett, 'Swedenborg and the Mystical Enlightenment in Late Eighteenth-Century England', *Journal of the History of Ideas* 45 (1984) 67–81; Harrison, *The Second Coming*; James K. Hopkins, *A Woman to Deliver Her People* (Austin, 1982); W.H. Oliver, *Prophets and Millennialists: The Uses of Biblical Prophecy in England from the 1790s to the 1840s* (Auckland, 1978).

104. See Donna T. Andrew, 'Popular Culture and Public Debate: London 1780', *Historical Journal* 39 (1996) 405–23; Trevor Fawcett, 'Eighteenth-Century Debating Societies', *British Journal of Eighteenth-Century Studies* 3 (1980) 217–30; Mary Thale, 'Deists, Papists and Methodists at London Debating Societies, 1749–1799', *History* 86 (2001) 328–47.

105. Thale, 'Deists, Papists and Methodists', 334.

106. Joseph W. Reed and Frederick A. Pottle (eds), *Boswell: Laird of Auchinleck 1778–1782* (New York [1932] 1977), p. 327.

107. *Daily Advertiser*, 30 September 1789; Donna T. Andrew (ed.), *London Debating Societies, 1776–1799* (London Record Society, 1994), p. 264; *The Times*, 24 March 1790.

108. Andrew, *London Debating Societies*, p. 352.

109. *The Times*, 5 July 1790.

110. *The Times*, 5, 12, 19 and 26 April 1790. For further reference to Mrs Williams see Davies, *Witchcraft, Magic and Culture*, pp. 238, 254.

111. *The Times*, 26 April 1790.

112. *Morning Post*; Andrew, *London Debating Societies*, p. 217. See also *Daily Advertiser*, 7 May 1794; Andrew, *London Debating Societies*, p. 328.

113. See Davies, *Witchcraft, Magic and Culture*, pp. 20–2.

114. *The World*; Andrew, *London Debating Societies*, p. 229.

115. *The Times*, 5 April 1790.

116. See Alex Winter, *Mesmerized: Powers of Mind in Victorian Britain* (Chicago, 1998).

117. Karl Von Reichenbach, *Researches on Magnetism, Electricity, Heat, Light, Crystallization and Chemical Attraction in Relation to the Vital Force*, 2nd edition, trans. William Gregory (Kessinger [1850], 2003), pp. 126–7.

118. Emma Hardinge Britten, cited in Oppenheim, *The Other World*, p. 219.

119. See Oppenheim, *The Other World*, pp. 207–24; Finucane, *Ghosts*, pp. 179–80.

120. Louis Alphonse Cahagnet, *The Celestial Telegraph; Or, Secrets of the Life to Come, Revealed through Magnetism* (New York, [1850] 1851), p. 6.

121. The point is well made in R. Laurence Moore, 'Spiritualism and Science: Reflections on the First Decade of the Spirit Rapping', *American Quarterly* 24, 4 (1972) 488; Malcolm Gaskill, *Hellish Nell: Last of Britain's Witches* (London, 2001), p. 89.

122. On ectoplasm see Gaskill, *Hellish Nell*, pp. 89–100; Marina Warner, 'Ethereal Body: The Quest for Ectoplasm', *Cabinet* 12 (2004); Rosemary Ellen Guiley, *The Encyclopedia of Ghosts and Spirits*, 2nd edition (New York, 2000), pp. 116–17.

123. Alex Owen, *The Darkened Room: Women, Power and Spiritualism in Late Victorian England* (London, 1989), pp. 103–4.

124. Edmund Gurney, Frederic W.H. Myers and Frank Podmore, *Phantasms of the Living*, abridged edition (London, [1886] 1918), p. lv.

125. F.W.H. Myers, *Human Personality and its Survival of Bodily Death* (London, 1903). See Carlos S. Alvarado, 'On the Centenary of Frederic W.H. Myers's Human Personality and its Survival of Bodily Death', *Journal of Parapsychology* 68 (2004) 3–43.

126. Paul Tabori, *Harry Price: The Biography of a Ghost-Hunter* (London, [1950] 1974), p. 231.

127. Kenneth D. Pimple, 'Ghosts, Spirits, and Scholars: The Origins of Modern Spiritualism', in Barbara Walker (ed.), *Out of the Ordinary: Folklore and the Supernatural* (Utah, 1995), p. 79.

CHAPTER 5

1. Mr. Addison [pseudonym], *Interesting Anecdotes, Memoirs, Allegories, Essays, and Poetical Fragments* (London, [1793] 1797), pp. 38–9.

2. Haywood, *The Female Spectator*, vol. 2, p. 298.

3. *The Entertainer* 11 (12 November 1754), cited in E.J. Clery and Robert Miles (eds), *Gothic Documents: A Sourcebook 1700–1820* (Manchester, 2000), p. 30.

4. Elizabeth Bonhôte, *The Parental Monitor* (London, 1788), vol. 2, p. 149.

5. 'Notes on Folklore', *Folklore* 27, 3 (1916) 308.

6. Defoe, *History and Reality of Apparitions* (1727), p. 375.

7. Joseph Lawson, *Letter to the Young on Progress in Pudsey During the Last Sixty Years* (Stanningley, 1887), p. 72.

8. *The Times*, 26 October 1851, 17 December 1872.

9. Elisha Coles, *An English Dictionary* (London, 1677).

10. William Fulke, *A Goodly Gallerye with a Most Pleasant Prospect* (London, 1563), p. 12.

11. Gideon Harvey, *Archelogia Philosophical Nova* (London, 1663), p. 375.

12. Fulke, *A Goodly Gallerye*, p. 13.

13. W. Derham and Tho. Dereham, 'Of the Meteor Called the Ignis Fatuus, from Observations', *Philosophical Transactions* 36 (1729–30) 204–5.

14. Harvey, *Archelogia*, p. 376.

15. See, for example, *The Shepherd's Kalender: Or, the Citizen's and Country Man's Daily Companion*, third edition (London, c. 1725), p. 37–8.

16. Baring-Gould, *Further Reminiscences*, p. 122.

17. *The Times*, 15 October 1804.

18. Augustin Calmet, *The Phantom World*, edited and translated by Henry Christmas (London, 1850), p. 131.

19. Charles Ollier, *Fallacy of Ghosts, Dreams, and Omens* (London, 1848), p. 93.

20. *The Times*, 26 May 1863.

21. *Apparitions, Supernatural Occurrences, Demonstrative of the Soul's Immortality*, p. 5; Andrew Baxter, *An Enquiry into the Nature of the Human Soul* (London, 1733), p. 298.

22. Erasmus Darwin, *Zoonomia; Or, the Laws of Organic Life* (Dublin, 1796–1800), vol. 2, p. 311.

23. Johann Georg Zimmermann, *A Treatise on Experience in Physic* (London, 1782), vol. 2, p. 277.

24. John Locke, *Some Thoughts Concerning Education* (London, 1693), p. 159; *The Spectator* 1 (1712) 69.

25. Darwin, *Zoonomia*, vol. 2, p. 312.

26. *The Compleat Servant-Maid: or, the Young Maiden's and Family Daily Companion* (London, 1729), p. 11.

27. *London Journal*, 7 October 1732; Ollier, *Fallacy of Ghosts*, p. 9; *Gentleman's Magazine* 2 (October 1732) 1001.

28. Bonhôte, *The Parental Monitor*, p. 148.

29. Joseph Collyer, *The Parent's and Guardian's Directory* (London, 1761), p. 3.

30. Scot, *Discoverie*, book xv, ch. 39.

31. *The Pleasing Instructor: Or, Entertaining Moralist* (London, 1756), p. 194.

32. *Gentleman's Magazine* 2 (October 1732) 1002.

33. Joseph Taylor, *Apparitions: Or the Mystery of Ghosts, Hobgoblins and Haunted Houses* (London, 1815), p. iii.

34. *The Times*, 13 September 1828.

35. See Davies, *Witchcraft, Magic and Culture*, pp. 157–60.

36. Sarah Trimmer, *The Family Magazine; Or, A Repository of Religious Instruction, and Rational Amusement* (London, 1789), vol. 3, pp. 42–7.

37. [Richard Johnson], *False Alarms: Or, the Mischievous Doctrine of Ghosts and Apparitions* (London, 1805), p. 49.

38. For a concise history of the concept see Roy Porter, *Madness: A Brief History* (Oxford, 2002), pp. 42–55. A more in-depth consideration is provided by Jennifer Radden (ed.), *The Nature of Melancholy: From Aristotle to Kristeva* (Oxford, 2000).

39. See Thomas, *Religion and the Decline of Magic*, p. 691.

40. Burton, *The Anatomy of Melancholy*, pp. 252–3, 260, 367.

41. On Burton consulting Forman see Barbara Howard Traister, *The Notorious Astrological Physician of London: Works and Days of Simon Forman* (Chicago, 2001), p. 48.

42. Traister, *Notorious Astrological Physician*, pp. 69, 116.

43. Michael Macdonald, *Mystical Bedlam: Madness, Anxiety, and Healing in Seventeenth-Century England* (Cambridge, 1981), pp. 157, 203.

44. Hobbes, *Elements of Philosophy*, p. 300.

45. Defoe, *History and Reality of Apparitions*, p. 100.

46. *The Power of Conscience Exemplified in the Genuine and Extraordinary Confession of Thomas Bedworth* (London, 1815), p. 9.

47. *The Power of Conscience Exemplified in the Genuine and Extraordinary Confession of Thomas Bedworth*, pp. 10, 11.

48. Details of his trial were recorded in *Effect of Jealousy! The Whole Proceedings of the Trial of Thomas Bedworth* (London, 1815).

49. *The Times*, 31 December 1887; 22 February and 13 March 1888. For another similar case see *The Times*, 18 April 1877.

50. Terry Castle, *The Female Thermometer* (Oxford, 1995), p. 177.

51. For discussions on dreams in ancient, early Christian, medieval and early modern history see Lyndal Roper and Daniel Pick (eds), *Dreams and History* (Hove, 2004); Lisa M. Bitel,

'"In Visu Noctis": Dreams in European Hagiography and Histories, 450–900', *History of Religions* 31, 1 (1991) 39–59; Jacques LeGoff, 'Dreams in the Culture and Collective Psychology of the Medieval West', in Jacques LeGoff, *Time,Work, and Culture in the Middle Ages* (Chicago, 1980); Steven Kruger, *Dreaming in the Middle Ages* (Cambridge, 1992); Thomas, *Religion and the Decline of Magic*, pp. 151–3.

52. See Alice Browne, 'Descartes's Dreams', *Journal of theWarburg and Courtauld Institute* 40 (1977) 259–73; Michael H. Keefer, 'The Dreamer's Path: Descartes and the Sixteenth Century', *Renaissance Quarterly* 49, 1 (1996) 30–76.

53. Thomas Tryon, *A Treatise of Dreams andVisions* (London, 1689), pp. 68–77.

54. Nashe, *The Unfortunate Traveller*, p. 211.

55. See Lucia Dacombe, '"ToWhat Purpose Does ItThink?": Dreams, Sick Bodies and Confused Minds in the Age of Reason', *History of Psychiatry* 15, 4 (2004) 395–416.

56. Bitel, '"In Visu Noctis"', 49; Flint, *The Rise of Magic*, pp. 193–5.

57. Nashe, *The Unfortunate Traveller*, pp. 218–19.

58. Hobbes, *Leviathan*, p. 7.

59. Hobbes, *Elements of Philosophy*, p. 299.

60. John Locke, *An Essay Concerning Human Understanding* (London, 1690), p. 42.

61. Robert Macnish, *The Philosophy of Sleep*, 3rd edition (Glasgow, 1836), p. 147.

62. For discussions of the historical significance of the nightmare experience and references to key biomedical research see David Hufford, *The Terror that Comes in the Night: An Experience-Centred Study of Supernatural Assault Traditions* (Philadelphia, 1982); Hufford, 'Beings Without Bodies: An Experience-CentredTheory of the Belief in Spirits', in Walker (ed.), *Out of the Ordinary*, pp. 11–46; Davies, 'The Nightmare Experience', 181–203. See also Jorge Conesa Sevilla, *Wrestling with Ghosts* (Xlibris Corporation, 2004).

63. Edmund Gardiner, *Phisicall and Approved Medicines* (London, 1611), p. 55.

64. Lawson, *Progress in Pudsey*, p. 68.

65. Hufford, *The Terror that Comes in the Night*, p. 211.

66. Tryon, *A Treatise of Dreams andVisions*, p. 24.

67. Raine, *Depositions from the Castle ofYork*, pp. 28–9.

68. It is worth mentioning that Gurney, Myers and Podmore, in *Phantasms of the Living* (p. 332) noted that three cases had been sent to him in which 'a subjective hallucination seen on waking was accompanied by inability to speak or move'. Green and McCreery (*Apparitions*, p. 127), though apparently unaware of the biomedical studies of sleep paralysis, identified that bedroom paralysis was found in 3 per cent of their respondents' experiences.

69. *Taunton Courier*; reprinted in *The Times*, 27 August 1810.

70. *Bath Chronicle*, cited in *Manchester Guardian*, 18 June 1851.

71. Reprinted in *The Times*, 25 March 1844.

72. *Athenian Oracle*, 3rd edition (London, 1728), vol. 3, p. 293; Thomas Willis, *Dr.Willis's Practice of Physick, being theWholeWorks of that Renowned and Famous Physician* (London, 1684), p. 142. On Willis see the *NewDNB*.

73. Trenchard, *Natural History of Superstition*, p. 20.

74. Nicholas Culpeper, *The English Physitian* (London, 1652), p. 193.

75. Bryan Cornwell, *The Domestic Physician* (London, 1784), p. 505; Philip Woodman, *Medicus Novissimus; Or, the Modern Physician* (London, 1712), p. 194.

76. William Buchan, *Domestic Medicine*, 2nd edition (London, 1772), p. 556.

77. Macnish, *The Philosophy of Sleep*, pp. 262–3. See also G.E. Berrios, 'On the Fantastic Apparitions of Vision by Johannes Müller', *History of Psychology* 16, 2 (2005) 229–46.

78. Walter Scott, *Letters on Demonology and Witchcraft* (London, 1830), p. 34. For discussion on Coleridge's scientific activities and ideas on the optics of ghosts see Frederick Burwick, 'Science and Supernaturalism: Sir David Brewster and Sir Walter Scott', *Comparative Criticism* 13 (1991) 103–4.

79. For these quotes and good synopses of the ideas of Ferriar and Hibbert see Castle, *The Female Thermometer*, pp. 163–4; Srdjan Smajic, 'The Trouble with Ghost-Seeing: Vision, Ideology, and Genre in the Victorian Ghost Story', *English Literary History* 70 (2003) 1114–15.

80. James Sully, *Illusions: A Psychological Study*, 4th edition (London, [1881] 1905), p. 185.

81. David Brewster, *Letters on Natural Magic* (London, 1832), p. 11.

82. On criticisms of Brewster's theory see Burwick, 'Science and Supernaturalism', 99–103; Smajic, 'The Trouble with Ghost-Seeing', 1115–17.

83. John Alderson, *An Essay on Apparitions* (London, 1823), p. 20.

84. Alderson, *An Essay on Apparitions*, p. 33.

85. Alderson, *An Essay on Apparitions*, p. 52.

86. See the entry for Catherine Crowe in the *NewDNB*.

87. Allan Ingram (ed.), *Patterns of Madness in the Eighteenth Century: A Reader* (Liverpool, 1998), p. 198.

88. Macnish, *The Philosophy of Sleep*, pp. 272–4.

89. Ollier, *Fallacy of Ghosts*, p. 10.

90. See, for example, Davies, *Murder, Magic, Madness*, pp. 132–5; Davies, *Witchcraft, Magic and Culture*, pp. 41–4.

91. *The Times*, 23 March 1846.

92. *The Times*, 6 March 1890.

93. *The Times*, 24 March 1834.

94. Philip Breslaw, *Breslaw's Last Legacy: Or, the Magical Companion* (London, 1784), p. ix.

95. Priestley, *Original Letters, by the Rev. John Welsey*, p. xiv.

96. Fred Nadis, *Wonder Shows: Performing Science, Magic and Religion in America* (New Brunswick, 2005), p. 117; Davies, *Cunning-Folk*, p. 47.

97. *The Times*, 12 May 1789.

98. For excellent histories of ventriloquism see Connor, *Dumbstruck*; Leigh Eric Schmidt, *Hearing Things: Religion, Illusion, and the American Enlightenment* (Cambridge, Mass., 2000); John A. Hodgson, 'An Other Voice: Ventriloquism in the Romantic Period', *Romanticism On the Net* 16 (November 1999).

99. *Annual Register* (1763), p. 143.

100. Thomas Blount, *Glossographia* (London, 1656), cited in Schmidt, *Hearing Things*, p. 141.

101. John Aikin, *General Biography* (London, 1801), vol. 2, p. 310.

102. The story was reiterated in several English publications such as *The Young Philosopher; Or, Instructive Entertainer* (Huddersfield, c. 1799), pp. 12–13.

103. Françoise Levie, *Étienne-Gaspard Robertson: la vie d'un fantasmagore* (Paris, 1990), p. 116.

104. Robert Thoroton, *The Antiquities of Nottinghamshire* (Nottingham, 1790), vol. 2, p. 149.

105. *The Times*, 11 July 1796, 10 August 1799.

106. Stebbing Shaw, *The History and Antiquities of Staffordshire* (London, 1801), vol. 2, p. 75.

107. [William Belcher], *Intellectual Electricity, Novum Organum of Vision, and Grand Mystic Secret* (London, 1798), p. 27.

108. Francis Hopkinson, *The Miscellaneous Essays and Occasional Writings of Francis Hopkinson* (London, 1792), vol. 1, p. 144; Thoroton, *Antiquities of Nottinghamshire*, vol. 2, p. 149.

109. Connor, *Dumbstruck*, p. 249.

110. Thoroton, *Antiquities of Nottinghamshire*, vol. 2, p. 149; Gerhard Ulrich Vieth, *The Pleasing Preceptor; Or, Familiar Instructions in Natural History* (London, 1801), vol. 2, p. 228.

111. Alderson, *An Essay on Apparitions* (1823), p. 46.

112. The most detailed account of the Rannies is Charles J. Pecor, *The Ten Year Tour of John Rannie: A Magician-Ventriloquist in Early America* (Glenwood, Illinois, 1998).

113. Leigh Eric Schmidt, 'From Demon Possession to Magic Show: Ventriloquism, Religion, and the Enlightenment', *Church History* 67, 2 (1998) 296; Pecor, *The Ten Year Tour*, p. 21.

114. Schmidt, *Hearing Things*, p. 157.

115. Elihu Palmer, *Principles of Nature: Or, a Development of the Moral Causes of Happiness and Misery Among the Human Species* (New York, 1801), chs 8 and 22.

116. William Frederick Pinchbeck, *Witchcraft or the Art of Fortune-Telling Unveiled* (Boston, 1805), p. 26.

117. William Frederick Pinchbeck, *The Expositor; Or, Many Mysteries Unravelled* (Boston, 1805: limited edition reprint, 1996), pp. A2, 93.

118. See Rita Shenton, *Christopher Pinchbeck and His Family* (London, 1976); New DNB; Edwin A. Dawes, *The Great Illusionists* (Secaucus, 1979), pp. 36–8. The Pinchbecks' shop seems to have been attractive to thieves. See <www.oldbaileyonline.org>.

119. Dawes, *The Great Illusionists*, pp. 186–7.

120. Nadis, *Wonder Shows*, p. 120.

121. See Iwan Rhys Morus, *Frankenstein's Children: Electricity, Exhibition and Experiment in Early Nineteenth-Century London* (Princeton, 1998), esp. pp. 80–2; During, *Modern Enchantments*, pp. 142–9.

122. See, for example, *The Times*, 16 April 1863.

123. Simon During, *Modern Enchantments: The Cultural Power of Secular Magic* (Cambridge, Mass., 2002), p. 146; *The Times*, 6 January 1877.

124. Advertisements for his work for Bland and the Polytechnic can be found in *The Times*. See, for example, *The Times*, 1 January 1867.

125. Christian Fechner Magic Collection, auctioned by Swann Galleries, New York, 2005.

126. On Pepper see J.A. Secord, 'Quick and Magical Shaper of Science', *Science* 297 (6 September 2002) 1648–9; New DNB.

127. *The Times*, 2 April 1872.

128. Colonel Stodare, *Colonel Stodare's Hand-book of Magic, Or, Conjuring Made Easy* (London, 1862). This rare book was reprinted along with a brief biography of Stodare in Edwin A. Dawes, *Stodare: The Enigma Variations* (Washington, 1998). For an explanation of the Sphinx see Jim Steinmeyer, *Hiding the Elephant: How Magicians Invented the Impossible* (London, 2004), pp. 83–6.

129. For a poster of their first show see the British Library Evanion Collection, Evan.3036.

130. See George A. Jenness, *Maskelyne and Cooke: Egyptian Hall, London, 1873–1904* (privately printed, 1967); During, *Modern Enchantments*, pp. 156–61; Steinmeyer, *Hiding the Elephant*, pp. 94–111; Nadis, *Wonder Shows*, pp. 119–20.

131. *The Times*, 1 November 1864.

132. See E.M. Wood, *A History of the Polytechnic* (London, 1965); 'Quintin Hogg', New DNB.

133. Jung, 'Foreword', in Jaffé, *Apparitions and Precognition*, pp. vi–vii.

134. On Freud's interest in the occult see Roger Luckhurst, '"Something Tremendous, Something Elemental": On the Ghostly Origins of Psychoanalysis', in Peter Buse and Andrew Stott (eds), *Ghosts: Deconstruction, Psychonanalysis, History* (London, 1999), pp. 50–71.

135. Ernest Jones, *On the Nightmare* (London, 1931), pp. 112, 346. See also Donald Tuzin, 'The Breath of a Ghost: Dreams and the Fear of the Dead', *Ethos* 3, 4 (1975) 555–78.

136. John W.M. Whiting and Irvin Child, *Child-Training and Personality: A Cross-Cultural Study* (New Haven and London, 1953), pp. 295–304; John W.M. Whiting, 'Sorcery, Sin and the Superego', in M.R. Jones (ed.), *Nebraska Symposium on Motivation* (Lincoln, Nebraska, 1959); Gustav Jahoda, *The Psychology of Superstition* (London, 1969), pp. 84–5. See also Melford E. Spiro, 'Ghosts: An Anthropological Inquiry into Learning and Perception', *Journal of Abnormal and Social Psychology* 48 (1953) 376–82.

CHAPTER 6

1. Lang, *Cock Lane*, p. 126.
2. John Bale, *The First Two Parts of the Actes or Unchast Examples of the Englysh Votaryes* (London, 1551), pp. 69–70; Scot, *Discoverie* (1651 edition), p. 105; Samuel Harsnett, *A Declaration of Egregious Popish Impostures* (London, 1603), p. 135; John Melton, *Astrologaster: Or, The Figure-Caster* (London, 1620), pp. 59–60; Lavater, *Of Ghostes and Spirites*, p. 43. The latter story was repeated in Henry More, *A Modest Enquiry into the Mystery of Iniquity* (London, 1664), p. 134.
3. John Gee, *The Foot Out of the Snare with a Detection of Sundry Late Practices and Impostures of the Priests and Jesuits in England* (London, 1624), p. 109.
4. John Gee, *New Shreds of the Old Snare Containing the Apparitions of Two New Female Ghosts* (London, 1624), pp. 4–5. For further analysis of the case see John Newton, 'Reading Ghosts: Early Modern Interpretations of Apparitions', in Newton, *Early Modern Ghosts*, 57–9. On Gee see the New DNB.
5. See Alexandra Walsham, '"The Fatall Vesper": Providentialism and Anti-Popery in Late Jacobean London', *Past & Present* 144 (1994) 36–87.
6. *Seasonable Present to the Renowned Society of Ghost-Mongers*, p. 10.
7. Scot, *Discoverie* (1651 edition), p. 113.
8. Marshall, 'Old Mother Leakey', p. 98.
9. Thomas Potts, *The Wonderfull Discoverie of Witches in the Countie of Lancaster* (London, 1613), p. K3r; Richard Bernard, *A Guide to Grand-Jury Men* (London, 1627), p. 199.
10. [Richard Baddeley], *The Boy of Bilson: Or, a True Discovery of the Late Notorious Impostures of Certaine Romish Priests in Their Pretended Exorcisme* (London, 1622).
11. Scot, *Discoverie* (1651 edition), p. 113.
12. Erasmus, *Twenty-Two Select Colloquies*, pp. 185–95.
13. Erasmus, *Twenty-Two Select Colloquies*, p. 191.
14. Cecil L'Estrange Ewen, *Witchcraft in the Star Chamber* (London, 1938), p. 15.
15. *Annual Register* (1762), p. 80.
16. *The Times*, 28 April 1804.
17. *Herts, Huntingdon, Bedford, Cambridge & Isle of Ely Mercury*, 16 and 23 October 1830.
18. *Cumberland Pacquet*; reprinted in *The Times*, 7 December 1844; *The Times*, 7 February 1888.
19. *The Times*, 29 September 1885.
20. *The Times*, 7 December 1872.
21. *Cheltenham Journal* 17 May, 1830.
22. Spring-Heeled Jack has been the subject of poor research and much misleading speculation, some of it stemming from Peter Haining's flawed book *The Legend and Bizarre Crimes of Spring-Heeled Jack* (London, 1977). In 2001 the folklorist Jacqueline Simpson wrote a brief research note on Spring-Heeled Jack that made some pertinent comments

regarding contemporary legends: 'Research Note: "Spring-Heeled Jack"', *Foaftale News* 48 (2001). However, the definitive and scrupulously researched work on the topic, which corrects numerous errors and fabrications, is the work of Mike Dash. See his 'Spring-Heeled Jack: To Victorian Bugaboo from Suburban Ghost', *Fortean Studies* 3 (1996) 7–125. A version of this is also available at <www.mikedash.com>.

23. *The Times*, 9 January 1838.
24. *The Times*, 11 January 1838.
25. *The Times*, 22 February 1838.
26. *The Times*, 23 February 1838.
27. *The Times*, 2 March and 3 March 1828. In his extensive research Mike Dash failed to find any further reference to the case.
28. See Dash, 'Spring-Heeled Jack'.
29. Reprinted in *The Times*, 14 April 1838.
30. L'Estrange Ewen, *Witchcraft in the Star Chamber*, pp. 23–4.
31. *Hertford Mercury and General Advertiser*, 4 November 1826.
32. Lackington, *Memoirs*, pp. 28–9.
33. *The Times*, 16 November 1857.
34. Lavater, *Of Ghostes and Spirites*, p. 29.
35. *The Times*, 27 October 1823.
36. Priestley, *Original Letters, by the Rev. John Wesley*, p. xiv.
37. James Plumptre, *The Truth of the Popular Notion of Apparitions, or Ghosts, Considered by the Light of Scripture: A Sermon* (Cambridge, 1818).
38. *The Times*, 13 December 1825.
39. *Somerset County Herald*, 18 May 1878.
40. *Somerset County Herald*, 1 August 1868.
41. *The Times*, 29 October 1823.
42. Priestley, *Original Letters*, p. xiv.
43. *Somerset County Herald*, 28 August 1886.
44. *Morning Chronicle*, 10 January 1804.
45. *The Times*, 26 August 1815.
46. *The Times*, 27 November 1839.
47. *The Times*, 16 November 1857.
48. *The Times*, 19 December 1839.
49. On the possession of girls and young women in early modern England see James Sharpe, *Instruments of Darkness*, pp. 190–211, and his detailed case study *The Bewitching of Ann Gunter* (London, 1999).
50. Gauld and Cornell, *Poltergeists*, p. 226; David J. Hess, 'Ghosts and Domestic Politics in Brazil: Some Parallels between Spirit Possession and Spirit Infestation', *Ethos* 18, 4 (1990) 431–2.
51. The point is well made in Hess, 'Ghosts and Domestic Politics', 434.
52. Augustin Calmet, *Dissertations Upon the Apparitions of Angels, Dæmons and Ghosts* (London, 1759), p. 141.
53. *Bucks Gazette*; reprinted in *The Times*, 28 April 1834.
54. *Observer*; reprinted in *The Times*, 15 September 1817.
55. *Maidstone Journal*; reprinted in *The Times*, 20 December 1859.
56. *The Times*, 9 October 1839.
57. Calmet, *Dissertations*, p. 141.

58. *The Times*, 11 January 1838.
59. *Liverpool Standard*; reprinted in *The Times*, 23 August 1838.
60. *Scoggins Jestes* (London, 1613), p. 38. The story is presumably based on a similar story told in Lavater, *Of Ghostes and Spirites*, p. 43.
61. Charles Johnson, *A General History of the Lives and Adventures of the Most Famous Highwaymen, Murderers, Street-Robbers, &c* (London, 1734), pp. 110–11.
62. *The Times*, 2 September 1836.
63. L'Estrange Ewen, *Witchcraft in the Star Chamber*, p. 15.
64. *Old Bailey Sessions Papers*, January 1810, Margaret Conners (t18100110–39).
65. Johnson, *A General History of the Lives and Adventures of the Most Famous Highwaymen*, pp. 12–13.
66. *The Times*, 26 August 1815.
67. *Manchester Guardian*; reprinted in *The Times*, 19 October 1835.
68. *The Times*, 27 November 1839.
69. Latham, 'Some West Sussex Superstitions', 21–2.
70. *Morning Chronicle*, 21 January 1804.
71. *Leeds Intelligencer*; reprinted in *The Times*, 12 February and 11 March 1834.
72. Lackington, *Memoirs*, p. 39.
73. *Gentleman's Magazine* 2 (October 1732) 1002; Fowler Haywood, *The Female Spectator*, vol. 2, p. 297.
74. *Westmorland Gazette*, 10 October 1818.
75. *The Times*, 28 November 1825, 13 December 1825.
76. Reprinted in *The Times*, 21 February 1834.
77. Calmet, *Phantom World*, p. 131.
78. Andrew Oehler, *The Life, Adventures, and Unparalleled Sufferings of Andrew Oehler* (Trenton, 1811); Erik Barnouw, 'The Fantasms of Andrew Oehler', *Quarterly Review of Film Studies* 9 (1984) 42.
79. *The Times*, 8 July 1830.
80. *The Times*, 10 October 1947.
81. *The Times*, 18 December 1830, 10 January 1831.
82. *The Times*, 24 December 1856, 23 March 1857.

CHAPTER 7

1. Agrippa, *Three Books of Occult Philosophy*, Book 1, ch. 6, p. 15.
2. Cited in Hermann Hecht, 'The History of Projecting Phantoms, Ghosts and Apparitions: Part 1', *New Magic Lantern Journal* 3 (1984) 4.
3. Giannbattista della Porta, *Natural Magic* (London, 1658), pp. 364–5.
4. Cited in Laurent Mannoni, *The Great Art of Light and Shadow*, trans. Richard Crangle (Exeter, 2000), pp. 10–11.
5. R. Colie, 'Cornelius Drebbel and Salomon de Cause: Two Jacobean models for Salomon's House', *Huntingdon Library Quarterly* 18 (1954); Donna Coffey, '"As in a Theatre": Scientific Spectacle in Bacon's New Atlantis', *Science as Culture* 13, 2 (2004) 259–90.
6. S.I. Van Nooten, 'Contributions of Dutchmen in the Beginnings of Film Technology', *Journal of the Society of Motion Picture and Television Engineers* 81 (1972) 117.
7. See, M.J. Gorman, 'Between the Demonic and the Miraculous: Athanasius Kircher and the Baroque Culture of Machines', in D. Stolzenberg (ed.), *The Great Art of Knowing* (Stanford,

2001). An unabridged version of the essay is available at <www.stanford.edu/group/shl/Eyes/machines>.

8. Van Nooten, 'Contributions of Dutchmen', 118–21; W.A. Wagenaar, 'The True Inventor of the Magic Lantern: Kircher, Walgenstein, or Hurgens?', *Janus* 66 (1979) 193–207; Mannoni, *Great Art*, pp. 34–42; Koen Vermeir, 'The Magic of the Magic Lantern (1660–1700): On Analogical Demonstration and the Visualisation of the Invisible', *British Journal for the History of Science* 38, 2 (2005) 129, n.7.

9. Mannoni, *Great Art*, p. 40.

10. Samuel Pepys, *Diary*, 19 August 1666.

11. Van Nooten, 'Contributions of Dutchmen', 119.

12. Van Nooten, 'Contributions of Dutchmen', 119; Mannoni, *Great Art*, pp. 39, 58.

13. Oligerus Jacobaeus, *Musaeum Regium*, 2nd edition (1710), cited in Mannoni, *Great Art*, p. 51.

14. Mannoni, *Great Art*, p. 59.

15. Charles Patin, *Travels thro' Germany, Swisserland, Bohemia, Holland, and Other Parts of Europe* (London, 1696), pp. 232–6, cited in Mannoni, *Great Art*, p. 60.

16. Daniel Defoe, *History of the Devil* (London, 1728), pp. 343–4.

17. For a good account of Schröpfer see Mervyn Heard, 'The History of Phantasmagoria', PhD thesis, Exeter, 2001, ch. 2.

18. William Hooper, *Rational Recreations*, 2nd edition (London, 1782–38), vol. 2, pp. 43–7. See also John Gale, *Gale's Cabinet of Knowledge* (London, 1796), pp. 200–1. Gale borrowed heavily from Hooper.

19. See Gorman, 'Between the Demonic and the Miraculous'; Vermeir, 'The Magic of the Magic Lantern'.

20. Cited in Mannoni, *Great Art*, p. 35.

21. Cited in Vermeir, 'The Magic of the Magic Lantern', 154.

22. Cited in Gorman, 'Between the Demonic and the Miraculous'.

23. Clark, 'Reformation of the Eyes', 148.

24. Vermeir, 'Magic of the Magic Lantern', 142, n.41.

25. Quoted in Heard, 'The History of Phantasmagoria', p. 31.

26. Mayhew, *London Labour*, vol. 3, p. 73.

27. *The Times*, 2 January 1799.

28. Levie, *Étienne-Gaspard Robertson*, p. 55.

29. Levie, *Étienne-Gaspard Robertson*, p. 55.

30. For general histories of the phantasmagoria and lantern shows see Laurent Mannoni, 'The Phantasmagoria', *Film History* 8, 4 (1996) 390–415; Mannoni, *Great Art*, pp. 136–76; Hermann Hecht, *Pre-Cinema History: An Encyclopaedia and Annotated Bibliography of the Moving Image before 1896* (London, 1993); Levie, *Étienne-Gaspard Robertson*; Heard, 'The History of Phantasmagoria'; Terry Castle, 'Phantasmagoria: Spectral Technology and the Metaphorics of Modern Reverie', *Critical Inquiry* 15, 1 (1988) 26–61.

31. See Mervyn Heard, 'Paul de Philipsthal and the Phantasmagoria in England, Scotland and Ireland', *New Magic Lantern Journal* 8, 1–2 (1996) 2–7, 11–16.

32. *Britannic Magazine* (London, 1794–1807), vol. 9, p. 225.

33. *The Times*, 23 December 1801.

34. *The Times*, 5 January 1802.

35. *The Times*, 22 January 1802.

36. Heard, 'The History of Phantasmagoria', p. 192; *The Times*, 7 January 1802.

37. The Times, 8 October 1802, 17 April 1802; Richard Altick, The Shows of London (Cambridge, mass., 1978), p. 218.

38. X. Theodore Barber, 'Phantasmagorical Wonders: The Magic Lantern Ghost Show in Nineteenth-Century America', Film History 3 (1989) 73–86.

39. Schirmer and Scholl, Sketch of the Performances at the Large Theatre, Lyceum (London, 1805), pp. 7, 20, 22.

40. Brewster, Letters on Natural Magic, Letter IV.

41. Levie, Étienne-Gaspard Robertson, pp. 115–17, 240, 243–4, 144–5.

42. Cited in Barnouw, 'The Fantasms of Andrew Oehler', 43.

43. Mannoni, 'The Phantasmagoria', 394.

44. Heard, 'Paul de Philipsthal', 4.

45. Mannoni, 'The Phantasmagoria', 394, 397, 399.

46. The Times, 23 December 1801.

47. Barber, 'Phantasmagorical Wonders', 79.

48. Terry, 'Phantasmagoria', 30.

49. The Times, 26 October 1801.

50. Johann Samuel Halle, Magie oder die Zauberkräfte der Natur (Berlin, 1784), pp. 232–3, cited in Mannoni, 'The Phantasmagoria', 392.

51. During, Modern Enchantments, p. 103.

52. Oehler, The Life, Adventures and Unparalled Sufferings of Andrew Oehler. The relevant passages regarding his phantasmagoria show are discussed in Barnouw, 'The Fantasms of Andrew Oehler', 40–4.

53. The Times, 16 January 1804.

54. The Times, 17 January 1804.

55. Morning Chronicle, 21 January 1804.

56. The Times, 24 January 1804.

57. Crista Cloutier, 'Mumler's Ghosts', in Clément Chéroux, Andreas Fischer, Pierre Apraxine, Denis Canguilhem and Sophie Schmit (eds), The Perfect Medium: Photography and the Occult (New Haven and London, 2004), pp. 20–8.

58. For a detailed account of Mumler's trial see Michael Leja, Looking Askance: Skepticism and American Art from Eakins to Duchamp (Berkeley, 2004), ch. 1.

59. See Andreas Fischer, '"A Photographer of Marvels": Frederick Hudson and the Beginnings of Spirit Photography in Europe', in Chéroux et al., The Perfect Medium, pp. 29–36; Ronald Pearsall, The Table-Rappers (London, 1972), ch. 10.

60. Oppenheim, The Other World, p. 46; John Warne Monroe, 'Cartes de visite from the Other World: Spiritism and the Discourse of Laicisme in the Early Third Republic', French Historical Studies 26, 1 (2003) 129, n.29.

61. For a detailed account of Buguet and his trial see Monroe, 'Cartes de visite', 129–37.

62. The Times, 10 April 1863.

63. Cited in Helmut Gernsheim and Alison Gernsheim, The History of Photography (London, 1969), p. 258.

64. The Times, 8 September 1857.

65. The Times, 16 December 1857.

66. See, for example, The Times, 16 December 1857.

67. For a discussion of this trend see John Harvey, 'The Photographic Medium: Representation, Reconstitution, Consciousness, and Collaboration in Early-Twentieth-Century Spiritualism', Technoetic Arts 2, 2 (2004) 109–23.

68. *Quarterly Review*, quoted in Allen W. Grove, 'Röntgen's Ghosts: Photography, X-Rays, and the Victorian Imagination', *Literature and Medicine* 16, 2 (1997) 143. See also Linda Dalrymple Henderson, 'X Rays and the Quest for Invisible Reality in the Art of Kupka, Duchamp, and the Cubists', *Art Journal* 47, 4 (1988) 323–40.

69. Levie, *Étienne-Gaspard Robertson*, p. 144.

70. *Old Bailey Session Papers*, February 1817, Joseph Hudson (t18170219–7).

71. John Henry Pepper, *Scientific Amusements for Young People* (London, 1861); Henry Negretti and Joseph Zambra, *The Magic Lantern, Dissolving Views* (London, 1865); *The Magic Lantern: How to Buy, and How to Use It* (London, 1865).

72. Mayhew, *London Labour*, vol. 3, p. 74.

73. *The Times*, 21 December 1793, 29 December 1820.

74. R. Ebsworth, *A Popular Treatise on Astronomy, Intended to Accompany a New Series of Astronomical Diagrams* (London, 1825).

75. Elizabeth Shephard, 'The Magic Lantern Slide in Entertainment and Education 1860–1920', *History of Photography* 11, 2 (1987) 91–100; Thomas L. Hankins, 'How the Magic Lantern Lost its Magic', *Optics and Photonics News* (January 2003) 34–49; G.H. Martin and David Francis, 'The Camera's Eye', in H.J. Dyos and Michael Wolff (eds), *The Victorian City: Images and Realities* (London, 1973), vol. 1, pp. 239–40.

76. George R. Tweedie, *Gossip about Ghosts: A Lecture to Accompany a Series of 50 Lantern Transparencies* (Bradford, 1894), pp. 3, 24. My thanks to Richard Crangle and the Magic Lantern Society for providing a copy of this rare publication. For brief details on Tweedie see the Open University's Biographical Database of the British Chemical Community, 1880–1970, <www.open.ac.uk/ou5/Arts/chemists/>.

77. See John Henry Pepper, *The True History of the Ghost* (London, 1890); Henry Dircks, *The Ghost! As Produced in the Spectre Drama* (London, 1863); George Speaight, 'Professor Pepper's Ghost', *Theatre Notebook* 43 (1989) 16–24; Steinmeyer, *Hiding the Elephant*, ch. 2; Secord, 'Quick and Magical Shaper of Science', 1648–9; *New DNB*.

78. *The Times*, 8 May 1863.

79. *The Times*, 20 May and 21 November 1863.

80. Dircks, *The Ghost!*, p. 26.

81. *The Times*, 31 December 1863, 3 February 1864. One wonders whether Linguarde was a member of the Lingard family of Victorian music-hall singers.

82. Robin's real name was Henri Joseph Donckèle. See Laurence Senelick, 'Pepper's Ghost Faces the Camera', *History of Photography* 7, 1 (1983) 69–72; Laurent Mannoni, 'La lanterne magique du Boulevard du Crime. Henri Robin, fantasmagore et magicien', *1895* 16 (1994) 5–26; Edwin A. Dawes, *Henri Robin: Expositor of Science and Magic* (Abracadabra Press, 1990); Steinmeyer, *Hiding the Elephant*, pp. 41–3.

83. Senelick, 'Pepper's Ghost Faces the Camera', 72.

84. Altick, *Shows of London*, p. 505; *The Times*, 26 December 1868.

85. *The Times*, 8 May 1863.

86. Dircks, *The Ghost!*, p. 29.

87. Mervyn Heard, 'Giving up the Ghost', unpublished conference paper, available at <www.thegalloper.com/backstories/0702ghosts.html>; 'Fairground Photographers and Travellers of Ghost Shows & Other Visual Exhibitions', <www.users.nwon.com/pauline/photo.html>.

88. British Library Evanion Collection, Evan. 2559, 2559.

89. *The Times*, 20 January 1876.

90. See Vanessa Toulmin, *Randall Williams: King of Showmen — From Ghost Show to Bioscope* (London, 1998). See also the website 'Randall Williams: The King of Showmen', <www.users. nwon.com/pauline/randall.html>.

91. Toulmin, *Randall Williams*, p. 7.

92. On early trick films and their makers see Erik Barnouw, *The Magician and the Cinema* (Oxford, 1981); Rachel Low with Roger Manvell, *The History of the British Film 1896–1906* (London [1948] 2003), pp. 78–85. See also the British Film Institute's website, <www. screenonline.org.uk>; *New DNB* entries for R.W. Paul, George Albert Smith and Cecil Hepworth.

93. For a list of early ghost movies see the American Film Institute Catalog, <http://afi. chadwyck.com/home>. See also the following websites: <www.missinglinkclassichor- ror.co.uk>; <http://us.imdb.com>; <www.eofftv.com>; <www.huntleyarchives.com>; <www.screenonline.org.uk>; <www.bfi.org.uk/nftva>; <www.silentera.com>. There is also a useful list in Emily D. Edwards, 'A House that Tries to be Haunted: Ghostly Narratives in Popular Film and Television', in Houran and Lange, *Hauntings*, pp. 102–19.

94. Quoted in Michael Chanan, *The Dream that Kicks: The Prehistory and Early Years of Cinema in Britain* (London, 1980), p. 31.

95. For details of Smith's life and psychic adventures see Trevor H. Hall, *The Strange Case of Edmund Gurney* (London, [1964] 1980). On his films see Frank Gray, 'George Albert Smith's Visions and Transformations: The Films of 1898', in Simon Popple and Vanessa Toulmin (eds), *Visual Delights: Essays on the Popular and Projected Image in the 19th Century* (Trowbridge, 2000), pp. 170–81.

96. See Hall, *The Strange Case of Edmund Gurney*, pp. 169–71.

97. Low and Manvell, *History of the British Film*, p. 19.

98. Low and Manvell, *History of the British Film*, pp. 45, 79.

99. To see this film, visit <http://memory.loc.gov/ammem/edhtml/edhome.html>.

100. Edwards, 'A House that Tries to be Haunted', pp. 86–7.

101. Lawson, *Letters to the Young on Progress in Pudsey*, p. 72.

CHAPTER 8

1. On ghosts in Elizabethan and early Jacobean drama see, for example, F.W. Moorman, 'The Pre-Shakespearean Ghost', *Modern Language Review* 1 (1906) 85–95; F.W. Moorman, 'Shakespeare's Ghosts', *Modern Language Review* 1 (1906) 192–201; John Jump, 'Shakespeare's Ghosts', *Critical Quarterly* 12, 4 (1970) 339–51; Kristian Smidt, 'Spirits, Ghosts and Gods in Shakespeare', *English Studies* 5 (1996) 422–38; Stephen Greenblatt, *Hamlet in Purgatory* (Princeton and Oxford, 2001), ch. 4.

2. See Howard Baker, 'Ghosts and Guides: Kyd's "Spanish Tragedy" and the Medieval Tragedy', *Modern Philology* 33, 1 (1935) 27–35.

3. Ruby Mildred Hickman, *Ghostly Etiquette on the Classical Stage* (Cedar Rapids, 1938).

4. Moorman, 'The Pre-Shakespearean Ghost', 86.

5. *The Second Tragedie of Seneca Entituled Thyestes, Faithfully Englished by Jasper Heywood* (London, 1560); *The Eyght Tragedie of Seneca*, trans. John Studley (London, 1566); *Seneca, His Tenne Tragedies* (London, 1581).

6. See, Jackson I. Cope, 'Peele's Old Wives' Tale: Folk Stuff into Ritual Form', *English Literary History* 49, 2 (1982) 326–38.

NOTES **283**

7. Thomas Lodge, *Wit's Miserie and the World's Madnesse* (London, 1596), p. 56.

8. Quoted in Smidt, 'Spirits, Ghosts and Gods in Shakespeare', 427.

9. Stephen Greenblatt, *Hamlet in Purgatory*, p. 200.

10. Moorman, 'The Pre-Shakespearean Ghost', 95.

11. *The Entertainer* 11 (12 November 1754), cited in Clery and Roberts (eds), *Gothic Documents*, p. 31.

12. Alfred Roffe, *Essay upon the Ghost-Belief of Shakespeare*, p. 3.

13. Richard Ellman, *Oscar Wilde* (New York, 1987), p. 251, quoted in Alan Ackerman, 'Visualising Hamlet's Ghost: The Spirit of Modern Subjectivity', *Theatre Journal* 53, 1 (2001) 125.

14. L.W. Rogers, *The Ghosts in Shakespeare: A Study of the Occultism in the Shakespeare Plays* (Chicago, 1925), p. 39.

15. Elmer Edgar Stoll, 'The Objectivity of the Ghosts in Shakespeare', *Publications of the Modern Language Association of America* 22, 2 (1907) 232.

16. Stanley Wells, 'Staging Shakespeare's Ghosts', in Murray Biggs et al. (eds), *The Arts of Performance in Elizabethan and Early Stuart Drama* (Edinburgh, 1991), pp. 51–2.

17. Michael Hattaway, *Elizabethan Popular Theatre: Plays in Performance* (London, 1982), pp. 87, 112.

18. Hattaway, *Elizabethan Popular Theatre*, pp. 85, 112.

19. For an overview of stage symbolism see Charles R. Forker, 'Symbolic Staging in Shakespeare and its Importance to the Classroom', *Rocky Mountain Review of Language and Literature* 38 (1984) 3–11.

20. Diana Macintyre Deluca, 'The Movements of the Ghost in *Hamlet*', *Shakespeare Quarterly* 24, 2 (1973) 150.

21. Arthur Colby Sprague, *Shakespeare and the Actors* (Cambridge, Mass., 1944), p. 103.

22. Deluca, 'The Movements of the Ghost in *Hamlet*', 152; Wells, 'Staging Shakespeare's Ghosts', p. 52.

23. Wells, 'Staging Shakespeare's Ghosts', p. 52.

24. *The Times*, 18 October 1822.

25. See Henry Schnitzler, 'The Jesuit Contribution to the Theatre', *Educational Theatre Journal* 4, 4 (1952) 283–92; Coffey, '"As in a Theatre"'; Gorman, 'Between the Demonic and the Miraculous'.

26. Jump, 'Shakespeare's Ghosts', 342.

27. Philip Massinger, *The Unnaturall Combat. A Tragedie* (London, 1639), sig. Lr.

28. *The Ghost: Or the Woman Wears the Breeches* (1653), p. 39.

29. Thomas Shadwell, *Epsom-Wells. A Comedy* (London, 1673), p. 79; John Vanbrugh, *The Relapse; Or, Virtue in Danger* (London, 1697), p. 72; Peter Anthony Motteux, *The Novelty. Every Act a Play* (London, 1697), p. 46.

30. J.M. Armistead, 'Occultism in Restoration Drama: Motives for Revaluation', *Modern Language Studies* 9, 3 (1979) 60–7. See also James Anderson Winn, 'Heroic Song: A Proposal for a Revised History of English Theater and Opera, 1656–1711', *Eighteenth-Century Studies* 30, 2 (1996–97), 130.

31. John Dryden, *The Indian Emperour* (London, 1667), p. 17.

32. John Dryden, *Oedipus: A Tragedy* (London, 1679), epilogue.

33. George Villiers, *The Rehearsal, As it is Now Acted at the Theatre Royal* (London, 1709), pp. 35–6. For a contextual discussion see Steven E. Plank, '"And Now About the Cauldron Sing": Music and the Supernatural on the Restoration Stage', *Early Music* 18, 3 (1990) 392–407.

34. John Dryden, 'Of Heroique Playes. An Essay', in *The Conquest of Granada* (London, 1672), sigs A4v–A4r.

35. A similar burgeoning of popular ghost literature at this time has been identified in Lutheran northern Europe; Jurgen Beyer, 'On the Transformation of Apparition Stories in Scandinavia and Germany, c. 1350–1700', *Folklore* 110 (1999) 45.

36. *Original and Genuine Letters Sent to the Tatler and Spectator* (London, 1725), vol. 2, p. 176.

37. Priestley, *Original Letters, by the Rev. John Wesley*, p. 134. Dunton was a well-known London bookseller.

38. *Strange and Wonderful News from Lincolnshire. Or, a Dreadful Account of a Most Inhumane and Cruel Murther*, p. 4; *A True Relation of the Horrid Ghost of a Woman*, p. 8.

39. For example, *A Dialogue betwixt the Ghost of Charles the I Late King of England and Oliver the Late Usurping Protector* (London, 1659).

40. See William E. Burns, *An Age of Wonder: Prodigies, Politics and Providence in England 1657–1727* (Manchester, 2002), pp. 100–8.

41. See also *Sh—— Ghost to Doctor Oats. In a Vision* (London, 1683).

42. *The Ghost of Tom Ross to His Pupil the D. of Monmouth* (London, 1683).

43. *The Spectator*, No. 44, 20 April 1711.

44. Roger Boyle Orrery, *The Tragedy of King Saul* (London, 1703); Aaron Hill, *Elfrid: Or, the Fair Inconstant. A Tragedy* (London, 1710); Benjamin Griffin, *Injured Virtue: Or, The Virgin Martyr. A Tragedy* (London, 1715).

45. Joseph Addison, *The Drummer; Or, the Haunted House: A Comedy. With a Preface by Sir Richard Steele* (London, 1722); Price, *Poltergeist over England*, p. 44.

46. See Grant, *The Cock Lane Ghost*, pp. 83–7.

47. Clery, *The Rise of Supernatural Fiction*, p. 17.

48. Henry Fielding, *The History of Tom Jones, a Foundling* (London, 1792), vol. 2, p. 73.

49. Benjamin Martyn, *Timoleon. A Tragedy* (London, 1730), p. 47. Entry for Martyn in the *New DNB*.

50. James Miller, *Harlequin-Horace: Or, the Art of Modern Poetry* (London, 1731), p. 27.

51. George Alexander Stevens, *Distress upon Distress: Or, Tragedy in True Taste* (London, 1752), p. 59.

52. John Gay, *The What D'Ye Call It: A Tragi-Comi-Pastoral Farce* (London, 1715), p. 17.

53. Gay, *The What D'Ye Call It*, p. 3.

54. Cited in Robert P. Reno, 'James Boaden's *Fontainville Forest* and Matthew G. Lewis' *The Castle Spectre*: Challenges of the Supernatural Ghost on the Late Eighteenth-Century Stage', *Eighteenth-Century Life* 9, 1 (1984) 90.

55. *The Times*, 19 September 1811.

56. See Clery, *The Rise of Supernatural Fiction*, pp. 38–45.

57. Joseph R. Roach, 'Garrick, the Ghost and the Machine', *Theatre Journal* 34, 4 (1982) 431–40.

58. James Boswell, *The Journal of a Tour to the Hebrides*, 2nd edition (London, 1785), p. 31.

59. *The Times*, 25 August 1787; *The Times*, 18 November 1796.

60. *The Times*, 21 January 1793, 8 September 1794, 13 July and 25 September 1801.

61. *The Times*, 12 November 1812.

62. Clara Reeve, *The Old English Baron: A Gothic Story*, 2nd edition (London, 1778), pp. vi–vii.

63. Madame de Genlis, *The Knights of the Swan* (Edinburgh, 1796), vol. 1, p. 44. For reactions to the book see Angela Wright, 'Gothic Technologies: Visuality in the Romantic Era: Haunted Britain in the 1790s', *Romantic Circles* (2005), available at <www.rc.umd.edu>.

64. Mary Alcock, *Poems, &c. &c. by the Late Mrs. Mary Alcock* (London, 1799), p. 91.

65. Macnish, *The Philosophy of Sleep*, pp. 139–40.

66. See Reno, 'James Boaden's *Fontainville Forest*', 99–100.

67. Reno, 'James Boaden's *Fontainville Forest*', 97–8.

68. Fielding, *Tom Jones*, vol. 3, p. 177.

69. On Loutherbourg's various talents see the *New DNB*; C.L. Baugh, *Garrick and Loutherbourg* (1990); Robert W. Rix, 'Healing the Spirit: William Blake and Magnetic Religion', *Romanticism on the Net* 25 (2002).

70. See Bristol Record Office, Theatre Royal Cat. ref. 8982.

71. On the staging of the play see Paul Ranger, *'Terror and Pity Reign in Every Beast': Gothic Drama in the London Theatres, 1750–1820* (London, 1991), pp. 116–25.

72. Jonathan Glance, '"Fitting the Taste of the Audience": Matthew Lewis's Supernatural Drama'.

73. *Analytical Review*, cited in Jonathan Glance, '"Fitting the Taste of the Audience Like a Glove": Matthew Lewis's Supernatural Drama', <www.Litgothic.com/Authors/lewis_essay_ jg.html>; Sean Gaston, 'Romanticism and the Spectres of Disinterest', *European Romantic Review* 15, 1 (2004) 119.

74. Reno, 'James Boaden's *Fontainville Forest*', 101.

75. *The Times*, 3 September, 15 October 1804. The reports probably referred to the clothes-ripping ghost mentioned by Benjamin Smith.

76. *The Times*, 1 April 1823.

77. *The Times*, 18 November 1823.

78. Michael Booth, *English Melodrama* (London, 1965), p. 82.

79. S. Rosenfeld, 'Muster Richardson, the Great Showman', in D. Mayer and K. Richards (eds), *Western Popular Theatre* (London, 1977), p. 114, cited in the entry of Richardson in the *New DNB*.

80. Booth, *English Melodrama*, p. 84.

81. Leeds Playbills, <www.Leodis.info>.

82. *The Times*, 7 January 1863.

83. See Paul Buczkowski, 'J.R. Planché, Frederick Robson, and the Fairy Extravaganza', *Marvels & Tales: Journal of Fairy-Tale Studies*, 15, 1 (2001) 57.

84. *The Times*, 23 April 1807.

85. *The Times*, 19 September 1811.

86. Marc Brodie, 'Free Trade and Cheap Theatre: Sources of Politics for the Nineteenth-Century London Poor', *Social History* 28, 3 (2003) 350.

87. See Antony Taylor, 'Shakespeare and Radicalism: The Uses and Abuses of Shakespeare in Nineteenth-Century Popular Politics', *Historical Journal*, 45, 2 (2002) 357–79.

88. Mayhew, *London Labour*, vol. 1, p. 15.

89. Plumptre, *The Truth of the Popular Notions of Apparitions*, p. 4.

90. Mayhew, *London Labour*, vol. 1, p. 275.

91. Leeds Playbills, <www.Leodis.info>.

92. Charles Hindley, *Curiosities of Street Literature* (London, 1871), p. 26.

93. *Notes & Queries*, 2nd series, vol. 3, no. 74 (1857) 434.

94. Hindley, *Curiosities of Street Literature*, p. 19.

95. *Notes & Queries* 11, 2nd series, vol. 11, no. 277 (1861) 316. On the trial see *The Times*, 27 September, 3 October, 27 October, 13 November, 14 November, 20 November 1860.

96. For example, *Ghosts! &c! A True and Particular Account of the Disastrous Circumstances Attending the Horrible and Most Awful Appearance of a Ghost* (1827). This can be accessed at the National library of Scotland's website, <www.nls.uk/broadsides>. The broadside reproduced in Finucane, *Ghosts*, plate 5, also reproduces a newspaper report.

97. Dircks, The Ghost!, p. 64.
98. The Times, 15 March 1814.
99. The Times, 15 March 1814.
100. 'John Palmer', New DNB.
101. Michael R. Booth, Theatre in the Victorian Age (Cambridge, 1991), p. 78; Steinmeyer, Hiding the Elephant, pp. 23–4.
102. The Times, 18 November 1823.
103. Booth, Theatre in the Victorian Age, p. 90.
104. Tracy C. Davis, '"Reading Shakespeare by Flashes of Lightning": Challenging the Foundations of Romantic Acting Theory', English Literary History 62, 4 (1995) 933–4.
105. Reno, 'James Boaden's Fontainville Forest', 99; The Times, 9 September 1817.
106. The Times, 18 October 1823.
107. Liverpool Mail; reprinted in The Times, 2 October 1838.
108. Heard, 'The History of Phantasmagoria', pp. 203–4.
109. Altick, Shows of London, p. 219.
110. K. Petroski, '"The Ghost of an Idea": Dickens's Uses of Phantasmagoria, 1842–1844', Dickens Quarterly 16, 2 (1999) 71–93; William Main, 'Charles Dickens and the Magic Lantern', History of Photography 8, 1 (1984) 67–73. See also Graham Holderness, 'Imagination in a Christmas Carol', Études Anglaises 32, 1 (1979) 28–45.
111. Dircks, The Ghost!, p. 24.
112. The Times, 8 September 1879.
113. Dircks, The Ghost!, p. 63.
114. See Speaight, 'Professor Pepper's Ghost', 21, 22.
115. The Times, 31 March 1864.
116. Sprague, Shakespeare and the Actors, p. 325.
117. Speaight, 'Professor Pepper's Ghost', 22.
118. London Metropolitan Archives, ACC/0809/LB.
119. Rachel Low and Arnold Manvell, The History of the British Film 1906–1914 (London, [1948] 1973), p. 225.
120. <www.screenonline.org.uk>.
121. The Times, 26 January 1804.

THE FUTURE FOR GHOSTS

1. <www.mori.com/polls/2003/666-heavenandearth-top.shtml>; <www.icmresearch. co.uk/reviews/2004>; <www.populuslimited.com/poll_summaries/2005_06_20_sun. htm>.
2. Figures taken from <www.mori.com/mrr/2003/c030610.shtml>; Geoffrey Gorer, Exploring English Character (London, 1955); pp. 263, 276; R. Gill, K. Hadaway and P. Marler, 'Is Religious Belief Declining in Britain?, Journal for the Scientific Study of Religion 37 (1998) 513.
3. Gill et al., 'Is Religious Belief Declining in Britain?'; <www.populuslimited.com/poll_summaries/2005_06_20_sun.htm>.
4. Gorer, Exploring English Character, p. 252; Gill et al., 'Is Religious Belief Declining in Britain?', 509; <www.populuslimited.com/poll_summaries/2005_06_20_sun.htm>.
5. <www.populuslimited.com/poll_summaries/2005_06_20_sun.htm>.

6. <www.mori.com/polls/2003/666-heavenandearth-top.shtml>.

7. See Hazelgrove, *Spiritualism*; Davies, *Witchcraft, Magic and Culture*, pp. 69–72.

8. Gorer, *Exploring English Character*, p. 263.

9. Bennett, *Apparitions*, p. 6.

10. Gorer, *Exploring English Character*, p. 263.

11. Data from Humphrey Taylor, 'The Religious and Other Beliefs of Americans 2003', *Harris Poll* 11 (26 February 2003); Daniel Boy, 'Les français et les para-science: vingt ans de mesures', *Revue française de sociologie* 43, 1 (2002) 35–45; <www.tns-sofres.com/etudes/pol/110203_diable_r.htm>.

12. Sara Horsfall, 'The Experience of Marian Apparitions and the Mary Cult', *Social Science Journal* 37, 3 (2000) 375–84.

13. See, for example, Eloïse Mozzani, *Magie et superstitions de la fin de l'Ancien Régime a la Restauration* (Paris, 1988), pp. 112–16, 207–12, 339–45; Judith Devlin, *The Superstitious Mind: French Peasants and the Supernatural in the Nineteenth Century* (New Haven and London, 1987), pp. 88–92.

14. Marie-Catherine Mousseau, 'Media Coverage of Parapsychology and the Prevalence of Irrational Beliefs', *Journal of Scientific Exploration* 17, 4 (2003) 709–11.

15. See, for example, Gill et al., 'Is Religious Belief Declining in Britain?'; Grace Davie, *Religion in Britain Since 1945: Believing without Belonging* (Oxford, 1994); Grace Davie, 'Religion in Modern Britain: Changing Sociological Assumptions', *Sociology* 34, 1 (2000) 113–28; Steve Bruce, *God is Dead: Secularization in the West* (Oxford, 2002); Steve Bruce, 'The Truth about Religion in Britain', *Journal for the Scientific Study of Religion* 34, 4 (1995) 417–30; Callum Brown, *The Death of Christian Britain* (London, 2000).

16. Bruce, 'The Truth about Religion in Britain', 423.

17. Davie, 'Religion in Modern Britain', Table 1; <www.statistics.gov.uk>; <www.populuslimited.com/poll_summaries/2005_06_20_sun.htm>; <www.mori.com/polls/2003/666-heavenandearth-top.shtml>.

18. Gorer, *Exploring English Character*, p. 276; D.J. Davies, C. Watkins and M. Winter, *Church and Religion in Rural England* (Edinburgh, 1991), p. 250; Davies, *Death, Ritual and Belief*, p. 173.

19. Leea Virtanen, 'Have Ghosts Vanished with Industrialism?', in Reimund Kvideland (ed.), *Folklore Processed: In Honour of Lauri Honko* (Helsinki, 1992), p. 231.

20. It is also worth noting how numerous ghost legends formed around abandoned industrial sites in parts of nineteenth- and twentieth-century America. See Judith Richardson, *Possessions: The History and Uses of Haunting in the Hudson Valley* (Cambridge, Mass., 2003), pp. 160–72.

21. Gorer, *Exploring English Character*, p. 263.

22. John Richards, *But Deliver Us From Evil: An Introduction to the Demonic Dimension in Pastoral Care* (London, [1974] 1988), preface.

23. Richards, *But Deliver Us From Evil*, pp. 199–200.

24. Donald Omand, *Experiences of a Present-Day Exorcist* (London, 1970); Dom Robert Petitpierre, *Exorcising Devils* (London, 1976); J. Aelwyn Roberts, *Holy Ghostbuster: A Parson's Encounter with the Paranormal* (London, 1990).

25. Roberts, *Holy Ghostbuster*, p.15.

26. Mike Higton and Stephen R. Holmes, 'Meeting Scotus: On Scholasticism and Its Ghosts', *International Journal of Systematic Theology* 4, 1 (2002) 67–81.

27. W.R. Matthews, 'Foreword', in Bennett, *Apparitions*, p. ix.

28. For a discussion of James's inspiration and literary gift see Jacqueline Simpson, '"The Rules of Folklore" in the Ghost Stories of M.R. James', *Folklore* 108 (1997) 9–18.

29. For recent literary and cultural critiques of cinematic ghosts, which I have no space to summarise in depth here, see, for example, Lee Kovacs, *The Haunted Screen: Ghosts in Literature and Film* (Jefferson and London, 1999); Katherine A. Fowkes, *Giving Up the Ghost: Spirits, Ghosts, and Angels in Mainstream Comedy Films* (Detroit, 1998); Jeffrey Andrew Weinstock (ed.), *Spectral America: Phantoms and the National Imagination* (Wisconsin, 2004).

30. Kovacs, *The Haunted Screen*, pp. 166–74.

31. For background see T.J. Worthington, 'There is a Ghost in My Horse' (June 2003), <www.offthetelly.co.uk>.

32. Information obtained from Bournemouth University's TVTiP: TV Times Project, <http://tvtip.bnfrc.ac.uk/index.php>.

33. *The Times*, 8 May 1967.

34. For a discussion of this genre see Marla Harris, 'Contemporary Ghost Stories: Cyberspace in Fiction for Children and Young Adults', *Children's Literature in Education* 36, 2 (2005) 111–26.

35. See Warren Bareiss, 'Ghost-Hunting, Mystery, and the Rhetoric of Technology' (2002), conference paper available at <www.hu.mtu.edu/aarst/2002/warren_bareiss.pdf>.

36. See, for example, Paul Devereux, *Haunted Land: Investigations into Ancient Mysteries and Modern Day Phenomena* (London, 2001), pp. 141–2.

37. There is a considerable amount of literature on these legends. For an overview and detailed analysis see Gillian Bennett, 'The Vanishing Hitchhiker at Fifty-Five', *Western Folklore* 57 (1998) 1–17; Bennett, *Alas, Poor Ghost!*, pp. 159–67. See also Michael Goss, *The Evidence for Phantom Hitchhikers* (Wellingborough, 1984).

Index